Richard Kadrey has published seven novels, including *Sandman Slim*, *Kill the Dead*, *Aloha From Hell*, *Devil Said Bang*, and more than fifty stories. He has been immortalized as an action figure, and his short story 'Goodbye Houston Street, Goodbye,' was nominated for a British Science Fiction Association Award. A freelance writer and photographer, he lives in San Francisco.

RichardKadrey.com

By Richard Kadrey

Sandman Slim
Kill the Dead
Aloha from Hell
Devil Said Bang

ALOHA HELL FROM

RICHARD KADREY

HARPER
Voyager

Copyright © Richard Kadrey 2011

Richard Kadrey asserts the moral right to
be identified as the author of this work

Grateful acknowledgement is made to reprint lyrics from the following:
"Aloha from Hell", by Erick Lee. Purkheiser and Kirsty Mariana Wallace.
Copyright © 1985 Songs of Windswept Pacific. Vengeance Records. All rights reserved.
"At the Devil's Ball," by Irving Berlin, 1913.

A catalogue record for this book
is available from the British Library

ISBN: 978-0-00-744602-5

Printed and bound in Great Britain by
Clays Ltd, St Ives plc

MIX
Paper from
responsible sources
FSC
www.fsc.org
FSC™ C007454

FSC™ is a non-profit international organisation established
to promote the responsible management of the world's forests.
Products carrying the FSC label are independently certified
to assure consumers that they come from forests that are managed
to meet the social, economic and ecological needs of present
and future generations, and other controlled sources.

Find out more about HarperCollins and the environment at
www.harpercollins.co.uk/green

To Suzanna S, always inspiring

ACKNOWLEDGMENTS

Many thanks to Ginger Clark, Diana Gill, Holly Frederick Sarah LaPolla, Nicola Ginzler, Suzanne Stefanac, Paul Goat Allen, Pat Murphy, Pamela Spengler-Jaffee, Jessie Edwards, Will Hinton, and Carol Schneck.

Thanks to Wild Bill and Vidocq for not smothering me in my sleep. Thanks to Bart Ehrman, Raymond Chandler, Lustmord, Jon Hassell, Sergio Leone, and Guillermo del Toro.

Thanks also to everyone who follows me on Twitter and isn't a pornbot. Seriously bots, I have all the Russian mail order brides and barley legal Asian trannies I can handle.

I sat upon the shore
Fishing, with the arid plain behind me
Shall I at least set my lands in order?
– T. S. Eliot, *The Waste Land*

Gonna take a week off
Gonna go to Hell
Send ya a postcard
Hey I'm doin' swell!
Wish you were here . . .
– The Cramps, *Aloha from Hell*

"TELL ME," SAYS the Frenchman. "How long has it been since you last killed anything?"

He's fucking with me. He knows the answer, but he wants to make me say it. Father Vidocq taking confession.

"I don't know. What time is it?"

"That long, then?"

I shrug.

Vidocq and I are in a very dark room in a very large house full of very fashionable furniture and we're stealing something very valuable. I have no idea what and pretty much don't care. It's just nice to be hanging out and doing some crimes with the old man. Crimes where no one ends up zombie meat, shot, or annoyingly decapitated.

"It's been a while," I say. "Six. Eight weeks. Somewhere around there."

I slipped us into the house through a shadow. Vidocq is working on the wall safe. He's good with safes. He's had over a hundred years of practice.

"So, no crusades? No great wrongs that need to be righted?"

I reach into my pocket for a cigarette, then remember there might be smoke alarms.

"Nothing worth killing for. I'm no cop. The Sub Rosa has their own Mod Squad to deal with the small stuff."

I like watching Vidocq work over a safe. He has hands like a surgeon. Nimble. Precise. He could thread a needle while being shot out of a cannon.

"*Incroyable*. Perhaps you're reaching something of a rapprochement with your angelic half and it's having a moderating effect on your disposition."

Right. I'm part angel. Half, if you want to get picky about it. It's great. A halo and five bucks will get you a cup of coffee in L.A.

"Maybe. The angel screams at me sometimes, mostly at night when I'm tired and he can ambush me with one of his Give-Peace-a-Chance, no-smoking, veggie-bacon sermons. But he isn't trying to run the show single-handed anymore. We reached a kind of MAD pact the other day."

Vidocq looks at me.

"MAD?"

"Mutually Assured Destruction. I told him that if he ever tried to push me out of my brain and turn me into a clean-living choirboy again, I'd have to do something, you know, unreasonable."

"Such as?"

"I told him I'd get hammered and go through the Room of Thirteen Doors to the Pearly Gates. Then I'd find the Archangel Gabriel and thunderbolt-kick him in the cojones in front of all the other angels."

"Whereupon the other angels would draw their swords and kill you."

"Exactly. Mutually Assured Destruction."

"That sounds much more like the old you."

"Thanks."

Technically, I'm what you call a "nephilim." Half human, half angel. And I'm the only one. The others are all dead. Suicides mostly. Some people call my type freaks. If you're one of heaven's lapdogs, you'll probably call me "Abomination." I say, call me either of those things to my face and you'll get to see what your lungs look like as throw pillows.

The angel half of me got shaken loose a while back when a High Plains Drifter—that's "zombie" to you—bit a chunk out of my hand. The human half of me almost died and the angel half thought that was its chance to take over. It was for a while, but then I got my strength back and I locked the angel upstairs in the attic like Joan Crawford in *Whatever Happened to Baby Jane?* It still bangs on the door and shouts, but I've learned to ignore it most of the time. Some of the time. It depends on the day.

Vidocq goes back to work on the safe. Over his clothes, he's wearing a tailored gray gabardine greatcoat. Looks like his girlfriend Allegra's been dressing him again. He looks like the doorman at a speakeasy in the Kremlin. The greatcoat tinkles gently when he moves, like he's smuggling wind chimes. The sound of the hundred or so little potion bottles he has sewn into the coat's lining. I have my guns, my knife, and na'at. Vidocq has his potions.

"What exactly are we stealing?" I ask.

"A golden brooch or device in the shape of a scarab. It's quite ancient. There is a clockwork mechanism inside. Perhaps it's God's pocket watch."

"He doesn't need a watch. He needs a compass so he can find his own ass."

There's a click and the front of the safe swings open.

Vidocq moves his hands in a graceful TV-spokesmodel arc in front of the safe.

"Et voilà."

"You are the man, Van Damme."

He squints at me.

"Jean-Claude Van Damme is Belgian, not French."

"There's a difference?"

"Fuck you."

I like how Vidocq pronounces "fuck": "fock."

He whispers, *"C'est quoi, ça?"*

"Anything wrong?"

"No. It's very interesting. The owner of this safe is a very paranoid man. The inside is etched with spells and runes."

"Can you still get the swag?"

He flashes a small LED light around the inside of the safe.

"I don't see anything in here that should stop us. They mostly seem to be containment spells. He must have been afraid of this shiny scarab walking away."

He reaches into the safe and pulls out a polished ebony box the size of a cigar box and pushes up the lid. A beautiful gold scarab lies on bloodred silk. He hands me the box and begins packing his tools. I slip it into my coat pocket.

I say, "I have to admit, it doesn't feel bad, but it feels a little weird not raising a hand in anger this long. I can pretty much just talk humans and Lurkers out of doing stupid shit to each other these days."

"See?" he says from the floor. "By embracing your angelic half, the mere force of your personality is enough to keep the peace."

"I think killing all zombies in the world in one night helps."

"Yes, that could be a factor."

"And Lucifer and the Vigil aren't around paying me to be a hit man rent-boy bitch."

Vidocq scrolls his gear into a leather tool roll and stands up.

I ask him, "Are we cool?"

He smiles and says, "As the North Star on Christmas Eve. But we aren't quite done."

He takes two potion bottles from inside his coat and pours their contents onto the floor where we were standing and on the safe door, trying to shampoo away any magic or forensic dandruff that might lead back to us. When he tosses the contents of a third bottle into the safe, I hear the scratching.

"You heard?" he asks.

"Get out of the way, Eugène."

He doesn't. Vidocq has a scientific mind. Instead of getting out of the way, he looks inside the safe.

It wouldn't be my fault if the back of his stupid French skull blew out like a five-dollar retread, but I pull Vidocq out of the way just before the demon cannonballs out of the safe and hits the far wall.

The demon's carapace gleams like blue-black gun steel. The big bug doesn't have eyes, just two sets of jaws at an angle to each other and two huge hooked front claws. The moment it hits the wall, it starts tunneling through it. That's what this particular type of demon does. It's a digger. A greed demon. It'll protect anything it thinks it owns. Like the contents of a safe. It's why the safe had containment spells on the interior. To keep the demon inside. Smart. Your basic bad guys—us, for instance—will maybe test for eaters, but who's going to worry about a brainless digger until it's excavating the Panama Canal through your intestines?

Vidocq bumps against the desk when I pull him to his feet. The digger freezes and turns. It's blind but it has great hearing. I can slow my heart and breathing, but in a few seconds the demon's going to zero in on Vidocq. I step back from him, leaving him exposed to the digger. He turns and looks at me with wide horrified eyes.

Sorry, man. This is how it has to be.

The digger turns. It has Vidocq's heartbeat. It hooks its two huge digging claws into the wall and uses them to slingshot forward. A metallic blur, four glittering jaws, and arm-size hooks going right for the old man's chest. He doesn't look at it. He never takes his eyes off me.

As the digger's body blurs across the desk, I whip the na'at out. Twist the grip out from the body into a hair-thin serrated whipsaw.

The digger hits the na'at like a meteor with teeth. I twist the na'at's cutting edge into its body and the bug splits in two lengthwise. The halves come apart and smash into the wall on either side of Vidocq, embedding themselves deep into the wood and plaster.

Vidocq swivels his head, checking out the giant insect shanks that flank him.

I say, "What do you know? I do remember how to kill things. Good news for our side."

"Fuck you, boy."

An alarm goes off when a naked fat man kicks open the office door. I'm going to roll the dice and guess he's the home owner. He points an exquisitely made-over and -under shotgun at us. It might even be a Tullio Fabbri. A hundred and seventy-five grand worth of etched steel with a carved walnut stock and accurate as a cruise missile. I'm almost tempted to ask him, but his pupils are dilated and I smell the excitement in his sweat because he thinks he's finally going to get to use that Fort Knox popgun on actual human beings.

Through the angel's senses I hear the infinitesimal scrape of metal over lubricated metal as the fat man applies pressure to the shotgun's trigger. I grab Vidocq in a bear hug and jump through the window just as the gun goes off.

Davy Crockett here isn't Sub Rosa, but he must know some because he has an antimagic cloak over his house and the grounds outside. What that means is no one's supposed to be able to throw any hoodoo or hexes around here. Whoever built the cloak probably pegged him for a mark right off. I figure they got him to pay a bonus to build it big enough to cover the whole estate, the perfect way to turn a cloak into something as reliable as a marshmallow condom. Antimagic shields are powerful things when you do them right, and part of that's knowing they can only be so big. Blow them up too much and the skin stretches thin. Keep blowing and they can pop right out of existence. That's what Davy the Rube paid for: a one-hundred-thousand-dollar soap bubble.

The cloak is stretched so thin I can throw all kinds of

hoodoo in here. Like when we climbed the fence onto the grounds, I could take us into the house through the Room of Thirteen Doors. But I can't get us off the grounds that way. Of course, I could have used some hoodoo to wrap Davy Crockett's shotgun around his neck like a mink stole and swung him around like a carousel pony while I shot the shit out of his office, but I didn't do any of that. Someone else might think that would earn them karma points down the line, but I know better. Karma is just loaded dice on a crooked table. Celestial pricks with wings and halos make the rules and the house always wins. Always.

So Vidocq and I are falling. Tinkling glass falls with us like razor-blade snowflakes.

When you're jumping two floors with a civilian whose broken bones won't heal overnight like your own, you need to remember a couple of things. One, cushion the fall as much as you can, and two, be prepared to use your body as an air bag. That means controlling the fall enough so the other, usually extremely startled, person lands on top of you. Does it hurt? Go outside, get a friend to drop a garbage-can-ful of bacon fat on your chest, and see.

Trying to control a fall is no tea party when you're holding on to someone who's thrashing around like a Tasered octopus. But it's not impossible. The trick is to grab them just under the ribs and squeeze so they can't breathe. Then you let go just as you hit the ground so they breathe out hard when they hit. It helps absorb the shock, though it still hurts. Especially if you're the one on the bottom.

There's a tree below Davy's window. I aim for it, rolling

us into the branches, hoping it'll slow our fall a little. It does. Coming down into the hedges helps, too. We still have some momentum to burn off, so I keep rolling and we end up on the lawn that Davy was kind enough to lay out with fresh soft sod in the last few days. Thanks, man. I'll send you a honey-baked ham for Christmas.

I pull Vidocq to his feet and we run for the wall like a couple of spooked raccoons. I look back over my shoulder and Davy is standing in the broken window with the shotgun at his shoulder. Wishful thinking. We're too far away for him to hit anything but the air.

Don't sweat it, Davy. Vidocq and I aren't going to touch your safe or wreck your office again. But I might have to come back some night for that Tullio Fabbri and you can try to shoot me with something else. I am in severe need of something like that. It's so quiet and peaceful out here I'm getting bored with breathing. Maybe we'll get lucky and the world will go to Hell again. Fingers crossed.

I PARKED THE stolen Lexus half a block away. Vidocq is limping. He stops and opens his coat like a flasher. There are dozens of pockets sewn into the lining. Each holds a different potion. Batman has his utility belt. Vidocq has his coat. I have guns and a knife. None of us will be on the cover of *GQ*.

Satisfied that Vidocq's little glass vials aren't broken and leaking about a hundred hexes into his underwear, we head for the car. The old man is limping, but when I put a hand on his arm to help him, he shrugs it off. Another grateful customer. I have a knack for pissing people off, especially my friends.

He still won't talk to me, but at least when we get to the

Lexus he lets me help him into the car. I start to close the door, but he blocks it with his hand.

"Who is that?" he asks.

I turn and see a man a few yards away. He's standing in the shadow of a big shade tree on someone's lawn. He doesn't move when I look at him. I reach behind my back and pull a Smith & Wesson .460, making sure he sees it. He doesn't flinch. I put the gun back and start toward him. Now he moves. He comes right at me.

"Is this Disneyland?" I say. "Are you Mickey Mouse? I always wanted to shake hands with giant vermin."

Not a peep. Maybe he's a Daffy Duck fan.

There's something wrong with his face. I can't make out any ears and there's a deep slit where his nose should be, like he's healed up from third-degree burns. Must be a tough bastard to go through that and still walk.

We both stop about six feet apart, having a Sergio Leone stare-down.

"I don't know if you're looking for directions or a date, but we're fresh out of both. Take a walk and stare at someone else."

He's fast for a guy who looks like he just escaped from a deep-fat fryer. He lunges and grabs my arms over the biceps. He's strong for a cripple, but nothing I can't handle.

Then my arms are burning. Literally. My coat sleeves smoke and burst into flames where he's holding me. I have heavy Kevlar inserts in the sleeves, but in just a couple of seconds the heat is almost through and down to my skin.

I step back and bring up my forearms in an outward circle from underneath and hit his arms hard. Standard self-defense stuff every high school kid knows. It doesn't work. It's like hitting Jell-O. And now my forearms are burning. Wrestling this guy is like waltzing with lava. I try to form hoodoo in my mind to knock Smokey the Asshole across the street or at least make him let go, but the pain makes it hard to think straight.

I bark some Hellion I learned back when I was fighting in the arena. If you do the hex right, it's like a garbage-can-size gut punch that hits in a blaze of purple light and bores like an oil-rig drill through just about anyone or anything. I get it just right. The purple explosion, the whirlpool of power. Smokey's midsection collapses in on itself. And goes through and out his back, dragging a long strip of lava flesh with it like burning taffy. The prick doesn't even seem to notice.

The guy isn't a burn victim. His face churns like thick liquid as we wrestle. Stupid. I should have known this asshole wasn't human.

The heat is down to my skin, cooking my arms. Being hard to kill means a lot of things. I have a high pain threshold, but it's not infinite. Not when something a volcano shit out is trying to give you an Indian burn. Being hard to kill also means that you don't go down fast, so whatever's cutting you, shooting you, or burning you alive is something you get to experience for a good long time.

Being hard to kill isn't the worst thing that can happen to you, but it sure as shit isn't the best, and right now it isn't even fun.

Something clear and hard spins past my shoulder and hits Smokey in the face. He jerks his head away like I have bad breath. But he doesn't let go. Another vial flies past. And another. Smokey lets go this time. Vidocq is behind me, limping over and tossing potions like a pitching machine.

Smokey backs away, his arms pulled in close to his body. Something's hurt him. Good. He starts to shake like someone stuck a vibrator in a bowl of cherry Jell-O. I step back and grab my gun, but before I can use it, Smokey melts like the Wicked Witch of the West, leaving a circle of scorched black earth on the green lawn.

Vidocq grabs my shoulder and pulls me back to the car. He bunny-hops on his good leg into the passenger side and I slide into the driver's seat, jam the black blade I carried back from Hell into the ignition, and we peel out.

"What the hell kind of burglar alarm was that? Why can't rich people have rottweilers like everyone else?"

"I don't think that was an alarm. That was a demon."

I glance at him. My arms are throbbing now, and between each throb they still feel like they're burning. I smell something, but I don't know if it's the coat or me.

"I've never seen a demon like that before."

"Neither have I, but the potion that hurt the creature was a rare type of poison. A toxin formulated to affect only demons."

I drive at a moderate speed. I pause at stop signs and obey every light.

"Think it was after us?"

Vidocq shrugs.

"Possibly. But who knew we'd be here tonight? And why would someone attack you now? You've been a good boy for weeks."

I roll down the windows to let out the smell. I'm stinking up the Lexus, but who cares? I hate these luxury golf carts. Gaudy status symbols with as much personality as an Elmer's-Glue-on-white-bread sandwich.

I say, "Maybe someone was settling an old score. Hell, maybe it was after you."

Vidocq laughs. "Who would send a demon for me?"

"I don't know. The few thousand people you've robbed over the last two hundred years?"

"It's more like a hundred and fifty. Don't try to make me sound old."

"'Course, sending a demon for something like that sounds like overkill. Especially something rare enough that neither of us recognizes it."

"I'll look into it tomorrow when I'm certain I'll be able to feel my right leg again."

"Whiner. Your girlfriend is the best hoodoo doctor in town. She'll give you an ice pack and conjure you some kangaroo legs. Then you can do your own second-story work."

Vidocq pats me on the shoulder.

"There, there . . ." like he's patting a five-year-old with a skinned knee. "I would have thought you'd be happy. You got to have a fight. Draw a little blood. Isn't that what you've been wanting?"

I think it over.

"I suppose. And you killed it, not me, so my not-slaughtering-things record is still intact."

"Unlike your arms."

"A little Bactine and they'll be fine by the morning."

"Judging by the look of them, they'll hurt in the meantime. Take this. It will help you sleep."

He reaches into his coat and hands me a potion.

"No thanks. Dr. Jack Daniel's is coming by tonight. He's got all the medicine I need."

He slips the vial into my pocket.

"Take it anyway. He might be late."

"Yes, Mom."

"And don't forget to brush your teeth and say your prayers."

"Fuck you, Mom."

WE DRIVE ACROSS town, near what the city fathers call the Historic District, an ironically named area in a city that has no history but has seen more shit go down than a lot of countries. It's all right to forget all the Mansons, the celebrity ODs, the brain-boost religions, the UFO religions, the tinhorn Satanists, the rock-and-roll suicides, the landgrabs, the serial killers, the ruthless gangs and even more ruthless cops, the survivalists with cases of ammo, cigarettes, and freeze-dried beans in their desert compounds, as long as we remember to bring the family downtown to grab a latte and admire the knockoff Mickey Mouse T-shirts.

We ditch the car in the Biltmore Hotel parking lot and start the four-block walk to the Bradbury Building. This is flat-out stupid, but Vidocq insisted that he could walk off whatever happened to his leg in the fall. I've seen plenty of injuries. I know he can't, but I let him hobble until he grabs my arm, huffing and puffing before falling against a newspaper box full of local porn papers. I didn't know those things were still around.

"Want to take the shortcut?" I ask.

"Please," he says.

I put one of his arms around my shoulder and lift him off the box. We limp to the corner and around the side of a Japanese restaurant. I pull him into a shadow by the delivery entrance. We go into the Room of Thirteen Doors and I pretty much carry him out the Door of Memory and into Mr. Muninn's place.

Every good thief needs a fence and Mr. Muninn is Vidocq's. Muninn's regular shop, the one he keeps for his vaguely normal clients, is in the old sci-fi–meets–art-deco Bradbury Building on a floor that doesn't exist. He serves a pretty select clientele—mostly Sub Rosa and über-wealthy L.A. elites. But if you ever stumbled into his store and could afford a Fury in a crystal cage, the seeds from Eve's apple, or Napoleon's whalebone cock ring, he'd let you in. Mr. Muninn's a businessman.

The really interesting stuff he keeps in a deep cavern beneath the Bradbury Building. His secret boutique for only the oddest and choicest items in the world. That's where we come out.

When he sees us Muninn holds his arms out wide like he's giving a benediction.

"Welcome, boys. What a pleasure to see you two working together again."

Vidocq says, "Just like the good old days. I'm limping and he was just on fire."

Vidocq drops into a gilt armchair that probably belonged to King Tut.

I stamp my foot on the stone floor a few times, shaking loose shotgun pellets that have embedded themselves in the soles of my boot.

"On fire is my best look. Ask anyone."

Muninn shifts his eyes to Vidocq and then back at me.

"How may I ask did a simple robbery turn into a Greek drama? And were there any witnesses who might make things complicated later?"

I say, "The drama started and ended with demons. One in the house and one in the street."

"The only witness is the man who owned the scroll you wanted," says Vidocq. "His residence was badly cloaked and there was a guardian demon in the safe. He'll be too embarrassed that he paid for a worthless shield to tell anyone. No doubt he knows that leaving a demon mantrap where an innocent party might stumble on it is a serious violation of Sub Rosa precepts. No, I believe he'll lick his wounds and not tell a soul about tonight."

Muninn smiles and does his benediction thing again.

"And there we are. An adventure complete with just a few scars to make the memories all the more vivid. And then there's your reward. Not a bad night's work, I'd say."

I take the box out of my pocket, then peel off the charred remains of my coat and drop it on the stone floor. If it was anyone else, I'd stomp him for his attitude, but Muninn doesn't think like regular people. I don't know if he's the oldest man in the world, but I'll bet there isn't anyone else within midget-tossing distance who's seen multiple ice ages freeze and thaw the world. He's a nice guy for someone who thinks like a Martian. And he's always fair when it comes to business. If you ask me, we could use a few more like him. You never know what's going to come out of his mouth and he always pays on time.

He rummages around his endless maze of shelves crammed with books, bones, strange weapons, the crown jewels of kingdoms no one's ever heard of, and ancient scientific devices. Does even he know what they do? They could be Krishna's gumball machine for all I know.

He comes back with a handblown green glass bottle and three small silver cups, takes them to his worktable desk, and pours drinks. He hands us each a glass and raises his own.

"To God above and the devil below."

Vidocq says something pithy back in French.

Great. Now it's my turn to sound smart. The angel in my head chimes in with something, but I shove Beaver Cleaver back into the dark.

"You owe me a coat," is all I can think of.

He smiles and nods, pouring more drinks.

"A man of many thoughts but few words. Lucky for us all that it's not the other way around."

Vidocq laughs and turns away, pretending he's looking at the shelves so I won't see him.

Muninn says, "I hear that when you're not playing *le voleur* with Eugène, you're rebuilding your movie house."

"Rental place. We don't show them. We just pimp them. And yeah, Kasabian and I are rebuilding and expanding Max Overdrive with all the Ben Franklins that vampire bunch, the Dark Eternal, gave me."

Muninn looks down, contemplating his glass.

"I expect they would be grateful for you clearing out the revenants. Zombies can't have much nutritional value for vampires."

"According to the news, it never happened. It was mass

17

hysteria. Drugs in the water or weaponized LSD. Between tourists, traffic cams, and private security, there's a million video cams in L.A., but there's not one good minute of zed footage anywhere, just blurry cell-phone shit. We might as well say we were attacked by Bigfoot."

It stinks of the feds like ripe roadkill. Like Marshal Wells.

Until I snuffed the zeds, Homeland Security had heavy muscle in L.A. I mean, they had a goddamn angel on staff. Aelita. The meanest celestial rattlesnake I ever met and I've partied with Lucifer. Aelita is Ilsa, She-Wolf of the SS, but not as good-natured. She was the organ grinder and Marshal Wells was the monkey. They're exactly the kind of bastards with connections to levels of occult and law enforcement power who could make thousands of hours of video disappear overnight.

Washington spanked Wells hard after the zeds got out of control. Aelita strolled away, so he got to be the fall guy. DHS closed him down out here. Who knows, if he plays nice and eats his vegetables, maybe the Men in Black will send him back. They might even let him resurrect the Golden Vigil, his and Aelita's private jackboot army. Heaven's Pinkertons on earth.

Muninn waves his hand.

"It was bound to happen. Most ordinary people's desire to forget what they can't comprehend is virtually infinite. It's more comforting to disbelieve their own eyes than accept the possibility that the dead can walk the streets. I can't say I blame them."

I raise my glass.

"To reality. The most overrated and underpaid game in town."

We all drink.

"So, what will you do until your movie palace is complete?" asks Muninn. "Are you considering carrying on as an investigator? You seem to have a flair for it. No one else figured out the nasty little secret behind the revenants."

"That was a onetime thing. And I got lucky. If Brigitte and I hadn't been bitten, I wouldn't have done any of it. I would have taken her and blown out of town."

Brigitte is a friend from Prague. A trained High Plains Drifter—that is, a zombie—hunter. I might have fallen for her if we'd met at a different time, under different circumstances, and on another planet. I screwed up and let Brigitte get bitten by a Drifter. She almost turned. If it hadn't been for Vidocq and his alchemy hoodoo, she would have.

"That's not true and you know it," says Vidocq. "Perhaps you'll turn your attention back to Mason? If I remember correctly, finding him was the main reason you returned from Hell. I understand, of course, your getting distracted, what with saving the world and all."

"I did find Mason. And I locked him up good and tight Downtown."

"Which is what he wanted all along," says Vidocq. "I'm not sure you can call that punishment."

I give the old man a look. I don't like having my own stupid confessions thrown back at me. Of course he's right. Mason wanted to go to Hell and he wanted to go there alive, just like I did. And I walked up to him like a backwoods rube with a corncob pipe and put him there. Not many people know about that. I couldn't walk the streets if they did. I couldn't look people in the eye if they knew I'd sent the most dangerous man in the world to the worst place in the universe so he could raise an army to kill them all. People get murdered for mistakes like that. Sometimes they don't wait for someone else to do it. If someone else tries it, they might get it wrong and leave you in a coma, only half dead. That would be even worse. Someone might feel sorry for you and that's something I couldn't take.

"Kasabian still has access to Lucifer's book, *The Daimonion Codex*. He keeps an eye on Downtown twenty-four/seven. If Mason makes a move, I'll know about it."

"Why not simply go yourself?"

"I've tried a few times. Even changing my face with a glamour, there's always some Hellion or other who spots me and I have to de-ass the place fast. There's got to be another way to get to him, but I haven't figured it out yet."

I'm lying. I've tried it a couple of times and I was so nervous that the glamour wasn't even half-baked. I thought I could walk back Downtown like Patton riding a tank. But I can't. The smell and the heat hit me and I'm back on the arena floor, ripped open and bleeding, hoping my guts don't slip out into the dirt. Or I'm covered in thick Hellion blood, playing hit man for another Hellion while he tells me Alice will be safe as long as I keep killing for him. And then she's dead and all I am is a murderer. So I close the door to Hell and I slink back home, sitting at my favorite bar long enough that the smell fades and Kasabian won't know what a coward I've become.

What's more useless than a weak-kneed killer?

"You'll find a way in," says Vidocq.

I nod and finish my drink, putting on my serious, thoughtful face.

"I hope it's soon. Since I can't play Hannibal Downtown, the angel in my head wants me to roam the streets at night looking for bad guys like Batman. I got so pissed one night that I actually did it. Know what happened? Exactly nothing. Looking to get mugged is crazy and bad guys walk the other way when they see crazy coming. What I need is angel Valium to shut this Boy Scout up."

Muninn nods.

"I know how it feels to constantly be at odds with those closest to you. Eventually you reach the point where none of you can stand the sight of each other anymore. My brothers and I are like that."

"Brothers?" says Vidocq.

That's more interesting than a two-headed calf singing "Some Velvet Morning" in tight harmony. I have about a million questions, but most aren't real discreet. I go with the easiest.

"Are they like you? Live in caverns and know everything about everything?"

Muninn shakes his head, lost in thought. He stares at the green liquor bottle.

"I have four brothers, and no, none live in caverns. None of us is even the slightest bit like the others. I haven't seen any of them in years. Centuries. Occasionally I miss them, but the truth is that I have no real interest in tracking any of them down. I daresay they feel the same thing about me."

No one says anything. We've hit into one of those weird silences that happen when someone drops something too real into the middle of a conversation that should just have been about drinking and patting ourselves on the back. Somehow, while we were talking, Muninn has opened the box and extracted a scroll from the scarab. I pick it up.

"What's so special about this that we had to bust open Fort Knox to get it?"

Muninn's eyes lighten. He smiles.

"Yes, that. The scroll is for a gentleman in, let's say, investment banking. A man like that can do extraordinary damage to his soul. Maybe even several souls. He is always on the market for new souls to wear until he ruins them too. Even L.A.'s many soul mongers can't keep up with him. The price of souls is going up for everyone. And Los Angeles is a town that needs all the souls it can lay its hands on."

"So, the scroll is a soul?"

"No. It's a bit like . . . What do you call the elixir that restores hair?"

"Rogaine?"

"Yes! Rogaine for the soul. It restores and replenishes the user's original umbra. A re-souling will last him a year or two I hope. Buyers can become testy when they want a new soul and you have to tell them that the cupboard is bare."

"Suddenly I don't feel so bad about my life."

Vidocq says, "If you feel so good, why not come take a trip with me tomorrow?"

"Another job?"

"That's for you to decide. I sometimes do work for a private investigator. Today she called and asked about you. She has a job that she believes you would be perfect for."

I finish my drink and smile.

"Get mixed up in a total stranger's problems for no good reason? Sounds like a scream, but I think I'll pass."

"Maybe doing something for a stranger will settle down your angel," says Muninn.

The moment he says it, the haloed bastard starts squirming around. It tickles the inside of my skull and not in a good way. I try to push him back into the dark, but he smells a hero moment and won't budge.

"And there's my poor, abused knee," the old man says, patting his leg. "You owe me for tossing me through a window tonight."

I turn from Vidocq to Muninn.

"Never save a Frenchman's life. He'll hold it against you for the rest of yours."

I look at Vidocq and screw up my face into the least sincere smile I can make.

"What the hell? I haven't done anything truly stupid in weeks."

THE BEAT HOTEL is in a typically glamorous area, near the corner of Hollywood Boulevard and North Gower.

Across from the hotel is the Museum of Death, a fenced gray bunker with a ten-foot painted skull out front. Next to it is the long-dead Westbeach Recorders, an empty studio local acts used to record and where Pink Floyd recorded part of *The Wall* (I believe that like I believe Jesus invented chili dogs). Down the street a car dealership is dying in the desert sun, the parboiled cars like beached fish carcasses slowly cooking to squid jerky. A couple of strip malls and empty parking lots on the corner. The front of the Beat Hotel is painted a pale industrial green. Maybe green paint was on sale that day or maybe it's supposed to be ironic. I've never been sure.

If any of this makes you think I don't like the Beat Hotel, you're wrong. It's like a cross between a seventies swingers no-tell motel and the kind of hipster hot spot where rock stars stay when they don't want to be seen bringing home good smack or bad strippers. The rooms are comfortable in a Zen halfway-house kind of way. But the kitchens are decorated in bright primary-colored vinyl like a *Playboy*-chic burger joint. The place looks like where David Lynch would meet Beaver Cleaver's mom for secret afternoons of bondage and milk shakes. I love it.

Kasabian and I have been there about three weeks. I rented us a room for the month. At the end of the month I'll probably do it again. You're not supposed to stay for more than a week, but I pay the right people to change my name on the registry so it looks like someone new moves in every Saturday.

I had to get out of Max Overdrive for a while. All the rebuilding going on after the zombie riots—the saws and hammers and especially the stink of new paint—was making me feel kind of stabby. None of it bothered Kasabian, of course. He'd put on headphones, crank up the volume on *Danger: Diabolik,* and peck away on his computer. The smell didn't bother him because he doesn't have lungs, so he doesn't breathe.

Kasabian and I have a lot in common. Like me, he's a monster; only he wasn't born that way. I made him one when I cut off his head with the black bone knife I brought back from Hell. The blade that didn't let him die. Now he's a chain-smoking, beer-stealing pain in my ass. To get specific, Kasabian is a head without a body. And he won't shut up about it. He gets around on what to a civilian would look like a polished mahogany skateboard with a couple dozen stubby brass Jules Verne legs underneath. Really, it's a hoodoo-driven prosthetic for a guy who's wandering around with nothing but a bad attitude below his neck. It's his own fault. When I came back from Hell, the idiot shot me, so I cut off his head. It seemed like a good idea at the time. Now I'm stuck with him. We've gotten as used to each other as a couple of monsters can be. But I'll never get used to a roommate surfing around on a magic plank like a beer-swilling Victorian centipede.

And that's the other reason we're at the hotel. I don't want some schmuck carpenter wandering upstairs and getting an eyeball-ful of Kasabian's disembodied cranium. When the guy's brain explodes, our insurance would go through the roof.

I go right to the game room set up for the guests. There's an "Out of Order" sign outside. I rap on the door using the secret knock Kasabian insisted on. (He's been watching too many spy movies.) *Knock. Pause. Knock. Knock. Pause. Knock.* A second later I hear something scrape behind the door and it opens a few inches. I look around to make sure no one can see me and slip inside. When I get in, Kasabian uses his little legs to wedge a wooden chair under the doorknob, then tells me to throw the lock.

I say, "You're riding the paranoia pony pretty hard today, Alfredo Garcia."

"Blow me, biped. I have to be security-conscious or I'll end up freak of the month on YouTube."

"Don't sweat it. We're both going to end up a couple of pickled punks in the Museum of Death someday."

"Yeah, but I'm not looking for it to happen tonight."

He clambers on top of the pool table and gives me a sometime-today-asshole look. I roll the cue ball and we lag for break. Kasabian wins. I rack the balls and step back to light a Malediction, Lucifer's favorite cigarette. You can only get them Downtown, and since I haven't seen Lucifer in a while, I'm running low. It might almost be worth chancing going back down to snatch and grab a pack or three. Almost.

Kasabian shooting pool is as graceful as a lobster playing soccer. He scuttles around the green felt tabletop, lines up his shot, and kicks the cue ball with his stubby metal legs. I'm not sure if him playing like that is fair, but you've got to pick your battles, so I let it go. Besides, it gets him out of the room and makes him happy and that makes him easier to live with.

"What's that smell?" he asks.

"Me. I got parboiled by a demon when I was out with Vidocq."

I shrug off the rifle frock coat Muninn gave me and show him the burns on my arms. I'm doing my best to ignore the pain, but I'm going to need a drink soon. Getting tossed in a meat grinder every now and then is part of what I do. I came back to earth to kill things, so I have to expect things to fight back occasionally.

"Nice. New scars to add to your collection. You collect getting fucked up the way old ladies collect state spoons."

Kasabian takes a shot and sinks the nine, eleven, and four. Two stripes and a solid.

He says, "I'll play stripes. Thirteen in the corner," as he lines up the shot. He sinks it.

I puff on the smoke. I get the feeling he's not going to leave me much else to do.

"So what kind of a demon was it?"

26

I shake my head.

"Damned if I know. I'd never seen one like it before."

He creeps around the table, not looking up.

"What did it look like?"

"Not much. I mean, from a distance it looked like a guy in a cheap suit. But when it got closer, it was all Jell-O and acid. When it grabbed me, bang, I was burning."

He takes one of the blue chalk cubes from the side of the table and uses it on his stubby legs.

"Sounds like a Gluttire."

"A what?"

"Gluttire. A glutton. He wasn't burning you. He was trying to dissolve you. Gluttons are pretty rare and mostly eat other demons. You been around any recently?"

"Yeah. The guy whose house we hit had a digger in the wall safe."

"There you go," he says, and sinks the fourteen. "He smelled the digger."

"I need to start bringing cologne on robberies."

"There's a ton about demons in the *Codex*. There's a lot more kinds of them than you think, but Gluttires are the rarest. Most people never get to see one."

"Lucky me."

Things get quiet for a minute. He knows what I'm going to ask.

"Talk to me about Downtown. Got any gossip? Marilyn Monroe dating the Antichrist? Is Lovecraft being tortured by sexy octopuses?"

"What makes you think Monroe's Downtown?"

"Wishful thinking."

Kasabian lines up another shot and sinks it. I'm not even paying attention to which balls anymore.

I say, "So?"

Kasabian doesn't look up when he answers, keeping his eyes down on the table.

"The weather's hot with a chance of chain saws and bullshit blowing up from the south."

I walk over and put my hand over the cue ball. Kasabian looks up at me, not at all happy.

I'm bugging him about the one thing he controls. His one little domain. *The Daimonion Codex*. It's Lucifer's Boy Scout manual, Google search engine, and secret angelic ball-buster cookbook all in one. The most valuable thing in Hell besides the horned one himself. It contains every bit of dark, esoteric-stuff-you-don't-want-to-know-about-if-you-ever-want-to-sleep-again knowledge in the universe. As far as I know, Kasabian is the only one on earth who can read it.

He glances down at my hand and I take it off the cue. He sinks another ball. The little prick has been practicing when I'm not around.

Kasabian used to look things up in the *Codex* for Lucifer when he was too busy, which was 90 percent of the time. Of course, nothing in Hell works the way it's supposed to. That's why they call it Hell. The magic gear down there is like buying Russian souvenirs. The samovars are pretty, but you know they're going to leak all over your mom's chintz tablecloth.

What that means is that Hell's half-assed gear hacks pretty easy. Take the *Codex*. Kasabian's supposed to get a peek Downtown just wide enough to read the book. But it doesn't work right. He's like one of those traffic surveillance cams that catch you running red lights. If he squints just right, he can see a lot more than the book. He's like a whole series of traffic cams wired together and he can spyglass all over Hell. Not all of it, but a lot. It's the one thing he has over me and he never lets me forget it.

He says, "The usual Chuck E. Cheese ball pit-party games. Since Lucifer pissed off back to heaven, Mason's completely taken over. Lucifer's generals are having slap fights over battle plans. Mammon and Baphomet have been sabotaging each others' troops. Poisoning their food and shit like that. All so they can suck up to Mason. Semyazah is the only general who refused to kiss Mason's ass, so he's had to blow town."

"Smart move."

"Mason's getting ready for something. He's pulling troops in from everywhere, but they're scattered all over Hell, so it'll take a while. In the meantime he's got some other game going, but I haven't figured out what it is."

I can walk through shadows and come out almost anywhere I want, passing through the Room of Thirteen Doors, the still-central point of time and space. I can get into the Room because years ago one of Lucifer's generals, the one who wanted me as his personal assassin, stuck a key in my chest. I'm the only one in the universe who can get into the room because I have the only key. But while the Drifters were tearing through town like graveyard locusts I found out that Mason was trying to make his own key.

"Is it the Room of Thirteen Doors? Has he found a way to get in?"

"I don't think so. If he did, he'd be up here already gnawing on your skull."

Kasabian is right. Mason isn't shy or subtle. If he could escape from Downtown, even if it was just for a minute, he'd do it and try to kill me.

"So, what's he up to?"

"You tell me. You talk to the guy every night. It used to be Alice, which was creepy enough, but now it's Dr. Doom."

He shoots at the twelve. It bounces off the cushions and doesn't drop. My shot.

I set down the cigarette, lay the cue down on my thumb and index finger, and line up a shot.

"What does that mean?"

"Back at Max Overdrive you used to talk to Alice in your sleep. Since we got here, though, whenever you're asleep you start spinning like a rotisserie chicken and talking to Mason."

"What do I say?"

I bank the one off the rail and sink it in a corner pocket.

"Aside from 'Fuck you' and 'I'll kill you,' you mumble a lot in Hellion, so it's hard to tell."

"Buy a dictionary."

He walks around the edge of the table, a fleshy spider circling a fly.

"There's something else. It doesn't really change anything, but you might want to know."

"What?"

"No one's all that scared of you Downtown anymore. You used to be the bogeyman who kept them up at night. Now they talk about you like you were the high school bully."

"So they've forgotten about me."

"I didn't say that. What I mean is, Mason is the new scary

human in town, and you've been gone so long, he wins badass title by default."

I take a shot at the three, but hit it too hard and it rolls back into the center of the table.

I pick up my cigarette and Kasabian crawls back onto the table.

"First he sends me to Hell and then he won't even let me keep my rep. The little prick wants everything."

Kasabian lines up a shot.

"So go down there and kill something. Slit some generals' throats. You're the monster who kills monsters. Be creative."

I shake my head.

"Everyone knows my face, and Mason's put wards on all the entrances I use to get into Hell. He'd know the moment I stuck my big toe down there."

"Worrying about shit like that doesn't sound too Sandman Slim to me, if you don't mind my saying."

"I do mind, but you already said it."

"Just go down and kill him already! You've done lots crazier shit than that before."

"It's not the right time. I need to shut down everything he's doing. Battle plans. Backroom deals with generals. All of it. I need more chaos. You murder someone at the Ice Capades and the place goes apeshit. You blow someone's head off in a war zone, people step over the body and have a snack."

"Maybe. A few months back you'd have John Wayne'd your way in there and started your own war. I think that angel in your head's made you soft. You've been Glenda the Good Witch too long."

He's right. Mason talked to me once. He possessed other people's bodies and talked to me through them. He's getting stronger and he's working on a key. He's rallying troops. I should be Downtown murdering him and giving fallen angels new nightmares. I wasted the last six, seven months skipping rope with Wells and the Vigil, drinking myself stupid and losing my edge.

After all this time, I still don't understand this world. It's soft and stupid and full of soft and stupid people. Why aren't they all crazy and ripping each other to bloody confetti? They want to. I can read their eyes. Hear their hearts beating. Smell the fear sweat. The anger sweat. The fury inside they can never let out. I'm turning into one of them. It's the price of living in this world and trying to fit in.

The angel in my head is part of it. On the other hand, is the angel even there? Maybe I'm going crazy and it's my Tyler Durden. Maybe I've always been crazy, and coming back here let it loose. Hell was my Haldol and without it I'm slowly going schizo. Hearing voices. Taking orders from something that might not even exist.

Alice isn't here and this place will never be anything but a desert without her. But I'm connected to people now. Vidocq. Allegra. Candy. Carlos. Kasabian. Even Brigitte, who dumped me. They're the cinder blocks dragging me to the bottom of the ocean. Knowing them, giving a damn about them, sucks the marrow out of my bones. Makes me weak. They want me sane and clean, but the monster in me wants to hear Hellion necks snap and pop like champagne bottles on New Year's.

Kasabian sinks one ball and lines up another. Am I playing stripes or solids? I can't remember. I finish the last of my cigarette and drop the butt in an abandoned soda can under the plastic "No Smoking" sign.

"Maybe you should start something here. Go beat up some more skinheads. Fight a dragon. Or a Kissi."

I look at him, trying to read him. He doesn't breathe or sweat much, so it's hard. He's concentrating on his shot, so I can't see his eyes.

"What made you say that? The Kissi are gone."

I know it because I'd killed them, the whole race of deformed, half-finished angels. Well, almost the whole race. I saw one, he calls himself Josef, a few weeks back. He's alive and he knows where there are other Kissi. We talked about that for a long time.

Kasabian stops and looks at me. We've lived together long enough that he knows when I'm being . . . well, deadly serious.

"Cool out," Kasabian says. "It was a joke."

He gives the fifteen a solid kick and it slams into the hole. He moves around fast, trying to get things back to normal. Back to the game. He sinks another.

I say, "Don't joke about them. I don't like it."

"Whatever you say, man. If I hurt your feelings we can watch *Fried Green Tomatoes* and eat a pint of Häagen-Dazs."

I can't stand it anymore. I take out Vidocq's pain potion and down the whole thing in one gulp.

"No. Let's watch *The Wild Bunch* and pay strangers to bring us Korean ribs."

"Well, fuck me with Lloyd Bridges's dick. You're still alive in there after all," he says. Then, "Corner pocket."

He lays down a solid kick, bounces the eight ball off the far rail, and sinks it in the corner pocket at my end.

"You pay," he says.

"I always do."

I PUT KASABIAN in his bowling bag so I can carry him to the room without the other hotel residents having a nervous breakdown. I close the bag all the way, but he always unzips it a few inches so he can see out.

On the way across the parking lot I spot a Nahual beast man grab a little blonde's arm. She sounds Scandinavian when she shouts at him. She has on the traditional surfer tank top and shorts all foreign exchange students seem to wear. The Nahual isn't showing his beast face, so she has no idea that the guy she's arguing with isn't human.

I set Kasabian down on a bench and walk over. The Nahual lets the girl go when he sees me. I shove his head through the windshield of a shiny rental car and bounce his face off the dashboard a few times. When I stop hurting him he runs like hell. The Scandy girl hasn't moved an inch. Her eyes are fixed on the broken windshield. She doesn't say thanks when I go past, but I don't expect her to. Between the Nahual and me, she's too shell-shocked to say anything at all. Welcome to L.A., darlin'.

As I carry Kasabian upstairs he says, "That's exactly what I was talking about."

IN THE MORNING it feels like my brain ran away to join the circus, got mauled by a lion, and rolled over every bump and boulder coming home. The pain juice Vidocq gave me doesn't mix well with Jack Daniel's, unless you enjoy feeling like someone parked a Saturn V on your eyeballs.

Weird whiskey dreams last night. I dreamed about the old *Faces of Death* movies. Sideshow pseudo-documentary mash-ups of real and obviously fake footage of people being killed in interesting and creative ways. A real carnage rodeo. And each of my dream segments starred Alice being mangled in wide-screen Technicolor.

After all this time I still don't know how she died. I know that Parker, a magician, professional asshole, and Mason's favorite hoodoo thug, murdered her and that Mason ordered it. But I don't know how Parker killed her. The question always hovers at the back of my mind whenever I think of her. When I'm asleep my dreams play out different scenarios. Everything from a quick bullet in the back of the head to being stabbed and bleeding out. Her death scenes get mixed up with dreams of being back in the arena. Whatever beast I kill morphs into Alice dying at my feet.

I know it's a kind of betrayal to hide from the truth of how she died, but I know Parker's mind and I doubt that he made it quick. Parker's the kind of guy that makes you want to believe in reincarnation. I already murdered him once, but if I had the chance I'd never stop killing him. Killing Parker would be my circuit training. My racquetball game. I could build a whole new healthy lifestyle running him to the ground and snapping his neck three times a week.

Vidocq comes by with a cab around ten. On my best days, the sun isn't my friend. This morning, hungover and still wearing yesterday's clothes, all I can do is cover my head and run from shadow to shadow like a vampire that forgot to wind its watch.

When I get to the cab, Vidocq is waiting by the front passenger door, which is weird. We usually ride in the back so we can talk. I look through the window into the back and see why he's up front. Candy is inside.

"What, are you playing matchmaker?"

Vidocq grabs the door and starts into the cab.

"*Oui*. You need to talk to someone besides me and that chattering jack-o'-lantern in your room."

Vidocq slides in next to the driver. I get in the back with Candy.

She's in her usual ensemble of white T-shirt, a beat-up and just a little too big leather jacket, Chuck Taylors, and black jeans about to completely give up at the knees. She looks like Joan Jett's little sister. She's got on a pair of kid's sunglasses, like something you'd pick up in Little Tokyo. The frames are white with blue flames and there are flying robots down the sides. When I sit down she doesn't say hello. She touches the middle of the frames just above her nose. The sunglasses start singing the theme song to some Japanese kiddie cartoon in a tinny robot voice. It makes my skull throb.

"Did you wear those just to torture me?"

She touches the frames and the robot song starts again.

"Not everything is about you, but yeah, pretty much. And I always wanted a robot sidekick."

"Can it be a quiet robot?"

The song stops. She holds a finger over the frames.

"Don't make me use my super-awesome robo powers on you again."

Candy is like me. A monster. Specifically, she's a Jade. Jades are sort of like vampires, only worse. They dissolve your insides and drink them like spiders. But she's a good girl and is trying to kick the human milkshake thing with a special potion. Blood-and-bone methadone. Besides being cute and dangerous, she saved my ass from joining the living dead after a Drifter bit me. I was far gone and didn't want to take the cure, so she stabbed me with a knife coated in the stuff. Yeah, it hurt. And yeah, I'm glad she did it.

I throw up my hands.

"You win. Take our lands and gold but leave me my virtue."

"Those are my only choices?"

"If you're going virtue hunting, you better bring a backhoe and dynamite. You're going to have to dig deep."

"I'll bring a strap-on."

I look at Vidocq in the front seat.

"Make her stop. I'm hungover and she has a robot. It's not fair."

"Life is fair only in the grave and in the bedroom. This, you will notice, is neither."

"That's why I don't take cabs."

I look out the window. The cabbie takes us down Hollywood Boulevard for a few blocks and then U-turns on Sunset and heads back the way we came.

"Where are we headed?"

"The Bamboo House of Dolls."

"What the hell, man? It's just a few blocks. We could have walked."

"But then you might have walked away. You'll notice I told our driver to take the long way so that I could talk to you. The woman we're going to meet thought you'd be more comfortable discussing business there."

"What woman?"

"Julia Sola."

"Never heard of her."

"Marshal Julie, you used to call her. One of Marshal Wells's agents. You liked her. You said she was the only one in the Golden Vigil who treated you like a human being."

I sit up.

"Are you fucking kidding me? Just cause she didn't ice-pick me doesn't mean I want to work with her. Or any other Homeland Security. Stop the car. I'm getting out."

"Keep going," Vidocq says to the driver. He turns back to me.

"Stop behaving like a child. The Vigil is dead and Homeland Security isn't here anymore. You know that. Julia has opened her own private investigation business. Trust me. Do you think I'm so stupid that I would work for someone without investigating them?"

"With who? Your little thief pals?"

"Who better to know who works for law enforcement and who is a free agent?"

I'm not sure what to think. Vidocq has a nose for cops. He knows how they think, how they work. A hundred years ago he taught the French police forensic analysis techniques he'd picked up from his science and alchemical books, and transformed them from a bunch of medieval thumb breakers into actual cops that could do real criminal investigations.

The cabbie has the radio on. Patti Smith is singing "Ask the Angels."

Pounding devotion, armegeddon, and rock and roll. A song to die to.

"This situation is total bullshit."

Candy looks at me, presses the button, and her robot glasses are singing over the radio. I'm back in Hell.

WHEN WE GET to the Bamboo House of Dolls, Vidocq comes around to my side of the car and opens the door fast like he thinks I'm going to bolt. Hands the driver a twenty and doesn't wait for change. The three of us go inside, where it's dark and cool. Carlos is behind the bar setting up glasses for the night's business. He nods at me when we walk in. It's weird seeing the bar at this time of day with no music playing. The tiki dolls and coconuts look as bleary as I feel.

Carlos says, "Funny seeing you awake. I thought you'd melt like the Wicked Witch if someone tried to wake you up before dark."

"You, too. Are you part of this conspiracy, too?"

"I'm just the hired help. Ask the pretty lady in the bathroom what's going on. She booked the place at this unholy hour. Is it your birthday or something? You should have told me."

"No. This is just me being shanghaied, is what it is. If that's coffee I smell, I don't want any. I'm not staying long."

Julia comes out of the back. Her dark hair is longer than I remember and she's wearing it up. She has on a sensible black skirt with a power-color bloodred blouse. She looks like a sexy librarian, but moves like someone who could casually dislocate your knee or crack some ribs with a tactical baton.

She stops when she sees me. Smiles a little and comes over to the bar.

The last time I saw U.S. marshal Julia Sola was here in the bar. She told me how Wells had taken the fall for the Drifters' tearing the city apart. Homeland Security had shut down its L.A. branch, disbanding the Golden Vigil and recalling Wells to Washington. She told me she was quitting the marshals' service to open her own investigation company. Just the general awkward bar chatter between two people who barely knew each other, but had seen a lot of the same craziness and slaughter over the last few days.

"Hello, Stark."

"Marshal."

"I wasn't sure you'd come. I had a bet with myself that you wouldn't."

"Looks like you lost."

"I guess I owe myself five dollars."

She holds out a hand to shake. I give her a quick polite one to make Vidocq happy. He wants me to be a gentleman. I want him to be quiet about it.

"It's not 'Marshal' anymore. It's just 'Julia.'"

"Well, Julia, truth is I wouldn't have come if I'd known who we were seeing."

That night, while Julia and I were talking, her voice had changed. Dropped an octave and turned snotty. It was Mason's voice coming out of her mouth. He couldn't get himself out of Hell, but he'd conjured up a way to turn people into meat puppets for a few seconds. Mason hopped in and out of maybe a half-dozen different bodies, making threats and generally being the first-class asshole he always is. When he was gone, Julia didn't seem to remember a thing. *Seem* being the important part.

Carlos sets a cup of black coffee on the bar. She says, "Thank you," and picks it up. "You don't even want to know why I got you here?"

"Not even a little."

She smiles and I smile back, looking for Mason's shadow behind her eyes. But I can't find him. It's just her in there and I can't pick up anything that feels like deception. Julia looks at me like she's waiting for me to say something else. Maybe she's just sizing me up. I let the silence hang to see if the tension makes Mason reveal himself.

She sets down the coffee.

"Eugène must have told you that we've worked together a few times."

"He mentioned it."

"I know you feel a certain reluctance to talk to someone involved with DHS or the Vigil."

"That's putting it mildly."

Carlos says, "Wait a minute. She's with those people who got you beat up and fucked over? Lady, if I'd known that, you wouldn't have set foot in my place."

She looks at Carlos and then at me.

"I know I could tell you that I'm not with them from now until the end of time and you wouldn't believe me. But for what it's worth, I'm not and I won't ever be again."

"Is that supposed to impress me?"

"I thought maybe Eugène vouching for me would mean

something, but you never let facts get in the way of your judgment, do you?"

"Mrs. Robinson, are you trying to seduce me?"

Vidocq bumps me with his shoulder from behind.

"Listen to what she has to say."

Candy comes up beside me. I don't have to look. I can smell her slightly inhuman scent. I once killed the pimp who ran a Hellion brothel. He lit the place with burning amber and it smelled like burning pine and smoke. Candy kind of smells like that.

"So tell me why you wanted me here."

"I have a job I think you'd be uniquely suited for."

"What kind of job?"

"It might be dangerous."

"I figured that when you wanted me and not Vidocq or one of your marshal buddies. What you want is someone disposable. Someone off the grid who won't be missed when whatever this is goes balls-up."

"You're way off. I want you because I think you're the only person in L.A. with the skill set needed to handle this particular situation."

"When someone says 'skill set' I get nervous. Just tell me what this is."

"It's a demonic possession. An exorcism went wrong and a boy is missing."

I get up to leave.

"Thanks for getting me here for nothing. I'm gone."

Candy puts a hand on my shoulder.

"You, too?" I say.

"Just let her finish."

I look at Sola.

"I don't do exorcisms or bounty-hunt demons. The Vigil got me mixed up in a demon skip trace and it ended with me and Brigitte gnawed on by a roomful of Drifters."

She nods.

"I know. But that was Wells and this is me. There are no tricks here. No hidden agendas. Just a kid who needs your help."

"I don't think so. I think you're the one who needs help. You sent the kid a demon jacker, but he blew it and the kid ended up worse than before. Now you want someone to clean up your mess."

She picks up her coffee, takes a sip, and sets it back down. She doesn't look at me when she starts talking.

"You're right. Okay? There. I said it. I need you to fix up my screw-up."

The muscles in her shoulders and the back of her neck are tight. Her breathing has gone a little shallow and rapid. Her heartbeat's up. If I trusted her, I'd swear she's telling the truth.

Sola shakes her head.

"I don't know what happened and neither does Father Traven. Have you heard of him? The Vigil had him on retainer for freelance exorcisms. He's the real deal. A genuine old-school demon ass-kicker. Only this time the demon kicked back harder."

"Why come to me? Why not get another priest? Or a houngan or one of those old *nyu wu* witches in Chinatown? They love this kind of thing."

"I tried to get another priest, but when word got out that I was working with Father Traven, none of them would talk to me."

"Now you've finally said something interesting. What's wrong with your snake handler?"

"He was excommunicated."

I turn to Vidocq.

"Did you know about this? You were a nice Catholic boy. This is big-time stuff. Is there anything worse than an excommunicated priest?"

"Yes. One who's not excommunicated."

I get out a Malediction and light it. I look at Carlos. State law says I'm not supposed to smoke in here, but he gives me a don't-sweat-it shake of his head.

"What did Traven do? Skim from the collection plate? Oil-wrestle altar boys?"

Julia shakes her head.

"Nothing like that. Father Traven is a paleolinguist. He specializes in translating ancient religious texts and deciphering dead languages."

"Let me guess. Instead of collecting stamps for a hobby, he translated a book the Church didn't approve of and got nailed for it."

"Something like that. It was one book in particular that got him into trouble, but he won't talk about it. However, none of that has anything to do with the fact he's an experienced and extremely successful exorcist."

"So what went wrong with the kid?"

She sits down on one of the bar stools. Shakes her head and drops her hands to the bar.

"Your guess is as good as mine. The exorcism seemed to be going well, and Hunter—Hunter Sentenza, the possessed boy—was doing well. His color was coming back. The voices had stopped. There wasn't a trace of fire."

"Fire?"

"We didn't actually see it, but there was a symbol burned into the ceiling over his bed. There weren't any matches or lighters in his room. We think it was done by the demon possessing the boy. His hands and face were blistered."

"What's the symbol look like?"

"Old. I didn't recognize it. Father Traven can tell you more about it."

"What happened next?"

"It felt like we were reaching the end. Traven was sure that he had the demon under control and almost had it out. Before that, Hunter had been speaking in tongues. But then he seemed all right. He was calm and breathing normally. All of a sudden he grabbed Father Traven and tossed him across the room. Hunter levitated a few feet over the bed and shouted, 'I won't be locked in.' After that, things got weird."

"After that?"

"Hunter fell back onto the bed and didn't move. I didn't know if he was passed out or dead. As I helped Father Traven to his feet, the kid started singing."

" 'Puff the Magic Dragon'?"

She shakes her head, a knowing little smile curling the edges of her lips.

"It was an old Chordettes song. It went, 'Mr. Sandman, bring me a dream, make him the cutest that I've ever seen.' "

I can't help but laugh.

"That's what this is. You think the demon knows me."

"Any idea who it might be?"

"I haven't had much experience with them." I try to think. Run over all my kills. There are so many. They run together like a dark stinking river.

"I might have killed a demon every now and then, but it's not like they have distinct personalities. They're like bugs. Who remembers stepping on a bug?"

"Maybe the song was a fluke, but I doubt it. The question is, what are you going to do about it?"

I look her in the eye, take a drag on the Malediction, and blow it out.

"I'm going to Max Overdrive and find an Andrews Sisters musical. Then I'm going to the hotel, put it on, and drink steadily for the rest of the day."

I stand up to leave, but Vidocq grabs my arm. He might look old, but he's been using his muscles for over a century. His grip is like a claw lifter at a wrecking yard.

"Give me the folder," he tells Julia.

Sola pulls a beige manila envelope from a shoulder bag she'd left on the bar.

Vidocq pushes me over to the bar and pulls something out of the folder. It's a picture of a teenage boy in a school robe. Maybe a high school graduation shot. He's smiling at the camera. Straight white teeth and messy brown hair under the graduation cap. He looks like the kind of kid who'd be captain of the track team. I hate him. Healthy, happy, popular jock. My natural enemy in school. On the other hand, he's not someone I'd pick to square-dance with demons.

Vidocq says, "This is the boy we've been discussing. His

name is Hunter. He's nineteen. The same age you were when you were dragged to Hell. Tell me, Jimmy, did that experience improve your life? I don't think so. Are you going to walk away and let what happened to you happen to this boy?"

There's acid in the back of my throat. A whirlpool of anger and fear in my head as the nineteen-year-old kid I keep buried under the floorboards in my head, way deeper in the dark than the angel, struggles up to where I can't help but look at him. Total Nam flashback time and I'm feeling things I didn't know I could still feel. The dry, brittle arms gliding out from under the floor in Mason's house, wrapping around me and dragging me Downtown. Sensations of falling. Crashing onto a blood-and shit-stained backstreet in Pandemonium. Trying to clear my head and focus as a thousand new smells, sounds, and the perpetually twilight sky hit me. Then the slow realization of where I was and the gleeful looks on the Hellions' faces.

I toss the photo back onto the bar.

Lying there in that Hellion street, I had a strange sensation, like some primal and essential thing inside me had cracked and everything I ever was or ever might have been— my name, my hopes, Alice, my whole ridiculous life—was turning black and falling apart like rotten fruit. When it was done there was nothing left inside me but the numb hopelessness of a corpse. Not much to build a new life on but it was all I had when I realized the Hellions weren't going to murder me right away. Maybe that's why killing is so easy for me and why I've been hiding with a dead man in one room over a store since I crawled back here. There's not enough of me left to do anything else.

I drop the rest of my cigarette into Sola's coffee cup.

"I don't like being manipulated. You fucked this thing up. You fix it."

I get up and walk out.

I CROSS TO the other side of the street, where it's darker and I can keep the sun out of my eyes. Candy just about catches up with me halfway down the block.

"Wait up, will you," she says.

I keep walking.

She catches up and walks beside me.

"I sent Vidocq to the clinic and told him to take Allegra to breakfast. Want to have breakfast with me?"

"This is why Vidocq bought you, isn't it. I'm the asshole who walks out and you're the angel who's supposed to bring me back in."

"Of course. Is it working?"

"Not that I've noticed."

She gets in front of me at the corner.

"Come on. Just have breakfast with me. We don't have to talk about any of this."

"No thanks."

"Why do you have to make everything so hard? Let's do something. Just us. We kissed that night at Avila and the timing has been so fucked between us trying to get to know each other ever since. But we're here now and I don't have to save Doc and you don't have to save the world. Can we just try to be like normal people for an hour?"

"I thought not being normal people was why we got along. Monster solidarity."

She puts a hand on my chest.

"Then we can pretend. A couple of wolves eating blueberry waffles among the sheep."

"Keep your waffles. I need grease to kill this hangover. Lots of bacon or ham. Maybe a chicken-fried steak."

"Anything you want."

I take a step back from her.

"Let's get one thing straight. You never play games like this or lie to me again. About anything."

She nods.

"I promise."

"Okay."

She loops her arm in mine and pulls me down the street.

"Roscoe's on Gower, then. They have fried chicken and waffles."

Candy is a little shorter than me. I look down at her smiling in those stupid sunglasses. Sometimes just seeing a woman smile is like a knife in the heart. It hurts and it rattles your whole system, but against all your instincts you swallow the pain and keep looking. After a while you realize it doesn't hurt as much as you thought it would.

"Okay. Roscoe's."

WE SIT IN a booth in the back of Roscoe's, me with my back to the wall. It's an old family habit after Wild Bill caught one in the spine back in Deadwood. Neither of us had to look at the menu to order. Roscoe's specializes in fried chicken and waffles in a heroin-addictive gravy. You eat there because the food is great, and if you live in L.A. and aren't going to flatline on a speed binge, you might as well check out with arteries the color and density of concrete.

I've been trying to ignore my arms all morning, but I can't stand it anymore. I heal fast, but it's just a fast-forward version of how everyone heals and that means almost-healed skin itches like hell. I lean back against the wall, scratch one arm and then the other. It feels great. I want to dig underneath the red skin and new scars and hack away at the nerves with my fingernails so they'll shut up.

Candy says, "Have you been sleeping in pet-shop windows? You look like you have fleas."

"A Gluttire demon made me his chew toy last night."

"You have all the fun. I've never even seen one of those."

"Unless you see it through binoculars from an air-conditioned bunker, you don't want to. The bastard burned the hell out of my arms."

"Let me see."

I shrug off my coat and push my burned sleeves out of the way. (I really need to change clothes soon. It looks like I stole my clothes from a hobo arsonist.) I hope there aren't any nice families looking over here right now. They might have to bag up their chicken and finish it at home.

Candy leans across the table and pokes my raw red left arm.

"Hey. That hurts."

"You big baby. It doesn't look so bad."

"I'll send the next Gluttire to your place to give you a massage and a skin peel."

Our drinks arrive. My coffee and Candy's Coke. I haven't eaten with her before, but I hear that Jades have a real sweet tooth.

In between sips of soda she says, "After breakfast we should see Allegra. She'll have something to fix you up."

"That's not a bad idea. Even if it's only something to stop this damned itching."

Candy takes the straw from her drink and wraps it around her finger.

"Let's start the job interview. Mr. Stark, what's your favorite color? Your favorite movie? Your favorite song?"

"Are you fucking serious?"

"It's called speed dating. You have five minutes to see if you like someone, then a permed-bitch control freak rings a bell and you have to move on to someone else."

"You're serious. You've done this?"

She makes a face and shakes her head.

"Hell no. But I want to see you squirm. And I have lots worse questions than those. If you were a tree, what kind would you be?"

Someone remind me why I came back to earth.

"Christ. Okay. Ask me the questions again."

She gives me a wicked smile.

"Favorite color, movie, and song."

I glance at the kitchen, willing our food to arrive so I can stuff my mouth and not talk.

"Hellion gray, *Herbie versus Godzilla,* and 'The Star-Spangled Banner.' "

"Okay. Now me."

"If this is how speed dating works, I think I'll stay home with Kasabian."

"Go on."

"Okay. Favorite car, movie, and way to use a knife."

Our food arrives while she's answering. Thanks to whatever monsters are watching over me. This will be over in a minute.

"Shelby Mustang and *Evil Dead II*. I've never used a knife except to cut bagels."

"Wrong. The correct answer is a '71 Impala Super Sport. *Once Upon a Time in the West*. And from behind, your right arm around the throat and an upward thrust with your left so the blade slips between the ribs and into the heart."

The waiter is laying out the plates when I answer. He freezes for a second then puts down our cutlery and glasses of water. He turns and walks away slowly, like from a rabid dog, trying not to draw its attention or piss it off. What a pro. I'm leaving him a massive tip.

"How are the waffles?"

"Perfect. How about your chicken?"

"Smoothing over this hangover like a road grader."

We don't talk for a while. Just eat our food like a couple of civilians who haven't killed enough people to populate a small city. It's been six months since that night at Avila when we were both in monster mode, ripping our way through some of L.A.'s most elite millionaires and politicos, all of them Mason's accomplices as he tried to open the gates of Hell. Candy and I did kiss each other that night. A hard, long kiss while we were covered in other people's blood, a couple of monsters who recognized each other and weren't afraid of what they saw. And then nothing. Candy went back on the wagon, taking Doc Kinski's potion to keep from turning back into a killing machine. Then the Drifters invaded. And someone was looking to kill Doc, so she went on the road with him. I don't know if there's anything between us really, but it sure as hell feels like someone sprinkled mayhem and saltpeter all over creation to make sure we never find out.

I feel a little guilt bubbling up in the back of my mind. It's the same feeling I always get when I look at a woman who isn't Alice. But like Candy said, we're here now. Let's just see what happens. I can't live in the shadow of Alice's absence every moment of my life. I don't push her away, but let her drift back where she was. Not forgotten, but not making me wish I was dead. I don't let the picture of the Sentenza kid get to me either. Julia found one exorcist, so she can find another. Hell, I could point her to some Sub Rosa demon hunters.

My phone buzzes. A text comes through.

> *The girl is delicious. You're right to be with her.*
> *Leave the case alone. Forget you heard about it.*
> *Stay with the pretty girl.*

I push the plates away and get to my feet, storming through the restaurant looking for anyone holding a phone. A guy in blond dreads and a sleeveless T-shirt is looking at his. I'm across the room in two long steps and snatch it from his hand. A woman's voice comes out of the speaker. He's listening to his voice mail. I slam the phone on the table and stomp out of the emergency exit, setting off the alarm. There's no one on the street. A dusty station wagon and a VW Bug pass each other in the road. Only one passenger in each and neither of them has a phone.

I push back into Roscoe's through the front door. Everyone in the place is looking at me like they're expecting the crazy man in the coat to set off the bomb he's obviously hiding.

I go to the table and show Candy the message.

"Tell me this isn't you or Vidocq. Or something one of you set up with Julia."

She shakes her head.

"Vidocq wouldn't and I didn't," she says. I look at her and let the angel out for a second so he can look, too. He sees what I see. She's telling the truth.

I take a couple of the hundreds I grabbed from my stash of vampire money last night. Drop the money on the table and nod for Candy to follow me out. We double-time it back to Hollywood Boulevard to get lost in the tourist crowd before one of the solid citizens back at the restaurant dials 911.

I say, "Do me a favor."

"What?"

"I'm a little agitated and don't want to have to explain anything. Do me a favor and call Vidocq. Tell him I want in on the case. I don't like threats and I hate crank calls."

Candy puts her robot glasses on.

"At least whoever it was thinks I'm pretty."

"Even assholes can have good taste."

THERE'S A PARKING lot less than a block from the Beat Hotel. Vidocq hates riding in stolen cars, so I look for one that will make him the least unhappy and settle on a brown Volvo 240, one of the most boring cars in the world. No one, especially a cop, will look twice at a Volvo, especially one the color of a Swedish turd.

I leave Candy in the idling car, go into the room at the hotel, and ditch my burned shirt for a clean one. I always have the knife and na'at with me, but on the way out I grab the Smith & Wesson .460. You don't have to shoot an elephant with a gun this big and powerful. You just hit it on the knee with the butt and the elephant will give you all of its lunch money. When he sees me slip the gun into my coat pocket, Kasabian shakes his head, which, in his case, is his whole body.

"I knew they'd drag you in. You can't stay away from trouble."

"Can I help it if trouble has me on speed dial?"

"Have fun, sucker."

"*Vaya con Dios, Alfredo Garcia.*"

Sola already gave Vidocq the Sentenza family's address, so I pick him up and we head north on the Hollywood Freeway.

STUDIO CITY IS the kind of place where the poor have to settle for two-million-dollar "luxury properties" instead of mansions. The only difference between them and the genuinely rich in the hills is that they have to get by with one pool and they can't park a 747 in their two-story living room, though they can probably squeeze in a decent-size blimp. There are fake villas with fake Roman mosaics out front and fake castles with wrought-iron gates like Henry VIII is going to stop by with guacamole for the keg party.

Lucky for everyone, the address Julia gave us belongs to a place on Coldwater Canyon Avenue with nothing but a long snaking driveway. No monarchist gates, armed guards, or a giant hermetically sealed *Jetsons* dome.

At the end of the drive, a gold Lexus is parked next to a clean but well-used Ford pickup. There are streaks of mud and dried cement around the truck's wheel wells. We get out and follow a stone path to the front door. I ring the bell.

A woman opens the door a second later. She's obviously been waiting for us. She's about fifty and pretty, with short dark hair and a high-quality chin tuck.

"Oh," she says, all the hope and brightness disappearing from her eyes.

It's Hunter's mom. I can see the resemblance from one of the photos back at the bar. Mom takes one look at my scarred face and I can practically see the words *home invasion with multiple fatalities* spinning around her brain like the dragon in a Chinese New Year's parade.

I say, "Mrs. Sentenza. Julia Sola sent us."

She relaxes. The storm in her brain clears and her blood pressure drops to below aneurysm levels. Her little freak-out probably shaved a good five years off her life, but they're the shitty ones at the end, so no big deal.

"Oh. You must be Mr. Stark and Mr. Vidocq. Julia said you'd be dropping by." She stops, staring at Candy in her robot sunglasses.

I say, "This is my assistant, Candy."

Mrs. Sentenza gives Candy a thin smile.

"Of course she is. Please come in."

The inside of the house is bright, with light coming through a million windows and reflecting off the polished tile floor. Obsessive California chic. Like they own the sky and are goddamn well going to use every inch of it. Hunter's father is waiting for us by the stairs leading to the upper floor of a two-story living room. (I told you.)

"This is Hunter's father, Kerry."

"Nice to meet you all. Call me K.W."

Handshakes all around. His grip is firm and serious. He has rough laborer's hands, like he actually works for a living.

"Are you three exorcists, too?" he asks.

"No. Father Traven holds the prayer beads. We're more like spiritual bouncers."

"Well, if you can fix this, we're willing to try."

There aren't any hoodoo vibes coming off these people. Nothing shifty and hidden. They come across like straight-arrow civilians who wouldn't know a Hand of Glory from an oven mitt. They're not responsible for calling a demon into the house. Unless they're a lot more powerful than they look and can throw up a glamour powerful enough to even fool the angel in my head. Their eyes are dilating and their hearts are racing. I smell Valium and alcohol in Mom's sweat. Most of what I'm getting off them is heavyweight fear for their kid and confusion and a meek mistrust of us three. No surprise there. They don't run into people like us on the golf course at the country club.

Vidocq looks around the place. Like me, he's looking for any traces of magic, in his case mystical objects.

"You have a very lovely home," says Candy. "It looks like a happy place."

"It was," says Mom.

I say, "Can we see the room?"

"It's Hunter's room. His name is Hunter."

"Hunter. Got it. Can we see Hunter's room?"

Mom isn't sure about Candy and Vidocq, but I can tell she hates me already. I'm not sure about Dad. He looks like the kind of guy who didn't come from money, and now that he has it, he's always a little on edge waiting for someone to try to take it away. That means he'll have a handgun or two in the house.

K.W. leads us to Hunter's room while Mom trails behind.

"Don't take this the wrong way, but did Hunter take anything like antidepressants? Or was he ever locked up for, you know, behavior problems?"

"You mean, was our son crazy?" asks Mom.

"Was he?"

"No. He was a normal boy. He ran track."

So that's what normal is. I should write that down.

"Did he take any recreational drugs?"

Mom's attitude has gone from hate to stabby.

"He'd never touch those. He's an athlete. Besides, when Hunter was a boy he saw Tommy, his older brother, destroy himself with drugs. He hallucinated. He was scared all the time and couldn't sleep for weeks on end. And it kept getting worse. Then Tommy died. Hunter saw all of it."

"He didn't die. He hanged himself," says Dad. His face is set and hard, but it's clear that admitting this hurt.

"Don't say it like that," says Mom. The tears come fast, an automatic reaction when her other son's death comes up.

These people are unbelievably easy to read. They don't have any magic. There aren't any spells that will hide it this thoroughly.

K.W. puts an arm around his wife's shoulders.

"Jen, why don't you put on some fresh coffee for our guests?"

Mom nods and heads down the hall.

When she's gone K.W. turns to us.

"Sorry. This thing has us both a little crazy, but it's hit her worse. How are you supposed to live after one son's suicide and your other son's . . . well, whatever the hell this is. What's normal again after that?" he says. He swallows hard. "I still don't know what we did to ruin our boys."

"You didn't ruin anyone," says Candy. "Things just happen sometimes. It's easier to fall off the edge of the world than you might think. Even for nice people."

K.W. looks at her. His eyes are wet, but he's fighting hard not to let it go any further. I hate being reminded that rich people are still people.

He pushes open the door to Hunter's room.

"This is it," he says. "Look around at anything you want. We don't have any secrets."

Mom comes back.

"I put coffee on."

She looks past us into the ruined room.

She says, "Julia told us not to touch anything, so we haven't."

I scan the wreckage inside.

"You haven't done anything? Like a spilled glass of water or class photo?"

"No."

"Good. Never clean up after monsters."

"My son isn't a monster."

"I'm not talking about your son."

Vidocq goes into Hunter's room.

"What my associate is saying is that when powerful super-natural forces are at work, without proper preparation any encounter can be extremely dangerous. My advice would be to not enter the room at all and to keep it locked unless Julia or one of her associates is here."

Jen nods and stares, a little surprised at Vidocq's accent. She relaxes a little. Even in a pile of splintered furniture Vidocq is a charmer.

Candy and I go inside while Mom and Dad watch from the hall.

I kneel down, take some packets of salt I lifted from Roscoe's, and sprinkle a white line across the entrance. Vidocq sticks iron *milagros* down one side of the door frame with some green hardware-store putty.

"I have to close the door for a second," I tell the Sentenzas.

I get out the black blade and carve a protective rune into the wood on the inside of the door frame.

Vidocq reaches for my hand like he wants to stop me, but he's too slow.

"Why are you destroying their house further? Why not put an ash twig over the door?"

"Why don't we send the demon roses while we're at it? I hate hippie hoodoo."

Vidocq rummages in his coat and finds ash powder in one of his vials. He reaches up and sets it on the frame over the door.

"Okay," I say to K.W. and Jen when I open the door. "Nothing should get out of here."

"Thank you," Jen says.

The room is a wreck. It looks like it was worked over by Linda Blair on a crack binge. One of the windows is boarded up. There are holes in the wall where it looks like someone punched through. The place hums with residual dark hoodoo, like there are wasps in the walls. I don't think the Sentenzas can hear it, but Candy, Vidocq, and I can. Something bad was stomping around in here, but I have no idea what. Vidocq is blowing some kind of powder into the air and watches it settle on the floor and furniture. He looks at me and shrugs. Candy is over by Hunter's closet. I look at her and she shakes her head.

Vidocq prowls the room, trying different powders and potions, trying to identify the magic residue. Candy paws through Hunter's closet and dresser.

I ask, "How did the whole thing start?"

"I guess it started with the migraines," says K.W. "His head would hurt and he'd get real sensitive to light. He said there were ants eating their way into his brain. I get migraines sometimes, too, so I'd give him some of my Imitrex and put him in a dark room. Sometimes it helped, but other times it made things worse. I'd hear him talking and he said it was to the voices in his head. After a week of that, things got really bad."

Jen picks up the story.

"Hunter stopped sleeping. He said he had horrible dreams. Things were chasing him. Not to hurt him, just to have him. He drank coffee and energy drinks to stay awake, but he'd fall asleep anyway. There would be marks on the walls where he clawed them. His hands would be bleeding. It was like Thomas all over again."

Hunter's bed is just a bare mattress. The scene of the exorcism. All four corners are stained with blood. The kid cut himself on the restraints during the ritual. The rest of the mattress is stained with every fluid a human body can produce. There are deep claw marks by the head of the bed. Even some bite marks.

"Did he ever take anything more powerful to stay awake? Speed? Amphetamines, I mean."

K.W. says, "I know what speed is. And no, not that I'm aware of."

Candy stands at the foot of the bed looking. It's the sigil Julia told us about, which was burned into the ceiling. I can't place it, but I'm sure I've seen it before. I snap a picture with my phone.

Neither parent has moved from the door. Jen has one hand over her mouth as she watches us ransack her younger son's room.

"What you've told me so far could be anything from a bad batch of acid to a brain tumor. When did you start thinking it was supernatural?"

Jen says, "There was the time I found him floating in midair."

Vidocq stops pouring his potions.

"Julia didn't mention that," he says.

Jen turns away so she doesn't have to look at us.

"Tell us what you saw," says Candy. She has a good instinct for this kind of work, for knowing when it's best for a woman to ask another woman a painful question.

"It was early in the morning. It was still dark out. I couldn't sleep, so I came by Hunter's room to check on him and I saw that."

She nods at the scorched symbol on the ceiling.

"You saw him making it?"

She nods.

"He was floating there over his bed, smiling like he was the happiest boy in the world. He was digging that symbol into the ceiling with his fingers. There was blood all over his arms. He looked at me and then back at the ceiling. Then his whole body convulsed like he was going to throw up. He opened his mouth and out came a jet of flame. It spread all across the ceiling. I thought it was going to burn the house down. When he stopped, all that was burned was the symbol. After that he fell onto the bed and lay there like he was asleep. That morning we went looking for someone who could help."

K.W. squeezes her shoulder.

"It smells like coffee is ready. Would you go and bring us some?"

She nods and disappears down the hall, her arms wrapped around herself.

When she's out of earshot K.W. says, "Hunter did take drugs. Jen doesn't know about it. It was Hunter's and my secret. We made a deal. I'd pay for rehab and we'd never let his mother know. After Thomas, it would have killed her."

"What was he on?"

"Some new thing. Akira, he called it."

"I haven't heard of it."

"I have," says Candy. "It's a hallucinogen. Real popular with the Sub Rosa cool kids."

Vidocq nods.

"I've heard of it, too. It's supposed to enhance a user's psychic ability. However, Akira seems to work on anyone, so it's moving out into the civilian world."

Candy says, "A bunch of kids take it together. The high comes from being able to touch other users' minds."

Brilliant. Teenyboppers use condoms to fuck safe and then they bore psychic holes in their heads so that anyone or anything can get inside.

"Were you here during the exorcism?" I ask K.W.

"Jen and I were in the living room. We could hear it, but we didn't see anything until Father Traven got hurt. He was on the floor. Hunter was already gone."

He nods to the boarded-up window.

"We haven't seen him since."

While I talk to Dad, Vidocq examines the smoking patches some of his potions have left on the floor. They spread out in spider legs, each one a different color. I have no idea what it's telling him, but it looks impressive.

I give Candy the last packet of salt and she lays down a line beneath the window.

K.W. gives us a half smile and shakes his head.

"Seeing you three reminds me of Tommy's friends. They were into magic. Claimed to know about these kinds of things. Some of them called themselves Sub Rosas. It just seemed silly at the time. You know, kids dabbling in old stuff no one understands to impress their friends and bug their parents."

His smile gets broader, like he's found a memory that doesn't hurt.

"You're not quite like them, though," he says. "You look like you might have a clue."

"Thanks," I say.

I wish we had a fucking clue right now. I go to where K.W. is standing. He's still in the hall. Hasn't so much as stuck a toe into Hunter's room.

"Let me make sure I have this straight. Thomas, your older

son, was heavy into magic with his fashion-victim friends. Did Hunter want to play Merlin, too? Even something small and silly like a Ouija board."

K.W. shakes his head.

"Not after he saw what it did to Tommy. He was just a kid at the time, but he remembers. Hunter's into sports, Xbox, and girls."

"You sure? You didn't know he was taking drugs."

He waves a hand, palm up. A dismissal.

"That's different. You can hide drugs. When Tommy was into that stuff, there were magical books, crystals, twigs, and potions all over his damn room. When Jen asked him to clean up, he said his friends were the same way. There's a picture of him and a bunch of the kids. Would that help you?"

"You never know."

He still won't come into the room.

"You, lady," he says to Candy. "By your left foot, there's a photo in a frame. Would you bring it to me?"

She gets it and hands it to K.W.

He looks at the photo for a minute, not sure he wants to show it to us, an intimate thing he doesn't want to share. Finally, he hands it to me.

"See what I'm talking about?"

There's a group of six kids. *Harry Potter* by way of *Road Warrior*. My neck hurts and my stomach is in knots. I hand him back the shot. Take out my phone and pretend to look at the time.

"Mr. Sentenza, before we go any further, I think we should talk to Father Traven. Thanks for letting us have a look around."

"That's it? That's all you're going to do?"

"We'll know how to proceed after consulting with the father. Don't want to piss off any spirits by coming at them the wrong way."

"That makes sense, I guess. So, you'll call when you know more?"

"Exactly. Thanks." I turn to the others. "Let's go."

Vidocq and Candy look at each other, but follow me out. Vidocq shakes K.W.'s hand.

"Thank you for your hospitality. Please say good-bye to your wife for us."

I'm heading for the door, leaving the two of them to catch up with me.

"You'll call back soon, right? Hunter is still out there somewhere."

I turn and give him what I hope is a reassuring smile.

"We'll call right after we confer with the father."

I head back to the Volvo and fire it up. I already have it in gear when the others get in.

"What's wrong with you?" asks Candy. "Why are we running out on that family?"

I don't answer until we're down the driveway enough that I can't see the house anymore.

"I need to get clear of that place. I've got to think."

"What's wrong?"

Vidocq is in the front seat. He's looking at me hard.

"Thomas, the older kid in that photo? Hunter's big brother? He's TJ."

"Who's TJ?" Candy asks.

"He was in my magic Circle with Mason. He was there

66

the night I got dragged Downtown. I never even knew his name was Tommy. I was going to kill him with the others when I came back, only Kasabian told me he'd already killed himself."

Vidocq nods.

"It seems more likely now that the demon who sang that 'Mr. Sandman' song knows you after all."

"Doesn't it just? But I can't think of any demons I've pissed off. I kill Hellions and hell beasts."

"People, too," says Candy.

"They usually deserve it most."

Vidocq says, "Perhaps at Avila. Or something you did for the Golden Vigil. Perhaps you killed or injured a possessed person, ruining the demon's host. That might be enough for it to want revenge."

"Then why wouldn't the demon come after me? Or you or Candy or Allegra? Even Kasabian? Someone I give a damn about."

"Perhaps the father can answer that question. Let's hope so."

I cut around cars and thousand-dollar mountain bikes cruising Studio City's quiet, privileged streets, running the Volvo away from TJ's Haunted Mansion ride and onto the freeway. The exhaust fumes and clogged lanes are like a welcome-home party. The knots in my stomach are getting worse. I feel cold. I hold the steering wheel tight enough I feel it bend and get close to breaking. The angel in my head moves back into the dark. It recognizes this kind of anger and knows it's not going to talk me down. If it speaks or touches, it might burn up in the heat.

"This is what I get for going soft. For backing off. I don't kill anything for a while and the world starts coughing up this shit. Okay. I get the message loud and clear."

"You need to calm down if we're going to talk to the father," Vidocq says.

"I *am* calm. I don't know what exactly is going on, but what I do know is that someone or something is daring me to find them and maybe this preacher can tell me what. I'll do it old-school. No bullets. Just the knife and the na'at, like back in the arena."

"You scare me when you're like this, Jimmy."

"Not me," says Candy quietly from the back.

"Good, because when I get this thing figured out, I'm going to bring down all kinds of Hell on these assholes and this city."

I'VE CALMED DOWN a little when we reach Father Traven's place near the UCLA campus.

Vidocq's been playing navigator, running us up and down every little side street in the county. He can read a map as well as anyone, but I think he's been buying time, hoping that if he drags out the drive long enough, I won't storm into Traven's place like it's D-Day. The plan sort of works, but mostly it's seeing where the father lives that brings down my blood pressure.

Traven has an apartment in an old art deco complex from the thirties and the place really shows its age. It was probably beautiful once, back before reality TV, when lynching and TB were the most popular pastimes. Now the building's best quality is that it stands as a big Fuck You to all the developers who wake up with a hard-on every morning dreaming of plowing the place under and turning the land into a business park or prefab pile of overpriced condos. If I ever find out who owns the place, I'll buy them a case of Maledictions.

Father Traven lives on the top floor. In a normal building, that would be luxury central. The penthouse suite. In this one, it's pretty much a sock drawer with a view. The original architect had the brilliant idea of putting storage and utility areas at both the top and bottom of the building. Maybe elevators didn't work that well back in the thirties. Maybe he was anal-retentive. Sometime in the long history of the building, someone chopped up those top-floor spaces and tried to convert them into apartments, only they weren't designed to be a happy place for anything except rats and mops. The ceilings are too low and are at funny angles. The untreated wooden floors are warped. You'd have to call in Paul Bunyan to chain-saw the top of the building off and rebuild it from scratch to make Traven's bachelor pad into something anyone but a ghost or an excommunicated sky pilot would love.

We take the elevator up to the floor below Traven's and walk up a set of bare, uncarpeted stairs. Traven's apartment door is open a few inches when we get there. I don't like unexpected open doors. I knock and push it open, my other hand under my coat on the .460.

Traven is sitting at a desk scribbling away on yellow paper that looks old enough to have Spanish Inquisition letterhead at the top. He stops writing and lifts his head, speaks without turning around.

"Ah. You must be God's other rejects. Please, come in."

Traven gets up from a long desk piled high with books. Really, it's the kind of fold-up conference table you see in community centers. I don't know if he's getting ready for work or a church bake sale.

As we come in, Traven extends his hand. He gives us a faint smile, like he wants to be friendly but hasn't had any reason to be for a long time and is trying to remember how to make his face work.

"I'm Liam Traven. Good to meet you all. Julia has told me a lot about you."

He turns to Candy.

"Well, about two of you."

She takes off her sunglasses and beams at him.

"I'm Candy, Mr. Stark's bodyguard."

Traven grins at her. He does it better this time.

"It's very nice to meet you all."

He steps out of the way so we can get farther into the place.

The apartment is small but neat and brighter than I expected. Whoever cut up the place installed a couple of big picture windows overlooking UCLA. There are books, scrolls, and folded sheets of vellum, mystical codices, and crumbling reference books everywhere. Even some pop-science and physics textbooks covered in highlighter marks and Post-its. Brick-and-board bookshelves line the walls and there are more books on the floor. Vidocq heads right for them and starts eyeballing the piles.

"I owned many of these years ago. Not here. I had to leave my library when I left France. I haven't seen some of these texts in a hundred years."

He kneels and picks up a bound manuscript from the floor. It's so old and worn it looks like someone sewed dried leaves together and slapped a cover around them. Vidocq opens it carefully, flips through a few pages, and turns to Traven.

"Is this the old Gnostic *Pistis Sophia*?"

Traven nods and walks over to Vidocq.

"There it is. I've been looking for that. Thank you. And yes, it's the *Pistis*."

"I thought there were only four or five of these left in the world?"

Traven gently takes the book and puts it on a high shelf with other moldering titles.

"There's more than that if you know where to look."

I say, "Maybe there's one less now that you're not punching the clock for the pope. I bet that wasn't a going-away present."

Traven glances up at the manuscript and then to me.

"We do rash things at rash moments," he says. "Later, we sometimes regret them. But not always."

"God helps those who help themselves," says Candy.

"Especially the ones who don't get caught. Don't worry, Father. We don't have a problem with rash. The first thing I did when I got back to this world was roll a guy for his clothes and cash. He threw the first punch and I'd recently woken up on a pile of burning garbage, so I figured God would understand if I helped myself to some necessities."

Father Traven is in his fifties, but his ashen complexion makes him look older. His voice is deep and exhausted, but his eyes are large and curious. His face is lined and deeply creased by years of doing something he didn't want to do, but did anyway because he thought it needed to be done. It's a soldier's face, not a priest's. There's something else.

He's definitely not Sub Rosa—I would have known that the moment I touched his hand—but I can feel waves of hoodoo coming off him. Something weird and old. I don't know what it is, but it's powerful. I bet he doesn't even know about it. Also, I think he's dying. I smell what could be the early stages of cancer.

"The lucky among us might get the same deal as Dysmas. Dysmas was one of the thieves crucified next to Christ. When he asked for forgiveness, Christ said, 'Today you will be with me in paradise.'"

Candy and Vidocq wander around the room. I'm still standing and so is Traven, protectively, in front of his desk. He likes seeing people, but values his privacy. I know the feeling.

"I know a dying story, too. Ever hear of a guy named Voltaire? Vidocq told me about him. I guess he's famous. On his deathbed the priest says to him, 'Do you renounce Satan and his ways?'"

"And Voltaire says, 'My good man, this is no time for making enemies,'" says Traven. "It was a popular joke in the seminary."

Framed pictures of old gods and goddesses line the walls. Egyptian. Babylonian. Hindu. Aztec. Some jellyfish-spider things I haven't seen before. Candy likes those as much as Vidocq likes the books.

"These are the coolest," she says.

"I'm glad you like them," says Traven. "Some of those are images of the oldest gods in the world. We don't even know some of their names."

The angel in my head has been chattering ever since we

got here. He wants to get out of my skull and run around. This place is Disneyland to him. I'm about to slap a gag on him when he points out something that I hadn't noticed. I scan the walls to make sure he's right. He is. Among all the books and ancient gods there isn't a single crucifix. Not even prayer beads. The father lapsed a long time ago or he really holds a grudge.

"Would you like some coffee or hot chocolate? I'm afraid that's all I have. I don't get many guests."

"No thank you," says Vidocq, still poking at Traven's bookshelves.

"I'm fine, Father," says Candy.

He didn't mention scotch, but I get a faint whiff of it when he talks. Not enough for a normal person to notice. Guess we all need something to take the edge off when we're booted from the only life we've ever known.

"I'm not a priest anymore, so there's no need to call me 'Father.' Liam works just fine."

"Thank you, Liam," says Candy.

"I'll stick with 'Father,'" I say. "I heard every time you call an excommunicated priest 'Father,' an angel gets hemorrhoids.

"What is it you do exactly?" I ask.

He clasps his hands in thought.

"To put it simply, I translate old texts. Some known. Some unknown. Depending on who you ask, I'm a paleographer, a historical linguist, or paleolinguist. Not all of those are nice terms."

"You read old books."

"Not ordinary books. Some of these texts haven't been

read in more than a thousand years. They're written in languages that no longer exist. Sometimes in languages that no one even recognizes. Those are my specialty."

He looks at me happily. Is that the sin of pride showing?

"How the hell do you work on something like that?"

"I have a gift for languages."

Traven catches me looking at the book on his desk, pretends to put a pen back into its holder, and closes the book, trying to make the move look casual. There's a symbol carved into its front cover and rust-red stains like blood splattered across it. Traven takes another book and covers the splattered one.

I sit down in a straight-back wooden chair against the wall. It's the most uncomfortable thing I ever sat in. Now I know what Jesus felt like. I'm suffering mortification of my ass right now. Traven sits in his desk chair and clasps his big hands together.

He tries not to stare as the three of us invade his inner sanctum. His heartbeat jumps. He's wondering what he's gotten himself into. But we're here now and he doesn't have the Church or anywhere else to run to anymore. He lets the feeling pass and his heart slows.

"Before, you said, 'When I got back to this world.' You really are him, then? The man who went to Hell and came back? The one who could have saved Satan's life when he came here?"

"God paid your salary. Lucifer paid mine. Call it brand loyalty."

"You're a nephilim. I didn't know there were any of you left."

"That's number one on God's top-forty Abomination list. And as far as I know, I'm the only one there is."

"That must be very lonely."

"It's not like it's Roy Orbison lonely. More like people didn't come to my birthday party and now I'm stuck with all this chips and dip."

Traven looks at Vidocq.

"If he's the nephilim, you must be the alchemist."

"*C'est moi.*"

"Is it true you're two hundred years old?"

"You make me sound so old. I'm only a bit over one hundred and fifty."

"I don't think I'd want to live that long."

"That means you're a sane man."

Traven nods at Candy.

"I haven't heard about you, young lady."

She looks at him and smiles brightly.

"I'm a monster. But not as much as I used to be."

"Ignore her," I tell him. "She's just showing off and hardly ever eats people anymore."

Traven looks at me, not sure if I'm kidding.

"If you're in the exorcism business, you must know a lot about demons."

"Qliphoth," he says.

"What?"

"It's the proper word for what you call a demon. A demon is a bogeyman, an irrational entity representing fear in the collective unconscious. The Qliphoth are the castoffs of a greater entity. The old gods. They're dumb and their lack of intelligence makes them pure evil."

"Okay, Daniel Webster. What happened at the exorcism?"

Traven takes a breath and stares at his hands for a minute.

"You should know that I don't follow the Church's standard exorcism rites. For instance, I seldom speak Latin. If Qliphoth really are lost fragments of the Angra Om Ya, the older dark gods, they're part of creatures millions of years old. Why would Latin have any effect on them?"

"How, then, do you perform your exorcisms?" asks Vidocq.

"My family line is very old. For generations we served communities the Church hadn't reached or wouldn't come to. I use what I learned from my father. Something much older than the Church and much more direct. Best of all, God doesn't have to be involved. I'm a sin eater, from a long line of sin eaters."

Candy comes over.

"I don't know what that is, but can I be one, too?"

I give her a look.

"How does it work?"

"It's a simple ritual. The body of the deceased is laid out naked on a table in the evening, usually around vespers. I place bread and salt on the deceased. I lay my hands on the body. The head. The hands. The feet. I recite the prayers my father taught me, eating the bread and salt.

"With each piece, I take in the body's sins, cleansing the deceased until the soul is clean. When my father died, I ate his sins. When his father died, he ate his sins, and so on and so on, back centuries. I contain all of the accumulated sins of a hundred towns, hamlets, armies, governments, and churches. Who knows how many? Millions I'm sure."

I take a pack of Maledictions from my pocket and offer one to Traven.

"Do you smoke, Father?"

"Yes. Another of my sins."

"Light up and we'll ride the coal cart together."

I light two with Mason's lighter and hand one to the father.

Traven takes a puff, coughs a little. Maledictions can be a little harsh if you're not used to them. Really, they taste like an oil-well fire in a field of fresh fertilizer. Traven sees the pack in my hand and his eyes widen a fraction of an inch.

"Are those what I think they are?"

"The number one brand in Pandemonium."

He holds the Malediction out and looks at it.

"It's harsh, but not as awful as I thought it would be."

"That's Hell in a nutshell," I say. "Tell me about Hunter."

"It seemed to be going well. You see, a Qliphoth can only possess an imperfect and impure body, one that's sinned. Of course, that describes all humans except maybe for the saints. When I eat a possessed person's sins, their body returns to a pure and holy state. With nowhere left to hide, the Qliphoth is ejected like someone spitting out a watermelon seed."

"Where did it go wrong?"

"I'd laid out the bread and salt and I was saying the prayers. Not in Latin, but in an older language supposedly spoken by the Qliphoth and possibly the Angra Om Ya."

Traven opens his mouth and what comes out is all humming, gurgling, and spluttering, like he's drowning and speaking Hellion at the same time.

"I felt the Qliphoth being drawn out as I swallowed Hunter's sins. It knew what was happening and fought back hard. No doubt you've seen the wreckage. Toward the end of the ritual, the Qliphoth tried to drag the boy's body into the air.

I shoved bread and salt into Hunter's mouth, hoping it would draw out the creature. I prayed and ate the bread. That should have worked. It's always worked before, but something went wrong. Imagine that I was erecting a castle to push the Qliphoth out and keep it out. Something went wrong and it burst through the walls and back into Hunter's body. That's the last thing I remember before Julia helping me to my feet. By then, Hunter was gone out the window."

"Did you recognize the demon?" I ask.

"No. It's none I've ever encountered before. It wasn't angry or frightened until it realized that I knew how to force it out. That's unusual for Qliphoth. They're incomplete creatures and they know it, so it makes them fearful and vicious. This one was patient and thoughtful."

Traven walks to the windows and opens them to let the smoke out. I follow him so I can flick my ashes outside over the university.

I say, "I think we're going to need more information before we try the exorcism again. We're missing something important."

"I've been going through my books trying to identify the specific creature, but I haven't had any luck."

"Perhaps I can help you with your research," says Vidocq. "I have my own library, if you would like to see it."

"Thank you. I would."

"You two can play librarians. I'm going to make some calls and break some people's toys until one of them starts giving us answers."

"Cool," Candy says.

"Father, I know you must use the university library. Have you ever heard anyone talk about a drug called Akira?"

"Of course. It's popular among some of the students. Artists. New Agers. Those sort of thing."

"Do you know anything about the drug itself?"

"Not really. All I remember is that it seemed like it was harder to get than other drugs. That there were only a few people who sold it."

"Thanks."

I shake Traven's hand and I let Vidocq and Candy go out ahead of me. I start out, stop, and turn. It's an old trick.

"One more thing, Father. Julia never told us why you are excommunicated."

He's thinking. Not sure he wants to answer.

"I'll tell you if you promise to talk with me about Hell sometime," he says.

"Deal."

Traven goes back to his desk and picks up the book he'd hidden earlier.

"I don't like other people to see this particular book. It seems wrong for it to be a mere curiosity."

"I saw you cover it up."

The spray of red on the front of the book nearly covers an ancient sigil.

"I don't recognize the symbol."

"It's the sign of one of the Angra Om Ya cults," says Vidocq, looking over my shoulder.

Traven nods.

"You'll understand why the church was so angry with me. They have an unswerving policy that there is no God but their God. There never was and there never will be. But there are some who believe that there's more to Creation than what's in the Bible and that the stories in this book are at least as convincing as those."

"You translated the Angra Om Ya's bible. No wonder God doesn't want you whacking his piñata anymore."

"Certainly the Church doesn't."

"It isn't all bad, Father. I own a video store. Come around sometime. The damned get a discount."

He gives us one of his exhausted smiles.

"That's very kind of you. Since leaving the Church, I've come to believe that it's the little, fleeting pleasures like watching videos that mean the most in this life."

"Amen to that."

WHEN WE'RE BACK in the car I call the Sentenzas. K.W. answers.

"K.W., it's Stark. Did Hunter ever tell you where he got his drugs? Maybe give you a name?"

A slight pause.

"It was a girl. Not a girlfriend exactly, but someone he spent time with. Hang on a minute."

Over the phone comes the sound of things being moved. Furniture scrapes. K.W. curses. Then he's back on the phone.

"I knew he'd written it down somewhere. Her name is Carolyn. Carolyn McCoy."

"Is there an address?"

He reads it to me.

"Okay. Thanks. We'll be in touch."

I call up the phone's map app and punch in the address. It's off the Golden State Freeway in Sun Valley.

Vidocq is in the backseat. I turn to look at him.

"How did you hear about Akira? Did you ever try it?"

He shakes his head.

"No. What Hunter's father said at the house was wrong. Akira is nothing new. Like all drugs, it goes in and out of favor. I haven't heard it mentioned for perhaps two years. It sounds as if it's coming back. I'm a bit surprised."

"Why?"

"It's not an easy thing to fashion. The chemistry must be precise. Even a small mistake and you will not have synthe- sized Akira, but a very potent *neurotoxine*. Also, many of the elements are not readily available. Some of the plants and herbs required can only be cultivated in native soil. A mountaintop in China. A rain forest in Brazil. You must find a reliable source of the pure ingredients even to attempt to formulate Akira."

"How is it you know so much about it?"

"I was once asked to manufacture it. I was offered quite a large sum of money, in fact. I refused, but they asked again. Each time they asked, the amount of money increased, but I still refused." He turns and looks out the window. "Finally I said yes. Not because I wanted the money, but because I'm a coward, and when they grew insistent, I was afraid to keep saying no."

"Was it Mater Leeds? I heard that she and her people are big dope suppliers to the Sub Rosa."

He shakes his head and looks at me.

"No. It was Marshal Wells. The Golden Vigil wanted Akira."

I frown and look at Vidocq. He nods.

"What would a bunch of Homeland Security Bible-thumpers want with Akira? Were their office parties better than I thought?" I ask.

"I suspect they were interested in the drug's psychic aspects. They had many staff psychics, but mind reading has never been a precise art and subjects can resist. Now imagine that you had a drug that made a psychic link pleasurable. A drug that made the subject being interrogated feel as merry as New Year's Eve."

"Wells would love that. It sounds like something Aelita would love. Or Lucifer."

They tried something like that on me Downtown. For a while I was fighting in the arena so much that they gave me quarters in the basement. They made a big deal of it. Really it was just another holding pen, but it had four walls and a door and I had it to myself. I was so grateful I kicked and punched my guards harder than ever when they came for me. It was worth taking a beating to keep them from knowing that the filthy room made me happy.

When I was in Hell a funny thing happened. Every time I got beaten, burned, stabbed, or impaled in the arena, it just made me stronger. When I discovered I was a nephilim, it all made sense. But at the time I didn't know why it was happening. The Hellion fight masters and soldiers wanted to know why I didn't have anything useful to tell them and they beat me more. Which only made me stronger. Hellions aren't always clear on cause and effect.

Then they started the mind games. They'd spike my food with a kind of Hellion Ecstasy and send in the damned soul of a pretty murderess to play concubine. We'd work each other for a while, and when I was good and relaxed the questions would start. I didn't even realize I was being interrogated, it felt so good talking to another human. But I still couldn't answer their questions because I didn't have any answers. They tried young women and old ones, boys and oiled-up beefcake. They still didn't get any answers and by then my body had grown used to the drugs. But I could fake it. When the last devil doll didn't get any answers, a gaggle of disappointed guards bum-rushed my cell and did the hokeypokey on my head. I'd been in my Folsom Prison mansion a few weeks by then. I'd found the weak bolt in the iron door on my second night. I'd worked it out with my nails and teeth and had been sharpening it on the stone walls ever since.

I shoved it through one guard's ankle and kept going north, peeling off his calf muscle. That caught the other guards by surprise and they stopped kicking me for a second. Just enough time for me to get hold of one and shove the bolt into his thigh, opening up an artery that painted my walls and the last two guards with glistening black Hellion blood. It looked like we'd struck oil in there. They didn't try the pleasure principle on me again, which was nice, but a couple of days later I lost my private suite and got moved back to the bunkhouse with the other cattle. Moo, motherfucker.

"So you made it for them."

Vidocq nods.

"Yes. To give myself just a little credit, I did it rather badly. After several attempts in which I produced mild forms of the drug and pure poison in one case, I convinced the marshal that the ingredients he had acquired were of too poor a quality. I suppose he believed me because I remained alive and unincarcerated."

"That's good news, then," says Candy.

I look at her.

"If it's so hard to make and there are so few dealers, that means it's a small operation, right?"

"Or a bunch of lousy ones," I say.

Vidocq shakes his head.

"No. If people had died from Akira, there would be rumors everywhere. Candy is right. Akira is a specialized business. Possibly as small as one or two labs."

"See," Candy says. "I'm a good detective too."

"Just like Philip Marlowe. He's the one with the robot glasses in *The Maltese Falcon,* right?"

Candy sticks her tongue out at me. The sight of it is more distracting than I want it to be.

"Thanks for the talk. I think I've got things clearer. Now both of you get out. I'm doing this thing alone."

Silence. Then Vidocq pipes up.

"Do you think that's wise? You're not in the best frame of mind today."

"That's why you're not coming. Call a cab."

"Stark—" says Candy. I cut her off.

"I mean it. You're both reasonable and I don't want reasonable around when I talk to an Akira dealer."

Neither of them moves. Candy's up front with me. I reach across her and open the door.

"Go. I'll talk to you later."

"I'm calling you in one hour," she says. "If you don't like it, tough."

Candy and Vidocq get out. I leave them on the curb and head for the 405.

I can already picture Carolyn as one of those seductive damned souls that used to hover around my room under the arena. Getting me high. Getting me talking. Treating me like the soft fool I was back then. I'm not soft now and I'm even less forgiving. I don't know if Carolyn's blood is red or black, but if things go right, I just might find out.

CAROLYN McCOY LIVES on Cantara Street in a run-down tract home surrounded by a low metal fence and a half-dead lawn where patches of bleak grass break through the bare soil. Her house is right across the street from Sun Valley Park. Prime real estate for a small-time dealer.

I knock on her front door. It takes a while for anything to happen. I can hear someone banging around inside. I surprised her. She's hiding her stash.

The front door opens. Carolyn doesn't open the screen door, but stands there blinking in the sun like a not very bright groundhog. I've seen exhumed corpses with better tans.

"Who the fuck are you?" she says.

I lean close to the screen and smile.

"Hi. I'm a young college student trying to earn extra money selling magazine subscriptions door-to-door. Would you be interested in a ten- to twenty-year subscription to *Possession with Intent to Sell,* and its sister publication, *I'm Going to Burn Your House Down While You're Asleep in Bed Tonight*?"

She stares, her mouth open a little, like she's trying to form a question but forgot how to speak English in the last three seconds. I pull the screen door open and brush past her inside. She stands there, turns, and watches me invade her living room.

Carolyn has short dry hair that frames her face perfectly. She'd be pretty if she didn't have deep bruise-colored rings around her eyes and her skin wasn't the texture of sandpaper. There are red welts on the inside of her arms where she's been compulsively picking at the skin. I can smell not-quite-metabolized meth in her sweat. Her heart's jacked up and her eyes are pinpricks, but that's the drugs and not me. The angel in my head wants me to go easy so the back of her skull doesn't blow off and take her brain with it. That's a good idea. On the other hand, she's dealing DHS black-box psychic poison to teenyboppers who don't have a clue that demons, Kissi, and other brain-sucking assholes are out there waiting to get a claw hold in their cortex.

Carolyn stands by the door, arms crossed. When the clockwork in her brain kicks back in, she follows me into an avocado-and-orange living room with overstuffed chairs, throw pillows, and a long rattan sofa. It looks like the set for a seventies snuff film. She stops a few feet away and looks at me with a jittery stare, trying to figure out if she should know me. If she owes me money. If I owe her.

"Sit down," I say.

She doesn't. I take a step toward her.

"Sit down," I say again.

She walks around me and sits on the sofa, knees together, hands folded in her lap like she just graduated from charm school. I sit across from her on a cushioned green chair. I pull it over to the sofa so we're sitting face-to-face. The chair springs are long gone and my ass tries to sink below my knees. Not a good look when you want to come across as intimidating. I slide forward and sit on the edge of the chair.

"Are you a cop?" she asks.

"Do you think I'm a cop?"

"No."

"Then maybe we should go from there and see where it takes us. Is that all right with you, Carolyn?"

"Fine. Whatever. If you're not a cop, who are you?"

"I lied earlier. I'm not a college student."

She starts picking at the skin on her left arm.

"Stop that. You dig that arm open and you're going to get gangrene in a dusty shithole like this."

"What do you care?"

"I don't, but it's annoying to look at."

"What the fuck is it you want? You want money? Do I look like I have any money? Look around."

She waves a hand at the general wreckage. It's not so much that the place is a mess, it's that nothing is where any sane person would put it. It's like everything she owns, from furniture to coffee cups, she's used once and then dropped where she was when she was done with it.

"I don't have to look, Carolyn. I know that whatever kind of pig wallow you live in, you have money because you're a dealer," I say. "I can see it in your eyes and hear it in the tiny catches in your voice. You're also strung out and about six months from a fatal stroke. You know you have high blood pressure, don't you? That doesn't mix well with meth."

She lifts her head, still eyeing me.

"How do you know that?"

She gnaws on her thumb. Her fingernails have all been chewed down to the quick. There's plaster dust on her fingertips.

"It's just a trick I do. I know things about people. Like how all the money you say you don't have is stuffed in a hiding place in the wall."

The look she gives me is halfway between anger and dumb wonder.

"When did you come in my house?"

"I've never been here before. That was just to show you that lying isn't going to get you anywhere fun."

"If you want the money, take it. I'm sick. I can't stop you."

"I don't want your money. I just want a name or two."

"What name?"

"Before we get to that, did you sell Akira to Hunter Sentenza?"

She leans forward, resting her elbows on her knees, jacked up and exhausted at the same time.

"I didn't sell it to him. I gave it to him. We're like, you know, friends. We're going to get clean together."

I look at her. Her brain is vibrating so fast I can't read her. I go another way.

"Why not? You've got yourself a nice rich-boy client who was going to pay for your treatment. What was the plan? You take a walk your second day in and pocket whatever refund money you can con out of the clinic?"

She shakes her head and her straw-dry hair sways around her cheeks.

"It's not like that. Hunter and me are friends. We're going to do it together. For real this time."

"Then you haven't heard about him."

She sits up. Alert and for the first time somewhat focused.

"Something happened to Hunter?"

"He's missing. It was that last dose of Akira. His brain threw a rod. He jumped through a window and now he's missing."

"Oh God. Oh God. Oh God."

She covers her face with her hands. That was dumb. Never tell meth heads the truth. The whole reason they're high is they're severely reality-phobic. I snap my fingers in front of Carolyn's face. Lightly slap her arms.

"Come back to earth, Carolyn. We need you. Hunter needs you."

"Will he be okay?"

"I don't know. It depends entirely on what you can tell me. I need the name of your supplier."

"Why do you need that? Why aren't you out looking for him?"

"Do you know where to start looking?"

"No."

"Neither do we. What we do know is that Hunter used Akira without any problems and then all of a sudden he went psychobilly. I have a bad feeling that maybe there was something wrong with that last batch. Hunter's reaction wasn't a regular OD. It was real specific, so I want to know what was in there, who put it in there, and why."

She sits up and shakes her head. Draws her hands close to her body.

"I can't tell you that."

"Yes, you can. You're Hunter's friend and you want him found so the two of you can get better together."

"I can't."

I scoot forward on the chair and lean close to Carolyn. She freezes, trying to keep her eyes from meeting mine.

"Or maybe you're not Hunter's friend and you gave him a hot shot. Is that what you did, Carolyn? Did someone give you a special dose of Akira just for Hunter?"

Stop digging, boys, we struck oil.

Carolyn's brain is still humming like a tuning fork, but at least she's focused on something now. It's there in her eyes. She's beating herself silly trying to make all the contradictions and lies in her life add up to something sane. She really believes she's Hunter's friend, but the meth fog she lives in lets her justify giving Hunter drugs she knew were bad because someone up the food chain promised her more drugs or more money or the chance to settle a long-standing debt. Whatever her reasons, she feels guilty as hell. The addict self-pity tears start pumping out of her red and bruised eyes. I want to smack her to see if it snaps her brain back into gear, but I just pat her lightly on the shoulder. I keep my voice low, like I'm speaking to a child.

"Who gave you the special Akira?"

"I can't tell you."

"Sure you can. Just give me a name, I'll go, and you can get back to turning your brain to fish food."

"Fuck you."

She practically spits the words. Her whole body changes. She was a limp jellyfish a second ago and now she's ready to put her fist through the wall. We're on to the next step in this soap opera. She's not thinking like a tame little user now. She's moved into dealer mode. Hard-core. Defiant.

"Do you believe in magic, Carolyn?"

"Get out of my house, faggot."

"I don't mean kid-party magic. I mean the real thing. Witches on brooms. Love potions. Hexes and demons. Do you believe in that?"

"You know, one phone call and you'll be smoked before you get back to Hollywood."

I run through some ideas. There are a lot of scary things I learned in the arena, but I only used them on Hellions and Lurkers. Ninety-nine percent of what I learned I've never tried on a civilian and I don't particularly want to because I'm pretty sure they'd go off like a gerbil in a microwave.

Her hands are shaking from the drugs, but she's past scared and is deep into gangster territory.

She puts on her best Scarface sneer and says, "You just going to sit there staring at me? I know you. Pussies like you talk and talk, but you won't do anything. You don't know the kind of people I know. They have balls."

She sniffs and wipes the snot from her nose with the back of her hand.

I take out Mason's lighter, thumb it open, and spark a flame. Her eyes flicker to mine and then zero in on the lighter.

"I'd like to show you a magic trick. Would you like to see a magic trick, Carolyn?"

She gets up. I grab her arm. She twists and tries to sucker punch me. Puts her whole body into it. I don't try to stop her. I'm faster than any civilian, so she's moving in exquisite slo-mo. When she's a few inches from making contact, I lean back slightly and let her fist sail past. Grab the wrist and twist so her arm bends out like a chicken wing and every muscle and tendon in her shoulder feels like it's going to snap. Carolyn goes down face-first onto the sofa and rolls herself into a little ball, squeezing her aching shoulder. I wait. Eventually, she sits up. There's a half-finished cigarette in an ashtray on the arm of the sofa. She takes it, puts it between her lips, and starts looking around for matches. I'm still holding the lighter. I hold the flame out to her. She leans forward. I pull the lighter back and she follows a few inches. When she realizes I'm fucking with her, she stops and gives me a dirty look.

I say, "Let me get that for you for real."

There's one thing you have to remember about threats: when you make one, mean it. This is especially true with addicts. Their brains aren't designed to absorb new information and they're used to being slapped and stomped, so that doesn't scare them anymore. If you need to impress upon an addict the gravity of their situation, you need to make a threat that doesn't seem like a threat, but more like God pissing on them from a mountaintop.

I hold the lighter to my hand and my skin bursts into flames. Fire is fire and this isn't fun hoodoo, but I can stand the pain long enough to make my point.

Carolyn jumps back at the sight of my burning mitt. I play it up. Let the meat cook black until it flakes, and crispy skin drifts onto the carpet. I could let it get down to the bone, but I really don't want to do that. I move my hand toward Carolyn. She presses herself against the back of the sofa, trying to put as much distance as she can between us. I touch the tip of a finger to her cigarette until it glows.

"This is what I meant by magic. I know worse tricks than

this, but let's focus on this one for the moment. What do you think would happen if I held you with this hand and used you to mop up this messy, messy house? Does that sound like fun? I think it would hurt. Maybe as much as it hurt Hunter when that shit you gave him turned him into a demon's chew toy. I'm going to ask you one more time, and if you fuck with me, things are going to get drastic. Who gave you the Akira for Hunter?"

"Cale," she says.

She takes a long breath after she says it. Rubs the sores on her arms. She wants to pick at them, but she knows I don't like that.

"Cale what?"

She shrugs.

"I don't know. Just Cale." She nods at my still-burning hand. "I've seen him do weird shit like that, too. Like magic and shit."

"Where can I find Cale?"

"Downtown. At Dead Set. It's a club on Traction Avenue near Hewitt. You can't miss it. At night they show old zombie movies on the side of the building."

"What's Cale look like?"

"Tall. Skinny. He wears big boots to look taller and he wears one of those, like, Nazi-officer trench coats. His hair is bleached all white and there's like these runes or some kind of voodoo shit tattooed on the sides of his head."

I whisper some Hellion and the flames on my hand flutter and disappear. There's most of a flat can of beer on the floor next to the sofa. I pour it over my aching hand. The beer bubbles and steams away. I hand Carolyn the empty can. She clutches it to herself like it's a holy relic. I wipe the beer off my hand on the sofa and get up.

"Remember what I said, Carolyn. Go see a doctor about your blood pressure. You're about to lose your supplier, so your job is going to evaporate. The good news is that Cale won't be asking for any of that money you have in the wall. Take it and use it to clean yourself up. Dying isn't the worst thing in the world, but dying because you're stupid is."

I head out the front door. I'm halfway across the doomed lawn when I hear Carolyn yell something. I go back to the house. Behind the bright mesh of the screen door Carolyn looks like a ghost child.

"I'm sorry," she says.

She leans forward so that her face is almost touching the screen and whispers, "Tell Hunter I'm sorry. I didn't mean to . . . you know."

I nod.

"Sure. I'll tell him."

WHEN I GET back to the hotel, I find Candy in the room and Kasabian holding forth on Terrence Malick's *Badlands*.

"See, what Malick did wasn't tell us the story of a couple of kids on a cross-country murder spree, but to tell us a dream about it. Like the whole thing is a shared fantasy in the kids' heads and ours, which, from what I've heard, is pretty close to what it was like for Charlie Starkweather to kill all those people."

She smiles up at me from the foot of the bed as I come in.

"Hey there. I'm getting Film 101 from your boss."

"My boss?"

"That's what he said."

I look at Kasabian.

He says, "What do you know about accounting, insurance, inventory control, and, you know, running a video store besides watching movies all day?"

"Not much."

"Then I'm the boss."

I sit down next to Candy.

"You can't argue with that logic," she says.

"I could, but it would end in tears and divorce lawyers, and I can't stand paperwork."

Candy leans gently into me so our shoulders are touching. I pull a wad of cash from my pocket and hand it to her.

"Why don't you get us another room where we can talk? If the night manager gets weird, use my name and give him too much money. He'll set you up."

She bounces off the bed onto her feet and goes to the door. On her way out she blows Kasabian a kiss.

"I'll be back for your master class on Monte Hellman."

He beams at her as she leaves.

"Now that's the kind of girl you shoplift beer for."

He whizzes around on his skateboard to face me.

"Good thing you got here when you did. I was going to rock her world with some surfboard moves. She would have been mine."

"You're the boss and I don't surf. You could probably have her in Mexico by now with a preacher and a cut-up fishnet stocking for a wedding veil and a donkey for the witness."

"*Badlands* was probably too cerebral for a first date. I

should have gone with something sexy and scary like *Suspiria*. Next time."

"Sure. Next time."

I start to say something about delusions of grandeur, but keep my mouth shut. I haven't seen Kasabian this happy in probably ever.

I'm out of cigarettes. I reach into the nightstand and get a fresh pack of Maledictions. There aren't too many packs left. Kasabian's happy. He doesn't need to know that. I light two and stick one between Kasabian's lips.

"I need you to look up something for me in the *Codex*."

"That sounds like work. Didn't you see the sign? I'm closed for the evening."

"You may be the boss, but I pay the beer bills and rent, so pull a little overtime for me."

Kasabian puffs on his cigarette and frowns. His little legs take the Malediction out of his mouth and tap ashes onto the floor.

"What do you want to know?"

"I need to know about a . . . Qlifart? Qlifuck? Screw it. Demon. This one is different. It's confident. Maybe even smart. It does possessions, but it doesn't automatically attack unless it feels threatened. I thought for a while it might be a Kissi, but I know them, and this doesn't feel like their work."

He shakes his head.

"That doesn't make sense. If it's a demon, it's dumb. All demons are dumb. Which means they have an inferiority complex that makes them trigger-happy."

"If it made sense, I wouldn't ask you to look in the *Codex*."

"Why are you dragging me into this thing? I don't like

demons. Just because you're feeling magnanimous doesn't mean I am."

I sit on the end of the bed and smoke. I flick the ashes onto the carpet, too. Got to give the maid something to do when she comes in so she won't notice the dead man on the skateboard.

"Yes, you are. Candy's working with me on this. Do it for her. Dazzle her with your kung fu."

"Nice try. I was kidding before."

"She's a Jade. You never know what kind of fetishes they have."

Faint traces of cigarette smoke drift from the bottom of Kasabian's neck and hang around his face like mountain mist.

"I was going to watch *Blue Velvet* and order chicken wings. What more could a guy want?"

"How about a body?"

His eyes narrow.

"Is this case of yours going to get me one?"

"I doubt it. But fucking off in here isn't either. The more hoodoo work we do, the more likely one of us will stumble on a fix-it spell for your situation."

"My situation," he mumbles. "You put me in this situation."

"After you shot me."

He smacks the keyboard and the computer wakes up.

"Asshole. Here I was, talking to a pretty girl, content as Jayne Mansfield's pasties, and you come in and want me to flip burgers on the night shift."

"You'll check the *Codex*?"

"I'll check."

"Cool."

I get up to go out. He yells something at me.

"I need highly concentrated carbs to do this brain work. Get me something cold and I'll make you Employee of the Month."

I go to the kitchen and get a six-pack from the fridge.

I set it on his table and say, "You want a soufflé or something, too? I'll need to warm up the oven."

"This will do. Don't forget to punch out when you leave."

"I'm about to punch something."

I ASK THE night manager what room Candy is in and head upstairs to the last one at the back. It has a nice view of a used-car lot.

I stop for a second before going in, feeling a little strange. Candy and I have been dancing around each other for months, but we've hardly ever been alone together. Maybe the one and only time was when she stabbed me in the heart to give me the zombie serum. Does that count as a first date? And if so, on what planet? I'm thirteen again, trying to figure out how to talk to a girl. This is ridiculous. We've killed and fought side by side and kept the gates of Hell from opening. I should be able to string enough words together not to drool on myself.

I open the door and Candy is waiting for me, standing naked in the middle of the bed. I barely get the door closed when she jumps all the way across the room and lands on my chest, pinning me against the wall. A pure predator ambush.

Candy's skin is as corpse cold as I remember from the first time she pecked me on the cheek outside Doc Kinski's clinic.

But she warms up when we fall onto the bed and I'm on top of her and we're kissing like it's the cure for cancer.

She shreds my shirt with her nails and I barely get my pants off before she destroys those, too.

Candy wraps her legs around me. I slip inside her and the world goes black and hot. Her teeth wolf into my shoulder. I pull her hair as her nails dig into my back. I pull harder and bend her head back so I can see her face. I catch a glimpse of the Jade lurking just under the skin. Her nails extend into claws and our grinding bodies torpedo us from this soft and stupid human world to someplace where monsters can tear and bite. No one's afraid of it and all the groans and pain and craziness are beautiful.

The hotel bed makes a sound like a bullet and collapses beneath us. I pull her legs onto my shoulders and push deeper inside her. When she throws back her arms, her hands smash through the cheap wall paneling. She shifts her weight and rolls on top of me. My elbow comes down on the nightstand, cracking it and demolishing the phone.

We fall out of bed and onto the floor. Candy is on her hands and knees and I'm in her from behind. She doesn't hold the Jade inside anymore. Her body starts its transformation but she holds it halfway. Not quite girl and not quite beast. She moans and snarls as one clawed hand rips the stuffing and springs out of the sofa next to us.

The mirror on the dresser falls and shatters on the floor. I'm not really sure which one of us did that.

We crawl back onto the bed. Candy crawls back on top and thrusts down on me hard enough to crack the San Andreas Fault. I swear I hear plaster falling from the ceiling in the room below us. I don't care. All that matters is the girl and the monster thrusting down against me.

In the dim distant parts of our brains that can still form thoughts, I know we're both thinking the same thing.

This has been a long goddamn time coming.

LATER WE LIE in the ruins of the room. We push some debris out of the way and move the bed so it's at least flat on the floor. We lie down, wrapping ourselves in torn sheets and what's left of the bedspread.

"I like this hotel. The rooms are simple, but kind of pretty," says Candy.

"I think we broke this one."

"Want to do it again?"

"Sure."

Later, when Candy falls asleep, I put on my pants and boots and go back to the other room to get a new shirt. Kasabian hasn't moved from the computer. Beer cans are piled under his table.

"Your shoulder is bleeding," he says. "Let me guess. On the way over you ran into a midget with an armful of razor blades and barbed wire."

"I don't kiss and tell."

"You don't have to. I could hear you all the way over here. The whole hotel could hear you. Everyone was out of their rooms. They thought it was a gang fight. The hotel manager called 911."

I find a clean Max Overdrive T-shirt and put it on.

"Cops are coming?"

Kasabian shakes his head.

"Relax. I routed the call to a phone-company all-circuits-are-busy message."

"You know how to do that?"

"I'm on this computer all day. Making it do bad things is the only fun I have. Did you really think I spent all my time looking at video catalogs and porn?"

"Yeah. I sort of did."

His eyes narrow at me.

"See. That's exactly the kind of thing I expect from you. No respect whatsoever. After all the research and information I've found for you."

"That's not how I meant it. I just never pictured you as the high-tech type."

"I have to be. All my magic goes into keeping this goddamn skateboard upright. I don't have extra for anything else, so I have to use machines."

"That's actually a real smart way to deal with things. You're a credit to your race, Alfredo Garcia."

"Hey, don't call me that when you're off getting laid and I'm in here keeping LAPD off your back," he says, pissed and with a right to be.

"You're right, man. I owe you."

"You're goddamn right you do." He leans toward me and speaks in a whisper like maybe the CIA is listening. "Is she as cute naked as she is with clothes on?"

"Don't even start."

"Come on. I saved you both. And you just said you owe me. Get me a Polaroid."

I crack a smile at that.

"You know, she just might think that's funny enough to do. She's not shy."

"Seriously?"

"I'm not going to ask her for you. You want it so bad, you do your own begging. And I don't want to see you Photo-shopping her head onto porn stars."

"What's her e-mail address?"

"I don't even know if she has one."

"You hick. I'll find it myself."

I take the Smith & Wesson out of my coat and reload it with special rounds I made with cut-down .410 shotgun shells. I might not need them, but fortune favors the prepared mind that thought to bring a really big gun.

I say, "Don't crash out on me. I'm looking for information right now and that'll probably lead to more questions. I might quiz you now, but I need to make a call."

"You know where to find me."

IF YOU'VE EVER wondered if your life has run off the rails, here's a handy quiz.

Is the only person left in the universe you can go to for help someone even God doesn't want to talk about?

Is the only alliance left to you with a gang that eats and shits chaos?

Are you about to drunk-dial the only guy in Creation who's probably more despised than you?

If you answered yes to any of these, then you should seek psychiatric help. If you answered yes to all of them, you're me.

I WALK OUT the front of the hotel and a block down Hollywood Boulevard.

On the way I get out my phone and thumb in a number I've had for a while but never dialed before. I let it ring once and hang up without waiting for an answer.

"It's about time we heard from you."

I spin around, toward a vinegar stink. When they aren't trying to pass as regular people, Kissi have a very particular smell.

"Goddamn you're fast."

He's blond, with the kind of sky-blue eyes that don't happen in nature. His cheekbones look like they were sculpted by a fascist Michelangelo. I don't know if he was grown in a petri dish or assembled from dead SS rent boys. I can't stand to look at him.

I say, "I told you I didn't want to see you wearing that Nazi face anymore."

"I don't remember my appearance being part of our bargain," says Josef.

"Wear your real face next time. It's easier looking at a burn-victim bug than Dr. Mengele."

You can't be subtle when you're dealing with a Kissi, even their leader. And he's the least psychotic one of the bunch.

The Kissi and I have one major thing in common. We shouldn't exist. We're both part of God's Misfits of Nature traveling show. When the Big Bopper created angels at the beginning of time, he fucked it all up. The blowback from conjuring all those angels created both angels and their opposite. The Kissi. They don't live in heaven with Daddy, but way out in the boiling chaos at the edge of the universe.

In their true form Kissi are fish-belly white and have a faint bottom-of-the-ocean-fish glow. They look like a cross between a regular angel and a six-foot-tall grasshopper dipped in wax and left in the sun to melt. If you've ever seen one, that's enough to last a lifetime, and I've seen a whole world of them. That was back when I destroyed their Honeycomb Hideout way out in the ass end of Chaosville. Yeah, it's hard to justify trying to kill off a whole species, but they were collaborating with Mason in his plan to take over Hell and then the rest of the universe. So basically, fuck 'em.

Most of them went spinning off into space and died when I wiped out their home world, but enough survived that Josef has assembled a small army of them. He did it because I asked him to. We made a deal with this particular devil a while back. I wasn't happy about it then and I'm not happy about it now, but when you're an Abomination, you can't trust Hell, and Heaven hates you, so you don't always get to choose who you dance with at the prom.

"Why are you wasting time chasing drug dealers over a dead boy? That's not what we agreed to."

"One, I don't think the kid is dead. And two, whatever is going on with the kid has to do with Mason and Aelita. You should thank me for finding out what it is."

When I first got back, the Golden Vigil's main obsession wasn't Lucifer, it was monitoring the Kissi. The Vigil saw Lucifer as a gelded pony. More of an annoyance than any kind of threat. The Kissi were the real danger in the universe. The only thing that could tilt all of existence toward total chaos. That's one more thing I have in common with the Kissi. They hate the Vigil almost as much as I do.

"You promised us a war. We're tired of waiting," Josef says.

"I know, but remember, you being impatient is why I beat you last time. When we made this deal, you agreed to wait for my signal before doing anything. My game. My rules. What we're planning is going to take some time to set up. If you don't want to play in my sandbox, then fuck off back to Limbo."

I'm tall, but Josef is taller. He straightens so he can look down his perfect nose at me.

"We'll wait, but not forever."

"Calm down. The big plan is still down the road, but I might have some fun for you in the meantime."

"What kind of fun?"

"Your favorite. Chaos and destruction. Loss of life and property. Burned toast and spoiled milk."

"I hope you're not lying to me."

"Is that a threat? That's big talk for a guy who ended up with his head and body in separate zip codes the last time we went at it."

Josef stares at me. Maybe the Nazi face is right for him after all. Like all good goose-steppers, Kissi think they're better than everybody else. In their minds they're high-rolling, comped-in-Vegas true angels. God, on the other hand, thinks of them as being like the black sludge that rolls into sewers. When he thinks of them at all.

"We're done for now. I'm going inside. Keep your phone on," I tell him, and start back to the hotel.

"The beast in your room is very pretty," says Josef. "Her true face is, at least. Much better than that human you wasted your time with before. You should thank Mason for getting rid of her for you."

I head back for him, trying to decide if I should rip out his tongue or stomp his ribs into marmalade. But he's gone before I even turn around. Like I said, Josef is fast.

I go to Candy's room, climb over the broken furniture as quietly as I can, and lie down next to her. I'm exhausted from getting up early, fighting the hangover, and torching my hand. A club like Dead Set won't open its doors until at least eleven and I'm betting Cale won't be there before one. There's time to get a few hours of sleep.

Candy stirs when she feels my body hit the mattress. Takes one of my arms and wraps it around her, pulling me onto my side until my front is pressed against her back. It feels strange to be in a bed with another person. Strange in an okay way. The kind of strange a person could get used to.

I don't even feel sleep coming on, but the room goes soft around me and I'm somewhere else.

I'm making coffee in the kitchen of the old apartment. Alice is on the sofa doing a crossword puzzle. *Miyuki-chan in Wonderland,* a weird fetish anime version of *Alice in Wonderland* is on TV with the sound off. X is playing "The World's a Mess It's in My Kiss" from a little boom box on the counter.

Alice says, "What's an eight-letter word for 'bountiful flora'?"

"I have no idea. You know I hate crosswords."

" 'Genocide,' " she says, and fills in the squares.

"What?"

She doesn't look up.

"How about a five-letter word for 'Pinocchio's kin'?"

"I don't know."

" 'Sheol.' "

I leave the coffee and walk over to the sofa.

"What kind of a crossword is that?"

" 'Saints' bones.' Seven letters. 'Armageddon.' "

I sit down next to her. On the TV, a dominatrix version of the Mad Hatter is coming on to cartoon Alice.

My Alice looks up, smiles, and kisses me lightly on the lips.

"Here's one that's two words for 'a makeshift mantra.' "

I look over her shoulder at the puzzle. It's completely normal except that she's filling in all the answers in strange runes or pictograms I've never seen before.

" 'Orphée.' "

"Is this a dream?" I ask her.

She shrugs.

"You tell me. This is in your head. Would you be more comfortable if I was a dancing midget?"

"In another dream, before the Drifters hit the city, you warned me about something that was going to happen to me. Is this one of those dreams?"

"What's a five-letter word for 'banker's holiday'?"

The X song starts up again. She must have it set on loop.

Go to hell see if you like it
Then come home with me
Tomorrow night may be too late
The world's a mess it's in my kiss

" 'HOLOCAUST,' " she says.

"I'm going to make this right, you know. I'm going to make Mason pay for what he did to you and me."

Alice finishes the puzzle and sets it on the coffee table. I can see it better now. Even though she was coming up with different answers, the puzzle is filled in with the same seven symbols, over and over again.

She leans over and puts her arms around me. Rests her head on my shoulder, watching the TV.

"That's one fucked-up movie," she says.

"I don't know why I picked it."

"Yeah, why would you possibly pick *Alice in Wonderland*?"

"Oh. Right."

She pulls me closer.

"You know I love you, right?"

"Yeah."

"Then you need to stop goddamn obsessing all the time. I'm dead. Boo-hoo. You're Sandman Slim. Boo-hoo. The universe is a lot bigger than us."

I shake my head. Reach for a cigarette. She lets go so I can lean forward and grab the lighter.

"I know all that. But a lot of little stuff still hurts like Hell."

"You're telling me? I'm the one who got a knife in the back."

She says it right after I light up. I try to move away, but she holds on to me.

"That's really what happened?"

"Yeah. You've got to give Mason credit for that. Sending Parker to do it fast. The guy knew how to do it. I hardly felt a thing."

"If you know that, then this isn't a dream."

"Maybe not a hundred percent. But it's still a dream."

"For a long time I was afraid of knowing what happened to you."

"Gee, I hadn't noticed. Now you do know. It's time to get your ass past it."

I take a drag off the cigarette. She takes it from my hand and puffs. Hands it back to me. Her fingertips are blue to the point of almost being black. They don't look like a living person's hands.

"I don't know what to do next."

Alice punches me on the arm.

"Were you even listening to the crossword, dumb-ass? It's all finally happening. What you knew was going to happen. You can either keep watching movies until the sun burns out or you can stop running from who you are. You're Sandman Slim, goddammit. You're that or you're nothing. Your choice."

"Isn't there a curtain number three? I don't mind a year's worth of Turtle Wax."

"Sorry. The money's all down. Betting is closed. Play or walk away."

I nod toward the crossword puzzle on the table.

"What's with the hen scratching? I can't read a damned word."

She glances at the crossword and shakes her head.

"It's a puzzle. You're supposed to figure it out. That's why they call it a puzzle."

"How?"

"Once again, it's called a puzzle for a reason."

"Okay."

Some kind of magic being, a stand-in for the caterpillar, I think, is hitting on Alice.

"You know I'm in bed with another woman, right?"

"It'd be pretty creepy if you were in bed with me, Ed Gein."

"It's okay with you?"

"I thought we went through this when you fucked Brigitte. Get on with your life."

"It's more like she fucked me. I was pretty much just an innocent bystander."

"Every guy tries that line at least once. It never works."

"Why did you pick that particular song?"

"Who says I picked it? Who says it's about me?"

Alice takes the cigarette from my hand, finishes it, and stubs it out on the sole of her shoe. She nods at the TV, where a barely dressed female Jabberwock is flying Alice across Wonderland.

"If you dream about me again, dream me like that Alice. She gets to fly around, have adventures, and isn't stuck in this fucking apartment forever."

"I'll work on it."

"Do that. You know I'd look good as an anime schoolgirl. I love you, but I'm over your moony guilt trip. Dream about that girl you're lying next to for a change."

She kisses me on the cheek, gets up, and walks away.

"See you around, Miyuki-chan."

"Later, alligator."

I wake up and take my arm from around Candy. I'm sweating. I go to the bathroom, run some water on my face, and wipe myself down on one of the hotel's rough white towels. I find my phone and check the time. Still early enough to get some sleep. I sit on the edge of the bed, letting my head clear. In a little while I lie down and put my arm back around Candy. She moves back against me.

Yeah, I could get used to this.

I WAKE UP around one and start putting my clothes on. Candy hears me and turns over.

"What's up?"

"I'm going to a zombie industrial club to track down a drug dealer. What are you doing?"

She throws off the covers and starts looking around for her clothes.

"No way I'm letting you tough-guy-solo it and hog all the fun."

"Then shake a leg, Modesty Blaise."

I KIND OF regret having ditched the Volvo in the afternoon. I have a bad feeling about where all this drugs-and-demon bullshit is heading, especially after talking to Alice. Or talking to myself. Or talking to some combination of Alice and my subconscious. I don't hate the dull anonymity of the car or, when I'm being honest with myself, the last month and a half of quiet. Things are changing and they're going to change faster. You'll be able to boogie-board on all the blood that's coming.

Tonight, though, the universe throws me a bone.

A BIKE RIDE is what I need to blow out the dust and clear my head, and what do you know? Someone's left a red Ducati Monster in the street just for me. Every day is Christmas if you know how to get around locks.

I look at Candy.

"You okay riding without a helmet?"

"What's a helmet?"

I take out the black bone knife, slice through the Cobra lock in one pass, and toss it away. I climb onto the bike. Candy gets on behind and puts her arms around me. I jam the knife into the ignition, turn, and gun the throttle. The Ducati purrs like a big mechanical cat. I kick up the stand, turn, and speed off to find Cale. At the corner I remember we're going across town and there might be cops. I grunt a little Hellion trickster hoodoo so civilians will see helmets on our heads. Sometimes magic is as dull as taking out the trash.

The wind feels good on my face and Candy is warm against me. Talking to Alice has taken a weight off my back, one I didn't even know I was carrying. I'm amazed I haven't been walking around like Chaney in *The Hunchback of Notre Dame*. I know some of what I'm feeling comes from Alice's tough-love, leave-me-alone-and-find-a girl-that-breathes pep talk, but the more important part is finding out how she died. Not knowing was killing me and I never had a clue. I'm not saying that knowing feels good, but it feels more human. I've broken things and killed people for what happened to her and I don't regret any of it. But now it feels like the bottomless fury that both pushed me forward and held me back might have an end to it. Or at least it won't be cranked up to eleven all the time. I'll never let go of Alice entirely and I'll never forgive what happened to her, but I know I don't have to destroy myself to make things right. I just have to kill Mason.

Sometimes, when I'm out at night and things are quiet, I take pity on the angel in my head and let it take the lead.

The angel can see in the dark, but not like it's an owl or has night-vision goggles. The angel sees the world the way God must see it. Nothing is solid. Objects don't exist except as strings of vibrating pearls of light. Molecules are interlocked Tinkertoys of atoms hiding in smudged electron fogs, all wrapped in the twisted folds of superstring taffy. Swirling and flowing, the universe folds in on itself in a multidimensional Technicolor Busby Berkeley dance of the celestial spheres. And that's just in the city. I wonder what the ocean would look like with these eyes? Waves within waves within waves within waves, a fractal whirlpool dropping down forever, past Heaven and Hell and what? Could eyes like the angel's see the Big Bang? Could I pick out the atoms of Alice's ashes where I dumped them by Venice Beach? No. None of that tonight. I'm alive and I'm driving and there's a pretty girl at my back. I'm a goddamn Bruce Springsteen song.

When we get near the club, I leash the angel and stuff him back in his doghouse. I need to see with my eyes now.

I stop the bike in the driveway of a gated warehouse down the block from Dead Set. The scene is pretty much what Carolyn said it was. The Goth industrial crowd wrapped in latex and chrome. Girls and skinny boys wearing boots with heels high enough to tickle Gabriel's ball sac mill around outside, smoking.

Dead Set is in a converted furniture warehouse. There's a projector on the low brick building next door splashing *Stacy,* a Japanese-schoolgirl zombie flick, across three floors on the side of the Dead Set warehouse. A horde of barely legal *shoujos* in bloody school uniforms stumble toward soldiers firing automatic weapons. It goes the way these face-offs usually do. Schoolgirls one. Soldiers zero. I light up a couple of Maledictions, hand one to Candy, and we wait.

"Shouldn't we go inside?" she asks.

"Too crowded. If we get into a tussle, all those extra bodies are just going to get in the way. A club like this only has one entrance. Give it some time. Cale will come to us."

"I love it when you talk all Sam Spade."

A cop car cruises by every half hour or so to let the crowd know they're there. I smell some undercover bacon in the crowd, too. Their sweat is different. They're excited, but it's not by the drugs or possibility of sex. It's at the possibility they might get the chance to put a beat down on the young and beautiful. The cool kids who wouldn't let them sit at their table in the lunchroom. Fucking cops. They're making me side with these preening assholes.

I have to wait around an hour for Cale to come outside. Yes, it's boring. You can only make so many catty comments about the crowd when everyone looks pretty much the same. Candy and I burn through more Maledictions than we should. Fuck Lucifer, too. I saved his life. He could have at least sent me a crate of smokes before he fucked off back to Daddy's condo in heaven.

I get back on the bike and gun the ignition.

"Follow me over on foot," I tell Candy.

I hit the throttle and blast across the street like a twin-cylinder RPG. Cale and his crew have come outside. I screech-skid to a hard stop inches away from him. However high he is, his reflexes are good enough that he jumps back a few inches when he sees me closing in on him.

"Hey, Cale. Long time no see. How've you been doing?"

"Do I know you?"

"Sure. Carolyn McCoy introduced us."

"Sorry. You've got the wrong guy. I don't know you or any Carolyns or any McCoys."

I'm close enough to see that yes, he does have runes and sigils tattooed on the sides of his head. I want a closer look, but the lights are shit and he's too high to stand still.

He turns and tries to walk away.

"Sure you know Carolyn. You're her Akira connection." I say it loud enough so that everyone nearby can hear.

Cale turns and heads back, his long lanky body moving with a dancer's practiced grace but a boxer's strength. I'm pretty sure he's armed, but I'm not sure what with.

"What did you just say?"

There are five in his crew. Three girls and two other guys. They spread out behind him, blocking the street in case I try to rabbit away.

"Akira. The Akira that Carolyn sells to stupid college kids and, for all I know, underage go-go dancers. Damn, how many felonies is that?"

"That's what she says? And you believe everything every dumb junkie cunt tells you?"

"I believe her because you said you didn't know any Carolyns, but you know she's a dumb junkie cunt."

He does a little grunting laugh.

"All these small-time bitches have habits. If I ever did know a Carolyn, I don't know her anymore."

"Why would you? She dosed the kid for you and that makes her too dangerous to keep around. What I want to know is whether you dosed Hunter Sentenza on your own or did someone pay you to do it?"

He doesn't say anything, but he doesn't walk away either. He's trying to decide if he wants to talk some more or fight.

"I'm guessing the second," I say. "If you wanted Hunter dead, you'd have sent one of your monkey boys to do it. That means you did it for someone. I want to know who."

Cale subtly shifts his weight, dropping it onto his back foot. He's trying to be subtle, but I know a fighting stance when I see one. His crew is showing a lot of teeth. Candy is behind them in the street. She keeps an eye on them while they keep an eye on me.

Someone screams off to my right. Two drunk girls have fistfuls of each other's coiffed hair and are rocking back and forth trying to hit each other. Drunk catfighting for the crowd's amusement. Every town has its arena.

But I shouldn't have taken my eyes off Cale. By the time I refocus, he's throwing a hex at me. And it isn't in the textbooks in Sub Rosa school. He's been hanging out with a bad crowd. I bet he cheats on his spelling tests, too. But there's no time to think about that. A buckshot hurricane of wasps blasts from his hands right at my face.

The first wave hits me square in the chest and face before

I can throw up a shield spell. The wasps are coming so fast that most of them don't have a chance to sting me. They splat and bounce off into the crowd. The young and the beautiful scream in pain and run. Fuck 'em if they're too dumb to get out of the way of a hoodoo street fight.

I get a shield up, covering my front from ground to head. The stream of wasps is coming at me so hard that I have to lean into them to keep from being blown onto my back. I expand the shield over and around Cale and his crew. Shouting in Hellion, I slam the shield shut, trapping them inside with Cale's ballistic bugs.

There's a couple of minutes of hilarious screaming and self-flagellation as Cale and his people crouch, crawl, and slap themselves silly trying to get the wasps off. Cale is barely in control of the hex, but finally turns off the bug spigot.

Cale is pissed. He shouts a string of hexes and chips away at the sides of my shield dome. I let him. I'll give the kid some credit. He's got some power and he's on his way to learning how to use it, but he isn't there yet. That's a dangerous place to be. It can make you do stupid things. Like now, for instance.

Finally, he blasts my shield dome into a million pieces of formless aether. A guy like this with lots of showy magic tends to forget the basics of fighting. The physical part. I rush him and get a hand around his throat before he can throw any more hexes.

Cale's boys just stand there like pricy mannequins. It's the girls who finally do something and make to throw some hoodoo my way. Candy is on them before either of them can get more than a syllable out. She puts the boot to them, but has enough control of herself not to go Jade on them.

I let go of Cale long enough for him to take a swing at me. Then I speak a single Hellion word.

He collapses. Not like he fell. More like a giant invisible foot from the sky is trying to squash him like a bug. He fights it, writhing and twisting. Almost pushing himself up on two arms and then collapsing again. His face is a few inches from the street when he starts vomiting blood. Some of it splashes onto his face and his bleached white hair. Cale's crew freezes. They don't run, but they don't try to help him either. Blood does that to people. I let him keep vomiting. In fact, I make him vomit more blood than any ten human bodies could possibly hold. Gallons and gallons of it. It spreads in a widening puddle in the street, covering him and threatening to touch his crew's expensive shoes. They want to stop the mayhem, but they're torn between their loyalty to their leader and their look.

One of the girls, Cale's squeeze I guess by her haughty high-toned look, rushes to his aid, but slips and ends up on her ass in the gooey red slip-and-slide pouring from her boyfriend's mouth.

I can hear the electronic beeps and boops of people dialing cell phones. Good citizens calling 911. I shout a bit of mind-control abracadabra. It's something you use on people and hell beasts, but it does weird things to electronics. I once blew out all the traffic lights on Hollywood Boulevard with it when I drove Allegra to Doc Kinski's clinic. This time it just fries some smartphones.

I let up on Cale. He can't breathe while puking and I don't want him to die of oxygen deprivation. The moment the blood stops, he sucks in big mouthfuls of air.

"Hurting your boss here is fun, but only one of you pricks

is going home alive, and it's the one who names your Akira supplier. The one who makes it. Just shout out a name and address and you get to walk away."

One of the boys who's gone even paler than when he came out of the club waves a bony arm in the air like a drunk praying mantis.

"It's Hunahpu," he says. "He runs the cookers."

"Where can I find him?"

"Shut your fucking mouth, Jonas."

It's Cale, still on the ground, but still in command. His latex glistens with blood. He's gone from platinum blond to *I Love Lucy* red.

Candy moves behind him in case he freaks and takes a runner.

Jonas says, "I don't want to die here."

Cale shouts, "Say another word and I'll kill you myself!"

"Who do you think is in better shape to kill you, Jonas? Cale or me? Tell me where to find Hunahpu."

"I'll tell you if you don't kill anyone."

I nod.

"Good boy. That's reasonable. Tell me. I'll know if you're lying."

"Hunahpu works out of a lab in West Hollywood. Bio-Specialties Group."

"What kind of lab is it?"

"I don't know. There's test tubes and shit. It's a lab."

"Will he be there now?"

"How should I know?"

"You got a number for him?"

Jonas's hands are shaking so much he can hardly get the

phone out of his pocket. The hoodoo I threw earlier should have just fried the part of the phone that makes calls. The address book and calendar still ought to work. Maybe.

Jonas nervously thumbs through a couple of screens. Cale's girl is up on her feet. She tries to grab the phone from Jonas's hands, but he shoves her back down in the blood. Candy kicks her hands out from under her when she tries to get up again.

"Jonas, you cocksucker, don't tell him anything," shouts Cale.

"I don't want anyone getting killed."

Jonas holds up the phone so I can read the number off the screen.

"Good boy. You are not a completely useless human being. Now get the fuck out of here."

"Cale? You okay? Cale?" calls his girl.

Jonas's chest explodes with wet red holes. The blood on his shirt is real and it's his. He collapses onto his knees and falls over onto his face.

I spin and see Cale pointing a .38 snub nose at me. Probably loaded with .357 rounds. He must have had it tucked in his boot. He has to use both hands to steady the gun enough to aim. The hammer is already halfway down. He gets off one shot. A body blurs by me. Candy has shoved one of the boys from Cale's crew in front of me. He catches the bullet just below his right ear and is dead before he hits the pavement.

Cale manages to get off one more shot. It goes through my right sleeve. I feel some heat and blood, but the bullet does more damage to the coat than to me. Cale doesn't know that, and too bad for him, neither does Candy.

She is on him and the blood isn't my hoodoo spell this time. She's gone full-on Jade and is tearing him apart.

"Candy, that's enough," I yell.

She turns to me. Her eyes are red slits in black ice. Her nails have grown out into curved claws and her mouth is full of sharp white shark teeth. Someone screams. Then a whole lot of people start screaming, which is the way it usually goes when people see a monster for the first time.

"Come on. He's not going to get any deader."

It takes her a minute to register my words. The beast is in control now and it takes a few seconds for the human part of her to get back online.

She walks over to me, her human face slowly replacing the Jade's. I put my arm around her, whisper, "Thanks for looking out for me," and kiss the top of her head.

Most of Cale's crew is long gone. Only his girl is still there. I walk over to his body and push his head to the side. He's a mess. When I wipe the blood away, I can make out the tattoos on his scalp and the rusty gears in my brain go *click, click, click.*

"What the hell is that doing there?" I ask Cale's girl.

The girl says, "That's the symbol for Sister Ludi. She's a protector spirit."

"I know what she is. What is she doing on Cale's scalp?"

"What do you mean?"

"Sister Ludi is fake. A gaff. She's something Sub Rosa touts made up to sell fake idols and potions to tourists. What's her symbol doing on the head of someone who had to know that?"

A better question is what does a demon have to do with a

fake goddess? I recognize it now. Sister Ludi's sigil is the same symbol that was burned over the bed in Hunter's room.

"Oh, that. It's for Hunahpu. He's really into Sister Ludi. He thinks saying she's fake is some kind of Anglo conspiracy. Cale wore it to show respect and Hunahpu gave him a cut rate on product."

She keeps looking at Cale's body with no way to process what just happened. I feel a little sorry for her. But I feel sorrier for Hunter.

"Was it Hunahpu who gave you the special Akira for the Sentenza kid?"

"I don't know who it was for, but yeah, Cale said there was a special batch for someone."

"That's all I needed to know."

I take her by the arm and walk her to a cab that's been waiting outside the club. Like everyone else, the driver is standing and gawking at the mess. I put Cale's girl in the backseat and close the door.

"Listen to me," I say, leaning in the window. "It's hard and nasty what you saw tonight, but you're lucky it happened now. Cale was never going to last doing what he does. There are people out there ten times harder and a hundred times meaner than Cale was ever going to be. He was always going to end up on his back with holes in him. The difference is if you'd stuck around much longer, you'd be lying in blood next to him, another dumb dead girl in a place that spews out more dumb dead girls than smog. Go home. Be sad for a while. When you're over it, fall in love with someone who has better tattoos."

I go around, give the driver some money, and tell him to take her home. Before he can get in the cab, I take out the

.460 and pop a few rounds over the crowd's head. The cut-down shotgun shells I'd loaded it with aren't filled with pellets, but with one of Vidocq's memory powders. It will scrub away the last hour from everyone's brain. I might have a bad temper and be dating someone who eats people, but I'm not stupid enough to leave witnesses.

Someone's dropped a coat on the ground. I pick it up, take Candy by the arm, and walk her around the corner. When we're out of sight of the club, I use the coat to wipe Cale's blood from her face and hands.

I say, "Thanks for saving me back there."

Her eyes are a little vacant.

"Wow. I haven't done that to a person for a long time."

"How are you feeling?"

"A little spacey, but okay. Are you okay? We should get you to see Allegra to get the bullet out."

"I'm fine. It barely grazed me and I've already stopped bleeding."

She leans against the wall, a little out of breath.

"He shot you. I wouldn't have done what I did if he hadn't shot you."

"I know."

She stares at me, her eyes still a little unfocused, but she's coming back to earth.

"Did I go too far?"

I shrug.

"Technically he did shoot me. And he did kill his friend, so we can assume he would have kept shooting until he killed me or I got him. So, yeah, you saved me, and from my point of view that's a good thing." I pause. "Next time, though, maybe you can just snack on the bad guys a little until we see just how much fight they have in them. We probably don't need to kill all of them."

"Don't kill everyone. Got it. You sure you're okay?"

"The arm's fine. The coat took most of the damage. It was brand-new. Now it's like all my damn clothes. Shot up and bled on."

She cups my face in her hands and kisses me hard. I kiss her back.

"What happens now?" Candy says.

"We go see Hunahpu. I know where the address is. We can leave the bike."

"How are we going to get there?"

I pull her away from the wall.

"Have you ever walked through a shadow?" I ask.

"Uh, no."

"Want to?"

"Sure."

"Don't let go of my hand."

I step into the ripe black darkness in the recess by a loading-bay door, pulling Candy with me into the Room of Thirteen Doors.

I take her out again near the address the kid gave me. It's on Fairfax a little north of Beverly Boulevard.

As we step from the shadow, Candy says, "Holy fucking god-damn fuck, that's cool. What was that room we went through?"

"It's called the Room of Thirteen Doors. I can go any-where in the universe through those doors, even to Heaven and Hell."

"Why did we drive to the club? If I had something that cool, I'd be running in and out of it all day and night just to mess with people."

I believe her. I'm glad I have the key and she doesn't.

"It feels weird using it in the city when I'm going somewhere the first time. Like the club tonight. I didn't know where it was or what was going to be there when we arrived. I like to drive because I like to get a look at a place the first time I go there."

"Why don't you just get your own car?"

"Are you kidding? People steal them."

UP THE STREET is a white two-story office building plastered together to look vaguely colonial. It's as bland and forgetful as any real-estate office.

The first floor is dark, but there are lights behind the windows on the second. It's almost three and there's barely any traffic in either direction. Candy and I walk across the street to the glass-and-aluminum front doors. BIO-SPECIALTIES GROUP is painted on the door in a reassuringly scientific-looking serif font.

In theory, I could step into a shadow here and come out on the second floor near the lights, but I don't want to do that. Drug cookers tend to be on the jumpy side and I've already been shot at once tonight. I take Candy around the side of the building and we use a shadow to get into the lobby. No alarms go off, so they don't have motion detectors down here. So far so good.

There's a locked wooden door at the top of the stairs with the company's name on it. I stand there for a minute.

"What are we doing?" asks Candy.

"Shh."

Light leaks from beneath the door where it doesn't quite touch the floor. I watch for moving shadows to see if people are moving around and how many there might be. Nothing moves past the door. I let the angel's senses expand.

There are voices off to my right. Seven, maybe eight. The clinks and taps of metal and glass. The whir of machines and whisper of small gas flames. That will be the lab. Off to my left, closer to the street, I get nothing. Probably offices, unoccupied at this hour. Everyone seems to be bunched up in the lab.

I say, "Keep your head down when we get inside." Then I take her hand and we slip inside through a shadow on the wall.

Behind the door is a reception area with a desk, computer, and phone. Wrought-iron letters spell out BIO-SPECIALTIES GROUP on the wall above the receptionist's desk. Either the company deals with a lot of amnesiacs or they really, really like the sound of their own name.

The office at the front of the building overlooking the street isn't set up to impress, but at least it looks like the lab is a legit business. It must do everything by courier or pickup them. There's a plain wooden desk that you'd see in any high school principal's office, piled with receipts, schedules, and undelivered lab results. A business phone with about ninety buttons, most unlabeled. A combination fax and copy machine. In the corner is a plant with shiny green leaves. It looks like the only thing in the office the occupant cares about.

We go into the next office. Hallelujah. This one is decked out for a bank president. Dark green walls with light trim. Very Victorian. An oak desk with inlaid leather, big enough to land cargo planes. A plasma TV on one wall and a glass-fronted cabinet on the other filled with framed certificates and trophies. It's all very nice and respectable looking and copied straight out of an executive furniture catalog, I bet. The wall to the left of the desk is why the nice office is back here and not up front with a view. This one has a window looking right into the lab.

I was right. There are eight people on the night shift. A collection of clean-cut MIT types and scruffy old-school meth cookers who have enough brain cells left to move up the food chain to the exotica market.

What's really interesting isn't the people but their gear. It isn't ordinary college-surplus Bunsen burners and Dr. Frankenstein bubbling flasks. The place is decked out like a TV starship. Smooth, sexy, and at times translucent Golden Vigil gear, a collection of advanced human tech tweaked by angels recruited by Aelita, the Vigil's psycho angel queen. The last time I saw her, she was quitting the Vigil so she could return to Heaven and, no shit, kill God, the dead-eyed neglectful dad who she thought had outlived his usefulness. Aelita might be the most vicious and craziest thing with wings I've ever met, but you've got to give her credit for ambition.

The window looking into the lab must be one-way glass because no one in there has noticed us. Candy has probably seen drug cookers and I know she's never seen anything like Golden Vigil tech. She's got her nose pressed against the window like it's her first visit to the zoo.

I sit down at the desk and dial Hunahpu's number from his office phone. That ought to get his attention. I look through the lab window, hoping Hunahpu is inside with the techs. I hear the cell ring, but none of the techs pulls out a cell phone. After the few rings, Hunahpu's phone cuts off. No voice-mail message. Nothing. A minute later the desk phone rings. I wait. A few rings and a recorder built into the phone kicks in. An amplified voice comes through the unit's speaker.

"Stark. Pick up. I know you're there."

Damn.

I pick up the receiver.

"Who is this?"

"It's who you wanted to speak to. So speak."

"How did you know I'd be here?"

"I know you saw Carolyn. And I know you're the kind of persuasive person who would get her to talk about Cale. If you have my cell and are calling from my office, something tells me you found him, too. Is he dead?"

"Entirely. Have you ever been to Donut Universe? They're open twenty-four/seven. Why don't we meet for coffee?"

"Let's not and say we did."

"I'm looking at your lab."

"Of course."

"You're what's left of the Golden Vigil, aren't you? I mean, any idiot could have bought stolen lab gear from when the Vigil closed down, but how many people would know how to use it?"

"We're not all of the Vigil. There are other cells scattered here and there. But we all lost our dental plans and 401(k)s when the government shut us down. It was either find a way to earn a living or go on food stamps, and like you, we hate filling out paperwork. "

I'm trying to place his accent, but there's nothing to get hold of. It's like he learned to speak phonetically. The Vigil or Homeland Security sent him to speech classes to erase any regional traces.

"Do I know you?" I ask.

"I saw you at the Vigil offices, but we never had any heart-to-hearts."

The angel in my head talks to me. He's a little Sherlock Holmes, which, I guess makes me Dr. Watson. I'm not wild about that. Better that he's Starsky and I'm Hutch. At least I get a cool car that way.

"Why do I get the feeling that somehow Wells is involved in this? He's coming back to L.A. and he wants his own private army. Maybe he wants to start a panic with a drug associated with hoodoo and get them to send him back."

Hunahpu makes a sound. At first I think it's a sneeze, but realize it's a little laugh.

"Don't be stupid. Wells flunked out because he was and remains a Boy Scout. He can't see the big picture. He doesn't want to because it's so big there isn't even anyone to arrest."

"There's you and your people in the next room."

"If he was coming, we'd know it. If he grabs us, he won't keep us long."

It's not a boast. I can read it in his voice. This guy is connected to something or someone higher than the clouds and probably just as hidden.

"So you're off on your own, causing trouble after your

boss takes a bullet. What does that make you? Do you think you're the forty-seven Ronin? Are you making a samurai movie in Grandma's backyard?"

"Fuck the feds. Sister Ludi set us up. We work for her now."

"You mean Aelita, don't you?"

I lean back in Hunahpu's chair. He hasn't said anything for a few seconds. I hit a nerve.

"Call her what you want, white boy. Sister Ludi came to me in a vision and I saw who she really was."

"You mean Aelita got inside your head and showed you what you wanted to see. She's good at that kind of thing. She's a fucking angel. And she's crazy. You know that, right?"

"She's doing the work that needs to be done, just like we are."

"Are you crazy, too, or just stupid?"

"You're hurting my feelings, Stark. If you really feel that way about Sister Ludi, I suppose you don't want what she left for you."

I sit up straight in the chair.

"I take it all back. Aelita is Florence Nightingale, Patti Smith, and Miss America all rolled into one. Now, what did she leave me?"

"A message. Listen. 'If you've made it this far, it's already too late.'"

I lean my elbows on the desk.

"What does that mean?"

"I assumed you'd know. It's pretty fucking funny that you don't, don't you think?"

"Why did you go after Hunter Sentenza?"

"She told us to."

I used to think Wells was a lapdog and a true believer, but this little shit's got a Ph.D. in celestial bootlicking.

"This is why the demon knows me, right? What demon is she using? At least tell me that."

"I'm a pharmacist. I don't know anything about demons."

Goddammit. He's telling the truth again.

"Aelita does. Do you think you're going to click your ruby slippers together and she's going to whisk you off to Heaven? She isn't going to kill God, and when she fails she'll drag you down the toilet with her, right down to the bottom of Hell."

"If the choice is you or her, I choose her."

"Answer one personal question. You're supposed to be a lab that analyzes things. DNA and AIDS tests, but you spend all your time cooking Akira and whatever else brings in money, right?"

"Close enough."

"Are you at least sending out the blood to a real lab so people know if they're sick or are you just letting them all die?"

"Of course we do," says Hunahpu. "We're not monsters. You're the monster, Stark. Or are you so comfortable with that now that you've forgotten?"

"I guarantee you I'm not going to forget your voice. We're going to run into each other down the road sometime, and when we do I'm going to pop you apart one rivet at a time."

"There's the monster. Hello, monster."

"I hope you have another lemonade stand stashed out back because this one is going out of business."

He sighs.

"With everything you know about the Vigil, you don't

think we'd put our whole operation in one location, do you? Do your worst. We'll be up and running again by the end of the week."

"My worst is a lot worse than you remember. Be sure to check the papers tomorrow. It'll be on the front page."

"I wouldn't expect anything less from you, Abomination."

Candy is looking at me when I hang up.

"What was that all about?"

"This place isn't just a drug lab. It's God's little terrorist angel army on earth. That was one of them on the phone. You know how you said not everything is about me? Well, this is. Aelita sent a demon after Hunter because she knew I'd find out that he's TJ's little brother. I bet it's one of these pricks who sent me the text knowing it would piss me off and get me on the case."

She raises her eyebrows.

"They sound like they have their shit wired tight. How can you go after people like that?"

"I'm not. Come on. We're getting out of here."

I take Candy outside through a shadow by a bookcase.

When we're on the street, I dial a number on my cell. No one answers. I don't leave a message. A second later the phone rings. There's silence on the line.

"Do you know where I am?"

"Yes," says Josef.

"The building and everything inside is yours. Be sure to make a mess."

"We've been waiting so long for something to do, a mess is inevitable."

The line goes dead.

We walk to the other side of the street and into an alley hidden from view. Normally I'd cut and run from a scene like this, but Candy will want to see it.

"Who was that?"

"A guy who's head I once chopped off."

"What is it with you and cutting off heads?"

"It's an old habit. The crowd loved it in the arena. If you do it right, the body does a twitchy little dance before it falls over."

"It's pretty fucked up that you know that. I like it."

"I know. I've been saving that one up for you."

She kisses me on the cheek.

A warm wind swirls down from the sky, kicking up garbage and whirlpooling it away. There's a roar behind it. Like the wind, but lower in pitch. Like a billion hungry locusts. Or a jet flying low. Maybe both.

I say, "Among God's many fuckups at the beginning of time was this. When he created the angels he created something else, too. They're called the Kissi. Watch close because we're not staying long."

The Kissi come down on the building like a black boiling fog. At first they look like a solid mass. It isn't until they start tearing the building apart that you can see individual ones. I'm behind Candy with my arms wrapped around her, not because it's cold but to prevent her from doing exactly what she's doing now. Trying to leave the alley to get closer to the carnage. She only does it for a few seconds then settles down against my chest. I can hear her heart beating like a speed-metal-band encore. Something explodes and she jumps back against me. One of the Kissi must have hit a gas line. The building already looks like Pompeii. Broken walls. Cracked stones. And everything on fire. The horrible-beautiful faces of individual Kissi are visible in the flames. That's enough fun for one night. I pull Candy back farther into the dark.

We come out by the hotel. She's holding on to my hands, which are wrapped around her.

She looks up at me.

"I don't have the words," she says. "You've seen a lot of that kind of stuff, haven't you?"

"Way too much for my taste."

She steps out from my arms and takes my hand.

"Let's go upstairs and finish off the furniture."

"I can't right now. Every bit of information I get makes this whole thing more confusing. I know Aelita is doing this to fuck with me, but that can't be all there is to it. She thinks too big for that. And what does 'If you've made it this far, it's already too late' mean? I need to talk to Kasabian. Want to come with me?"

She shakes her head.

"He talked my ear off before. He doesn't get out much, does he? I think I need to take a break before I dive back in."

"Okay. I'll see you upstairs in a little while."

She heads for the room.

"Take as long as you want. I'm starting without you. You'll just have to catch up."

"I'll bring my Jet Ski."

INSIDE, KASABIAN IS drinking a beer and watching *Las Montañas del Gehenna,* an obscure seventies Mexican spaghetti western. Kind of a cross between *Pat Garrett and Billy the Kid* and Jodorowsky's God-is-a-Freudian-shootist epic, *El Topo*. After a long drought hits their village, the residents decide to sacrifice a young girl to the ancient Mayan rain god. The girl's father and lover shoot up the village and rescue her. Later, a priest visits them at their hideout in the desert. He tells them that they have to find the gods and make it up to them for stealing their sacrifice. Midway into the movie, the girl and the two men ride their horses up a mountain of bleached human and animal bones to a cave that's the entrance to the Mayan underworld. The gods' minions grab the girl and lay her out on a stone altar while a priest holds an obsidian knife over her, ready to cut out her heart. The girl's father and lover have to play the traditional to-the-death Mayan ball game to see if they're all going to be sacrificed or they get to return to earth. I was watching *Las Montañas del Gehenna* the night Mason sent me Downtown, so I never got to see if any of them survived.

"Is that blood on your jacket? You got shot again. Are you a bullet magnet or just have a fetish for never wearing the same clothes twice?"

I don't want to see how *Las Montañas del Gehenna* turns out. I decided a long time ago that the girl makes it home and I don't want to find out I'm wrong. I turn off the set.

"Hey! I'm watching that."

"You can finish it later. I just found out that Aelita is mixed up in this Hunter thing."

He nods.

"I'm not surprised. I think she's got something going with Mason, too. An angel's been sneaking in and out of Hell, coming in from way out in the badlands where even

Hellions don't go. Who else is crazy enough to deal with Mason but her?"

"They're the ones that probably sent the Qlipots or whatever they're called. But why go after Hunter? And why get me involved? Maybe they're trying to railroad me into a trap."

"Were you just trying to say 'Qliphoth'? Look at you. You learned a big-boy word."

"Aelita can't have hit God already. That would shake the whole universe. They're not ready to invade Heaven, are they?"

"No way. Generals are still arguing over plans. Troops are still coming in from all over Hell. No way they're ready."

"Why would she be tiptoeing down to Hell?"

"Mason just got hold of something that's got him pretty excited. It's big, too. Like an oversized gold coffin carved with all kinds of binding runes and hexes. Aelita might have smuggled something out of Heaven. Maybe a weapon."

"Or something to help Mason make a new key to the Room of Thirteen Doors?"

"More likely something like the Druj Ammun. A passkey to a secret back door in Heaven. She's supposed to have allies upstairs, so it wouldn't surprise me."

"What if she didn't come straight from Heaven? If she sent that demon after Hunter, maybe she has more demons. Could she and Mason be raising a demon army?"

Kasabian smirks.

"Even Lucifer couldn't do that. Training demons is like herding cats on acid."

My gut is churning and I really want to hit something.

"This is all on me. I got too clever. I should have killed

Mason when I had the chance. That proves my theory that thinking's overrated."

"Get a grip. We can rule out Mason having a key. He'd have used it by now. He'd have come back himself or sent a Hellion hit squad. No. This is something else."

"It's got to be the thing I'm too late to stop. I need to talk to the Sentenzas again. I freaked out and left last time when I realized that Hunter is TJ's kid brother."

"TJ? Our TJ? That's fucking insidious."

"I missed something with them. I'll go back in the morning. You keep watching Downtown. Consider it self-defense. If Mason gets back here, it isn't just me he's going to snuff."

"Now you've piqued my interest."

I think about things for a minute.

"You know, you could have told me some of this before. And saved me a lot of bullshit time."

"Right. I never know how you're going to react to information. I don't need you going batshit and throwing me out or pulling a gun."

It's true. I've thrown the little weasel out and I've taken a few potshots at him. It's not like I didn't have my reasons. He was spying on me for Lucifer, and then there was that time he tried to kill me. But that was a while ago, and since then the angel has been whispering sweet nothings in my ear about not killing people when they get annoying. And it was before I figured that I need all the friends I can get in this world. Not that Kasabian is exactly a friend, but he has good taste in movies and we both want Mason drawn and quartered.

He scuttles over to the set and turns it back on.

"If you're going to shoot me, I want to finish my movie."

On the monitor, the two vaqueros are playing the Mayan ball game. They're slow and clumsy, falling all over each other.

"All right, man. Sure. Mea culpa. On occasion I've been known to express myself in uncouth ways, but I'm on the wagon for pulling guns on people I know."

He turns his eyes from the monitor and looks at me for a minute.

"So that's my apology?"

"I guess so."

He turns off the movie, picks up his beer, and drinks. A trickle leaks out from the bottom of his neck and into his bucket.

"Ever since Lucifer left, the place has been falling apart, and I don't mean the trash isn't getting picked up. I mean Old Testament falling apart. Earthquakes. Wild fires. Hellion food riots. That's something you don't want to see. No one's in charge. Mason has the army and local Pinkertons tied up with his war plans. It's like he doesn't give a rat's ass how Hell is going to . . . you know. Hell."

"Who's working with him?"

"Most of Lucifer's generals have defected. Abaddon, Wormwood, Mammon. They're all in Pandemonium. General Semyazah is the only holdout. He doesn't like the idea of being pushed around by a mortal. And he commands a shitload of troops. I don't know if they can pull off the attack without him or his troops."

I get a Malediction from my coat and pour myself a drink from a bottle of Jack on the nightstand.

"You know what's weird? This whole thing between me and Mason—I can't even remember what started it."

"Aside from the fact that you're exactly alike?"

"Fuck you."

"The truth hurts doesn't it, Tinker Bell?"

I rub my arm where the bullet grazed me. At least it helps me forget about the burns on my arms.

"I don't get this Heaven and Hell thing of his at all," I say. "It's stupid enough wanting to grab Hell, but why would Mason want Heaven, too? The dry-cleaning bills on all those robes must be murder."

Kasabian swigs his beer. It sounds like distant rain as it drains from his neck into the bucket.

"I don't think Mason wants to be God. I think he just wants to be in control," says Kasabian. "Look, man, just because you don't want anything doesn't mean the rest of us feel that way. You always hid or fucked around with your power. Mason took his seriously because he had to. He was part of a heavyweight Sub Rosa clan and Daddy wouldn't have it any other way."

"Boo-hoo. The rich kid had it rough."

"He was raised to take magic as seriously as anyone alive. He had to. He went to Hell, too, when he was a kid. He used to joke about it."

I stare at him. Kasabian widens his eyes and nods, pleased he caught me off guard.

"What do you fucking mean, Mason was in Hell?"

Kasabian rolls his eyes.

"Not that Hell. Metaphorical Hell. Christ, how can you not know any of this? Mason was famous when he was a kid. His parents were even more famous."

"I met his mom once. A dumpy lady with the Bettie Page hair and trophy-wife jewelry. She's famous?"

"That was his aunt. His parents were dead and regular civilian court appointed an uncle and auntie dearest to take care of him. They were happy to move into the house in Beverly Hills and spend as much of Mason's inheritance as they could. Maybe that's why he burned the house when he disappeared. It covered up what he did to you and it sent the Beverly Hillbillies packing."

"Tell me about Mason's metaphorical Hell."

Mason grunts. He's calling me a hick without actually saying it out loud.

"It started with Mason's father, old Ammit Faim. Ammit killed and hexed his way into running a big chunk of the California drug biz, and I don't mean aspirin. Why would he cozy up to civilian dope peddlers? Because drugs are power and influence, and Ammit and Gabriella, Mason's mom, were the ambitious type."

He swigs from his beer.

"You know what assholes rich Sub Rosas are. Everything is about status and building a dynasty. None of the other clans were into the drug biz, so there wasn't any competition. He imported the stuff. Set up operations to manufacture the complicated stuff and then cut and distributed it himself. He had a handle on Sub Rosa recreational drugs and most of the pot, meth, and Ecstasy in the state, but he didn't control heroin and opium. So he decided to go to the source. Ammit and Gabriella packed up the kiddies, that's Mason and his little sister—bet you didn't even know he had a sister—and off the family went to Burma."

"The drug connection has to be why Mason and Aelita dosed Hunter. Another joke or clue for me to figure out."

"Shut up," Kasabian says. "Ammit had enough connections to get a meeting with an opium general up north. He was an army officer who'd defected and took a lot of his troops with him. Formed his own private army and marched into the Golden Triangle. They paid the local farmers to raise poppies for them. The farmers didn't care. Crops are crops and they made more money than growing rice.

"Ammit and the general cut a deal for his product and for a while everything was champagne and Hot Pockets. Mason's father had a good source of dope and Mom kept the books. The general had a real businessman selling his stuff and the money rolled in. The Faims' power grew and so did the family's status. Then it got ugly.

"The reason the general and his men had originally gone into the hills was to hunt down guerrilla armies in the mountains. The Faims were in the hills visiting their dope crop when the rebels attacked.

"The general and his men were pros, but a bunch of guerrilla groups got together and all attacked at the same time. There were so damn many of them, they wiped out the general's army.

"These rebels were some mean Khmer Rouge–type pricks. Once the fighting was over, one by one the guerrillas cut off the heads of all the general's men. Eventually someone found Mason and the kiddies. Normally Ammit could have magicked the family out of there, but the general had local witches lay down all kinds of antihoodoo spells around their camp.

"It must have been a pretty good shock for those Burmese grunts to find a whole *Leave It to Beaver* family up in the mountains. Normally in a situation like that, the local army will ransom off Americans for cash. But not the rebel general. He took one look at these wealthy white foreigners financing his enemy and he started to kill them on the spot. But an old shaman stopped him. The guerrillas might have been fighting about politics and money, but they brought their old tribal magic and religion with them. Supposedly the old man made a beeline for Mason and took him aside. He pawed at the scared kid, checking him out, and the shaman saw something special in Mason. After the shaman and the general talked, the old man took Mason while soldiers hacked his whole family to death with machetes.

"The Faims weren't slackers when it came to magic, but the witches' spells worked and they couldn't fight back.

"When the shaman was done blasting their asses around the camp, the soldiers had fun hacking them to pieces. They killed Mason's little sister last. The Burmese have these big dogs up in the mountains and the rebels use them as war dogs. Mason got to watch as the general let his dogs loose on the big pile of hamburger that used to be his family."

"I don't believe a word of this."

"You'll like this part. It gets weirder," says Kasabian. "People eventually found out about the dead white people in the hills, but not about the little boy. Mason is gone. Off the radar for two or three years. UN workers found him when a local militia shot up one of the rebel groups.

"Mason got passed down the food chain to the U.S. embassy. Imagine what that was like for a kid. In just a few days he goes from eating bugs and learning ancient fucked-up tribal magic all the way back to L.A.

"That's when the aunt and uncle show up. Ammit had put together a tidy little nest egg from his drug business, and with Mason only being around ten at the time, the court set him up with a brand-new family."

"Why didn't anyone tell me any of this?"

"Because you're an asshole and you never wanted to know. Listen. The best part is coming.

"Mason settles into the whole home-sweet-home thing. He goes to private Sub Rosa school. He has money. He has nice clothes. But no friends. Nothing. He didn't talk to anyone, especially his new family. At school, he gets the same kind of generic magic training we all got. Only Mason is like you. Kind of a freak. He showed them the shaman's stuff. Dark magic they'd never seen before. They graduated him early just to get him out of there.

"After graduation he disappears again. He was gone for three months, and when he came home he wouldn't tell anyone if he'd been kidnapped or ran away or anything. But no one cares because all of a sudden he's acting like a normal kid. They let him back into upper grade school. He made friends and generally acted the way any idiot schoolkid was supposed to act.

"A few months later stories started popping up on TV about arms smuggling along the Burmese border and how there must have been a bad accident. Like a big ammo dump or even a small tactical Chinese nuke had gone off. The land in one area was fried. And part of a mountain was gone, like it was scooped out with an ice-cream scoop. The funny thing was no one saw or heard any explosions. It all got hushed up pretty quick by the local government because whatever happened had wiped out an entire rebel army along with their village, their families, their crops, and their animals. There was nothing but ashes for miles."

Kasabian finishes the beer and tosses the empty into an overflowing trash can.

"Mason went to Hell all right, but he got his revenge. That's why I'm sure what Mason wants is to be in charge. This time around he's not going to be dragged into the jungle while his family is chopped into dog food. He's going to be the dragger, not the draggee."

What do you know? Mason isn't Dr. Doom after all. He's Bruce Wayne, pining away for his long-gone *Partridge Family* lifestyle. I have no way of knowing if everything in Kasabian's tall tale is true, but he got at least one thing right. From the moment we met, I don't think it ever occurred to Mason and me to do anything but go at each other. It's not that we hated each other. It's more like how some people can't help but bring out the not necessarily righteous parts of your personality. Like how you meet someone and instantly know they're a full-time professional victim, and no matter how hard you try, something takes over and you can't help needling them. From day one Mason and I were playing King of the Hill. It all makes a sad kind of sense now. Sending me Downtown wasn't just Mason's play for power. It was his way of finally winning the stupid game we'd been playing since we met. Kasabian nailed it. Mason and I aren't anything special. Just a couple of angry toddlers out to crack the world over a playground punch-out.

"You okay?"

I look around. Kasabian looks concerned. Somewhere along the way I'd gotten to my feet. I guess I've been standing here for a while.

"I'm fine. Thanks for laying it all out for me. At least now I know why Lucifer thought Mason was the only other candidate to take his place."

"Maybe you ought to sit down and finish your drink."

"Good idea."

I'm feeling a little dazed. A little high. Mason and I are connected at the hip and the brain stem. Isn't that goddamn hilarious?

"Just be cool. You wanted to hear the story. Don't go getting mad at me."

"Don't sweat it. I'm glad I know."

I pick up my coat. Finger the bullet hole. It's not bad enough to throw the coat away. Besides, I heard that blood is the new black.

My cigarette has gone out. I drop it in a half-finished drink by the bed and light another.

"I get it now. Why Mason wants Heaven and Hell."

"What do you mean?"

"He's going to do it again. He doesn't want to be God. He wants to burn us like he burned that mountain."

"Why would he do that?"

I look at Kasabian. He's as mad as any human or Hellion I've ever met. Why can't he see it? It's because he's a lousy magician. Third rate when he gets a good tailwind. He never learned to dream big.

"Because the universe abandoned him. Mason was scared. He'd seen his family butchered. He needed help. He begged and groveled and prayed, but nobody came. Not his parents. Not the Sub Rosa. Not the army. Not God or Lucifer or one lousy angel. The little boy got tossed out like the trash and now he's going to burn the universe because when he was lost and pathetic and needed help the universe turned its back and took a planet-size dump on his head."

"How do you know this sick shit?"

"Because it's exactly what I was going to do. When I got back from Hell, I traded Mr. Muninn for something I have hidden in the Room of Thirteen Doors. Something that can fry every atom in Creation. Turn this whole peep show to dust. I thought that killing the Circle and sending Mason to Hell was going to fix me and the world would be full of sunshine and pretty girls and bluebirds that shit cold beer. But it didn't. Alice was still dead. God and Lucifer still gave me the silent treatment. And Wells, Aelita, the Golden Vigil, and everyone who worked for them still walked the streets."

I open my left hand. It hurts from being balled tight into a fist.

"So what changed your mind?" Kasabian asks. "From where I sit, the world is exactly as shitty as it was when you left."

"It was that night I killed the Drifters. It would have been so easy to sit down and have a cigarette and let them eat the city. But when it came right down to it, I didn't want to. It's as simple as that. I wanted to live and I wanted Vidocq and Candy, Allegra, and Brigitte to live. And if I murdered the world, I'd be Mason and I didn't want to be him."

"You're quite the humanitarian. By the way, thanks a fuck of a lot for leaving me off your who-to-save list."

"You're on it, Alfredo Garcia. I just didn't want to say it out loud and have you call me Nancy or Tinker Bell."

"Yeah, I would have done that."

"Behave yourself, and when I'm Downtown maybe I can find some Hellion alchemists who can stitch you onto a new body. You can have Mason's after I kill him."

Kasabian snorts.

"Yeah. That's what I want. Every time I pee I can look down and see Mason's dick in my hand. That won't give me nightmares."

"But think how upset the dick's going to be when it looks up and sees you."

IN THE MORNING Candy, Vidocq, and I head back to Studio City in Allegra's car. Vidocq borrowed it. He's on a kick about not riding in stolen vehicles all the time. For a people who invented absinthe and blow jobs, sometimes the French can be a drag.

After hearing Kasabian's story last night, I was itchy to talk to the Sentenzas and didn't want to wait until the A.M., but they have a skull-fucked-by-evil kid wandering the streets and I didn't want to have to haul them to an emergency room with matching coronaries.

Candy is a lot more of a morning person than I am, which is easy since I refuse to believe in the existence of a 10 A.M. But she's insistent enough and strong enough to drag my ass out of bed and pour me into some clothes. She even found a coffeemaker in the kitchenette that wasn't broken. Coffee isn't the perfect morning drug, but it'll do until someone invents French Roast adrenochrome.

What's pissing me off is that I'm going to have to dance around a lot of what I've learned about Hunter and his pals. K.W. and Jen aren't going to want to hear how close Hunter was to some really nasty drug peddlers. And I'm sure as hell not going to tell them about Aelita. I still don't know why she'd go after TJ's brother. It's not like driving the kid crazy threatens anyone I care about. Me included. I could walk away from this anytime and it wouldn't change a damn thing in my life.

We get to the Sentenzas' place around eleven. Their car and truck are both in the driveway. Nothing surprising there. K.W. seems like a real worker bee, but a missing kid will dull your work ethic. The three of us go up the stone walkway and I ring the bell.

A minute or so later Jen opens the door. She's in a red silk robe. Her hair is a mess and her eyes are red. She's been crying and it looks like she just got up. She doesn't say anything. She just stands aside and lets us in.

"This isn't good news, is it?" she asks.

"Why do you say that?"

"Hunter isn't with you and you don't look much better than I feel."

K.W. comes down the stairs. He's in a blue tracksuit. It looks like he slept in it.

"Have you found him?"

"I'm afraid not," says Vidocq. Bad news sounds better with his accent. "But we know a lot more than we did when we left here yesterday."

I say, "What happened to Hunter wasn't his fault. It was done to him. That might sound bad, but it's actually good news. If he was set up for the possession, it means someone wanted to make a point, one that hasn't been made yet. That means whoever did it still needs him. Wherever Hunter is, I'm sure that he's still alive."

Their bodies change when they hear that. I can feel their nervous systems unknot. Their breathing and heart rates get somewhere in the neighborhood of normal. K.W. even manages a minuscule smile.

"That's great news. So, why are you here? Do you need something else from us?"

Jen breaks in.

"Who would do something like that to Hunter?"

No way I'm answering that.

"We're not sure," says Candy. "That's why we're here. We need to ask you a few more questions."

"I'll put on some coffee," says Jen, and heads for the kitchen. K.W. nods in her direction and we follow.

The kitchen is big and spacious. Spanish tile and copper pans. It's flooded with light from a row of French doors that open onto a huge backyard with neat trees and a pool. We sit on stools at a serving island in the middle of the room. I doubt I could even afford the coffee filters Jen is fitting into an expensive German contraption. It looks more like something that fell out of the space station than a coffeemaker.

"What do you need to know?" asks K.W.

I figured out one thing last night. If Mason and Aelita are mixed up in this thing, then not only do they want the kid found, but they want me to find him. That means there's information I don't have yet. Since I don't know where to look, there's nothing to do but go back to the beginning.

"Was Hunter in touch with any of TJ's friends who were into magic?"

Vidocq and Candy look at me.

Okay, I'm starting somewhere a little self-serving. I want to know if the Sentenzas know that TJ and I are connected. And it's a legit question. TJ might have known some Sub Rosas outside our Circle. I doubt it, but you never know. Like I said, I'm grasping at straws and crabgrass.

"Not that I know of," says K.W. "Jen, do you know anything?"

She stands where she is by the coffeemaker. She's a long way down the counter from us, like she's afraid of catching a flesh-eating virus.

Jen shakes her head.

"Not that I know of. If he knew any of them, he was keeping it a secret."

"Was it his habit to keep secrets?" asks Vidocq.

"No. That was more TJ. Hunter is a good kid," says K.W.

"He was on the debate team at school one semester," says Jen, like it's proof that Hunter is an angel and that none of this is happening. "But he had to quit to go out for track."

I ask, "Did he do all right in school? No changes in his grades?"

"He was a hard worker," says Jen.

K.W. smiles ruefully and nods.

"He did all his homework and his grades were decent, but there wasn't much danger of him becoming a Rhodes scholar."

While the coffee burbles away Jen starts getting cups down

from the cupboard. She puts one down and stops. Her body has gone rigid again. Her heart rate is climbing fast. She's trying not to cry. Probably doesn't want to look weak in front of a bunch of strangers talking about her missing son like he's a stolen dirt bike. K.W. gets up and walks over to her, puts his hands on her shoulders.

"Why don't you go sit down? I'll get the coffee," he says.

She doesn't reply, but comes over and sits on the stool K.W. just vacated. Her arms are crossed and she's looking down at the counter.

Candy reaches out and touches Jen's hand lightly.

"We're very sorry to have to ask you all these questions."

Jen nods, still staring down.

This is bullshit. The kid was a jock with ambitious parents. They'd lost their smart son, TJ, and hoped that Hunter would take his place. But Hunter isn't TJ. If he joined the debate team, it was only to make his parents happy, and when he wanted off, he found a good enough reason that they couldn't get mad.

K.W. puts down cups for everyone. I sip mine.

"This coffee is good," I say to no one in particular.

K.W. nods.

"Yeah. It cost enough."

"You have a coffeemaker this good at work?"

"That's a funny question."

"It is, isn't it? But do you have a good coffeemaker at work?"

He shakes his head, still looking puzzled.

"Not this good, but the one in the office is okay. Most of the guys I work with wouldn't know good coffee from kerosene. They're the types who put on a pot on Monday and are still drinking it on Friday."

"What kind of guys are we talking about?"

"Construction mostly. I'm a property developer. Someone has a piece of land and wants something on it, they call me."

Makes sense. I remember seeing mud and cement around the wheel wells on the pickup in the drive.

"I have my own company. Some days I wear suits and some I'm out on the sites making sure the floor tiles are going in the right way up." He smiles like we're supposed to laugh. It's a joke he's used on a lot of clients. Now it's just a nervous tic.

"Depending on business, I'm either out in the field most of the time or back in the office having meetings."

"What kind of real estate do you develop?"

"Whatever a client asks for. Shopping malls. Business parks. Apartment buildings. Whatever a client wants."

"Is business good?" asks Vidocq.

K.W. shrugs.

"With development, it's always feast or famine. No one wants anything new. All they want is new electrics or pipes in old structures. Then someone wants a new hundred-apartment complex up in two weeks. And there are ten other companies behind that one who want the same thing."

"Was Hunter going to work for you when he finished school?"

"I don't know. We talked about it."

"Did he spend much time at the building sites?"

K.W. sips his coffee. Puts his hand on his wife's hand. Squeezes. She squeezes back.

"Not particularly. He liked the big construction machines when he was little."

Fucking fascinating. This family is in training for the Tedious Olympics.

"Are you developing anything new? Anything unusual?" asks Candy. Nice. She has good instincts for this Sherlock Holmes stuff. Me, I'm about ready to take her back to the hotel and break more furniture.

"What do you mean 'unusual'?"

"You're the builder," I say. "We don't know a dump truck from the Batmobile. You tell us."

K.W.'s eyes unfocus. Make microscopic movements back and forth in their sockets. It's an involuntary thing. The brain trying to access memories. If he was lying, his eyes would favor his left side, but they don't.

K.W. shrugs.

"Nothing out of the ordinary. We're finishing a housing development. Upgrading the fixtures in a strip mall. We're about to break ground on an office park near the 405."

"Okay, the jobs are boring. Are your clients? Any eccentrics? Odd requests? Anyone paying you in magic beans?"

He thinks again. His eyes stop and hold steady.

"There's only one thing I can think of and it's not really odd. It's just not something that happens every day."

"Tell us," says Vidocq.

"A client called for a fix-up on a business property. What was unusual was that I never met her or a rep in person. We did everything on the phone. It was like she was one person handling everything herself. That's unusual in this business."

"What was her name?" I ask.

He frowns.

"I can't remember. My secretary would know."

"What did she hire you to do?"

"She wanted us to renovate and restore an old commercial site in the Hollywood Hills. It was a big job, too. There was extensive fire damage, but she wanted us to fix it rather than tear it down. It was something historic. An old gentlemen's club. That I remember. It's not a phrase you hear too often these days."

I put down my coffee and Vidocq picks up his. Candy and I look at each other.

"Did she tell you the name of the club?"

"Maybe. I don't remember."

"Was it Avila?"

K.W. smiles.

"Yes, that's it. How did you know?"

The human brain is a very funny thing, and because of that, it can do very funny things to the human body. Take mine right now. My heartbeat just doubled. All my senses are cranked up to eleven. Even the angel in my head feels it. I hear Jen's breathing change. She knows my question and K.W.'s answer are important. I smell K.W. starting to sweat. He gets it that something he's said is connected to Hunter's disappearance. Vidocq and Candy are plain excited and trying not to show it. I'm as excited as any of them, but I feel cold, too. Like someone cracked open my chest and dumped a bucket of ice inside. But I don't show any of it. This is basic stuff. I could have had this information yesterday if I hadn't let the TJ thing get to me. But I guess getting to me has been the idea all along.

"How did you know the club's name?"

I sip my coffee. The room is practically vibrating from the tension. Candy is a furnace. She wants to run out and start gnawing on bad guys or the coyotes in the hills. Something.

"A lucky guess."

"I'll call the office and get you the woman's number."

I shake my head.

"Don't bother. It'll be turned off and she won't use it again."

Jen says, "You know who it is, don't you?"

"No," I say. It's the truth. I don't *know*. But yes, I know.

"I have an idea, but I don't want us to start getting ahead of ourselves."

The three of us get up and head for the door. The Sentenzas don't show us out this time. They stay in their bright and familiar kitchen, huddled there like the house is the *Titanic* and the serving island is the last lifeboat afloat.

Jen calls after us.

"What can we do?"

"Stay by the phone," I yell over my shoulder.

WHEN WE GET to Allegra's car, I say, "I'm driving," and Vidocq doesn't argue.

We get in and I tell the other two, "Get out your cells. You're going to make calls."

I start the car and back out of the driveway. I'm driving slow. Concentrating. I know what to do and I want to get to doing it, but I need to set it up right.

We head for the Golden State Freeway, but it's bumper-to-bumper, so I turn the car and we head to the city on surface streets.

I tell Candy, "Call Allegra. Tell her to clear out all the diaper-rash and splinter patients. We're bringing in a special case."

"You're that sure Hunter is at Avila?" she asks.

"I'd bet the pope's red shoes. Tell her to get out every piece of Kinski's hoodoo medical gear she has. The demon's been working over Hunter for days. He's going to be in bad shape."

I don't have to tell Vidocq what to do.

"I'll call Father Traven," he says.

I nod.

"Tell him to get his picnic basket together and be ready. I don't want to give whatever's in Avila the chance to know we're coming."

I get out my phone and dial the number Vidocq gave me for Julia. She answers on the second ring.

"Stark? How are things going?"

"I've got good news and bad news."

"What's the good news?"

"I know where Hunter is. We're on our way there right now."

"What's the bad?"

"Aelita is involved. It might be a trap and we all might die."

"Do I need to tell you to be careful?"

"It's always good to be reminded. I'll call you when it's over. If we're dead, I'll call collect."

I DON'T KNOW what to expect when we pick up Traven. How much bread do you need to bum-rush a demon out of *Ferris Bueller*? A baguette? A dump-truck-ful of biscuits?

Traven is waiting on the curb when we get to his place. He's all in black, with an old-fashioned high-collared coat that makes him look like Johnny Cash's stunt double. He's holding a battered canvas duffel bag. It's big, but he hefts it easily. I guess not that much bread after all.

I hit the brakes at the corner and say, "Let Traven sit up front. I want to talk to him."

Vidocq gets out of the car and takes Traven's duffel. He slides into the back with Candy. Traven gets in the front. I'm moving before he has the door closed.

"I understand you've found the boy. How's he holding up?"

I steer the car back toward the Hollywood Hills.

"We haven't seen him, but I know where he is. It was a place called Avila. In your line of work, you wouldn't have heard of it. They called it a gentlemen's club. Basically it was a casino and whorehouse for a very select group of über-rich assholes."

"Avila? After Saint Teresa of Avila?"

"Who's that?"

"Saint Teresa experienced an intense encounter with an angel. She describes it in sublimely intimate terms. The angel stabs her in the heart with a spear and the pain she describes is intense, but also beautiful and all-consuming."

"I didn't know saints went all the way on a first date."

He nods and purses his lips. He's heard it all before.

"A lot of people choose to interpret her description of religious ecstasy in simple sexual terms." He shakes his head. "Goddamn Freud."

"At least the name makes sense now. You see, Avila was a

huge secret. A real Skull and Bones kind of operation. If you were one of the handful of people in the know, one of the politically anointed or rich enough to use the same accountant as Jehovah, you got access to the club inside the club. You go to see what the club was really built for."

"And what was that?"

"They didn't keep human hookers in the inner sanctum. For the right price and a few blood oaths, you could fuck an angel."

Traven turns and looks at me, his face a blank mask.

"I'm not joking," I say. "No one knows who started the place or what kind of hoodoo they used to capture and keep them. L.A.'s a major power spot, so for all anyone knows, it might have been here in some form forever."

"And you think that's where the boy is being held?"

I nod.

"I knew the last angel that got dragged up there. Her name is Aelita. She ran the Golden Vigil. God's Pinkertons on earth. Real turbocharged assholes."

"Yes. I know about the Golden Vigil. You think this Aelita was taken there to become another prostitute?"

"No, she and the other angels were going to be sacrificed to open the gates of Hell. You see an old buddy of mine, Mason, has ambition the size of King Kong's balls. He wants to knock off Lucifer and take over Hell. Then he wants to stick a fork in God and grab Heaven. He's hard-core enough that he might be able to pull it off. You still with me, Father?"

Out of the corner of my eye I see Traven squinting. He doesn't know what to believe. I guess it's a lot to absorb when you've spent your life in church libraries, reading the books, learning the stories, and then finding out you have no idea how the universe really works. All these years he's been thoroughly shielded from everything but writer's cramp. Now he finds out that a real-life low-down biblical horror show was going on across town from where he brushed his teeth in holy water every night before bed. I can't blame him if his mind is a little blown.

"You want a cigarette?"

"That's would be nice," he says.

I hand him Mason's lighter and the pack of Maledictions from my pocket. Listen to him rustle the pack and spark the lighter. He coughs at the first puff but keeps smoking. Maledictions are easier to take when you're doomed.

"You were talking about a man named Mason trying to open Hell. I gather you stopped him."

"Something like that."

"And we killed an ass load of devil minions and dark magicians along the way," says Candy.

Traven turns in his seat to look at her.

"You were there, too?"

She smiles.

"Stark invites me to all his massacres. Isn't that right?"

She kicks the back of my seat. I look at her in the rearview mirror.

"You're not helping."

She smiles and settles down in her seat.

Traven puffs quietly on the Malediction, staring out the window as I steer us into the hills.

"So, because you stopped the sacrifice, you think that Hunter is in Avila?"

"Yeah. Mason and Aelita are behind this whole thing. They set the Qlipuffs on Hunter."

"Qliphoth. Why not send the demon after you?"

"Because Mason has a truly fucked-up sense of humor. I knew Hunter's brother and Mason would bust a gut using the kid to get me back up here. Aelita is helping just because she generally hates my guts."

"I thought you said you saved her."

"Yeah, when she found out I'm not exactly human, she got testy. A real racist."

"You know, yesterday if someone told me I'd be driving to an exorcism with a nephilim I would have been surprised. Today, though . . ."

He trails off and smokes the Malediction.

I wish I could read minds like Lucifer. I can hear Traven's heart beating fast. He's feeling the mixture of cold and fear that's excitement. He half knows what's coming and he's not sure if he can handle it. That's me in the arena, waiting for the gates to open to see what I'm going up against in this episode of *Kick Stark's Ass*. After a while you learn to live with the fear and ignore it, but it's never a hundred percent gone. But some kinds of fear can make you more than you are. You face down something bigger than yourself and maybe come out of it with scars, but you're a little stronger for it. There are other fears that are like a hole in your center where pieces of your soul go down the drain. That kind of fear has nothing to do with the knock-down-drag-out in the arena. That's the horror of finally knowing how things really are. Who has the power and how they love tossing it around at everyone who doesn't have it.

Every one of us, human and monster alike, lives with an angelic boot on our throats. But we don't see it, so we forget about it and limp along doing the stupid little things that make up our stupid little lives. Then the boot comes down on your gut, squeezing the air out of your lungs and cracking your bones like old matchsticks. And you know the only reason it's happening is because you're not one of the celestials on high. You're suffering with the worst curse of all. You're alive. We're just bugs on God's windshield. That's all we are. Annoying. Disposable. A dime a dozen.

Traven says, "You toss it all off so easily. Men enslaving angels. Humans challenging both Lucifer and God. And you say you're a nephilim, something I don't even know if I believe in."

"Don't worry, Father. I believe in you."

He's talking about me, but it's not what he means. I can hear it in the almost inaudible tremors in his voice.

"Ask the question, Father."

"What do I have to look forward to in Hell? Do they have special amusements for ex-priests?"

I should have gone easier on him. The poor guy is excommunicated. To him that means he already has one foot in the coal cart to the hot country.

"Don't sweat Hell, Father. There are Hellions down there and damned souls that owe me favors. I'll make sure you're taken care of."

The window is down a little on his side of the car. He pushes his hair back with a hand as lined and creased as his face. He does a little grunting laugh.

"I've read the most powerful and harrowing demonic texts

you can imagine, and this conversation is still the strangest thing I've heard. You really think you can make deals with fallen angels?"

"There are Hellions down there with more honor than half the humans I meet."

"That's not terribly comforting, but I suppose it will have to do."

"That pretty much sums up Hell."

The road smooths out as we near the top. I can just see Avila's blackened roof through the trees.

I say, "Too bad guys like us can't apply for unemployment. You think they have special forms for being fired by a deity?"

"I heard you worked for Lucifer. Lucifer isn't God."

"You don't spend enough time in Hollywood."

Traven looks up through the trees. He's spotted Avila, too. Candy is kicking the back of my seat again, bored with the talk and the drive. She wants to get her teeth into a demon. My kind of girl.

Traven says, "You've told me some of what you know about the universe; now let me tell you something. If you want to know why the world and all of Creation is so broken and afflicted, look up the word 'demiurge.'"

Traven turns to look at Vidocq.

"If I'm killed today, I want you to take my library. I trust you to take care of my books."

"I would be honored," Vidocq says. "But there will be no dying today."

"Demiurge?" I say. "That sounds like it has something to do with God, and not in a good way. Hell, I've burned so many bridges with the celestial types, I'd probably be better off cozying up to your Angra Om Ya pals than to any of the local celestial types."

"Then I think all you'll have to do is wait."

"I was joking. The Angra Om Ya are dead."

"What does death mean to a god?"

"You think the old gods are coming back?"

"I don't think they ever left."

I SWING THE car into the big circular driveway out front and park. We get out and Traven takes the duffel bag from Vidocq.

Avila has seen better days. Most of the roof has fallen in, leaving charred wood overhead, a puzzle palace of broken beams. The place has been thoroughly looted, trashed, and tagged by waves of squatters and skate punks. Moldy leather armchairs and silk-covered love seats surround the remains of a fire pit someone has chopped out of the driveway with who knows what improvised tools. A broken roulette wheel is almost lost in the grass that grows wild on all sides of the building. The ground glitters like a disco ball from all the broken glass. Even the walls are ripped open and the copper pipes inside are long gone.

"So this is what the gates of hell looks like," says Father Traven.

"No," says Vidocq. *"Le palais de merde."*

Even with everything that's been thrown at it since New Year's, the front door is still standing, like Avila's last dying gesture was giving the finger to the world. Maybe when we're done, I'll let Josef and his bunch loose on the place.

I gesture for the others to stay back, and push open the

door. I've never walked into Avila through the front before, only out, and that was just the one time. I mostly went into the place through shadows, and then only to kill people. The good old days when things were simpler.

I have the na'at and knife in my coat and the .460 cocked and locked up and ready to kill any spooky sounds or scary shadows.

Even though much of the roof is gone, it's dim inside, so I let my eyes adjust and then sweep the room. Nothing moves. Nothing makes a sound. It's as quiet as a pulled-pork-rib joint next to a synagogue.

I wave the others inside.

"It's safe to go in?" asks Traven.

"It's clear. I don't know about safe. I don't hear rats or even roaches in the walls. That's not a good sign."

"What does that mean?" asks Traven.

Vidocq says, "When even vermin abandon a building, it means that sensible people will stay out, too."

"Right now we're officially dumber than rats and roaches," says Candy.

"Welcome to our world, Father."

Traven starts to cross himself, catches himself halfway through, and drops his hand. Old habits die hard.

"Let's go. I'm pretty sure I know where the kid is, so I'm up front. Vidocq and the father in the middle. You okay watching our asses, Candy?"

"What do you think?"

"Here we go."

I lead them around the circular front room. We stay close to the walls. The place used to be full of antique furniture and Persian rugs. Now I can see down to the rock and grass of the hill where the floor has partially collapsed.

A couple of turns down a hall and the ceiling is intact. All of a sudden I'm missing the holes in the roof and their spooky shadows. With no lights back here, the place is pitch-black. As much as I hate it, I let the angel take the lead. Its vision is built for darkness.

The moment I ease back and let it run the show, Avila lights up like Vegas. I grab Vidocq's sleeve and tell Traven and Candy to hold on to each other. Then I walk them slowly around the circular corridors toward the sacrifice chamber.

It doesn't take long to find it. All roads lead here, the black nasty heart of the place. This is where I should have killed Mason. It's the room where I rescued Aelita. I don't think she's ever forgiven me for saving her. Maybe her thank-you note got lost in the mail.

The chamber's double doors are still open, still full of bullet holes and shotgun slugs from the New Year's Eve raid. Around here is where Candy and I had that first kiss on New Year's, shot up and covered in other people's blood. Good times.

A pale light comes from the room. I leave the others and step inside, sweeping the Smith & Wesson back and forth over debris from the partially collapsed roof. Going slow, I let my senses expand and fill the place, feeling for anything with lungs or a heartbeat. I feel something. I step lightly around bowling-ball-size chunks of marble that have fallen from the walls. A shaft of sunlight cuts down from a hole in the ceiling onto the stone sacrifice platform, and there's Hunter, stretched out like a boiled lobster, ready for the butter and claw crackers.

I wave Traven and the others in. They spread out around the platform. Traven goes right for the kid. We hang back, letting the father do his thing. Hunter is lying on his back. He's very still. His chest hardly moves. He looks like he's been beaten, left under a heat lamp, and dragged behind a truck. Patches of blackened skin are peeling away from his arms and face. The skin that isn't black or raw red is the greenish blue of tainted meat. Hunter's clothes would make any self-respecting wino jealous. Worn and splitting at the seams, they're covered in dried blood, shit, and vomit. He looks like he's been wearing the rags for weeks instead of a couple of days.

Traven leans in right over Hunter's mouth, listening for something. I'm waiting for the demon to take the bait and gnaw his ear off. But Hunter doesn't move.

Traven goes back to his duffel, unzips it, and lays out a bag of sea salt and bread on the floor next to him. Next he takes out a battered wooden box. Inside is a bottle of black sacred oil and a yellowed bone pen shaped kind of like a short, thick hockey stick. He dips the pen in the oil and scrawls symbols along all four sides of the sacrifice platform. He's creating a binding hex to keep the demon locked on the platform and away from us. I recognize most of the symbols. There's Hebrew and Greek. Some angelic script and even some Hellion cuneiform script. It's the last set of symbols that are the most interesting. Chicken scratches from some obscure heretical cookbook. I'll lay you odds they're from that Angra Om Ya book. Fine by me. Whatever hoodoo will keep Hunter and his demon on that side of the room and us over here in the cheap seats is fine by me. Now that I think about it, we should all be wearing body armor. Damn. Next exorcism for sure.

Traven's bread is a disappointment. It looks like an ordinary round loaf of French or sourdough. I was hoping for something belching fire and spinning like lowrider rims.

Traven rips the bread apart, setting a piece down every few inches from Hunter's throat to his crotch. He scoops up a handful of salt from the bag and drops a little mound of salt between each piece of bread. He sets the salt bag back in his duffel and moves it to the side of the room. He does it all in slow, practiced moves. A kind of moving meditation gearing up for the next step.

Traven points to Hunter's head, where he wants me to stand. He stations Candy by the feet. Vidocq is in the middle across from the father.

Traven says, "I understand that you carry potions with you."

Vidocq opens his coat like a flasher, showing Traven the dozens of pockets sewn into the lining.

Traven does his little smile.

"Do you have Spiritus Dei?"

"I didn't know the Church knew about or approved of such alchemical tricks."

Spiritus Dei is one of the best things in the universe. Like one of those all-in-one cleaners for your kitchen or hoodoo duct tape. It'll fix anything. It's a repellent for Hellions, demons, and pretty much any other nasty things with teeth. It'll Scotch Guard your panties from hexes and even cure some poisons. It's better than chicken-fried steak, but not by much.

"The church isn't here. I am. I'd like you to have some Spiritus Dei ready to throw if Hunter should get through the wards I've placed around the platform."

Vidocq nods.

"I'll be ready."

Traven looks at Candy and me.

"If he gets out, grab him and hold him, but try not to break him."

"I don't make rash promises. But he won't get away," I say.

Traven turns to the boy, holding his hands over him, palms down. His head is forward and eyes are closed. He's praying. To whom? I wonder.

Traven opens his eyes, raises his hands, and starts a chant. Another prayer, blessing the bread and salt. But I've never heard anything like what's coming out of his mouth, and I've heard drunk Hellions. Whatever language he's speaking is full of blurps, hisses, and deep Tibetan-monk throat drones and glottal stops. It sounds like a man drowning.

Hunter's eyes snap open. They're yellow and bloodshot, but alert. His heart is beating a million miles an hour, but his breathing is ragged. I don't know how both of those things can be going on inside him without him having a heart attack. His mouth slowly falls open. A vapor, as thin as fog but as bright as fire, drifts out. Guess Hunter's mother was telling the truth when she said he spit fire when he burned the symbol into the ceiling.

It doesn't surprise or impress Traven even a little. With one hand he pushes Hunter's head down. With the other hand, he picks up salt and throws it into Hunter's mouth. Then he shoves in a piece of bread to seal in whatever's trying to get out. Hunter goes completely batshit, thrashing and convulsing like he's being electrocuted. He flails his arms at his face, trying to knock out the bread, but Traven's magic has taken away a lot of his motor control. Traven keeps a hand over the kid's mouth, holding the bread in place. I grab Hunter's shoulders and Candy holds his feet to keep him from kicking.

Traven chants, and with one hand over Hunter's mouth he sprinkles salt over the lumps of bread and wolfs them down. Each time he downs bread and salt, Hunter goes wilder and wilder. I'm holding him tight. Candy is leaning over him, resting her whole weight on Hunter's legs.

All at once he stops moving. Goes completely limp. No one moves, in case he's playing possum. But Hunter doesn't twitch. Finally Traven nods to me and Candy and I let go. He takes some of the remaining salt and uses his finger to draw an elaborate sign on Hunter's forehead. He still isn't moving. I look at Candy and Vidocq and then back to the kid. I'm getting worried that the bread Traven shoved into Hunter's mouth has choked him. Traven takes the bread out of Hunter's mouth, cupping his hands around it. He holds it out with both hands.

Traven says, "The demon is in here. Use the Spiritus Dei."

Vidocq pops the top off the small vial with his thumb and upends the Spiritus on the bread. Traven squeezes the bread like a wet sponge so that some of the liquid dribbles into Hunter's mouth. Then Traven shoves the bread into his own mouth, chews, and swallows it quick. When it's down, he gets a funny look on his face.

I say, "What?"

"It doesn't taste right."

"What does that mean?"

"I should taste the remains of the demon. It's something, but it's not—" That's the last thing he gets out before Hunter's hand snaps up and grabs him by the throat.

The kid gets a good grip and lifts Traven from the floor. Traven flails at Hunter's arms, but he might as well be hitting tree trunks with a powder puff. I punch Hunter on the side of the head, digging a knuckle into his temple hard, but not hard enough to crack bone. He doesn't even react, just keeps squeezing Traven. Candy leaps from the end of the platform onto Hunter's chest. As she pushes him down, I give him one more shot in the head. I can't hit him any harder without scrambling his brains, so I aim low, hitting his floating ribs hard enough that I can feel a couple crack. That gets the message through. Hunter gasps and drops Traven, suddenly not able to breathe. Candy gives him a decent shot to the jaw before I pull her off. That knocks Hunter back onto his back. But not for long.

As we drag Traven away from the platform, Hunter starts up his Wild Man of Borneo routine. He tries to jump off the platform and follow us, but Traven's binding hex holds. Hunter punches, claws, and throws his whole body at the invisible barrier, but it knocks him back every time.

Vidocq rushes over, pulling another vial from under his coat. He pours the whole thing down Traven's throat. Traven coughs. His color goes from asphyxia blue to something human. He sits up and draws in a couple of wheezing breaths. He is alive, but he doesn't look all that happy about it.

"What's in there?" he says to no one in particular. "I've never seen a demon like this before. If the salt and bread didn't work, the Spiritus Dei should have paralyzed it."

Hunter is on his knees prowling back and forth along the platform like a pissed-off hyena waiting for its pack to arrive and kick our asses. The invisible barrier doesn't bother him anymore. He isn't even trying to get out. He's having fun. Licking it with his black tongue, spitting blood on it, and finger-painting with the clotted mess. At first it looks like he's just doodling, but a shape begins to emerge. In a minute he stops drawing, leans close to the bloody barrier, and opens his mouth. The fire fog that drifted from his mouth earlier flows out again. Flattening against the binding barrier, it spreads out like dozens of burning snakes. When it's done, he puffs out his chest and inhales the fire back down his throat. Then he collapses on the platform. This time I don't sense anything coming from him. I can usually feel life, a beating heart, even the shallowest breath, but this kid doesn't even feel dead. More like a black hole of life. Candy gets up and starts toward him, but I grab her arm. The hex barrier is still intact, but Hunter has burned a symbol into it. Sister Ludi's, the same symbol he burned over his bed.

And then I feel Hunter alive again. Still on his back, he turns his head and looks at me.

"Do you get it now? Please say yes. Don't make me embarrass you in front of your friends."

It takes me a minute to get past the face to the voice.

Hunter sits up. He stands, still a mess, but looking alert and calm.

"So, do you get it?"

I nod.

He's talking in Mason's voice.

"You're coming through loud and clear."

I reach into the barrier and run my hand through the burning symbol he drew until it drifts apart. Storm clouds and miniature fireworks.

"It's Sister Ludi's sigil. A fake goddess for a fake possession."

Hunter raises his hands and rolls his eyes heavenward in mock relief. He's a riot. Bob Hope with horns and a tail. But I deserve every bit of shit he serves up. Wells and Aelita foxed me like this once before, covering up a Drifter attack with a fake demon. Would I have fallen for the gag the first time if I was still on my game Downtown? No way. This stupid world is making me weak. Or maybe it's just reminding me of how weak I've always been. No more. Fool me once, shame on you. Fool me twice, you're dead.

Hunter—Hunter's body at least—shakes his head.

"I thought I was going to have to put on that medicine show forever. I mean Julia talked this idiot into exorcising me and it didn't work. Now you drag him back and it goes tits up again. I thought that would have set off a few alarm bells."

"It might have if I'd had time to think, but I was kind of busy with not letting your meat puppet kill him."

Hunter smiles. Black gums and yellow teeth. I flash back on the Drifters and feel the urge to rip out his spine.

"What's one Holy Roller more or less?"

"I like this one. He unfriended God on Facebook."

Hunter looks skeptical.

"You sure it wasn't the other way around? We have a lot of that type down here and I'm betting he's on the party list. I'm getting a definite whiff of sulfur off him."

He looks at Traven.

"You know all those suicides your Church condemns to Hell? There's nothing they like better than having one of

God's defrocked toadies to play with. I'll tell them to break out the party hats and get something special ready for you."

Traven is turning white. He's been through plenty of exorcisms, but having a rational, well-spoken demon threaten him personally is a whole new kind of fun for him.

"Don't listen to him, Father. That's no demon. It's the asshole I was telling you about in the car. My friend Mason, the one who thinks he's the new holy trinity—God, the devil, and GG Allin."

"That's the difference between us, Father. Ambition. He had none, so I had to have enough for both of us."

Traven is frozen on the floor. Candy's body vibrates, a low growl building in her throat. I put my hand on her back and shake my head. The last thing we need is for her to go full Jade.

"Don't be too impressed, Father. He's done this trick before. Talking through people on earth, but you don't have any real power here, do you, sunshine?"

Mason raises an eyebrow.

"What makes you think I can't pull this building down on you right now?"

"Because if you had any real power, you'd have made it through that binding hex by now."

Mason raps his knuckles on the invisible barrier.

"Good point," he says. "You've got me there. I suppose I'm helpless as a kitten."

He smooths down his filthy rags like he's getting ready for a date with Miss America.

"And here I thought you'd be occupied with your fantasy about attacking heaven. But you must have time on your hands to be pulling stupid tricks like this."

He shakes his head.

"I'm working twenty-four/seven on the big plan. Aelita, too. She came Downtown and brought some tchotchkes. She's a hell of a girl."

So it's true. That's not a combination I like thinking about. What do they have in common? One wants to kill God and one wants to be him, and I can't see Aelita approving of Mason taking the old man's place. Hell. Maybe they both want to be God and are going to do a set-up Pearly Gates time-share.

"You're bluffing," I say. "Aelita is a bitch on wings, but she's not stupid. She wouldn't have anything to do with a second-rate show pony like yours."

"Sure she would. We have the same hobbies."

"Like what?"

His face splits into a big grin. Those teeth again.

"Hating you."

"I'm flattered."

Traven grabs my arm and pulls me back a few feet.

"Stop talking to him. The demon is trying to confuse you."

"There is no demon. There's nothing in there but a little rich boy who wants to murder the world because some bad men took away his Etch A Sketch."

Mason clasps his hand over his heart like he's wounded. He spits some of Hunter's blood on the sacrifice platform and clears his throat.

"Answer me this, Jimbo. And I mean this sincerely. What you need to focus on right now is the key question of the night: Why is this happening?"

For all I'm bullshitting him, I know he's consumed with

his plans to attack Heaven, so, yeah, I'm kind of wondering what's really going on.

"Because you're trapped," I say. "Because you got yourself in way over your head. Because you're not Lucifer and not really in charge down there. You bribed a few generals into coming to your place for catered lunches and cigars. Big deal. Without General Semyazah, you're never getting close to Heaven. And you haven't been able to build a key to escape from Hell. You can't admit you're stuck down there. That's why this is happening. Hiding in other people's skin is as close as you'll ever come to getting home."

He stares at me, leaning his forehead on the barrier like a bored kid.

"You're embarrassing yourself again by thinking small. What's happening here is a formal invitation, but not from me. Listen."

Hunter's body goes slack. Mason has released control. A second later Hunter snaps back up. His eyes brighten and he looks around, but is unsteady on his feet. His lips move as he looks for his voice.

"Jim?" says Hunter.

No. Not this.

"Are you there? What's happening? Where am I?"

I can't see anything for a minute. It's like someone flipped a switch and my vision has gone out. This is what happens to people in deep shock or sudden anger. "Blind rage," they call it. It's a real thing.

"Don't listen. It's the demon," says Traven.

"Shut up."

Alice's voice comes out of Hunter's mouth again.

"Jim? I don't know where I am. An angel took me away and locked me up here. She said it was your fault. That you made her do it. I don't believe her, but I'm scared."

Hunter's body twitches.

"That's all you get of Little Miss Falling-Down-the-Rabbit-Hole for now."

"How did you find her?"

"Don't worry, Jimbo. She hasn't been here all along. Except for getting mixed up with you, Alice was a good girl and all good girls go to Heaven. But God isn't what he used to be. You should know that. So while good girls might get to Heaven, they don't always get to stay."

"Alice is what Aelita brought you."

"She dropped poor Alice here like a basket of muffins from the neighborhood welcome wagon."

"Why?"

He doesn't say anything for a long minute.

"Why? Because you made me do it," he says. "You could have come down here and we could have settled this like men, but you stayed up there with your quilting bee, drinking beer and getting soft. Now you have to come down and face me. Or not. You can always leave poor Alice alone down here with me. I know Kasabian can see us through the *Codex,* so you can see what happens like watching the Super Bowl in that bar you like." He smiles and takes a breath. "You thought Downtown was crazy when you were here? You ain't seen nothing, pal."

I start for the platform. Candy puts her hand on my shoulder. I shrug her off. She thinks I'm going to charge Hunter. I'm not. I just want to get close to see who I'm talking to.

Mason understands and kneels down so that we're eye to eye.

He says, "Now you have it. Your invitation. You have exactly three days from when I leave this body to find Alice and take her . . . well, I really don't care what you do with her. In the meantime, don't worry. She's in the safest place in town. The penthouse suite of the big asylum. Most of the inmates escaped weeks ago. The dangerous ones. Of course, the place is home to them, so they tend to wander back."

I can see him looking back at me through Hunter's eyes. No demon. It really is Mason.

"What's it going to be? Are you going to play my game or are you going to stay safe in L.A. playing Gary Cooper and wasting your time saving people who don't deserve it from things they'll never understand?"

I lean in close to Hunter's ear. Mason leans in to listen. I say a word in Hellion and he flies back, bouncing off the shield on the far side of the platform like he was hit with a sledgehammer. Vidocq and Candy get me from behind, throwing their full weight into me. Pulling me down. I let them. I don't want to kill Hunter because of what's inside him.

Mason staggers to his feet.

"You got me good, Jimbo. But that's all right. I'll take that as a yes. It'll be good to see you again."

He twitches.

"Jim? Are you still there? What's happening? I . . ."

And Alice is gone. Hunter collapses onto the platform. It's over.

Traven rubs away some of the binding hex marks. He and

Vidocq lift Hunter from the platform and lay him out on the
floor.

I'm stuck where I am. I feel a sucking sensation in my chest
and for a second I can't breathe. Gradually I feel Candy's
arms around me. I squeeze her hand and she lets me up.

Hunter is breathing. His eyes flicker open and closed. He
doesn't look like he's going to drop dead this minute, but he's
still pretty Linda Blair. Traven isn't looking so good either.
He's pale and his neck is dark with bruises and broken blood
vessels where Hunter grabbed him.

I pick Hunter up and tell Candy and Vidocq to help Traven.

"We're going out the fast way."

They get their arms around Traven's shoulders and steady
him. Vidocq is closest to me, so I grab his arm and walk the
few steps to the wall. We disappear into a shadow.

Come out again in the minimall parking lot. Pedestrians
pass us on the way to their cars with take-out pizza and new
manicures. A few of them stare. They must have seen us. Fuck
'em. The way we look, no one is going to tell anyone about it
without a doctor shoving Thorazine down their throat.

We head across the lot for Kinski's old hoodoo clinic. The
place Allegra has taken over. A sign on the door reads EXIS-
TENTIAL HEALING. Vidocq gets out his cell and dials Allegra.
I don't wait. I start pounding on the door.

A few good raps later, someone opens the doors looking
pissed. It's Allegra. She looks at Hunter and her eyes narrow.
Then she sees Vidocq and Candy holding up Father Traven.

"Jesus, Stark. You're like the Antichrist Santa Claus. Bring
in the presents."

We get Hunter inside and on the exam table. Allegra takes

over, looking at Hunter's eyes, shining a light into his blackened mouth. She turns and takes things out of a drawer. She presses one of them to Hunter's forehead. A silver crucifix. Nothing happens. Then she touches iron. Gold. A mixture of garlic and holy water. Nothing happens with any of them.

"Good," she says.

She rubs a yellowish salve on the inside of a mortar and tosses in thistle leaves, white ash bark, and things I can't identify. She holds a match to the gloop and the whole thing goes up in a *whoosh* of fire, leaving only ash. She dumps it into her hands and rubs the ashes across Hunter's forehead and eyes.

"Get me the glass, will you, Candy?" she says.

Traven is standing on his own now, so she leaves him and lifts several bundles of purple silk from a cabinet. Allegra takes one as Candy sets the rest on the exam table.

Allegra unwraps the first one and sets it over Hunter's heart. It looks like a heavy white stone. She sets other pieces of glass on Hunter's hands and diaphragm.

The stones are really pieces of ancient glass vessels saturated in divine light. Shards of the first stars. Kinski once used six of them to save Allegra. Now Allegra is the doctor, using them to save a kid she's never seen before and has no reason to care about. But she does it like she'd die, too, if the kid doesn't make it. It's a funny world.

Hunter shudders and opens his mouth. Vapor drifts from his mouth again, but it's the same gray now as the ash. Allegra nods.

"Whatever was in him is gone."

"You sure?"

She looks at me.

"I know what possession looks like. This one took more stones than usual. What was in him?"

I don't want to tell her. I'm feeling stupid and the last thing I want to do is have to hang around and explain anything.

"Candy and Vidocq can tell you."

"Well, whatever it was, it's gone now."

"Good."

She nods at Traven.

"What happened to him?"

"That's Father Traven, the exorcist. No hoodoo injuries. The demon just grabbed his throat and squeezed like it was trying to make orange juice."

Allegra looks past me at the father.

"Set him down in the lobby and let me get my instruments. I don't want to move the boy for a while."

Traven makes it to the lobby under his own steam, though Candy and I walk behind to catch him if he falls. He drops onto one of the plastic chairs. He leans forward, resting his face in his hands.

"I think I left my bag at that place," he says.

"Don't worry, Father. We'll retrieve it for you," says Vidocq.

I hand him Allegra's car keys.

"Sorry. I'd like to go back and get it, but I have things I need to do."

"I understand," he says. He looks at me like I'm ice and someone is about to toss boiling water on me. Will I explode or just melt?

He says, "We all heard what the demon said back at Avila. Don't do anything insane based on the word of a creature like that, Jimmy. They are masters of lies."

I shake my head.

"That wasn't the demon talking. That really was Mason. And he has Alice. I'm not going to do anything crazy. I'm going to do what I should have done all along."

"What?" he says, but I ignore the question.

"Call Hunter's parents," I say. "Tell them he's all right and give them the address. I need to go."

I catch Candy's eye and she follows me out into the parking lot.

"Where are you going?" she asks. There's a little catch in her voice.

I get close and say, "I know this is the most fucked situation I could have dragged you into, but I need to talk to someone. Please trust me. I'll meet you back at the hotel as soon as I can."

She looks up at me.

"You're coming back, right?"

"Of course."

"Promise."

"I promise."

She kisses me. I kiss her back, though in the back of my mind I'm already going to do what I have to do.

She takes a step back.

"You're going back, aren't you? Back to Hell."

"I don't have any choice. They snatched Alice out of Heaven because of me. I can't leave her down there."

Candy nods.

"I know. You have to do the right thing. Ride into the sunset and do your *Good, the Bad and the Ugly* thing. I think that's why I like you. You do the most fucked-up things for the best reasons."

"I'll see you back at the hotel. Scout's honor."

"Where are you going?"

"I need to talk to Mustang Sally."

BY THE TIME I make the corner, my hands are shaking. Even the angel is pissed, and that's not easy to do. I want someone to try to pick my pocket or pull a knife. I want an excuse. All I need is an excuse.

No one comes near me. I'm somewhere south of sanity right now and people can tell. Fuck it. I let the angel's senses reach out and read the street until they zero in on exactly the right car. It's stopped at a red light in front of me. Second from the front. A couple of gangbangers inside. They're either on their way to a drive-by or coming back from one. They're too high for the angel to be sure. That's good enough for me. I step into the stopped traffic and go around to the gang-bangers' car, a red midfifties Bonneville lowrider. I put the .460 to the side of the driver's temple.

"Do you want to keep the car or your head?"

There are two tough guys in the back. Real bruiser types. As big as linebackers. One of them wants to go for his gun. He stinks of coiled tension. I cock the .460 pressed against the driver's head and pull him out through the window. Toss him one-handed onto the hood of the car next to us. He leaves a nice dent as he hits and slides off. By the time I swing the gun back to the two toughs, they're scrambling out the passenger side. I get in and rev the engine.

I don't care that it's broad daylight, that a hundred people are watching, and that the traffic cams on the stoplights are recording everything. I want witnesses. I want them to see so that when I drag them from their cars, put a bullet in the gas tank, and let the explosion torch the street, they'll understand.

"This is the world. This is how it is," I'll tell them. "Jesus might have died for your sins, but a girl is burning for them. I'd trade every one of your fucking lives for one minute of hers. Don't you dare pray for her. Twiddle your rosaries and pray for yourselves, because if she goes down, I'm the Colonel, the fryer's hot, and you're my barnyard chickadees."

But I don't say it. I take the car and go. There's no way I could get the words out right now. I probably would have stood there hissing and twitching. Just another homeless schizo. Then I'd set the intersection on fire with some Hellion hoodoo and none of them would understand why.

The light turns green and I cut off the car next to me and pull a squealing and massively illegal left off Sunset, steering the Bonneville onto side streets and away from the cops.

The dinky little neighborhood streets with their speed bumps and stop signs are molasses-at-the-South-Pole slow, but eventually I get to Fairfax, where I stop for gas. When the tank is full I go inside the station to the little grocery. There's nowhere else you can get food like this. The donuts taste like diesel vapor and you have to smother the microwave hamburgers with mustard and onions to cover the taste of cancer. I spent a fair amount of time in places like this before I went Downtown. They're a solvent-stained oasis for people who drink till the bars close and are too brain-fried to find a Denny's for the grease injection they hope will soak up the poison they've been swallowing all evening. Here everything is poison and so full of preservatives that it will live forever.

This is junk-food Valhalla. I grab a plastic basket and prowl the aisles, filling it with the right mix of the sweetest, greasiest, most guaranteed-heart-attack stuff I can find.

I should have dealt with this long ago. How to get back Downtown now that Mason has pretty much made it impossible for me to get in. I hadn't counted on the little prick making friends so quick. He fast-talked his Hellion guards, their bosses, and their bosses' bosses, clawing and hoodooing his way up the Infernal food chain until he got to some of Lucifer's generals. With that kind of pull, it was easy for him to set up traps and guards at all my favorite entrances and exits in and out of Hell. And it's not like I can just pick a new entrance at random. Hell is a complicated place. I might come out in a swamp or the House of Burning Ice. And it's not like you can trust most of the maps of Hell. Lucifer was paranoid enough to put in fake landmarks and move mountains and towns around, so it's damned close to impossible to navigate outside the cities unless you already know where you're going. Or you have a guide. But I'm a little too famous down there to hop on a Gray Line tour bus and hope no one recognizes me.

I know every crawl space and backstreet in Pandemonium, but if Mason has Alice locked up in another city, I'll need help getting there. Hellions can be very cooperative if you pull out enough of their teeth, so I know I can get a guide. What I really fucking need is a fucking way in. There's only one person in L.A. who might know and who I trust enough to ask.

I take my basket of donuts, candy, chips, refrigerated burgers, and barbecue sandwiches up to the clerk. He's red-eyed and bored, trying to hide the *Hustler* he's been thumbing through the whole time I've been in the store. I let him take the stuff from my basket. My hands could get diabetes and a stroke just from touching the wrappers.

I say, "Throw in a carton of Luckies."

The kid sighs. I've ruined his day by asking him to turn around and pick up something.

"We don't sell cartons. Just packs."

"Then sell me ten packs and leave them in the box."

He thinks this over for a minute. I can hear the gears turning. The factory that runs his brain is spewing copious amounts of ganja fumes. Finally, he thinks of something that won't make him sound too stupid.

"You have any ID?"

"Do you really think I'm underage?"

He shrugs.

"No ID, no smokes."

I take two twenties from my pocket and slide them across the counter to him.

"There's my ID."

He has to think again. The workers are fleeing the factory. The boiler might blow.

The kid holds up the bills to see if they're counterfeit.

"Yeah, okay. Don't tell anyone."

"Who am I going to tell?"

He considers this for a moment, like it's a trick question, but it soon fades from his resin-clogged brain along with the state capitals and how to do math. He drops a carton of Luckies onto the pile of death snacks and rings them up, setting the well-thumbed *Hustler* on the counter as he counts out my change. Then realizes what he's done. He freezes. It looks like he might stay like that for the rest of the day.

I pick up my bag and say, "Keep the change. I respect a man who reads."

I go back to the Bonneville and set the bag on the passenger seat. Time to talk to the one person who might be able to help me get Downtown. Mustang Sally, the freeway sylph.

EVERY CITY HAS a Mustang Sally. Every town and jungle village with a dirt path. She's a spirit of the road, an old and powerful one. If you add up all the freeways, the county and city roads, in and around L.A., it means Sally controls twenty thousand miles of intense territory. And that doesn't even count the ghost roads and ley lines.

I steer the Bonneville onto the shoulder of the 405, the freeway that runs along Sepulveda Boulevard, the longest street in L.A. I break open the carton of Luckies, take out a pack, and slice it open with the black blade. I slide across the front seat and get out on the passenger side. This would be a lousy time to die.

Traffic blasts past at sixty per hour and no one even glances in my direction as I walk behind the car and scratch Mustang Sally's sigil into the freeway concrete. When I'm done I stand in the center of the mark, take out a Lucky, and light up. Passing cars pull the smoke in their direction, like it wants to follow them down the road. I smoke and wait.

Mustang Sally has been cruising L.A.'s roads twenty-four/ seven since they were nothing more than mud paths, horse tracks, and wagon ruts. As far as I know, she never sleeps and never stops except when someone leaves an offering. For the last hundred years she's been through every kind of car you can name. Of course, she never has to stop for gas. Sally eats, but only road food. Things you can find in gas-station markets and vending machines. She doesn't need to eat. She just likes it. It's like me and stealing cars. Sometimes you just want to feel ordinary. Like a person. She eats. I drive.

Twenty minutes later, a silver-and-black Shelby Cobra pulls onto the shoulder a few yards behind me. I stomp out of her emblem and hold the Lucky out to her.

Sally is taller than I remember. Taller than someone who spent all day and night comfortably in a compact sports car. Her hair is dark. Maybe jet black with blue highlights. She's dressed in a white evening gown and the highest spike heels this side of the Himalayas. I don't know how she drives in those things. She walks over to me slowly, sizing me up. She's running the show, and making me wait is part of it. She has on a pair of soft white calfskin driving gloves. From one hand dangles a small clasp purse rimmed in gold. She's every bit a goddess except for one thing. She's wearing what looks like a pair of round glasses with smoked lenses; the kind the blind wore a hundred years ago. They break up the goddess look. Like the *Mona Lisa* with a lip ring.

When we're just a couple of feet apart, she stops, peels off the driving gloves, and drops them into the clasp bag. She takes the cigarette from my hand and inhales deeply, letting the smoke drift slowly from her nostrils.

"Unfiltered. You sweet boy."

I wonder what's behind those dark glasses. I swear, even in daylight I can see a faint glow from underneath the lenses.

She could be sporting twin suns or headlights back there. You would not want to aim your road rage at this woman.

Mustang Sally cocks her head and stares at me for a few seconds.

"I know you. The charming Frenchman introduced us."

She has a low, purring smoker's voice, the kind you can almost feel in your chest when she speaks.

"You've got a good memory. That was my friend Vidocq. He was looking for Mickey the Hammer's grave and figured that since you'd been everywhere and see everything, you might have noticed where he was buried."

"Yes. He's an alchemist and Mickey was . . . what? A tracker? He left me a few offerings, too."

"Mickey was a scoria hound. He could trace anyone or anything through its trail in the aether. I guess he found the wrong person because he ended up dead. People said he was buried with a scroll explaining how to do it. You told Vidocq where to find his grave."

"And did he find what he was looking for?"

"The body was where you said it would be, but someone got there before us and picked it clean. It cost Vidocq a lot of donuts to find that body."

She shrugs and gazes out at the traffic.

"That's the way of the road. It's gas, gab, or food. Nobody rides for free."

I go back to the bike and bring her the bag of snacks. Sally smiles when she sees it. I hold it out to her. She doesn't take it. Just pulls the edge of the bag with a fingernail and looks inside.

"My. You must be looking for a diamond as big as the

Ritz." She smiles a tiger's smile. "Put it in the car and ask your question."

I go to where she's parked. The Cobra's seats are perfect. They look brand-new, but she must have logged thousands of miles in the thing. The only thing that gives away she lives and eats there is the trail of litter that stretches out behind the car for as long as I can see. Cookie boxes. Cellophane from around snack cakes. Crushed cigarette packs. Sally marks her territory and no one stops her. Not CHP. Not cops. No one.

I get back just as she grinds out the cigarette with the toe of one delicate shoe.

"I need a back door into Hell," I say. "A way in that no one will notice."

She curls her lips into a half smile.

"Sneaking into Hell. That's old magic. Beginning-of-the-world stuff. Back when the different planes of existence weren't so far apart that the residents of one don't even believe in the existence of the other."

"Is that a problem?"

"It depends on how you want to go in. There are places where this twelve-lane Möbius strip is the Hell parents tell kids they'll end up in if they don't behave. There are other places where this is Heaven."

She smiles.

"You don't want to go in that way. It's too unpredictable."

"Are there other ways in?"

"Don't be in such a rush. Give a lady a moment to think."

She takes another Lucky from the pack. I light it with Mason's lighter. As she breathes in the smoke, I swear the glow behind her sunglasses brightens.

"Nice car," I say.

"Thanks. It's pretty but it might be time to trade it in. It's getting too noticeable. These days, if you own something long enough, it becomes vintage and everybody wants one. In my day, when something was old, it was just old."

"I bet it handles these roads well."

She shrugs, unimpressed.

"Each road has its own way of going. You should have seen those few scratches in the dirt in the Fertile Crescent. The first roads that called me into being. Back then a decent pair of sandals was high tech."

She holds out the Luckies. I hesitate.

"It's all right," she says. "Half the job of being a spirit is knowing when to share."

I take the cigarette. She pulls a gold lighter from her bag and sparks the Lucky for me.

When she drops the lighter back in the bag, she says, "Do you know what it is you're asking? Do you have any concept of what Hell is?"

"I spent eleven years Downtown, so, yeah, I have a pretty good idea."

That gets her attention. She gives me a slow once-over with her eyes or whatever it is behind those glasses.

I say, "I was alive. The only living thing that's ever been down there and sure as Hell the only living thing that's ever crawled out."

"Oh. That's you. The monster who kills monsters."

Her body relaxes like we're chatting each other up in a bar.

"What a relief. For a minute there, I was afraid you were

a ghost. I don't like doing business with the dead. They leave pitiful offerings."

"I guess being all disembodied would make you a little skittish."

"That's not the half of it. Ghosts are whiners. When they don't like the answer I give them, some even try haunting me. Me. Can you imagine how annoying it is to have a ghost moaning away in your car? I banish them to road structures. Overpasses or cloverleafs. Let them watch the living go by for a hundred years or so and see if that improves their manners."

"I wonder if the bums that live in underpasses know they're pissing on the dead?"

Mustang Sally looks at me hard.

"Why do you want to go back? Escaping once was quite a feat. Are you trying to become famous by doing it twice?"

"I'm going to find a friend who shouldn't be there. And then I'm going to kill someone. If I have time, maybe I'll stop a war or two."

That makes her laugh. A full-throated husky howl.

"You're not frivolous. But you might be crazy."

"My friends wouldn't argue that point, so I won't either."

"This friend you're going to rescue, is she your lover?"

"Yeah."

Sally looks out at the road. Heat reflects off it, making the cars in the distance soft and dreamlike.

"Do you know what most people ask me when I stop for them?"

She waits. I'm supposed to ask the question.

"What?"

"You'd think it would be about where to find the boy who got away or the girl they left behind. But no. They want to know where they should go to be happy. How can I possibly answer that? The road isn't here to make you happy. It's here so you can find your own way. Because they bring me cigarettes, they expect me to cure their misery."

"What do you say?"

"I tell them to go to a gas station and buy the biggest map they can find. It doesn't matter if it's the city, the state, or the world. I tell them to open it, close your eyes, and drop your finger somewhere on the map. That's where you'll find what you're looking for."

"Running off into the unknown can sure clear your head. It sounds like pretty good advice."

"Thank you."

I smoke the cigarette as a highway-patrol car slows down and gives us the once-over. Sally throws the driver a tiny backhanded wave. The patrol cop's eyes go blank. He turns his attention back to the road and drives on.

"Any thoughts on my problem?" I ask.

"Yes. What you want isn't all that hard to do, but it isn't easy if you get my meaning. What you need is a Black Dahlia."

"And that means what?"

"You're going to have to die. And not a going-gentle-into-that-good-night death. It's going to be messy."

Story of my life.

"I was hoping for something a little more in the hocus-pocus area. Getting Downtown dead and being stuck there kind of defeats the purpose of my coming to you."

She flicks the Lucky butt out onto the road. It flies in a

perfect arc like a falling star. Marking her territory so more cops won't bother us.

"Silly boy. I said you had to die. I didn't say you'd be dead. Dying is just the offering you make to gain passage. Once you're on the other side, the debt is paid and you'll be you again."

"How violent are we talking about? I mean is the word 'entrails' involved?"

"Your death doesn't have to be quite as baroque as poor Elizabeth Short's Black Dahlia. A car accident should do it. At a crossroads, of course."

"Is there anything I need to do?"

"You'll need to carry an item worn by or touched by someone who suffered a violent death. Anything will do. A photo. A class ring. If the friend you want to find died violently, that's perfect. Get something of hers. Keep it close so it's touching your skin as you pass through. Love and death. There's no more powerful combination."

That's good news, but which of Alice's things should I bring with me? Maybe something she'd miss. Or is it too mean to remind her of her life here? On the other hand, it feels a little lame to bring the TV remote or her toothbrush.

"How do I find the right crossroads?"

"Elizabeth Short was murdered near Leimert Park. There was a nice crossroads there, but it's all suburbs now. Why don't you try the I-10 underpass at Crenshaw? That's a decent little crossroads. All you need to do is hit the accelerator and run the car into one of the concrete freeway supports. I'll be close by to give you a little push to the other side."

"Thanks. I appreciate it."

She nods and strolls to her car. I follow her over. She digs through the bag of snacks and comes up with a packet of jelly beans. She rips it open, offers me one, and when I shake my head, she spears one with a fingernail, takes it off with her teeth, and chews. She reaches into the packet, pushing the jelly beans around, looking for a specific one.

She says, "I'm only doing this because while you might be crazy, you're not stupid. You don't think you're Orpheus and can bring your friend back to the world of the living. That means you're willing to die and cross over to the worst place in Creation for someone you love but can never truly have. That's the kind of thing that can give even an old thing like me goose bumps."

"To tell you the truth, I'd rather be back running Max Overdrive."

"No, you wouldn't. You're like me. One of the night people. I'm the road. I give life and I take it. People like us don't get to close our eyes to the world and live cozy mortal lives."

Two men's faces slide into my memory. My real father, Kinski, a has-been archangel, and the father who raised me. One of the faces fades away. It's the other, not-quite-human one that stays.

"You make it sound so doomed and romantic. We should all be drinking absinthe as we die of consumption."

She shrugs her pretty shoulders.

"It's what you allow it to be. You can find beauty and joy in the dark places just as easily as civilians find comfort in the glow of their TVs. But you have to allow yourself to do it. Otherwise . . ."

"Otherwise what?"

"Otherwise, ten years from now, you'll be stopping me and asking a foolish question and I'll end up sending you to a gas station to buy a map."

"Ow. When you put it that way, Hell sounds just about right."

Sally touches my cheek. Her hand is warm, like the furnace burning behind her shades.

"Be a rock, James. Otherwise, you'll lose everything."

"How did you know my name was James?"

She swallows another jelly bean.

"It's just a trick I can do."

I shake my head.

"You sound like the Veritas sometimes."

"One of those little Hellion luck coins that insults you when you ask a question? I hope I'm not that mean."

"No. But what the hell does 'Be a rock' mean? It sounds like the kind of hoodoo warning that never actually means what it says."

Mustang Sally puts the jelly beans back in the bag.

"I always say what I mean."

She takes the white driving gloves out of her purse and puts them on. "Just like I always signal when I change lanes. I can't help if you don't see me coming and end up in a ditch."

Like a Howard Hawks freeway femme fatale, Mustang Sally slings the little purse over one shoulder and gets back in her car, revs the engine, and peels out. She blows me a kiss as she speeds by.

I DRIVE ACROSS town and beach the Bonneville in a no-parking zone in front of the Bradbury Building, that old art deco ziggurat and one of the few truly beautiful constructions in L.A. A group of schoolkids is on a field trip and I let them pass by before stepping into a shadow. I'm pretty sure a couple of the kids saw me. Good. Kids need their minds blown every now and then. It'll keep them from thinking that managing a McDonald's is the most they can hope for.

I don't come straight out into Mr. Muninn's cavern. I lean against the wall in the Room of Thirteen Doors. This is the still, quiet center of the universe. Even God can't text me here. In here I'm alone and bulletproof.

I've had one ace up my sleeve since this whole circus with Mason, Aelita, and Marshal Wells began. The kill switch. The Mithras. The first fire in the universe and the last. The flame that will burn this universe down to make way for the next. I told Aelita about it but she never believed me. She couldn't. I'm an Abomination and I could never get anything over on a pure-blood angel like her. So what good does that make the Mithras? A threat only works if people believe in it, which leaves me alone in this eternal echo chamber, not sure what to do. I can get behind Mustang Sally's beauty-in-darkness idea. That's half the reason Candy and I have been circling each other all these months. We're each other's chance to find some black peace in the deep dark.

Burning the universe was a lot more fun to think about when Alice was somewhere safe. Some puny hopeful part of me imagined that Heaven would still stand even if the rest of the universe turned to ash. But Alice is Downtown now and I know she was right and I have to let go of her, but I can't let her die down in Mason's crazy-house hellhole, and that's what will happen if I throw the kill switch.

I grab a heavy glass decanter from the floor and step out into Muninn's underground storeroom.

I yell, "Mr. Muninn. It's Stark."

He sticks his head out from around a row of shelves overflowing with Tibetan skull bowls and ritual trumpets made of human femurs decorated with silver. He wipes his brow on a black silk handkerchief as he walks over.

"Just doing a bit of inventory. Sometimes I think I should hire a boy like you to put this all on a computer, but then I think that by the time he's finished, computers will be obsolete and we'll have to do it all over again with brains in jars or genius goldfish or whatever other wonders scientists come up with next."

He sighs.

"I suppose in a place like this, the old ways work best. Besides, I know that while it looks like a jumble to other people, I know where each and every item is. I only do inventory as an excuse to revisit doodads and baubles I haven't handled in a century or two."

He sees the glass container in my hand.

"Oh my. You've brought it back. Let's sit down and have a drink."

Muninn's desk is a worktable covered in the kind of junk that would give the staff at the Smithsonian nuclear hardons. An early draft of the Magna Carta that included the emancipation of ghosts. Little floating and whizzing match-box-size gewgaws from Roswell. Cleopatra's lucky panties. For all I know, he has Adam and Eve's fig leaves pressed in their high school yearbook.

I set the decanter on the table between us. If you look hard enough into the glass, you can see a flickering match head of fire. It doesn't look like much, but neither do the few micrograms of plutonium it takes to kill you as dead as eight-track tapes and with a lot more open sores.

"You've changed your mind, have you? You're not going to set us all ablaze like the Roman candles on the Fourth of July?"

"When you put it like that, it sounds fun. Giving this back might be a mistake, but I don't think it's mine anymore."

I pick it up and look inside. I've had the Mithras all this time, but I've hardly ever looked at it. It's beautiful.

"I don't want this sitting in the Room in case Mason manages to make a key and can get in there."

"No. If there was anyone even more unsuitable than you to hold the Mithras, it would be him. No offense, of course. I would never have traded it to you if I thought that you were capable of using it."

"But I am. I was. I almost pulled that plug a hundred times."

"But you didn't. And that's why I let you have it."

I push the Mithras across the table in his direction. Muninn picks it up carefully, like a preacher who just found a Gutenberg Bible at a garage sale, and puts it on a nearby shelf where he can keep an eye on it.

He says, "If you see any of my brothers when you get to Hell, please give them my regards."

"Your brothers are in Hell?"

"One or two, I expect. I'm the only sedentary one. The others are restless sorts. They're bound to pop up anywhere. Some of them pass through Hell on occasion and send me trinkets for my collection."

He points to a shelf with Hellion weapons, a cup I recognize from Azazel's palace, and a chunk of the same kind of black bone that my knife was carved from.

"How will I know if I meet one of your brothers?"

He laughs.

"You'll know. We're twins except that there are five of us, so I suppose we're two and a half twins."

"I'm going to be moving pretty fast, so hello is about all I'll have time to say."

"You won't even have to say that if you're busy. Here," Muninn says.

He pulls a metal strongbox from under the table and takes a set of keys from his pocket. I've never seen so many keys in one place at one time. He flips through them, makes a face, and tosses them on the table. He gets out an identical set from his other pocket. A lot of the keys on this ring are bigger and older. He finds one that's so thick with rust, it's more like a twig that's been laying in the water and is covered with barnacles. He jams the thing into the strongbox lock and turns. It scrapes, groans, and whines, but after a minute of really laying into the thing, the box pops open. He reaches inside and pulls out a twelve-sided crystal and hands it to me. I hold it up to the light and look inside. Two pinheads, one white and one black, circle around each other in the center.

"What is it?"

"A Singularity. An infinitely hot, infinitely dense dot. Well, the two halves of it. Apart they'll circle eternally, but when they come together . . ." He raises his hands and makes the sound of an explosion with his cheeks. "In common parlance, it's the Big Bang. You gave me the end of the universe, so I'm giving you the beginning. I spirited it away with me when I left the family."

I heft the thing in my hand. It's light. Maybe half a pound. It seems kind of light for a universe.

"This was your hedge, wasn't it? In case you were wrong about me and I did set off the Mithras. If I killed off this universe, you could start it up again."

He closes the strongbox and puts it back under the table.

"I have a great deal of faith in you, but I've learned that it's always smart to have a backup plan."

"If you set off the Singularity, would it restart this universe or start another?"

"There's no way of telling until it happens. And in the end, does it really matter?"

"Not to me. Though I might miss cigarettes."

He points at the crystal in my hand.

"If you run into one of my brothers down there, give it to him. Do me this favor and I'll owe you a favor down the line."

He gets out a bottle of wine. Muninn always likes to seal a deal with a drink. It's one of the reasons he's good to do business with.

"In the meantime, keep the crystal safe. There's only one. Now, is there anything I can give you to help you on your journey?"

He pours us wine in two highball glasses with dancing girls etched into the sides. I feel like I'm in the Rat Pack.

"What have you got? I don't know what I'm going to be walking into down there."

Muninn rummages through a box of random junk on the corner of the table and pulls out something the size of an acorn. He sets it on the table and drinks his wine. The thing is small and speckled.

I say, "It looks like an egg."

Muninn nods.

"It is. The creature it comes from doesn't live in this dimensional plane, but don't worry. It's no more exotic than an archaeopteryx, so the egg is completely edible."

"Does that mean if I keep it warm, I'll get a flying lizard?"

Muninn's eyes brighten.

"Wouldn't that be lovely? No, the egg has medicinal properties. If you're hurt, it will help you heal and dull the pain. It has a very tough shell, so don't feel you have to be delicate with it. Just toss it in a pocket. If you need it, put it between your teeth and bite down hard. I've heard they taste rather sweet. Like white chocolate."

"You've never tried one?"

"I've never been hurt."

If I had more time, I'd definitely want to hear more about that, but I don't.

"By the way. There's a tasty '55 or '56 Bonneville parked outside on Broadway. I don't need it anymore and the people I took it from don't deserve it. It would look good in your collection."

"You're too good to me," he says, and comes around the table. "I'll be sure to collect it before it's towed away."

I drop the egg in my coat pocket and get up.

"I have some packing to do, so I should get going."

Muninn takes my hand and shakes it warmly.

"You keep my crystal safe and I'll keep the Mithras for you. I hope to see you back here very soon."

He waves at me as I step into a shadow by the stairs . . .

. . . AND COME OUT in the shadowed and semidiscreet entrance of the Museum of Death across from the hotel. It's technically getting toward evening, but only technically. The sun won't go down for another three hours and I'm very tired.

When I step out into the sun, the desert heat slaps me hard. It's funny. I've lived here most of my life, so I hardly ever notice the heat. Maybe I'm feeling it now because I'm coming out of Muninn's cool cavern. Maybe I'm noticing it the way someone with terminal cancer notices every leaf, every snatch of a song, every breeze from a passing car, and the color of smog over the hills as they wheel him to the hospice.

When I get back to the room, Candy has pushed and kicked most of the broken furniture to one side, leaving a minimalist scattering of chairs and lamps filling the cleared space.

"You got it real homey in here. Like a twister came through, not a full-on hurricane."

She uses the toe of her sneaker to push a couple of legs from a broken table under the pile of debris.

"I wanted to make a good impression on the hotel so they could admire all the stuff we didn't break."

She's looking at the junk and not at me.

"There's no reason you have to leave. You heard what Mason said. However this thing turns out it can't last more than three days."

She looks at me over her shoulder, kicking splinters and broken glass into the pile.

"You want me to just hang around here like you've gone out for cigarettes?"

"I'm coming back," I say.

She turns and faces me, arms folded and staring at her feet.

"Are you? You're not going to find something more important to do? Save the whales in Narnia or start a Hellion homeless shelter?"

"If you think I'm going to get back with Alice, you're wrong. I'm going back to save her. Those are two different things."

"Easy to say standing here when you can't see her and aren't all dewy-eyed. She's the love of your life and I'm just some girl with fangs you like to fuck."

I hate shit like this. This is when I want to be Downtown and stay there. This is what regular people call real life and I can't stand it. Give me a thousand Hellion throats to cut. It's better than this.

I say, "It's not like that and you know it."

There's a long pause.

"I want to think that."

"So do it. This is what it's like being around me. I don't get a lot of downtime."

I go over to her. She's still staring at her feet. Her arms are still crossed, but she doesn't move away. I rest my hands on her shoulders.

"Ever since I got back, people having been getting bloody because of me. Parker almost killed Allegra and Vidocq. A Drifter took a bite out of Brigitte. Doc Kinski is dead. Alice was dragged off to Hell. Now it's this Hunter kid and you."

She unfolds her arms and lets them drop to her sides.

I say, "I can't fix what's already happened, but I can goddamn well kill it at the source, and that's what I'm going to do. I'm not doing this for Alice or you or Doc or anyone else. I'm doing this for me because I'm tired of waiting to see what kind of heinous shit Mason dreams up next and who it's going to take down."

I move a hand up behind her head, feeling her shaggy Joan Jett hair.

"Don't stick around if you don't want to. Hell, I never even bought you the breakfast I promised. It'd be great if you're here when I get back, but I won't blame you if you're not. I don't know if I'd stick around this half-assed horse opera. So if I don't see you again, thanks for playing monster with me for a while. It felt good."

I turn and head for the door, but stop before I get it open. I don't turn around.

"You got a taste of blood when you bit that dealer back at Dead Set. Promise me you'll go to Allegra and get some of the potion that helps you control the craving."

"I promise."

I go out onto the balcony, closing the door behind me.

IN THE PARKING lot, foreign exchange students are playing basketball and eating burritos from a taqueria truck parked on the street. A couple have their laptops out and are video-chatting with their families back home.

I head to my room with Kasabian.

Someone taps me on the shoulder.

"Hey."

Candy comes around in front of me.

She says, "When you're born in a burning house, you think the whole world is on fire. But it's not."

"What is that?"

"It's something Doc told me. I didn't get it at first, but later on it made sense. I thought maybe it could help you."

"Thanks."

I nod at the door.

"You coming in?"

She smiles a little and nods.

We go in.

Vidocq, Allegra, and Father Traven are inside talking. Vidocq and Allegra are sitting on the bed and Traven is on a chair across from them. Kasabian is by his computer listening to them and smoking. Candy goes over and sits by Allegra.

There's a small single bed in the corner. It never gets used, so junk just gets piled there. Magazines. DVDs. Dirty clothes. A few bottles of Jack Daniel's. I sweep it onto the floor and think about sitting down, but it doesn't quite happen.

"Is this my going-away party or a wake? 'Cause if it's supposed to be a party, you're doing it wrong."

"We knew that you being you, you would just creep off into the night like a thief," says Vidocq. "So we decided to force our company upon you for a little while before you left."

I look at Vidocq.

"Yeah. You're right. I would have—so you don't have to watch me twitch until sundown."

"What happens at sundown?" asks Allegra.

"I make like Robert Johnson and go down to the cross-roads."

Candy says, "Is that what Mustang Sally said?"

"Yes. I can find a back door to Hell there."

"Who's Mustang Sally?" Allegra asks.

"The patron saint of road rage."

Vidocq puts a hand on her arm.

"A significant local spirit. I'll tell you about her later."

I'm standing in the middle of the room like an idiot. They're all gawking at me like I'm made of peanut brittle and might fall apart any second. I want to toss everyone out. I need to get my brain wired tight for Hell. And the Black Dahlia. I'm trying not to think about that. I've been nearly killed a hundred ways, but never in a car, and I never had to actually die to pull off any hoodoo before. What if it all goes wrong? What if I end up just another tangle of ground meat and chrome on the side of the freeway? I'd get a great obituary. "A suspect in the murder of his longtime girlfriend Alice, a man who was declared legally dead seven years ago, finally turns up really and truly dead in a stolen car wrapped around a freeway support while rushing to have tea with the devil."

Mason would love to have me stuck in Hell. Just another damned dead asshole. So would all the generals and aristo-crats I didn't get a chance to kill and the friends and families of all the Hellions I did kill. If I end up dead down there, it'll be one long endless Dante gang bang. Get out the chain saws and pass the mint juleps. It's party time down south.

"Why don't you sit down for a while?" says Candy.

Allegra chimes in, "Even Sandman Slim can't make the sun go down faster."

"I was going to stamp my feet and hold my breath, but you're probably right."

I sit down on the small bed.

"What happens now? Did anyone bring cake? Or is it a sleepover and we're going to do each other's nails?"

"Don't be like that," says Candy. "Your friends are just worried, is all."

"I appreciate that, but if you want to help, we should switch beds. I need to get some stuff from under that one."

Candy, Allegra, and Vidocq come over to the small one and I go around them to the big bed. It's a clumsy little square dance, but we make it. Candy squeezes my arm as she goes by and whispers, "Don't be a little bitch," in my ear.

That's the best advice anyone's given me all year.

I take off my coat and throw it on the bed. I pull everything out of the coat and my pockets. I toss the cash aside. It won't do me any good Downtown. A key to this room and Candy's. Toss those. My phone. Toss. A pencil-thin piece of lead I sometimes use for drawing magic circles. Another toss. I carry a lot of crap.

I pull a silver coin and a smooth pea-size piece of amber out of my pants pocket. The silver coin is about the size of a quarter and is old. Like ancient old. The kind of thing Doc would have carried. And there's the amber. It's not big enough to be worth anything. I've never seen either of them before. Someone must have slipped them into my pocket. I get it. Silver is protection from evil. Amber is for healing. I don't look over at Candy. I just put them back in my pocket.

Vidocq says, "Let me be sure I understand this. Your great plan is to do exactly what Mason told you to do?"

"Pretty much. I sneak in, grab Alice, stab Mason in the head, and I'm back in time to catch the Beatles on *Ed Sullivan*."

"Mason is a born liar and he hates you. Why would he possibly tell you the truth?"

I push the mattress out of the way and start pulling out weapons from where I hid them in the box springs.

"Because the truth is worse than a lie. He took Alice away once when he killed her. Now he wants to show how much better he is than me by doing it again. It's playground stuff, but that's all this has ever been."

It's funny seeing the guns and other toys all laid out. The old Navy Colt revolver, great-great-granddad Wild Bill Hickok's gun. The LeMat pistol. Kind of huge and useless, but I like it. There's a cut-down Clyde Barrow–style "Whippit" gun. There are souvenirs I've taken off Lurkers and lowlifes. A farmers' market of pistols. Tasers. Brass knuckles with valentine hearts on the business side. Chinese butterfly knives and weirdly shaped Lurker daggers shaped for nonhuman hands. A sharpened goat horn. My favorite is a silver stake made by a wannabe high school vampire slayer. She made it by sharpening a flat-head screwdriver and dipping it in a pot of melted dimes. The perfect weapon against shroud eaters. Only the little idiot didn't know that modern dimes are mostly copper covered in nickel. All she did was ruin a perfectly good screwdriver and prove that L.A. schools truly suck.

"You have nothing but his word. It isn't possible."

"Of course it is. Mason has Hell and now he wants Heaven. Aelita wants to murder God. Neither of them wants me stumbling around and maybe getting in their way."

"Searching for Alice will keep you busy while they carry out their plans."

"Right."

Traven says, "I understand how a mortal man might come up with a mad plan to rule the universe, but how does an angel fall so far from grace?"

"You're the preacher. You tell me."

He shakes his head.

"I suppose if I knew the answer, I'd still be part of the Church."

"Come on, Father. Angels have been going crazy since the beginning of time. They're another one of God's great fuck-ups. Look at me. I wouldn't even be in this world of shit if an angel hadn't fucked my mother."

"They didn't cover any of this at the seminary."

"It's comforting to know that God's schools are as rotten as the regular ones."

As fun as my weapon collection is, most of it's useless where I'm going. I have my na'at and the black blade. They kept me alive Downtown for eleven years. They'll probably do it again. I always feel better with a gun on my belt, but getting shot with any of these would just make a Hellion giggle.

I look at Kasabian.

"You want to jump in here sometime with any new info?"

He looks at the bed and says, "I'm going to have a mother-fucker of a garage sale if you don't come back."

"Thanks for your support. Is it possible that Mason is armed up enough to attack Heaven in the next three days?"

"Troops are still coming in from all over. There are a lot of deserters, but not enough to make a difference."

"You said Mason couldn't attack without Semyazah's troops. Did he go over?"

Kasabian shakes his head.

"He's not there, but that doesn't mean some other general hasn't been able to turn his troops. Like I said, there's enough fallen angels in Pandemonium to start a thousand boy bands."

I get out Muninn's Singularity and the funny bird egg, Mason's lighter, and the small white stone Lucifer gave me back at Max Overdrive and set them with the na'at and the knife.

Father Traven says, "If all this is true, then you can't go down there alone."

I look at him and then at Kasabian.

"You're having a weird day, aren't you?"

Traven's eyes flicker to Kasabian and away again.

"It's hard to say. I think I'm becoming immune to weird."

"Damn. You're one of us already. Well, welcome to the Grindhouse Rodeo, Father, where it's monster triple features all the time. The popcorn's stale and the drinks are watered down, but we're open all night and deities have to sit in the balcony with the winos and rubber-raincoat types."

Traven does his half smile.

"Thank you, I suppose."

"There used to be a secret handshake, but only Kasabian knows it and he's not talking."

"Fuck you, Susan Vance," he calls from across the room.

"One more thing," I say. "Nobody starts with the you-can't-go-alone stuff. That subject is dead and buried."

The angel in my head is telling me to be calm, but it's not trying very hard. It always wants me to slow down and consider all the angles, but it knows that the clock is ticking on Alice, and now that I'm tying up loose ends on earth, I need to move faster than ever. Momentum is my best strategy. Slowing down and considering the consequences of what I'm doing is doom.

Vidocq and Allegra are holding hands on the small bed. I don't need to listen to their hearts or breathing. They're radiating tension like a microwave oven. Kasabian has gone back to his computer, trying to ignore all of this. Traven looks a little lost. Candy's not much better.

I know carrying a gun is stupid, but I feel naked without one. For sentimental reasons I'd like to take great-great-granddad's Navy Colt, but it's too big. I look back at the pile of guns on the bed and find a small-frame .357 revolver. I can't even hit the ground with the thing if I'm more than ten feet away, but it's better than nothing. I get a roll of duct tape from a drawer and pull my pants leg up a few inches.

"Want to give me a hand?" I say to Candy.

She comes over and I hand her the tape.

"Wrap it around my ankle a few times to hold the gun. Don't be shy. Make it tight."

She squats down in front of me and runs the tape around my leg a few times. Tests to see if the gun is secure and tears off the end with her teeth.

She slaps me on the ankle.

"You're ready to go, Wild Bill."

She leans up, puts her hands on my face, and kisses me. It feels good and it's a relief. I was half expecting a gone-baby gone-death kiss, like the kiss you give a corpse before it rolls into a crematorium. But it's a normal kiss. A have-a-nice-trip, see-you-soon kiss. For once, even the angel in my head is happy.

"Can you hold on to the stuff in that pile?" I ask her. "The phone and keys and cash and whatever."

"Sure."

In the closet there's a box of Alice's things that I took from Vidocq's apartment. I pop the top and start taking things out. What's the appropriate trinket from a murdered girlfriend to wear to a suicide?

From the bed Candy asks, "What are you looking for?"

"I'm supposed to bring something from a murdered person with me. Alice qualifies there, and I figure if I bring the right thing, it might help convince her it's really me. I have a feeling they'll have been messing with her brain by the time I get to her."

"I wasn't murdered, but I'm a girl. Maybe I can help."

"Okay."

She sits down beside me as I pile Alice's things onto the floor. There's a pair of her favorite shoes. Some dime-store bracelets and necklaces from when she was a kid. An Altoids tin with fortune-cookie fortunes and buds of eleven-year-old pot. I set everything on the floor and Candy examines each object. I don't know if she's helping me or trying to figure out who Alice is.

I hear Kasabian putting a DVD into the player by his computer.

"What are you putting on?"

"The Wizard of Oz," he says. "It's about a dumb broad who flies off to somewhere weird and dangerous so she can wander like an asshole down a road she doesn't know and get attacked by monsters and fucked over by a magic man. It sounds strangely familiar."

I pull out more of Alice's things. A brush. A Weirdos T-shirt. Photos of a ruined motel by the water, part of Salton City, an abandoned town in the desert. We were going to take a trip there.

From behind me I hear Traven say, "I wanted to thank you for saving me today and taking me to Allegra's extraordinary clinic."

"How's Hunter doing?"

"Much better. He can go home tomorrow."

"Good for him."

"Is there anything I can do to help besides tape things?"

I get a pen and paper off Kasabian's desk and scrawl lines and shapes. My memory isn't a hundred percent on how the seven symbols Alice was writing looked, but I draw them as well as I can. I hand Traven the paper.

"Do you know what these are?"

He carries the paper over to a lamp and stares at it for a minute.

"This is a very rare script. It's a kind of cipher combining pictograms and letters. Each letter has a numeric value, but their meaning changes in relation to their position in relation to the other characters. Where did you see this?"

"A friend showed it to me. What is it?"

"It's the secret language the fallen angels used to plan their rebellion in Heaven."

"Do you know what it says?"

"May I borrow your pen? I'll need to do some calculations."

I toss it to him and he starts scribbling on the paper.

I'm on my knees next to Candy with Alice's life spread around me on the floor. It's like I've fallen into a Hank Williams song. I push the T-shirt, underwear, jewels, and address books around like I'm looking for the prize in a box of Cracker Jacks. Candy upends a pair of green dress shoes with one broken heel and something falls out. It's a small toy, a plastic rabbit with beard stubble and a cigarette jammed between its lips. Candy holds it up.

"What's this?"

"Alice said it was me in a former life."

Candy smiles.

"I think we have a winner."

"Eleusis," says Traven.

I look at him.

"What's Eleusis?"

He raises his eyebrows.

"I thought you'd be the one to know. It's a region of Hell."

"Never heard of it."

He comes over and hands me the sheet of paper. It's just chicken scratches and his calculations.

Traven says, "Dante wrote about Eleusis in the *Inferno*, though he didn't call it by that name. Some translations described it as the woods given to the virtuous pagans. Dante described it as a green and pleasant place for pre-Christian men and women who weren't sinners but couldn't get into Heaven because they weren't redeemed by Christ's sacrifice."

"Wait, Heaven is punishing those for being born too early?"

"It's not punishment. It's like Limbo. A work-around invented by the Church centuries ago. If humanity can only be redeemed by Christ's death, what happens to the virtuous prophets of the Old Testament? Eleusis in Greece was the site of ancient mystery rites and therefore a vaguely mystical region as good as any to dispose of the pagans."

I hand the paper back to him.

"Then Eleusis is where Mason has Alice."

"From what I recall, it's a long way from Pandemonium. Halfway across Hell in fact."

"Does going across Hell get me frequent-flier miles?"

I take my coat off the bed and load in the na'at, the knife, and the other gear.

It's still two hours until sundown.

"We can sit here and stare at each other or we can have a drink and send for some food."

"Food," says Vidocq, and the others agree.

Kasabian turns around. Suddenly we have his attention.

"What kind of food?"

"Chicken and waffles," says Candy.

"From Roscoe's?" says Allegra. "I don't think they deliver."

"Everyone delivers if you pay them enough," says Kasabian. He types something into the computer and a phone app opens on the screen. "Watch. I'm the king of overtipping."

I say, "As long as you're wasting my money, get Donut Universe to send over a wheelbarrow-ful of whatever's fresh."

Traven is staring at the paper with the angelic cipher.

"What's up, Father? Not a waffle fan?"

He says, "I'm horrified by what you're about to do, but I'm also a little envious. Hell is waiting for me when I die, but I don't know what it is, and that scares me. But you can walk its streets without being afraid. I'd give anything for that."

"If anyone ever makes you that offer, don't take it. It's a sucker's bet. And I told you. I'll show you around if you end up Downtown."

Traven taps the pen against the paper nervously. He doesn't even know he's doing it. He's picturing flames and oceans of boiling blood. If I tell him it's not like that, he won't believe me. No one ever really believes what you tell them about Hell.

"You and your friends have shown me more of the universe in the last couple of days than the Church did in years. I wish I could do more to show my gratitude," he says.

"Do you have a car?" I ask.

"Yes."

"Is it insured? Like, well insured?"

"It was my late mother's car. She was a careful driver and had every kind of insurance there is."

"Can I borrow it?"

Traven takes out his keys and hands them to me.

"How long will you need it?"

"Just tonight."

TWO HOURS GOES a lot faster with whiskey and food than it does without either.

By the time the sun's gone down, everyone is pretty much acting like a person again and not a mourner in training. Candy catches me looking out the window.

"You probably need to get going soon."

"Yeah, I do."

We get up from where we've been eating on the floor and I put on my jacket. I'm very aware of its weight on my body. Nervousness is all about heightened senses.

Traven is the closest to me. I shake his hand and he nods. Vidocq grabs me in a massive bear hug.

"No good-byes. I'll see you soon."

"Sooner than that."

Allegra comes over and pecks me on the cheek. It's sweet and she means it, but I don't think she's ever quite forgiven me for working for Lucifer a couple of months ago.

Candy loops her arm in mine and walks me to the door.

"Do you want me to walk with you to the car?"

"You should stay here with the others. From here on out, I need to not be Stark. I need to be Sandman Slim and a very bad person."

"You mean more so."

"Yeah. That's what I mean."

Candy puts the plastic rabbit in my hand and we kiss.

Before I go outside, I look at Kasabian. He's gone back to the beginning of the DVD and the opening credits for *The Wizard of Oz* are playing.

"See you soon, Alfredo Garcia."

He doesn't look up.

"Shut up. The movie's starting."

I open the door and look at Candy.

"Three days."

She nods.

"Three days."

I close the door and get out the car keys.

TRAVEN'S KEYS ARE for a Geo Metro, a glass-enclosed gum wad of fiberglass that's like a car the same way movie-theater nachos are like food. Holding the keys out in front of me like the world's most pathetic magic wand, I push the lock button. Something a few cars up chirps. The Geo is exactly like the kind of car that a preacher's mother would drive. It's blue and looks like something that should come free with a kid's meal at a burger joint. This isn't how I imagined I'd be leaving this world, but I don't have time to hunt and kill a real car. The only thing worse than driving a car like this is having someone see you driving a car like this. Naturally, that's when I see Medea Bava strolling over from across the street. I already have the door open, so I can't even pretend I was going to steal something else. I get the Maledictions out and light one. Going back to Hell may be the worst thing I ever do, but at least I'll be able to get decent cigarettes.

"Why are you bugging me, Medea? I'm leaving town and may not be coming back. Go buy yourself a new crown of thorns. You win."

Medea stops in the street so that cars have to drive around her. She just looks at me, her face sweeping through the phases of the moon, turning her from a beautiful young woman to an old crone and back again.

"You're as constant as the stars in a few things, Sandman Slim. For example, your stupidity and selfishness."

"I also steal cable. What's your point?"

"What you're planning is reckless beyond belief. War is coming from below and above. And you plan on inserting yourself into the middle of it? And for what? A personal vendetta. You've even involved the Kissi. That alone has made the situation a thousand times worse."

"What I'm doing is a lot more than a vendetta."

A minivan full of frat boys goes around her, hooting and flipping her off. Medea flicks her head at them and the van's windows explode inward. You can hear the frat boys screaming as the van rolls to a stop at the corner.

"The last time we met, who were you with? Ah yes, the Czech whore."

"Watch your mouth. Her name is Brigitte and the proper term you're looking for is 'porn star.' You're just jealous of her because you never had a three-way with a cosmonaut."

"And now you're debasing yourself with that rabid dog in your room."

"Candy and I are only at the shock and awe stage. Debasing is penciled in for next Thursday."

Medea glances up the street as the bloody frat boys stumble out of the van. She turns and looks at me.

"Now you're sacrificing yourself for dear sweet Alice."

"You already know that, and I want to be dead before one, so I'm leaving. Have a nice time playing pranks on civilians."

I get into the car, but suddenly she's next to me with her hand on the door.

She says, "Are you really going to sacrifice yourself to save your great betrayer?"

"What the fuck are you talking about?"

"You and Alice didn't find each other by chance. We sent her to you."

She lets that sink in for a minute. It doesn't. It just sits there staring at me, ugly and cold.

Medea says, "Do you think the Sub Rosa is so blind that it wouldn't notice a child as powerful as you being raised by ordinary parents? You were dangerous when a child and became more so as you grew. Then you chose to distance yourself from the Sub Rosa, its codes and bylaws."

"Codes and bylaws? What are you? The Rotary Club? Fuck off."

Medea leans in closer. A faint smile plays around her mouth as it morphs from a young woman's full lips to a crone's, as dry and cracked as a desert plain.

"When you left us we needed to know what you were up to. A simple spell wouldn't do. You would have broken it. So we sent something you would accept wholeheartedly. The girl."

"Alice wasn't Sub Rosa. She didn't have any magic. I would have known."

"You're right. Poor Alice was an invalid. But her parents had the gift. They're Sub Rosa, which makes her Sub Rosa, too. Alice's infirmity is what made her the perfect operative. With no magic of her own, you would never suspect her. And keeping watch over you was the one way she could contribute to her people's welfare."

Alice flashes in my memory. A thousand snapshots of her face. Her hands. Her body. There's nothing that reads as magic or lies.

"I don't believe you."

"The truth doesn't require your belief. Alice was never yours. She belonged to us."

"Did Mason put you up to this? Aelita? Maybe both of them. What did they promise you, Baba Yaga? Your own Kentucky fried-chicken-leg house?"

Medea laughs. Up the block frat boys are pulling glass fragments out of each other's faces. One sits on the curb staring at the phone in his hand. He can't think of who to call.

"I'm the Inquisition and the Inquisition is beyond the sort of desires that make bribery possible."

Medea takes something from an inside pocket of her coat and tosses it into the car with me. Wolf teeth and crow feathers bound in linen with horsehair. An Inquisition death sign. She even went to the trouble to dribble a bloody X on top.

She says, "You've used up your nine lives. Go back to your room and be with that animal you rut with. Be happy and ruin yourself quietly the way you should have done years ago. If, however, you continue on the course you're planning, the Inquisition will deal with you permanently. This is your last chance for redemption."

I toss the death sign over my shoulder and take a puff of the Malediction.

"Redemption? I want redemption about as much as I want to be one of the blue-blood Ren Faire masters of the universe you report to. Lucifer chose me to deal with this. Not the Sub Rosa or you or the Golden Vigil or Mickey Mouse. Me. I'm the one who can stop Mason. You get in my way and he wins. That will be the end of everything and it'll be your fault. So why don't you go back to your gumdrop house in the forest and eat some lost children, witch?"

Medea walks to the curb and swings out her arm like a maître d'.

"I won't stop you, but remember this. When your final judgment arrives, I won't come for you. You'll be the one who comes to me, and of your own free will."

"So no hug good-bye?"

I pull the door closed and turn the ignition. The Geo coughs a few times, but the engine finally catches. Medea knocks on the passenger window and I push the button to lower it.

"We'll see each other much sooner than you think," she says.

"Super. You bring balloon animals and I'll hire clowns. It'll be a party."

I steer the Geo around the wrecked van. The frat boy on the curb finally figured out someone to call. Blood runs down his forehead and drips onto his phone, but he looks relieved. There's a siren in the distance.

I turn right at the corner and steer the Geo onto the freeway.

THINKING ABOUT DEATH makes a ride go by fast. Thinking about your own death—even if it's supposed to be temporary— makes it fly by like a cheetah with a jet pack. I've done the grand tour of Hell. I've seen pieces of Heaven in God's parade of divine fuckups. Jackboot angels. Deranged Kissi. Hellions. Ex-archangels. And me, too. I'm about the biggest gag on the geezer's holy blooper reel.

You'd think that with all my connections to the celestial sphere, I'd have a better handle on death. But I don't know anything. I didn't die in Hell and since then I've lived through every kind of attack, abuse, and humiliation Hellions, humans, and hell beasts could pile on. After you've been shot, stabbed, slashed, burned, and almost zombified and survived it all, death gets kind of abstract. It's like valentines and diplomas. Something other people have to deal with. But now it's my turn to ride the pale horse and I have serious reservations about it.

Every day I walk down Hollywood Boulevard and see civilians making themselves crazy worrying about the meetings they're late for or did they put the rent check in the mail or is their ass starting to sag and I think, "I've seen the creaky clockwork that turns the stars and planets. I've gotten drunk with the devil and body-slammed angels. I've seen the Room of Thirteen Doors at the center of the universe. I know the taste of my own blood as well as you know your favorite wine. I've seen so much more than you'll ever see. I know so much more than you'll ever know." And then it hits me like a runaway semi. I don't know anything that matters. Here I am thinking how much better and smarter I am than all the stuffed-shirt meat puppets wandering L.A. and I remember that there's a billion people who haven't done a tenth of the things I've done but who know the big answer to the big question: What happens when you die? I've seen fragments of it. I stood in the desert of Purgatory with Kasabian after he died and before Lucifer brought him back. But that doesn't count. That was someone else's death and Purgatory was just a projection of the afterlife created by my spell. Not the real thing. I've seen death a thousand times, and almost snuffed it myself, but I've never made it through all the way, and that scares me.

Are sex and death connected? Hell yes. They're the two things in the world you can't explain. You only know them by experiencing them. Maybe that was my mistake. I should have asked Mustang Sally if I could trade this death trip for having to relose my virginity at the crossroads. Easy. Any fun girl would be up for that. Instead of driving to my doom in a mom's powder-blue shit wagon, I could be back in Hollywood, stumbling down the street with a grin, a beer, and a frustrated boner, trying to lure drunken dollies into a night of black-magic freeway lust. But no, I didn't think of that and now I'm stuck on a backed-up interstate with what Medea said about Alice banging around in my head and wondering what this steering wheel is going to taste like when my face smashes into it at a hundred miles an hour.

IT HAPPENS ON West Adams as I'm closing in on the crossroads underpass at I-10 and Crenshaw.

The light bar on top of a cop car flashes in my rearview mirror.

Maybe he's looking for someone else.

His siren bleeps twice.

"Pull over."

The cop's voice comes out of the car's bullhorn sounding like a bigger and angrier version of the robot in Candy's glasses.

"Pull over."

The one time I don't steal a car this is what happens. That's the lesson for tonight. Anytime I try to do something like a regular person, I get fucked for it. Never again.

I slow down, but I don't pull over. Every nerve in my body

is vibrating, telling me to jam the accelerator and leave these shitbirds in my dust. But I can stomp this accelerator from now until the sun burns out and there still won't be any dust. This three-speed rowboat would lose a drag race to a crippled monkey on a Big Wheel.

I pull over and cut the engine. The patrol car stops behind me. The driver aims the car's outside spotlight at my side mirror, blinding me. I unclamp the angel a little and its eyes cut right through the glare.

Two cops in the car. Both male. One is young and wiry with a close-cropped flattop. He's more excited than he should be at a simple traffic stop. Probably a recent cop school graduate.

The driver, the one getting out, is heavier. A bit of a donut gut, but he's got at least fifty pounds of muscle over his partner. The older cop showing a young pup the ropes. Shit. I'm probably one of his life lessons. Any other night, this *Romper Room* scene would be playing out somewhere else. I should have pulled over when I saw the lights go on.

I roll down the window. The cop comes up on me sticking close to the car. Smart. If he came in wide, I could reach for a weapon and shoot before he had a chance to get his gun out. Sidling up like he is, I'd have to turn around in my seat to get a shot off and he'd put six slugs in the back of my head before I could say, "Ouch."

The cop has his flashlight out, held in an underhand grip so he can swing it like a club. He shines the light in my face then lowers it a few inches, leaving me temporarily night-blind.

"Evening, sir. Did you know that your left taillight is out?"

"No, I didn't. Thank you. I'll get it fixed first thing tomorrow."

He's unmoved by my diplomacy.

"May I see your license and registration, please?"

"This isn't my car."

"Whose is it?"

"A friend's. He's a priest."

"Is he? May I see your license, then?"

Here it comes.

"I don't have a license."

The light goes back into my eyes. I turn my head this time so I won't go blind. When I look back, the cop has backed away a little from the car. He's lowered the flashlight and his other hand is resting lightly on the grip of his gun.

"Have you been drinking tonight, sir?"

"Nope."

"Please step out of the vehicle."

"I told you already. I don't have a license. None. No bank account. No credit cards. No insurance. No library card. No magazine subscriptions. I'm legally dead, so technically I don't need a goddamn license."

His hands close on the pistol grip. His breathing and heart rate are rising, but his mind is calm and focused. I can't read it, but I can get a feel, and he's all concentration. The young cop could do worse than learning from this guy, but I don't have time to compliment either of them on their keen professionalism.

"Step out of the vehicle, sir."

He says it with a lot more gusto this time.

I say, "Listen, man." But that's all I get out. The cop goes flying over the hood of my car and into the weeds on the other side.

I get out. Josef is there with his perfectly coiffed Nazi hair.

"Why are you wasting time with these people? Kill them and go on," he says.

"I wasn't going to kill them. I was going to knock their heads and lock them in the trunk of their car."

"You enjoyed killing Kissi so much before, but when you had nowhere else to go, you asked us for our help. Now we're on the same side and you won't kill a couple of humans who would happily shoot you."

I flick the burning Malediction butt at him. He looks more surprised at that than he did when I cut off his head.

"You and your whole race were off floating around in the universe like dust. You wanted my deal. And I killed Kissi before because you're unreasonable psycho fucks and you were on Mason's side."

I look over at the cop lying in the weeds.

"These guys I could have handled without anyone having to go to the emergency room."

Which reminds me.

A door opens and slams. The rookie cop is out of the patrol car, his gun cocked and ready. Josef heads right for him.

"Stop where you are!" the rookie shouts. "Stop or I'll shoot!"

Josef is almost on him.

"Stop!"

The rookie fires twice. Exit wounds punch fist-size holes out of the back of Josef's designer shirt, but he never stops moving. I can hear the rookie's neck snap from all the way over here. I go over to the curb to check on the older cop. He's unconscious, but his heart is beating.

"Get away from him and do what you came here to do!" shouts Josef.

He heads for me, but he's been shot and he's a little slow. I get to him first. Squeezing his throat with one hand and his balls with the other, I flip him up and over the front of the cop car. He rolls and smashes the windshield. Before he can scramble off, I grab his ankle and spin, tossing him into the back of the Metro. He bounces off it and takes a swing at me, but he's off balance. I slip his blow and punch him in the throat. He falls to his knees.

"Don't ever just walk in and take over a situation I have in hand. Understand?"

He nods, trying to remind his throat how to breathe.

"And don't tell me how to do what I do. I invited you here, but it's still my tea party. It might not look like it to you sometimes, but I know what I'm doing. Got it?"

Josef nods. Resting his elbows on the Metro, he pulls himself to his feet. He's still unsteady, so I lean him back against the car, playing concerned dad now that the kid's been put in his place. The truth is I don't know what I'm doing two-thirds of the time, but I'd never admit that to a Kissi. What I need to do is calm Hermann Göring down.

I say, "You're going to get to do a lot more killing soon. And against a lot more fun and interesting opponents than these two. When it's over, you'll have Hell and your own kingdom again. That is if you don't get trigger-happy and Fuck. Up. Everything. Do you know where Eleusis is?"

Josef nods.

"When I get Downtown that's where I'm heading. Wait for my signal there. Got it?"

"Yes," he says. If his eyes could walk out of his head, they'd march over here and strangle me with my own intestines.

I take his hand and drop Traven's car keys in them.

"Do you remember the hotel where you came to see me?"

"Yes."

"Drive this car over there and leave it on the street. Leave the keys under the driver's seat."

He looks at the keys like I just shoveled dog shit into his hand.

"Why would I do that? I'm not your errand boy."

"Because it's not an errand. It's a loose end and loose ends are what ruin plans and get people hurt. Understand?"

He takes the keys and gets into the Metro.

Before he closes the door he says, "Go to Hell."

"Why didn't I think of that?"

As he heads out I check on the older cop. His heart and breathing are on the low end, but steady. I take the car keys off his belt and go back to the patrol car.

Inside, I reach across the laptop bolted between the seats and unhook the mike from the dashboard.

"Officers down at the corner of Adams and Eleventh Street. One is alive but hurt and the other is pretty much dead. For the record, I didn't do either one of them, but you wouldn't believe me if I told you who did."

The cop's communication unit crackles. I look for an off button but can't find one, so I kick everything on the dashboard until the noise stops. While I'm in Hulk mode, I punch the shattered windshield out of the way. The safety glass comes out in one piece. I shove it across the hood and let it fall on the side of the road.

Sorry, boys. I really wanted both of you to go home tonight. But sometimes pianos really do fall from the sky and sometimes you're the Coyote and catch it in the teeth. I've been there plenty of times. If I see you on the other side, I owe you a drink. If not, maybe it'll help knowing I'm about to do something that's really going to hurt.

I start the patrol car and the Crown Vic's V-8 engine screams. This is what I need for a Black Dahlia. This is the right way to leave, like Vidocq likes to say, *le merdier.* I slam the car into drive and floor it, smoking the tires and fishtailing down the street before I get hold of the thing. Suicide is still a goddamn scary idea, but burning rubber in a cop car at least makes it a little more fun.

Crenshaw is up ahead.

Candy flashes in my head. Red-slash eyes in black ice. Mad-dog teeth in my shoulder. Yes, I'm leaving you for another woman, but she's dead and it's only for three days and I'm coming back. I promise.

Shut up. Not the time for that. I push her back with the angel.

When Alice's face rolls up, I don't run from it. I examine it from a dozen different angles. Was Medea telling the truth? Is it possible Alice lied to me the whole time we were together? To my surprise, the angel comes up with an answer: "Who cares?"

It's right. Even if she's Lizzie Borden, am I going to leave Alice down there?

No.

Am I going to give up a chance to twist Mason's head off when he sees I've rescued her?

No.

Don't think. Just go. There's no time. No thought. No consequences. Just a bright flash of pain and then I'm home. There's nothing but the rush.

When I can see where Crenshaw passes under I-10, I stop, shift into reverse, and drive back a half a block. I can see cop lights in the distance, heading for the officer-down call.

Fuck Bava. Fuck doubt. Fuck everything.

I stomp the accelerator and aim the car for a freeway support midway under the roadway, in the center of the crossroads. I take the plastic rabbit from my pocket and hold it in my teeth.

I hope you're up there, Mustang Sally. I never prayed to God, but I'm praying to you right now. *Please know what the fuck you're doing.*

I'm doing just a hair over a hundred and ten when I hit. Time slo-mos as the car jumps the curb and takes the last few yards airborne.

It doesn't really hurt when we hit. It's more like a supersonic body blow as all the air and fluids in my body explode out of me like butcher-shop fireworks. My eyes can't focus. The world is a liquid blur. I hear the scream and groan of metal as the Crown Vic pancakes against the support. The steering wheel twists upward and turns my skull to cake batter. The front of the car comes apart and a million metal and plastic razor blades rip my skin off the bones. My arms break as I flip over the dashboard and out the window. One knee catches and is torn apart on the way out. I glide over the car hood like an Olympic figure skater and into a whirlpool of flame as the engine explodes.

Time shifts again. Shoots back up to normal speed. I slide through fire and gas and come out the other side a limp ball of flame. My eyes focus long enough to see the freeway support. Funny thing. It doesn't look like I'm flying at it. It's like it's coming for me.

And the world goes away.

THERE'S GRIT IN my eyes. When I try to brush it away, I just grind it in more. I roll over so my face is to the ground and run my hand all over my face so whatever's there falls down and not back onto me. The grit is all over me, like I've been rolling around in kitty litter. When my eyes are clear, I work up a little saliva and spit, clearing more grit from the back of my throat.

That's it. That's as much as I can do right now. Did I save everything yet? Guess not.

The world goes away again.

WHEN I WAKE up things are a little better. It feels like this thing weighing me down might be my body and not a bag of wet cement. I open my eyes.

The world is a fuzzy indistinct place, like I'm looking at it from inside a vodka bottle.

From what I can make out, I'm still under the freeway. Sunlight streams in from both sides of the underpass. I roll onto my back. My left foot rests on the crumpled front bumper of the cop car. I focus my eyes on that one image. My foot and the car. Slowly, the world comes back into focus.

The car isn't a car anymore. It's a big metal cigarette butt a giant stubbed out in a six-lane concrete ashtray. I pull my leg off the bumper and let it drop to the ground. I was expecting a lot of blood, but there isn't any. I check my arms. No bones sticking out. I feel for the knee I left behind in the car. It's on my leg right where it should be. My clothes aren't even ripped. The plastic rabbit is laying in the grit by my head. I pick it up and wobble to my feet. Mustang Sally was right. I went through the Dahlia and came out me again. But where am I?

I'm still at the crossroads. Sort of. This isn't the underpass from last night. This one is an underpass and nothing else. There isn't any freeway on either side of it, just cracked hardpan in both directions. The concrete support and the car are half buried in sand, like they've been there a hundred years. The sun is so bright out in the open that I can't see anything. The only thing I'm sure of is that this isn't L.A. and it sure as hell isn't Hell.

I go out the far side of the underpass into the light. I have to close my eyes until my eyes adjust to the glare. When I can see, there's nothing to see, just sand and more sand. Big rippling dunes curving down to little dunes. They go on forever. There's a miserable path of compacted dirt leading between the sand hills. A few parched and poisonous-looking weeds stick up along the sides of the path. I go back through the underpass and check the other side. It's the same. I'm in the middle of a goddamn desert. And this side doesn't even have a little path, so I head back out the other.

When I'm out I grab hold of the rusted guardrail and pull myself onto the Twilight Zone slice of freeway. A road sign is suspended across all eight lanes. One of the support legs has fallen, but it's still readable. Big white letters studded with reflectors on a green background. Typical California freeway stuff. The sign reads:

WELCOME TO NOD
POPULATION 0

A second smaller sign points to where an exit might have been a million years ago. It reads:

EDEN 10 MILES WEST

The arrow at the bottom points in the same direction as the dirt path. I climb down and start walking.

IT'S AS HOT as a dragon's balls. I have my coat off and thrown over my shoulder before I've gone fifty yards. I don't do outdoors. I'll take the arena any day over this Miami damnation tanning contest.

Bava showing up and sticking her bony fingers in my skull really threw me at the end. If something has gone wrong and I'm stuck in an afterlife cow town somewhere between Nowhere and Fuck All it could be my fault.

Alice was a mole feeding the Sub Rosa intel about my life and me? I don't buy it. That's exactly the kind of psyops party trick Mason would come up with. Then he'd get Aelita to tell Bava because she's security and security believes anything a superior or a halo tells them.

I don't believe it, but the angel won't shut up about it. I think the Black Dahlia might have shaken something loose in its head. I'm the unreasonable one in this Laurel and Hardy act, but it's jabbering away in a frantic stream of What if? Could it be? And that explains everything.

Maybe the angel can't deal with being on this side of death or whatever this is. Have I blown its tiny feathered brain? This treasure hunt was going to be hard enough with Little Mary Sunshine whispering to me, but it's going to be a whole lot worse if I end up with a crazy person trying to claw his way out of my skull.

The simple truth of it is that Alice couldn't be a mole. I would have felt it if she was Sub Rosa. Alice is the only person I never bullshitted or lied to. She's the only person I ever really trusted. That means if she was what Bava says and I missed it, everything I've ever believed about my life or myself is wrong.

My human father, the one stuck with the lousy job of raising me after a certain angel called Kinski knocked up my mom, hated me. He even took a shot at me once when we were deer hunting. So much for the father-son three-leg race at the church picnic.

My mother loved me, but was lost at sea most of the time when I was growing up. The drinking and pills didn't help. I don't remember a single moment when she didn't seem lonely. She jumped at every sound in the yard or at the door like she was expecting someone who was never there.

There's Vidocq, who's been more of a father to me than my civilian father or Kinski. He's the only other person I trust as much as Alice. Trusted.

I don't see how Bava's bullshit could be true, but Alice did hold out on me at least once. One night she told me that she was rich and that she came from heavy money. She never said much else about her family, but I always took that to mean she was as far from hers as I was from mine. Was she about to confess that all that filthy lucre came from Daddy's late-night infomercial magic-wand business or youth potions from Elizabeth Báthory's blood?

Goddammit. How could I let Bava get to me like this? Was she throwing some hoodoo at me when we talked? No. I would have felt it, and if I didn't, the angel in my head would. It has to be a mind game and I'm ashamed that it's worked. Or maybe the bitch was telling me the truth.

And where in the goddamn middle of for fuck's sake am I? Is Mustang Sally in on Mason's cosmic scam? If there even is a scam.

Calm down. Deep breaths. Go to your happy place. Oh, wait. I don't have one. Slow down and think, but thinking is supposed to be the angel's job. Nice time to stop taking your pills, Saint Acid Test.

Fuck me, it's hot here.

There isn't even a decent enough shadow so I can slink into the Room and go home.

Maybe I'll get lucky and there will be a postcard stand somewhere. "Dear Everyone. Hope you don't mind being doomed. XOXO Stark."

The road disappears ahead. A dune has blown across it like the wall of a sand fortress. If the desert has eaten the rest of the road, things are about to get really interesting.

The dune is soft and loose. I can't walk. I have to crawl up it. It's slow and hot with the coat draped over my shoulder. I move one hand. One foot. The other hand. The other foot. If this is a joke and Sisyphus is waiting at the top to hand me his boulder, he can kiss my ass.

Halfway up and I'm getting very pissed off. The angel is freaking out and the clock is ticking. Even if Mason is lying about having Alice and just wants me chasing my tail all over Hell, I need to know. It means that he's ready to make his move on Heaven.

If I ever get out of here, I'm going to find whichever angel invented sand and make it eat this fucking desert while getting a Tabasco enema.

I reach up and get a handful of air. I'm at the top of the dune. I was right. The road is gone. But it doesn't matter.

Holy shit.

I think I just found the Garden of Eden. There's probably a soda machine and I left all my cash in L.A.

I stumble down the side of the monster dune toward the acres of cool green grass and sparkling waterfalls.

The gates in front are dazzling in the desert sun. I don't know what they're made of, but they shine brighter than anything I've ever seen on earth, but the reflection doesn't hurt my eyes. It's like the gates have an internal glow that evens out the sun. Even the chains holding them shut are glowing.

There's a lone angel to one side of the gate. He's like one of those Buckingham Palace guards. He stands like an idiot statue staring straight ahead at attention, like a filthy, sweating madman didn't just stumble in off the Mojave. I wonder how long he's been there. I put my coat back on to cover up some of the dirt and walk over to him.

"My GPS is out, but the AAA guide said there was a Denny's around here. Is this it?"

The angel doesn't move. I get in front of him and stick my face right into his. Close enough that our noses touch. Nothing. If I wasn't trying to stop the destruction of the universe, I could waste some time giving this guy a hotfoot or starting a tickle contest, but duty and getting out of this sun calls.

Mom always told me that God helps those who help themselves, so I head for the gates. I grab hold of the chains holding them closed and take out the black blade. Before I can swing it, the angel turns into a speeding blur and slams his shoulder into me like a supersonic linebacker. I go flying back to the dune.

He looks a little surprised when I get to my feet, but manages to stay in character, spreading his wings and pointing at me in that superior my-shit-smells-like-blueberry-muffins way angels have. His armor glows with the same light as the gates. His voice is low, louder than the cop bullhorn, and echoing. I wonder if heaven issues every angel its own reverb unit.

"Halt. Your kind may not enter the Malchut of Atzilut."

I walk back to him, brushing the sand off my coat.

"Did I get turned around? The sign said this was the way to Epcot."

The angel drops his hands to his side. He's a head taller than me with Josef's chiseled übermensch cheekbones, only his hair is jet black.

"If you mean the road to Gan Eden, then yes. But you are not permitted to enter the place that God gave to man and was lost to him. This is a holy place and only the righteous shall pass through the gate."

I get out a Malediction and light up.

"Here's the situation. I was dead a few minutes ago and woke up a little way over those dunes. That tells me that this is where I'm supposed to be. I'm not looking to hang around and track dust all over your daffodils. All I want to know is if there's a freight elevator or a crawl space or something? I'm trying to get to Hell."

He gives me his stern face, all steely eyes and smoldering passion. He could get a job as a romance-novel cover model.

"Once, only Heaven was here, but the sin of man befouled it."

"So I can get to Hell through there?"

"Yes. The serpent brought the seeds of Hell into this place, man tended it, and here it stays like a festering wound."

"Would you mind pointing out the scar tissue? I need to get going."

"What matter is Eden to you? No mortal man or woman may enter."

"How many mortal men do you get around here? Do you rent the place out for pool parties during spring break?"

The angel doesn't say anything and his smoldering act is starting to get old. I blow smoke in his face.

"Listen up, Hawkman, I'm going in there even if I have to pluck off all your feathers and stuff you like a teddy bear."

The angel waves the smoke away. He stretches and rubs the back of his neck. His voice rises to a normal octave and doesn't echo anymore.

"Listen, man. It's the end of my shift. I'm really tired and the sun's giving me a migraine. I can't let you in, but I don't want to get into a whole thing about it with you. Can you just hang around and work this out with my replacement?"

"I'm in kind of a hurry."

"He'll be here tonight. Tomorrow at the latest."

"I really can't wait."

He sighs.

"Yeah. I figured."

He manifests his Gladius, his angelic sword of fire, and takes a swing at my head. The attack is slow. Completely for show. Why shouldn't it be? He's an angel and I'm just a lost spirit who wandered in from nowhere. I manifest my own Gladius, block his blow, and cut a nice diagonal slice through his chest plate. He falls back, eyes wide.

April Fool, motherfucker.

His Gladius is on the ground, but I'm mad. He made me drop one of my last cigarettes. I move in fast and get my sword under his chin.

"What's your name?"

"Rizoel."

"Well, Rizoel, you know that I could kill you entirely here and now, right? I know fallen angels go to Tartarus when they die, but I'm not clear on what happens to nice angels. Given my natural inclinations, I'd like to slice and dice you just to see where you end up. Lucky for you there's a little angel that lives in my head and I know he won't shut up about it if I turn you into chum. So to sum up, this is your lucky day. Understand?"

Rizoel gives me a mininod, making sure not to let the Gladius touch his chin.

"Here's the deal. You can walk away but you have to do

something for me. What do you think? You ready to come on down off your high-and-mighty for a second and make a deal?"

"I don't seem to have a choice."

"Sure you do. But one of them isn't pretty."

The angel nods.

"All right."

I let my Gladius go out. The angel tries to stand, but he's favoring the side where I slashed him. I take his other arm and help him up.

"You're him, aren't you?" he says. "The nephilim. The monster who kills monsters."

"I'll give you an autograph, but if it shows up on eBay, I'm going to be mad."

"You are an Abomination and will not pass through these holy gates."

I should have seen that coming. Never trust an angel.

We both fire up our Gladiuses and go at each other. Even hurt, the angel is inhumanly fast and strong, but so am I. He's not going to fall for the same trick twice, so I stay in close to him. He can't get a good swing at me, and with his injured arm he can't push me back enough to put me in dissecting range. But he figures out what I'm doing and kicks my leg. When I stumble he gets an overhead shot at my back. I see it coming and turn my shoulders so he only gets a piece of me. Still, the blow burns like nothing I've ever felt before. It feels a lot like a magic flaming sword.

I snap my head up under his chin and knock him back. I swing at his shoulder, but the prick has been playing possum. He grabs my throat with what I thought was his injured arm, raises his sword with the other, and brings it down at my head. I kick out my feet and fall backward, pulling him down with me. As we fall I swing my sword up between us. The angel lands on top of me and my Gladius goes out.

He's big, and with all that armor it feels like chorus line decided to do a show on my chest. It takes all of my strength to roll him off me. Once he starts moving, he goes easily. In fact he loses some weight in the process. His left arm falls off where I sliced through it in the fall.

I manifest my Gladius again and swipe it lightly across his face, giving him a scar like one of mine. He stays on his back, staring up at me. Angels don't bleed, but something thick and clear is leaking out from where his arm used to be, closing the wound.

"You're lucky. I want you to do my favor more than I want to kill you. This is your second chance to stay alive. No one gets a third."

He closes his eyes for a second then turns his head to where his arm isn't.

"I agree."

"Swear, angel. Swear a holy oath you can't break."

He blinks twice. Stares into the sun. He's thinking, *Father why have you forsaken my ass?* Because he can't choose you over the other angels bootlicking hosannas. Or like the rest of us, you're just another bug on his windshield.

"I swear and make a holy pledge as a servant of the Lord to abide by the bargain we make."

I let the Gladius go out, grab his chest plate at the neck, and pull him up. Toss him back against Eden's gates and get up close to his face so he won't miss a word.

"Tell Lucifer I'm coming for him."

Rizoel looks at me.

"Lucifer was his name in Perdition. In Heaven, he's Samael."

"Call him Travis Bickle for all I care, just tell him I'm coming. And I'm bringing all of Hell with me. Got it?"

"What kind of man are you that you'd wage war on Heaven?"

"It was this or stay home and watch *The Wizard of Oz*, and I hate musicals."

I leave him where he is, flame on my Gladius, and slice through the chains on the gates. One kick and Eden is open for business.

Rizoel staggers back.

"I'm going to get written up for this, you know. It'll go on my permanent record."

"Shouldn't you be on your way somewhere?"

Rizoel is horrified at seeing an Abomination in the garden. One step. Two steps. He doesn't move. I think he was expecting me to turn into a pillar of salt. I turn, and when he doesn't move, I drag my Gladius through the rosebushes. They burst into flame.

He takes a couple of steps back, shaking his head. "You are such an asshole."

"Don't forget our deal. By the way, how do I get to Hell in here?"

The look of disgust fades as his lips draw up into a big Cheshire-cat smile.

"It's easy. Exactly the way the human part of you did it the first time."

Before I get a word out, Rizoel spreads his wings and throws himself into the ridiculously bright blue sky.

I take a look around the garden. It's just a fucking garden. Rizoel was too gleeful to just be mocking me. He was giving me a clue. Hell is in here somewhere.

I stroll around the garden like a tourist in the kind of flower prison that florists dream about. After a while all the plants look the same to me. Leaves. Got it. Stems and flowers. Got it. Bark and fruit. Got it. I'm Steve McQueen and the Blob is after me, only it's made of dandelions and begonias.

Where is Hell in here? I stomp through the rosebushes and under pine trees. Climb up snaky vines and dig up screaming mandrakes. That was a bad idea. I thought they might be carrots. I'm getting hungry.

There's nothing here. No doors. No rabbit holes. No hoodoo portals or sci-fi transporters. I'm stuck in a feed-store calendar and I'm getting just a little pissed off.

Fuck you, angel, and everyone who's been spewing cryptic crap at me. The way you did the first time. "Be a rock." "Click your heels three times and think of flying monkeys." The next thing that quotes me a fortune cookie gets turned into a novelty paperweight.

Time is passing. *Tick tock. Tick tock.*

There's nothing left to do. Hey, Heaven. I let your angel live, but you don't understand the concept of cutting someone slack, huh? Fine by me. When this is over, just remember that *you* set the rules. Not me.

There's only one thing to do with a garden if it won't give you what you want. Get rid of it.

I drag the flaming Gladius along the ground as I stroll

through the winding path that curves from the entrance through the orchards, the redwoods, the pines, the thorny jungle foliage, and the crayon-colored flower beds, cutting a flaming red scar behind me. God must have yanked all the animals out of here when he gave Adam and Eve the boot. Good. The life of one flea-bitten squirrel means more than one inch of this pussy-willow paradise.

Fuck this place and fuck your games. This is where you first failed us. You gave us minds and told us not to think. You gave us curiosity and put a booby-trapped tree right in front of us. You gave us sex and told us not to do it. You played three-card monte with our souls from day one, and when we couldn't find the queen, you sent us to Hell to be tortured for eternity. That was your great plan for humanity?

Whatever your reasons, you won't have Paisley Park much longer. All you gave us here was daisies and fairy tales and you acted like that was enough. How were we supposed to resist evil when you didn't even tell us about it? You wanted us innocent. But when Lucifer found a way around your rules and we weren't innocent anymore, you blamed us and tossed us out into the wasteland like garbage.

You lounge upstairs on your golden throne like you're the greatest thing since "Johnny Be Good," but to me you're just another deadbeat dad.

I hope you can smell Eden burning. I hope you choke on it.

Alice wasn't a spy. She wasn't part of the big lie. She was real and she was mine.

Eden is an inferno. Some of it went up so fast the foliage is already gone. I kick through the cinders, looking for a way

Downtown, but I don't find anything. Stay calm. This is important. It's worth waiting for.

I follow the course of the fire as it eats up the plants. I kick through the dirt behind every burned hedge and blackened bush. I don't find anything. There's nothing here.

I go to the big tree at the center of the garden. The one that started all the trouble. It's the only thing that hasn't burned. I've been saving it for last. I reach up to the lowest branch and snap off an apple. Shine it against my coat and bite into it.

It's good. It's sweet and juicy, but it's not worth losing paradise over. For that, you'd think the man upstairs would make the fruit taste like the greatest thing ever. Your tongue should have an orgasm and drunk-dial old girlfriends to tell them about it. Still, the juice is refreshing. It clears the smoke and sand from my throat. I toss the core into the fire and reach for another apple but can't reach one. They're all on the higher branches. I swing up the Gladius and slice off a limb. The wood collapses when I pull off the apple. I push at the cracked bark with the toe of my boot. The branch is hollow. I cut another branch. It's hollow, too. I hack off more. They're all the same. The branches are like props in a high school play. The tree is a fake.

I concentrate and it calms the angel in my head. He's been quiet since we entered Eden, and now that he's seen what I've seen, for once he's on my side.

I swing up the Gladius, concentrating. It burns bigger and hotter than it's ever burned. The tree trunk is big. I have to start the cut way back, like I'm batting in the World Series. I swing the blade and it goes through the tree like a bullet through a chocolate sundae. The tree creaks, cracks, and falls over.

I was right. Just like the branches, the tree is hollow. Inside, the two halves of the tree are different. Inside the top half is a winding silver staircase that winds up to Heaven. In the stump is what looks like a grimy diamond-plate-metal staircase going into an industrial subbasement.

The angel told the truth. I get to Hell the way we did the first time. At the tree. You could have just said that, Tweety Bird. Then I wouldn't have had to burn Dad's prize marigolds. But I probably would have anyway.

I climb into the stump and walk down the rusty stairs.

IT ISN'T A long walk to Hell. Shorter than the walk to Eden. No surprise there.

The stairs lead to a long passage that looks like an abandoned maintenance tunnel. Someone needs to sweep up down here. Here and there whole sections of the ceiling have crashed onto the cement floor. I have to half walk, half hopscotch around it to keep from tripping. In the flickering fluorescent light, I swear some of the rusted rebar looks like bones.

After an hour of wandering I come to another set of metal stairs. It's not the best feeling being this close to Hell again. But it's what I signed up for. If Mason has a Hellion bike gang with chains and knuckle-dusters stationed at the top of these stairs, I'm going to be pissed. I could have stayed home and let Medea Bava kill me while eating hundred-dollar chicken and waffles with Candy.

There are double doors at the top of the stairs, the kind you see in front of old buildings for deliveries. I push with my arms, but can't budge them. I go up a few more steps, brace my back against the doors, and push.

The doors feel hot against my back. I can't tell if it's the metal or if I still hurt from where Rizoel tagged me. I ignore the pain and keep pushing. Nothing seems to be happening, but then light shines down through a space between the doors. I bend my knees and spring straight up, knocking both doors open.

And I'm instantly on fire. I roll off the pile of burning trash and keep rolling until all the flames are out. I get to my feet and look around.

Fuck me.

I'm back in the Hollywood Forever Cemetery and it's on fire. All of L.A. is on fire.

EVERYTHING IS WRONG. This is exactly where I was when I crawled out of Hell eight months ago. Now I'm back. Only I'm not. Everything is wrong, from the smells to the sounds to the light.

The cemetery looks like it was worked over by drunk bikers with garbage trucks for feet. Tombstones are knocked over or snapped in two. A lot of them are just dust. Some of the graves are open and spouting fountains of blue flames, like a gas line exploded beneath them. Clothes are strewn across the blackened lawn from bodies nearby that were blown out of the ground when the line broke.

I walk to the cemetery gates but don't step outside. The last time I walked out of here, a Beverly Hills crackhead tried to mug me. I mugged him instead. It was quite a welcome-home party. This time I stay put and take in the situation from my own comfy Sheol.

To my right I can see the giant Hollywood sign hanging

over everything like a promise to a dead man. The hills and the tops of all the buildings are on fire. Someone must have thrown some hoodoo on the Hollywood sign. It isn't catching, but the hills behind it are glowing orange ash.

The fires haven't reached this neighborhood yet, but they're on the move. From here it looks like the whole horizon is burning. The sky Downtown used to be all bruised purples and bloody reds. A mean perpetual twilight. Now it's a solid mass of roiling black smoke. Lit from below, it looks like the belly of a black snake the size of the sky crawling over us.

So, where the hell am I? I was pretty crazy the last time I crawled out here. Wasn't even looking for home this time, but I got it anyway. And it looks like someone broke it when I had my back turned.

How long was I unconscious after the Black Dahlia? Am I Rip van Winkle? Was I semidead for so long that Mason won and the universe thought it would be a hoot to wake me up just in time for the Apocalypse?

I get a fistful of graveyard dirt and scribble runes on my forehead while growling Hellion hoodoo. A death glamour. With any luck, no one will notice that I'm alive. I drop my coat on the ground and grab a corpse's hoodie dangling from a statue of the Virgin of Guadalupe. I put on the hoodie and the coat over it. I do a last quick check outside the gates for muggers. Satisfied the street's clear, I pull up the hood, covering as much of my face as I can, and head toward the big cookout.

A CRACK RUNS up Gower Street starting at the cemetery. A deep slash, as ragged as a lightning bolt and wide as a bus. What looks like a pool of bright red blood bubbles at the bottom. It smells like sewage but worse. Rotten eggs and dead fish.

I keep moving north, skirting a sinkhole at Fountain Avenue. Hellion bodies bloat at the bottom. Broken clock-work hellhounds writhe and twitch, leaking spinal fluid. I kick in a few pebbles. Watch them sink into the cherry muck.

Trees have collapsed on roofs and cars, like the ground simply couldn't support them anymore. Cracks have ripped homes in half. A deep geologic rumble shakes the ground under my feet and the two broken halves of Gower move a few inches in different directions. Fuck me. These aren't cracks. They're fault lines. Have I mentioned lately how much I hate every-thing?

On the side streets some of the new faults must have been exposed for a while because locals have strung them together with half-assed rope and plank and bridges. Idiot militias toss rocks and spears across the chasms, fighting to see who gets to take the crossing tolls.

Sunset Boulevard looks like it was blowtorched from below. As far as I can see everything is gutted, fried, or melted in both directions. The only things still standing are the palm trees. They burn like votive candles in a dark nave, throwing more shadows than light. Smoldering fronds fall like burning snow.

THERE'S A RIOT on Hollywood Boulevard.

When I crawled out of Hell eight months ago, I'd been surprised at how the boulevard had become a monochrome wilderness. The street was dead quiet, like someone had dropped a blanket over it. All empty-eyed street kids and vacant storefronts. There'd been plenty of traffic, but even the cars sounded like they were running on cotton candy instead of gas. Something had sucked the life out of the place. Maybe the Kissi. I still don't know. This version of Hollywood Boulevard is livelier, but I'm already longing for the muffled gray-and-white version.

The mob is a punch-drunk mix of Hellions and damned souls. This isn't fun, let's-turn-the-Dumpster-over rioting. It's the kind where you go at each other with knives and pipes, fighting over food and water and drugs.

I've only walked a quarter mile from the cemetery and I can already tell that the place is as bad off as Kasabian said. Lucifer would never let this happen. If Mason had any god-damn sense, he wouldn't either. When you're riding herd on a kingdom of killer Hellions, the first thing you do is make sure they're well fed and at least half hammered most of the time. The way this bunch is tearing up butcher shops and stores, they're neither. (Yes, Hell has stores and bars. It might be Hell, but it's better than a dry county in Mississippi.) And who let all the damned souls run wild? I saw some crazy shit when I was trapped Downtown, but this is the first time I've ever seen a soul in Pandemonium that wasn't tortured, locked up, or on a leash. If this really *is* Pandemonium. If it's not, where the fuck am I?

A couple of hundred Hellion gendarmes take positions at opposite ends of the street, surrounding the crowd. Hell is all about power games and influence. Lucifer didn't like too much power concentrated in anyone's hands, so Pande-monium has two police forces with overlapping territories.

And they hate each other. Instead of slowing the riot, the cop gangs smash into it like two hundred icebreakers. With their riot guns and heavy body armor, they rip through the crowd to claim as much of the swag as they can for their side.

I don't stick around to see which side wins because I couldn't possibly give less of a fuck. I hope they slaughter each other fast and get out of my way.

I hunch my shoulders, tug the hood, and head back to Gower. Maybe if I grabbed a cop, I could twist him around in interesting ways until he told me where Eleusis is, but seeing as how there are two hundred of them, that'll have to wait for later. What I want now is to cut back to Sunset and do an end run around this particular shit storm. If this is really a fucked-up version of L.A., then Max Overdrive isn't far from here. I can hole up until the riot blows over and figure out a next move.

"Where you going?"

A hand shoots out from the alcove of an out-of-business sex-toy shop and latches onto my arm. The Hellion the hand is attached to is dressed in layers of ragged coats, tunics, and greasy shirts. A Hellspawn hobo.

I don't say anything. I stare and hope the death glamour holds.

The bum says, "Got anything from the shops you want to share?"

"Nothing for you, rummy."

He grins and licks his lips, showing off a jumble of craggy gray teeth, like someone hammered broken cement into his gums. Maybe that's how God keeps Heaven's other angels in line. A better dental plan.

"Got a smoke?" he asks.

Something squirms under his grimy face. It looks like my glamour isn't the problem. It's his. Too bad I'm so slow on the uptake. By the time I recognize what he is, he has something very pointy and very sharp against my throat. It's double-pronged. Probably what on earth they'd call a Heretic's Fork. This fucker isn't a regular Hellion. He's a Malebranche, one of thirteen horned bastards that Lucifer kept as his private gestapo and interrogation squad. Even other Hellions hate the Malebranche. My back still hurts from Rizoel's sword. The last thing I want is to go one-on-one with a professional flesh ripper.

I say, "Looks like you've hit hard times."

"You've hit worse unless you have something I want."

The riot seethes along in its merry way behind us, but the Malebranche and me are in our own cozy little world in the alcove. A bottle breaks above us and we both reflexively turn our heads to avoid the flying glass, but it was random. Even though no one is paying any attention to us, I keep getting hit from behind, which pushes my throat down onto the fork. I hope not enough to break the skin. Human blood would be a dead giveaway.

I look at the Malebranche's dirty face. His skin is bright red under the grime.

"Which one are you? Rubicante?"

His laugh is high and a little frantic.

"Oh my. Am I still that famous?"

"It's your pretty face," I say. "Maybe I have something for you after all."

I reach into my pocket, feeling Rubicante push the sharp prongs harder against my neck.

"Easy, friend. I wouldn't want to slip."

He gives a quick flick of his head at my hand.

"Bring that hand out slowly and bring out something tasty with it or I'll have to pop out one of your eyes for a snack."

The alcove is a dim place and the riot is reflected clearly in the glass behind Rubicante's head. I feel around in my pocket for a minute, trying to buy some time.

"Any day now, friend," he says.

I have to do this just right. Or completely wrong. That sometimes works.

I come out with the half pack of Maledictions and Rubicante's eyes go wide. I hold them out and he takes his eyes off me. I drop the pack and he watches it fall all the way to the ground. I glance at the reflection in the glass door and throw myself out of the way.

A riot cop tossed from the crowd smashes into the Malebranche and they go flying through the shop's glass door.

I leave Rubicante and the cop playing Twister in the sex shop, grab the Maledictions, and run for Sunset.

It feels like the fall reopened the wound on my back. I don't want to smell even vaguely alive, so I whisper a little hoodoo and crank up the fumes from my corpse hoodie until I stink like the Dumpster behind a used-ass store. This is going to be a pleasant way to travel.

I'm going to have a hell of a time finding Eleusis if the whole place is as twisted as it was back then. Not that that matters if I've been napping for twenty years, Mason has already won, and this really is L.A.

Sunset is as scorched and sterile as a nuke test site. Some of the burning palm fronds fall and others float over the buildings, carried away by weird convection currents.

I stand on the corner and let the angel out of the attic long enough to expand my senses and do a kind of quick minesweep to see if there's anything alive or lurking in the burned-out buildings. Sunset is dazzling through the angel's eyes. The smoldering street with its torched trees is like a line of suns down a glory road of trembling atoms and subatomic particles.

The first time I saw Hell, it was a very different story. I was dragged down through Mason's floor and landed in a naked heap on a main street in Pandemonium. I must have been out cold for a while, and when I came to, the first thing that hit me was the stink. Nothing human smelled like that. It wasn't just waste. It was filth that had been packed, compressed, and locked away for a million years. Hell is the bottom of the universe and Heaven isn't going to let Lucifer pollute the rest of existence with Hellion shit and candy wrappers. So they still bury it in the deep, deeper, deepest caverns in their craptacular kingdom, where it sits, cooks, and festers in its own juices until the end of time.

The angel gives the all clear. I shove it out of the way, but I don't lock it up. Unfortunately, I'm going to need all of me to get through this, and that includes my divine squatter.

I head west down Sunset so I can cut up Las Palmas to Max Overdrive. The angel better be right that it's clear down here. I'm not above self-trepanation.

I can still see the Hollywood Boulevard riot when I cross Vine Street. And Cahuenga.

Getting down Sunset is harder than the road by the cemetery. The fault lines are wider and the broken pavement is pushed up higher and at steeper angles. Sinkholes have opened around whole blocks, forming skyscraper islands with sewage moats. Maybe that's why everything feels so wrong. I've only gone a couple of blocks but I swear it feels like I've been walking for-fucking-ever. Who or whatever built this L.A. got the proportions all wrong. The buildings are right, but some of them are in the wrong place. The Cinerama Dome still looks like a giant golf ball dropped to the earth by aliens, but it's on the wrong side of the street. Some of the side streets that used to cut across Sunset have twisted around like asphalt taffy and now run parallel.

That is not good news. It means that even if someone tells me where Eleusis is, I might not be able to find it in these deranged goddamn streets. And I can't even use maps. Lucifer was such a control freak that most of the maps you find Downtown are wrong. He didn't want the riffraff knowing exactly which roads led where or which were wide enough to hold rebel troops. That means I'm going to need a tracker who can walk and take me to the doorstep of Alice's asylum.

A hell of a quake must have hit the concrete island ahead of me. An entire block of gleaming new office buildings has fallen in on itself and half disappeared down a massive sinkhole. The acres of broken glass and steel reflect the burning street like the last ice floe at the end of the world.

I check out Hollywood Boulevard at the next corner. It looks clear and there's no noise that way. I run the whole way.

Seeing the Boulevard here, it's easy to understand why the crowd is tearing things up down the street. The place is picked clean. The ground floor of every building is gutted and burned. Bloody Hellions with broken limbs wander through the rubble looking for food, potions, or pills to make the world stop hurting. Damned souls are scattered all over the street staring into space like shell-shocked children. Finding themselves free but still in Hell was too much for their already tortured minds. They don't react when I walk by, but the Hellions see me and scatter like roaches into the empty buildings. The universe has entered a new level of weirdness when Hellions are the ones afraid to be caught out after dark.

Half a block ahead is the only intact, well-lit building on the whole street. When I get closer I understand why.

Praise God and pass the ammunition. Now I understand. Now I know everything.

Peter Murphy was wrong when he said Bela Lugosi's dead. He's not. I just found his retirement home.

It stands where Grauman's Chinese Theatre should be. I mean it's still the Chinese Theatre—all supersaturated reds and golds—but it's a different version. It's twice as big as it should be. It's so wide that it takes up half the block and the golden pagoda roof looks like it's high enough to rip open stray blimps. A fifty-foot metal electrified fence marked every few yards with lightning-bolt warning signs surrounds the place.

I know this place. It doesn't look anything like it looked like in my Downtown. There it was a kind of King Arthur's castle, but with soft and twisted, almost organic lines, like it hadn't been carved from the rock but had grown there. This place might not be General Mammon's palace the way I'm used to seeing it, but his standard is suspended between the pagoda spires so everyone in Hell or L.A. or Mordor or wherever the fuck I am can see it.

This is what I've been looking for. The answer to all of life's little questions.

When Mustang Sally said that using the Black Dahlia to cross over was easy but hard, I thought she was talking about the dying part. Now I think she was really talking about this. It's why I woke up under that strange version of the freeway. Crossing over with the Black Dahlia isn't a true one-hundred-percent-normal crossing. It's a Convergence. A psychic melding of the place the traveler left and the place where the traveler is going. It's a smart work-around to keep Mason from noticing me tiptoeing Downtown, because even though I'm truly in Hell, it's not exactly the one where he's expecting me. Yeah, I know. These metaphysical states and dimensions of being give me a headache, too.

If you know the Convergence is coming, it can be pretty useful. Say you want to travel fast through another city or parallel dimension. You do a Convergence and you can find your way around the new place by following the layout of the city you left. Unless the new place has decided to sprout fault lines, rearrange its streets, and generally fall the fuck apart.

Right this second I don't know if being in a Convergence is a help or more bullshit in my way, but I'm sure of one thing. Someone inside knows where Eleusis is and I'll kill them one by one until someone tells me.

I get out the na'at and eye a nice shadow at the corner of the palace. Chances are that Mason is expecting me to use the Room to get into Hell and not move around inside it. I'll know in a minute. I step into the shadow and come out just inside Mammon's palace.

No alarms go off. I'm alone in a giant movie-theater lobby. They must buy carpet by the mile to cover this floor. The concession stand is the size of Vegas. I bet the screen is as big as the Rockies. Wish I had time to catch a feature.

It hits me right about now that even though my old slave master Azazel brought me to Mammon's tree fort plenty of times, this mutant version might not be laid out exactly the same way. Only one way to find out. This new version is too weird to navigate normally and I don't feel like going on walkabout. I step back into a shadow. I'll take my chances with the Room and open the Door of Fire, the door that always leads to chaos and violence.

I come out behind a pillar in a circular room that looks like what I imagine the Oval Office is like, only bigger and with meaner monsters. Across from me are floor-to-ceiling windows with a Cadillac-size wooden desk between them. There's a fireplace to the right and expensive-looking couches and coffee tables scattered around the place. I halfway expect Remington cowboy sculptures and a giant flat-screen playing football or wrestling or some other macho backslapping good old boy to inject just a little more testosterone into the place. I don't know if I'm in Hell or the CEO's office at Halliburton.

Mammon and five of his officers are clustered around a worktable in the middle of the room. All of them are in sharp suits, but none of the officers is stupid enough to have a suit sharper than Mammon's. The general wears a large gold inverted cross on a chain around his neck. It's probably a war medal, but it makes him look like Sammy Davis Jr. in his late Rat Pack period.

The worktable in front of them projects a floating 3-D map laying out different routes around the universe from Downtown to Heaven. It looks like a schematic of the coolest ride since Space Mountain.

I want to go right at them, but I need to lay out a little hoodoo first. Unfortunately, a good hex needs to be spoken out loud. Black juju likes to be mixed in with a little sputter and spit. However, it's easy to toss off white magic inside your head. Instead of wishing Mammon's backup band ill will, I do the opposite and throw a protective shield up around the entire room. Aside from saving them from torch-carrying peasants, it'll soundproof the place and keep any nosy guards from getting in.

Quiet as I can, I get out the na'at, snap out the business end like a bullwhip, and give it a little twist so it goes rigid. It hits the closest Hellion at the base of his skull and comes out his extremely surprised mouth. The officer next to him goes for his shoulder holster. Bad idea. He's left his front exposed. I bounce the sharp end of the na'at off the worktable and flick it up, catching him just above his crotch, slicing him open to his chest. He has an excellent view of his Hellion guts spilling onto the floor before he follows them down. I step back into a shadow as the rest of the crew tries to process what just happened. In a brilliant tactical maneuver, the three remaining officers decide to rush the spot where I'm standing just as I'm not there anymore.

I come out of a shadow behind Mammon, pull the black blade, and pig-stick him in the spine about six inches above his waist. His legs suddenly stop working and he smacks onto the floor like an Easter ham.

One of Mammon's brighter officers figured out my shadow trick and stayed close enough to Mammon to jump me.

She's a huge red-haired Hulk Hogan beast trying to get the barrel of her .50 pointed anywhere on my body. She gets off a couple of shots as we wrestle, but she can't hit me without hitting herself, so she's just blowing holes in the floor. I drive the na'at's pommel into her temple and knock the gun out of her hand while she's still cross-eyed.

Two officers, one in a slick black Hugo Boss and one in a white ice-cream suit, take potshots at us, but they can't really open up without hitting Mrs. Hogan. She lunges at me. I kick out at her, but she tagged me hard enough that I trip over a pricey antique chair and smack the back of my head into the wall. My brain feels like a Shamrock Shake. Mrs. Hogan is on her hands and knees, pulling a knife the size of a leg of lamb from under her suit jacket. Hugo Boss and the ice-cream man come in behind her, closing the distance so they can shoot me a hundred percent dead. I flick the na'at at the ceiling, knocking out one of the overhead lights. There's a feeble shadow behind the chair I tripped over. It's not much, but I dive for it just as a wave of bullets blast fist-size chunks of polished wood and plaster from Mammon's office wall.

I stay in the shadow for a minute, letting my head clear, when I hear Mammon say, "The battle plan, lady and gentlemen, is simple: Do better."

The officers go back-to-back, forming a protective triangle around Mammon, which means they're stuck there while I can move around. I'm lucky that none of them can manifest a

Gladius. Besides Lucifer, only a few of the heavyweight fallen angels still have the power. None of this crew has or they would have used it by now.

I duck into the room, moving from shadow to shadow, swinging the na'at at the overhead lights. I take them out one by one, creating more shadows for me to work from. The white suit shoots at me, but Hugo Boss is busy reloading. I feel two shots go through my coat just above my leg and dive back into the dark.

Half the room is in shadows and Mammon's officers are nervous. Mrs. Hogan doesn't have her gun, so I go for her first. Keeping most of my body in the shadow, I snap out the na'at, leaving it loose until it wraps around her ankle, then I pull it tight like a snare. I fade back into the wall while retracting the na'at and it pulls her across the floor like she's tied to a freight train. When she hits the wall I grab her lapels and pull her upright. The sight of even just my hands gets Hugo Boss itchy. He blasts away, only I'm back in the shadow and his redheaded teammate is suddenly full of holes. I pull back my hands and let her fall. The ice-cream man checks her body and I get the distinct feeling that he had something going with Mrs. Hogan, because when he sees her back full of smoking craters, he levels his pistol at Hugo Boss and blows his brains out.

Now it's just the ice-cream man and Mammon. He grabs Mammon by the back of his collar and drags him into the biggest pool of light, shouting for the guards. No one shouts back. He keeps shouting until Mammon backhands him from the floor.

"Stop shouting in my ear. If backup were coming, it would

be here by now. You might consider shooting him yourself before he kills us."

I step out behind the pillar where I first entered the room and shout, "He's right. No guards get in here without a permission slip from me."

The ice-cream man blasts into the dark.

"That's a clever ploy. Use up all your bullets shooting at nothing. Did they teach you that at military school?" says Mammon. But the ice-cream man isn't listening. He's not a soldier anymore. He's an angry boyfriend looking to get back at someone who got his girl killed. Join the club, fucker.

The ice-cream man shouts, "Show yourself!"

"I am," I say. "Don't look at the shadows. I'm right out in the open with you. Come and get me."

He's pissed enough about Mrs. Hulk that he lets go of Mammon and prowls around the edges of the light, listening, trying to figure out where my voice came from.

"Get back here," shouts Mammon. "He's goading you."

I take out Mason's lighter from my pocket and toss it onto the nearest couch. The ice-cream man spins and blasts the enemy furniture.

I throw the black blade. He sees it at the last second but can't get out of the way, and the blade buries itself in his right eye. He's dead before he hits the floor.

Mammon finally sees me as I step out from behind his floating map of the universe. The room is empty except for us. Mammon's dead officers have all winked out of existence and are on their way to Tartarus, the Hell below Hell.

I get Mason's lighter off the couch and put it back in my pocket.

From the floor, Mammon gives the room an expansive wave like he's addressing the multitudes.

"Lo, the prodigal coward returns. It's been a long time, assassin. How have you been? Enjoying your life upstairs? That's a breathtaking tan."

I take my time getting to him.

"You'll notice I'm not rushing over. I want you to get used to seeing the world from floor level."

He looks me over.

"Nice coat. But I hate the shoes."

"I like what you've done with the place. Is that why you threw in with Mason? He got you a good decorator?"

"I'm with Mason because I appreciate winners."

"Like the five I just slaughtered? Or was it that time when you threw in with Lucifer to take over Heaven. Face it. You're completely shit in the picking-winners department."

Mammon's legs are splayed at funny angles. He's propped on his elbows, trying to look comfortable. I circle him so half the time he's talking to empty air.

He shrugs.

"We were young back then and swept up in the excitement that we could throw out the old ways and rebuild the world. I'm older now and understand. Our plans weren't thorough enough back then. This time they are."

"I've got my fingers crossed for you, doughboy. I have a feeling if you fuck up one more time, there's nothing left for you but Tartarus. Unless you know somewhere lower than that?"

He keeps smiling, but his lips do a little involuntary microtwitch. Tartarus is the only thing that truly frightens all these

Hellion bastards. Even they don't know what's down there. Maybe Lucifer does, but he's not around to ask.

Mammon manages a little mocking laugh.

"What's so funny?"

"Nothing. It's a private joke. You wouldn't understand. There's wine and Aqua Regia on my desk. I hear you're quite the drunkard these days."

"Did you hear that when Kasabian was still spying for Lucifer? That intel is out-of-date. I'm strictly a social drinker these days."

"That's what all drunks say. In any case, enjoy yourself."

I give the bottles on his desk a sniff. They don't smell poisoned, but it's hard to tell with Aqua Regia since it's already mostly poison. I start going through his desk.

"Where are the Maledictions? I'd strangle the Pope for a smoke."

"Sorry. I quit."

"You're a Hellion. All you do is torture and smoke."

"You're right. I lied. But I'm out of cigarettes. Maybe if you let the guards in, one of them could bring some."

"How's the view from the carpet, Tom Thumb? Does the world smell different down there?"

I go through the rest of the drawers. There's a silver flask in a bottom one. I take it out, admiring Mammon's family crest on the front. I hold it up and he says, "Be my guest."

While I'm pouring Aqua Regia into the empty flask, Mammon says, "You're going to be dead tomorrow, you know."

When the flask is filled to the top, I tighten the cap and slip it inside my coat.

"Dead, huh? That sucks. How are your legs? Any pain yet?"

Mammon shakes his head.

"None, thank you."

"It'll start soon."

Metal scrapes near the wall.

I snap out the na'at to its full length and twist it so barbs sprout along its length. A scared, muffled voice screams where the na'at is pointing. It sounds like it's coming from a weird metal sculpture across the room. It's about six feet tall and covered in hand-hammered silver in roughly the outline of a human body. It looks like something from Muninn's discount bin. I get closer, letting the na'at keep some distance between us.

There are openings in the sculpture, like eye slits. There's movement behind them. I shove the na'at right up to the opening. The muffled screaming starts up. When I get closer I can see eyes inside the helmet. They're brown. The pupils wide and dilated with fear. They're human.

I point at the caged man.

"Who's the gimp?"

Mammon pushes himself up a little higher on his elbows.

"That's Mr. Kelly. Say hello, Mr. Kelly."

The Hellion upper classes love to talk about the damned with mock formality.

The slaved soul in the metal restraints squeezes out what I guess is a muffled greeting.

"Why's he locked up? Is he dangerous?"

"Only to your kind. He's a murderer."

"Is that what's in this year? Collecting killers instead of baseball cards?"

He tightens his lips in a look of mild disgust.

"It was Mason's idea. He issued senior officers 'interesting' souls so we might become more acquainted with human minds. The one he gave me was a bore, so I put him in storage."

The soul is in something like a Hellion suit of armor welded inside an external cage. I put away the na'at and start slicing through the bars with the black blade. With a little force the bars come off easily. When I get the front clear, I start slicing off the armor.

"Just out of curiosity, where's General Semyazah these days? I know he's on the run, but I also know you have spies. Where's he hiding?"

"You admire the fool, don't you? 'Semyazah, the lone Hellion general brave enough to hold out against Mason Faim, the dread usurper of Lucifer's throne!'"

"I just asked where he was. I don't need a campaign speech."

Mammon pulls himself around so we're looking straight at each other again.

"Remember the private joke I mentioned? I'll share it with you after all. When you so subtly threatened me with Tartarus, I laughed because that's where your hero is. Semyazah is Tartarus's newest and I daresay most famous guest."

If Mammon is telling the truth then the game is over. There's no game at all. With Semyazah out of the way, another general will have claimed his troops and there won't be anyone to stop Mason from launching his war. It was a long shot that Semyazah could do anything anyway. Now even that slim chance might be gone. Mammon could be lying, but the first thing I have to do is find Alice. I don't have time to run all over Hell checking out Mammon's bullshit. I wonder what happens to a non-damned soul if it's killed in Hell? If I can't find Alice in time and Mason murders her again, will she end up in Tartarus? Or worse, she might be saved from Tartarus but end up too far from Heaven to find her way back, and wander in the Limbo between them forever.

"Who killed Semyazah?"

Mammon shakes his head.

"That's the best part. You inspired Semyazah's fate. He wasn't killed. Mason said that we should send him to Tartarus alive, and so we did."

What a bunch of gold-plated idiots we are, Hellions and humans alike. Somewhere God is laughing at us. We're his private joke with himself. Why didn't he just wipe us all out and start over? Maybe it's more fun watching us run around bouncing off the walls.

"What? No more jokes, Sandman Slim? Here's an idea. Run back to your cozy home upstairs. Drink. Watch movies. Fuck whomever it is you fuck these days and let the grown-ups get on with their work. We're really awfully busy."

I cut the last few pieces of armor off the soul and pull him out of the cage. There's a metal restraint around his head holding a leather bit in his mouth. I slice through the lock and the restraint falls to the floor. I go back to Mammon, leaving the soul to rub his aching jaw.

"When is it happening?"

"When is what happening?"

I want to kick him in the throat but I don't want to kill him, so I just give him the toe of my boot in the jaw.

"That was me being nice. The next thing that happens is I start cutting off the parts of your body you can still feel, starting with your fingers."

Mammon rubs his jaw, considering his answer. When he answers, his voice is low.

"The troops are already massed. All that remains is to agree to the final details of plans and bring the troops under a single command. From there, Mason will lead us to Heaven."

"Do you really think you're going to win this time? Heaven has the high ground and they know you're coming. Lucifer will have told them everything."

His eyes narrow when he smiles.

"Lucifer is far from omniscient."

"So you have a secret. What is it?"

"What is what?"

I grab Mammon by the collar and toss him across the room onto his desk.

He waits until I'm close before he attacks.

I'm walking around the desk when he moves his arm in a very particular way. He's angel-fast, but I recognize what he's doing because these days I can do it, too.

Mammon swings his Gladius back over his head, trying to slice me in half as I come around the desk. I dodge it just in time. Feel it burn through my coat sleeve.

He swings again but I've already manifested my own Gladius. I block the strike. Mammon is flat on his back, not a prime defensive position. When I block his next shot, I slip my Gladius under his, shift my weight, and flip his sword over and down onto his chest. He screams and I stab my sword into his fighting arm as far as it will go. I hold it there until his arm blackens and his Gladius goes out. Hellions smell bad at the best of times. Burning Hellions are like a bonfire in a garbage dump.

He lies on the desk blinking at the ceiling.

"You still with us, General?"

He doesn't say anything. He just holds his burned arm with his good one. I don't have time for him to lie around and go into shock. I open the bottle of wine, lift him up, and hand him the bottle. He takes it in his good hand and drains half the bottle. I pick him up off the desk and sit him in his leather executive chair.

He's looking at me, but his eyes have the vacant stare of someone on a bad acid trip.

"What doesn't Lucifer know about?"

It takes him a few seconds to focus on me.

"The key. The key Mason was building to get into the Room of Thirteen Doors. It will never open the Room, but it will do something else. It will open Heaven to us."

"Maybe you've made a passkey, but how can you break through all of Heaven's defenses and get close enough to use it?"

"There's a weak spot. One of the protective seals is missing."

"You mean the Druj Ammun?"

His eyes go wide.

"How do you know about that?"

This time I laugh at him.

"Because I had it. Back in L.A."

He grabs my coat sleeve with his good hand.

"Where is it? Name any price."

"Too late. I traded it for some magic beans."

He drinks more wine.

"This isn't anything to joke about."

"I took the Druj Ammun off a dead vampire. A young girl. The only one of her kind I ever felt bad about killing. When I found out one of the Druj's powers was to mind-control Hellions, the plan was to come down and get you assholes to rip Mason to pieces for me."

"Where is it now?"

"I also found out that it controlled zombies, and as it happened, we had a substantial zombie surplus in L.A. right then. Instead of letting everyone get eaten, I destroyed the Druj. That killed every single zombie in the world in one night. By now your secret weapon is in a million little pieces clogging up the L.A. sewer system."

Mammon stares at the floor. I can't tell if he's listening or getting drunk. He lifts his head.

"It would have been good to have. We could have built a great weapon from it. Made it control the other angels," he says, and looks up at me. "Baphomet said if anyone was going to ruin this for us, it would be you. But you'd been gone so long many of us thought that you wanted to forget all about this place and wouldn't get involved. We should have erred on the side of caution."

"If it's any comfort, L.A. is completely zombie-free these days, so you can bring the wife and kids to Disneyland."

"It's too bad you killed your patron, Azazel. I would have enjoyed torturing him to death for creating you."

"So, even without the Druj, Mason has a backup plan he thinks will still get him into Heaven. How?"

"I don't know. It's the one thing he's kept secret from everyone, including his generals."

It's hard to read Hellions, but the angel and I agree that Mammon is telling the truth. Damn Lucifer for not being here. He might be able to figure out Mason's secret.

The Kissi stole the Druj thousands of years ago and dropped it on earth just to see what would happen. They like to create amusing chaos. It's their main nourishment. But Kissi are hit-and-run types, not known for their long-term planning. We always thought of them like a bunch of ADHD kids with superpowers. Always playing games and breaking things for the dumb joy of breaking them. But when they stole the Druj and dumped it on earth, did they have a secret of their own that no one ever considered? Maybe we've underestimated them this whole time.

Mammon finishes the wine and I set the bottle back on the desk.

"You're being awfully cooperative," I say.

"You've already crippled me. Torture is the next logical step. Why shouldn't I skip all the messiness and tell you what you want to know since none of it will help you?"

While we've been talking, Mammon's enslaved soul has been creeping over to the desk.

"We'll see. The truth is, the war isn't the main reason I'm here. I want you to take me to Eleusis."

He raises his eyebrows slightly.

"Don't be stupid. I don't drive, and even if I could . . ." He holds up his one working arm. "I'm not in racing shape."

Drive? In the Hell I remember, Lucifer's generals have their own private barges for getting around Hell's five big rivers. I guess a nice luxury car is about the same as a barge in L.A.

I turn my head and find the soul staring at me. He's a medium-size man with dark hair and brown eyes. He has rough workman's hands and his cheap shirt and thin black pants say he wasn't all that high in whatever trade he was in.

I point to him.

"Can the gimp drive?"

Mammon brightens at that, getting back some of his old high-and-mighty look.

"And dust and sing songs, too. All the menial things humans are so good at. Isn't that right, Mr. Kelly?"

Kelly nods.

"Give me the keys," I tell Mammon.

He opens a drawer, takes them out, and tosses them on the desk. I hand them to Kelly.

"You're the wheelman, Kelly. I'm riding shotgun and Dr. Strangelove here can sit in the back and navigate. Got it?"

Kelly just stares.

I look at Mammon.

"Does he speak English?"

Mammon nods.

"Quite well. He needs my permission before speaking to you."

"Give it so we can get moving."

"You may talk to him, Mr. Kelly, but be careful not to get too friendly. He's a monster. Isn't that right, Sandman Slim?"

I look at Kelly.

"You really can drive, right?"

Kelly nods. His gaze flickers from the floor and back to me.

"Yes, sir. Thank you, sir. I never operated an automobile when I was alive, but I've been well instructed since then."

He sounds English. Cockney maybe. Michael Caine playing Harry Palmer. A working-class guy.

"Good enough. And don't call me 'sir.' "

"What should I call you, sir?" He cringes when he says it like he thinks I'm going to hit him. "My apologies."

"Stark's fine."

"Why not Wild Bill?" says Mammon brightly. "I hear he likes that even less than Sandman Slim."

Mammon turns to me.

"He's here, by the way. Your great-great-great-granddaddy, Mr. Hickok. I could arrange a tête-à-tête."

There's no wheelchair in the room and there's no way I'm carrying this charred creep to the car, so I push Mammon into his office chair.

"Introduce me, and when this is all over, I might let you keep the other arm."

Mammon brightens.

"You see what I mean, Mr. Kelly? He wants us to see him as human, but what's the first thing he does when he gets in here? He takes my legs. And I didn't even attack him. Then he takes my arm and threatens me with further mutilation. That sounds much more Hellion than human, doesn't it? I don't think you'll be wanting to turn your back on this one. Not for one minute."

"Where's the garage?" I ask Kelly.

"Directly below, Mr. Stark."

"Mister." It's better than "sir."

I don't want either of them to see the Room, so I blindfold them both and take them downstairs through a shadow.

Mammon's barge turns out to be a pristine early-sixties Lincoln Continental limo with a drop top and suicide doors. I think more than a little of this world is put together straight from my unconscious. I'll know for sure if I end up in a motorcycle race against Steve McQueen.

The Lincoln isn't like a modern limo. The car is wide open on the inside. No partitions or sliding windows separating the passenger compartment from the driver. It's like a club or a prison cafeteria. Candy would love this heap. I can see her in the passenger seat with her feet up on the dash hitting the button on her robot sunglasses in time with the radio.

It still feels strange to have left her behind while I go chasing after another woman even if it's not for a romantic kind of love, but the kind that says if you've ever been deeply connected to someone, you don't let them get snatched to the underworld without doing something about it.

When this is over and if the universe is still standing, maybe I'll bring her down here. I wouldn't take her to the Hell I knew, but I could see her getting off on a weekend in the Convergence. It would be like the adventure vacations yuppies go on where they get to experience the great outdoors from air-conditioned buses and ten-thousand-dollar tents. We'll take over a floor of the Roosevelt Hotel and shoot paintballs at the wildlife.

I take Mammon from his chair and belt him in behind the driver's seat. Kelly and I get in the front. He starts the ignition and drives us smoothly through the garage to the gatehouse, where a guard is waiting.

I show Mammon the knife in my hand.

"Be cool or you lose the other arm."

"Of course," Mammon says.

We pull up and Mammon rolls down his tinted window just low enough to show his face. He nods at the guard and the guard pushes a button that rolls away the gate. Kelly steers us out of the palace and on to Hollywood Boulevard. It looks like even in Hell I'm destined to travel in stolen cars.

"Turn right," I tell him. "Things are messy the other way."

He makes the turn.

It's funny seeing Mammon sitting calmly with his bad legs and crispy arm. I got lucky back at the palace. I had no idea he could manifest a Gladius. Azazel didn't bother to mention that when he sent me to kill Mammon more than ten years ago. I don't know why he wanted me to do it and I don't know why he changed his mind. Maybe his TiVo was out.

"To the Phlegethon, Mr. Kelly," Mammon says.

Sinkholes and fault lines slice up the streets, making them impassable. Kelly cuts down La Brea and takes a roundabout route through residential streets and apartment-building parking lots to the 101.

Mammon tells Kelly to head south. The breakdown lanes on both sides of the freeway look like sets from old driver's-ed films. They're a solid mass of twisted and burned-out vehicles.

In regular Hell, the Phlegethon is a river of fire that flows and ebbs like water. The flames are just a light breeze from on board a barge. You don't get burned unless you're in direct contact with the river.

The Phlegethon does double duty in Hell. It's one of the big five rivers, so it carries a lot of traffic, mostly barges, passenger boats, and freighters. It's busy enough that it needs docks, buoys, depth markers, and all the other Moby-Dick bric-a-brac I don't understand. This is Hell. Why get artisans to make all that stuff when you have millions of dead souls lying around? Down the length of the Phlegethon, the damned float in the eternal fire as channel markers and buoys showing depth readings. Entire docks are made from spirits lashed together. There's similar creativity in this Hell. The freeway guardrails and the median fence in the center are staked-out souls. The reflectors separating the freeway lanes are the heads of souls who've been buried up to their necks in Hellion concrete. What happens if you blow a tire down here? Hellion AAA probably comes out and ties a few souls around your axle so you can get to a damned garage.

"So, who are you?" I ask Kelly.

He doesn't say anything.

"Tell him to talk to me. Tell him he doesn't ever need your permission to talk again."

Mammon says, "Talk to him, Mr. Kelly. Talk to him to your heart's content. But first take this exit and merge left."

Kelly says, "I'm Master Mammon's servant and resident human. I do whatever he asks, from talking about my life to performing whatever tasks I'm instructed to do in a way that best exemplifies human habits and behavior."

"I told you he was a bore," says Mammon. "You remove creatures like this from their environment and they wither. He might still be interesting if we let him loose as a killer down here like you."

"I wasn't a killer until I got down here."

Mammon makes a dismissive gesture with his good hand.

"Just because a baby spider hasn't bitten anyone yet doesn't make it any less of a spider."

Kelly steers us down the fire road. Mammon occasionally tells him to change lanes or follow a road that splits off from the main one. We're driving for at least an hour but we don't seem to be anywhere yet. If Mammon is leading us anywhere but Eleusis, I'm going to tie him to the back bumper and drag him to Mexico. If I can find it.

"What makes you so special that of all the souls down here, you rate being handed off to a general?" I ask Kelly.

"I don't know, sir. Stark, I mean. I'm sorry. It's a wretched habit to break."

"Don't sweat it."

"There are so many people down here more accomplished than I. I've accomplished nothing compared to some I've met."

"Don't be so modest, Mr. Kelly. Mr. Kelly was a murderer, and after some practice he became quite adept. More than even his pursuers knew," says Mammon. "But it was only dumb luck that kept you unincarcerated after those first few, isn't that right?"

"Yes, Master Mammon. Just as you say, sir."

We drive for what feels like another hour. Every now and then I see a flash behind us, like a light going out or a reflection off a mirror, but when I turn there's nothing there.

I've driven the 101 south to San Diego a hundred times, but I don't recognize this road at all. We could be driving to Oz or right into a trap.

"We're getting off here," says Mammon.

I look around, trying to get my bearings. All the road signs have been torn down or hacked to pieces. More of Lucifer's paranoia or just another example of L.A.'s ever-expanding nervous breakdown?

The exit sign has been torched and lies in a little slag heap at the edge of the road. I swear I see another flash behind us, but then I'm bracing myself against the dashboard. Kelly takes the exit too fast and has to tap the brakes hard when we come to a hairpin curve. That's when Mammon stabs me.

I should have stripped the fucker down at the palace, but the angel in my head felt sorry for all the maiming and frying I did. I went easy on him and this is what I get.

The inverted-cross medal he's been wearing comes apart and the lower half is a razor-sharp golden blade. He was probably going for my neck, but when Kelly hit the brakes, it ruined Mammon's aim. The knife went into my left cheek. A little higher and it would have hit my eye.

Mammon pulls the knife out of my face and slashes me in the shoulder before I can turn and grab him. He stabs me a second time in the cheek before I can pin his good hand. I have one hand braced on the roof as we turn under the freeway. Mammon lunges at me and buries his teeth in my hand that's holding him. I pull back reflexively and he gets his hand free. He swings the blade at me as the car fishtails, but ends up slashing Kelly's arm.

Kelly screams and we plow through a guardrail and down an embankment. The car flips and rolls. When we stop moving I'm not sure which way is up or down, but when I elbow open my door, my foot touches the ground, so I'm guessing we're right side up.

I step out and fall onto the dry dead grass. When my head stops swimming, I go around to Kelly's side and pull him out. His arm doesn't look too bad. I don't bother with Mammon. His neck is twisted 180 degrees, so he's looking out the back window at the road we just left. Probably nostalgic for when he wasn't dead. I guess he's technically not dead since he hasn't blipped out of existence to Tartarus, but if I was his secretary I'd cancel all his appointments for tomorrow.

I carry Kelly around the car and set him down leaning against the car.

Human souls don't breathe or have beating hearts, so I don't know how to check if he's okay. The angel in my head can see souls, but the dead are all soul, so that doesn't help much. But a double-dead human soul will end up in Tartarus as fast as any Hellion, so Kelly still being here is a good sign.

The side of my face burns. I touch it where Mammon stabbed me and my hand comes away bloody. Shit. Exactly what I don't need right now.

Kelly moans and starts to move.

It takes him a few minutes to get his bearings. He rubs the back of his neck and stares at the ground. When he sees the car, he sits up straight.

"You bloody berk!" he yells into the car at Mammon's broken body. "This is fucking perfect."

"Get a grip, man. This really isn't the moment to freak out."

"Of course. I'm sorry."

He holds his arm where Mammon stabbed him. It clearly hurts, but is more of a shock than a wound.

I say, "Wait here while I look around."

I walk up the slope to the freeway to see if there's any trace of a town or a sign or wandering Boy Scout with a compass. Three strikes. I'm out. We could be in Egypt for all I know.

When I get back to the car, Kelly seems a little more coherent.

"The master is still in the car," he says.

"Yeah. He doesn't really need any fresh air, if you know what I mean."

"But he's not dead, is he? I mean he's still there."

"He's still with us, tough old bastard. Do you know where we are, Kelly?"

He gets to his knees and looks around.

"Roughly," he says.

"Can you get us to Eleusis?"

"I believe so."

"How long will it take?"

"On foot? If we cut through the flats and we don't have to detour too far around holes and faults, less than a day. But it'll be rough going."

From the freeway I hear the unmistakable sound of tires. I grab Kelly and pull him to the ground beside me. A heavy Unimog rolls slowly by, running without lights. That's what I've been seeing behind us all night. Mammon must have signaled someone before we left the palace and they've been tracking us ever since. A spotlight flashes from the Unimog, playing over the dying trees and cracked road. The car is on the downhill side of an embankment. The light moves back and forth across the exit, but I don't think they can see us down here. A second later the spotlight goes out and the truck drives away.

We've got a posse after us. More good news. Like Mammon said, it's a good idea to err on the side of caution. I need to do something in case they catch up to us.

"Kelly. Will we be passing through any towns or settlements? Anywhere someone might see us?"

"It's hard to say. Things can change so quickly here. It's best to assume we will."

"That's what I was afraid of."

I open the car and drag Mammon out.

Don't die on me now, you prick. Give me a few more minutes.

I pop the lock on the trunk with the black blade and start tossing things. It's full of the usual car junk. A tire iron, spare tire, jumper cables. But there's also military gear. I go back to where I left Mammon with a sturdy leather satchel and drop it beside him. With the knife I cut a large square of fabric from his suit jacket and lay it out flat on the grass.

Kelly creeps over closer to see what I'm doing.

"You might not want to watch this," I say.

"If it's all the same to you, I'd rather stay. This looks like it might be quite interesting."

"Okay," I say. "Here's the situation. We have to walk to Eleusis and then get all the way to the asylum and back out again. I'm wearing a glamour so I don't broadcast that I'm alive, but I'm bleeding, so I need more. And if Mammon signaled a posse, he might have told them I was the one who took him. I can't look like me. Are you getting my point?"

Jack gives me a big wolfish smile.

"If you're about to do what I think you are, I wouldn't miss it for the world."

"Okay, but if souls puke, don't do it on me."

"I'll remember that, sir."

"And don't call me 'sir.'"

"Yes. Sorry."

I close my eyes and try to remember any binding spells I picked up along the way, something to keep Mammon here with us a little longer before he croaks. My head is still a little foggy from the crash, but I come up with a minor bit of hoodoo that should hold if I work fast.

The next part I've never actually tried myself, but I saw it done a couple of times by old juju priests I met through some Dharma bums in a New Orleans Sub Rosa clan.

I try to get the words and rhythms of the old houngans in my mind before I start working. The real spell is a complex combination of Yoruba and Louisiana Creole and I've forgotten a lot of the words, so I have to do a lot of bebop improv, but bullshitting hoodoo on the fly is my specialty. As I chant, I rub my temples, and when the words are flowing fast enough and the time feels right, I grab my face just below the scalp line and pull. The skin comes off like I'm peeling a banana. It sticks in a couple of places and I have to snip them with the knife, but it's not a big deal.

I put my face, bloody side up, on the cloth I cut from Mammon's suit.

I hear Kelly gasp. It's not in horror, but in a kind of fascination and awe. He's probably never seen high-quality Merlin stuff. This must be a hell of an introduction to magic.

I do the whole ritual again. When I peel off Mammon's face, I drape it over the raw and bloody place where my face used to be. The new flesh burns as it attaches itself. I close my eyes and breathe, working through the pain. I'm dizzy and slide over onto an elbow. I feel Kelly grab me so I don't fall. The inside of my head swirls around once more and then it's over. I touch my new face. There's no pain at all. Mammon's skin feels like it's been there forever. I open my mouth. Move my lips in mock smiles and frowns.

I look at Kelly.

"What do you think? I don't look too much like Mammon, do I? It's his skin, but my bones and muscles, so we shouldn't be twins."

Kelly shakes his head.

"You don't look at all like him," he says. He stares at me with a kind of beatific smile plastered on his face, like Saint Peter just gave him an invitation to the Christmas after-party in Heaven.

He says, "If it isn't being too forward, I'd like to say that you might have just become my personal hero, Mr. Stark."

"Okay."

He looks up at the rolling black clouds that cover the sky.

"I once thought that I was a master of flesh. But I see now that you have surpassed me in every way."

As my new face settles in, I wrap my real face in Mammon's cloth, put it carefully in the leather satchel, and sling it over my shoulder.

"That's real nice of you, Kelly, but what the fuck are you talking about?"

He stands. Looks at me and then at Mammon. The Hellion finally dies and his body disappears.

"I prefer Jack, if you don't mind," says Kelly. "That's what people called me in older, merrier days when I was still alive. Jack the Ripper."

Some crazy people must stay crazy even after they're dead. I met dozens of Judas Iscariots, Hitlers, and Jack the Rippers in the eleven years I spent Downtown, but always one at a time. I always wondered if they steered clear of each other out of professional courtesy.

There's one thing that makes me think Kelly could be for real. Mason chose him. Picking a simple back-alley cutthroat with delusions of grandeur isn't a mistake Mason would make.

Jack is leading us down the embankment and into the thick woods that line the freeway. The trees stand at crazy, impossible angles. It's like we're walking through still photos of the forest in the process of falling.

"Step lightly," whispers Jack. "And don't touch anything. Tremors have loosed the land under the trees. They're barely rooted. They'll come down on us with the slightest provocation."

Suddenly I'm sorry I'm wearing big steel-toe boots. I should be in Hello Kitty slippers.

I've never seen a real forest in Hell. Not one with trees and plants. I've seen places called "forests," but they're usually tightly packed mazes of saw blades and spinning pylons studded with needlelike Hydra teeth.

We walk maybe twenty yards until the forest gets tight and dark and wild. Old-growth backwoods. It's hard not to bump into limbs and the solid trunks of the drunken trees. Each time I hit something, I feel it give, and wonder if it's going to fall and which way to run and if running will make things better or worse by bringing down even more trees. Tree trunks crack and branches fall around us, but we make it through the forest and come out onto low sand dunes.

Jack points off into the empty distance and says, "There's Eleusis."

But I'm looking down. At the bottom of the dune Venice Beach stretches into the distance. Which doesn't make sense. Venice is west of Hollywood and we've been going south. I don't know what's going crazy faster, this city or me.

I look up to where Jack is pointing. There's something in the distance, but I'm damned if I know what it is.

Venice is shuttered and looks like it's been that way for fifty years. The only light in the area comes from the fires reflected off the belly of the endless black clouds overhead. Vents in the ground belch geysers of superheated steam. Fire twisters skitter in the distance, tearing up the empty beach houses. We head down to the long tourist walk.

"You're wondering if I'm lying about who I am, Mr. Stark. Or if I'm a nutter."

"Something like that."

"And you're wondering how someone might go about proving or disproving my claim."

"Right on the money."

Even by Hell standards we've pretty much pegged the bleak meter. There's nothing more depressing than a dead beach town. It's like all the loons and extroverts and dimwit fun in the world has been boxed up and tossed on a bonfire. Of course, this isn't really Venice. It's just the Convergence projection of it. Still, something big died here and the sight of it has sucked the wind out of me. Or maybe I'm light-headed from cutting off my face. We move past empty weight-lifting areas and out-of-business tattoo parlors.

Jack says, "It's impossible for me to prove who I am. Perhaps I'm mad. Perhaps I'm a liar. If you perhaps had a book about old Jack's comings and goings, you might ask me details of my past. But you don't have a book and even if you did, Jack is a famous man. His crimes are well known and well documented. I might have read the same books as you."

"Where does that leave us, Jack?"

"In the wilderness, I'm afraid. I can no more prove to you that I'm happy Jack than you can prove to me you're Sandman Slim."

"Excuse me? I just stepped out of a shadow and killed five Hellion military officers. I took a Hellion general prisoner. I manifested a Gladius."

Jack rubs his jaw and rolls his shoulders, still trying to work out the kinks. I wonder how long he was in Mammon's cage.

He says, "Maybe you did and maybe you didn't. I'm not a magical sort like you and some of these other folk, so I don't know how it all works, do I?"

"Use your imagination."

"You appeared to kill a number of soldiers and to dash through shadows, but it could have been a trick of the eye. I've seen stage magicians make furniture dance and spirits float in the air. And I've seen this lot make people see all sorts of things. Lovers, friends, parents. Spiders. Snakes. But they were mere phantasms. Trickery meant to fool the eye and terrorize the soul. For all I know, you twiddled your thumbs and tricked Master Mammon's staff into killing each other."

"That would still be a pretty good trick."

"Indeed it would be. I've seen demons and devils that could break a man's bones on the rack or his heart with a single word. But that doesn't make any of them Sandman Slim."

"When you get down to it, I don't really care who you are. If you can get me to Eleusis, I'll call you Jack the Ripper or Mott the Hoople if you want. Just get me there."

"Of course. And what will be my payment for this service?"

I stop and look at him. Jack walks on for a few steps before looking back at me. He puts his hands in his pockets and stands up straight. The whole deferential attitude is gone. He's a killer standing his ground.

"Payment? And here I thought saving you from a tin-can coffin might cover it."

"Perhaps. Let's put our minds to it as we go and see what we come up with, shall we?"

He starts walking and I follow, staring at the thick foamy sea that looks more like tar than water. I should have tried to get the car started. But on the road the posse would have caught up with us. So no, leaving it was the smart move.

"Okay, Jack, I've got to ask. Assuming you are old Leather Apron, what's your story? Did the clap eat half your brain? Were you a religious freak? Did a talking dog named Sam tell you to kill all those women?"

"There is no God and I know nothing about a talking dog, though I'd surely like to see one."

"You're an atheist? You were a fallen angel's slave. In Hell. And you're an atheist? Walk me through that, Jack."

"Why is it necessary for God to exist for Hell to exist? The problem is that when good people imagine Hell, they imagine it as the opposite of the real world and as remote as the stars. That's their delusionment. Hell and earth are the same thing. Separated by nothing more than a thin shroud of understanding that this is so. I lived in Hell every moment I dwelt on the other earth and I made it my business to bring Hell to all God-fearing souls to remind them that horror is the fabric from which the world was made."

"You didn't date a lot when you were alive, did you, Jack?"

"I don't consort with whores, thank you very much. I rip 'em."

"Fucking hell."

I get out the flask and have a drink. The Aqua Regia burns in just the right way going down. I start to offer Jack a drink because you always offer the other guy a drink, but I screw the top on and put the flask back in my pocket.

We're off the beach and heading inland, picking our way through the dead neighborhoods. At the corner of one of the main streets, where rows of burning palms converge on it like a weird offering to a glue-sniffing beach god, is an office building with a three-story clown sculpture in front. It's in white face with dark whiskers and is wearing a top hat, white gloves, and ballet slippers. I know it's supposed to look whimsical, but whimsy in a place like this is like jerking off at a funeral. Someone might enjoy it, but you wouldn't want to know them.

"Assuming that you *are* Sandman Slim, tell me about yourself and your work. I've heard your name many times. Hellions talk about you like the bogeyman."

"I might be a monster but I never mailed a kidney to a newspaper."

"Half a kidney. I ate the other half."

"Mom always said it's a sin to waste food."

"How many Hellions have you dispatched, Sandman Slim? How many humans and human souls?"

"No idea."

"How many women?"

"I yelled at a meter maid once."

Soon we're in a residential area. People in Venice are sun worshippers and most of the houses have huge windows. Some of the upscale places even have one or two glass walls. The glass is all gone. Shattered by earth tremors and fucked over by looters. Houses are tagged with spray-painted Hellion gang signs. Teenyboppers are assholes here, too. I hope Heaven's teens are idiots. Going joyriding in Dad's wings and TPing other angels' clouds.

A dust devil swirls down the street, pelting us with trash and broken glass. I pull Jack behind a burned-out car and wait until the twister passes. It turns at the corner and heads down another street like it's alive and has a sense of direction. A few doors later, it goes. The neighborhood isn't completely deserted. I don't want to know who or what still lives here. I pull Jack to his feet and we get moving.

I hear a different kind of rumble back the way we came. There's a light in the distance. A spotlight coming down the dunes to the beach. The posse must have circled back and found Mammon's limo.

"Is there a faster way, Jack?"

"Yes, but it's more dangerous."

"Let's go."

We make a few turns back the way we came and run right into a dust storm. I'm practically blind, but Jack pulls me through it like I'm a poodle on a leash. When we emerge from the storm we're in a different neighborhood. Winding hill roads. The steep grades and long driveways are chewed-up, ever-widening fissures. Ghost mansions come and go in the settling dust. We head downhill, just like this neighborhood is. If the cracks in the road hook up with other, deeper cracks, one good shake and the whole side of this hill is going to turn into Surf City. Hang ten and ride the mansions, Rolls-Royces, and manicured lawns all the way down to the flats and into the Pacific.

Jack looks at me, trying to figure out how we got here.

"You're navigating with your eyes," he says. "To navigate these days, you have to think like a worm or mole. You must know what's underground. This isn't a land of right angles or streets anymore. It's purely geologic. The sand back at the beach was probably used as landfill around here to flatten sections of the hills."

"I'm lucky I have you, then."

"Yes you are." He pauses. "You were telling me about how many people you've killed."

"No. I wasn't."

"Back in London, old Inspector Abberline and the rest of the Met think I only took five. I took plenty more than that, believe you me. There were a few in the country, but south by the coast was best. Like the lovely beach we just left. Do a day's excursion to Brighton or Portsmouth. I'd find saloon trollops and rip them down by the wharfs. Toss their innards to the birds and fill their bodies with stones to weigh them down. They'd slip into the sea like it was waiting for them."

"Enough, you twisted fuck."

We walk on, Jack staring at his feet. Each step leaves a shallow impression in the thick dust that covers the sidewalk. If the posse is behind us, we'll be easy to track, but I don't have time to worry about that now. Each step is a second hand on a clock ticking away the time. Jack said it would take a day to get to Eleusis, but I've already lost track of how long we've been walking.

"None of this is a coincidence, you know," says Jack.

"Yeah. You had a great personal ad on Craigslist."

"Assuming I'm who I say that I am and assuming that you are who you say you are, do you truly believe that two such infamous killers could cross paths through simple happenstance?"

"Are you talking about divine intervention, Jack? Because that kind of blows your no-God theory."

"Not God. Some other, more subtle force that's thrown us together toward a higher purpose."

"Listen, we're in Hell and there are about fifty billion killers down here, so I was bound to meet someone like you. It could have been the Boston Strangler, Ted Bundy, or Freddy Krueger, and every one of them would tell me exactly what you're telling me now. There's nothing special about our road movie. It's nothing more than the flip of a coin."

He slowly shakes his head.

"I don't believe that. There's a reason for this. We're fated to do something together."

"Yeah. You're going to take me to Eleusis. When we get there I'm going to shake your hand and we are going to go our separate ways."

"There has to be more to it than that."

"Trust me, there doesn't."

"Maybe our doing the thing is the payment I need."

"It won't work, Jack. Look at our histories. We're lone

wolves. We don't work with partners. When we get to town we go our separate ways. I'll be grateful I'm there and you'll be grateful you're not still a Hellion's paperweight."

A steam vent explodes nearby. The blast of heat and vapor knocks me back. I think I hear a rumbling behind us. There might be a truck coming or it might just be the sound of the vent. I push Jack and we break into a trot.

Jack says, "May I see your knife? I have a great fondness for knives."

"No."

I look back at our tracks in the dust. You could see them from space. Maybe Jack wants us to get caught. We need to get off this street. I take his arm and push him onto a side street that's clean of dust. The vent spews again and the street moves below us. A palm tree falls and crushes a dusty pickup truck. Jack pulls me back in the other direction.

We run to the street we'd been on before. The air is full of dust and we can't see where we're going, but we run anyway. If there are any sinkholes or faults in front of us, we're fucked. We can barely see each other. But the tremors and the noise die down after a minute and the street goes back to being solid.

Jack looks at me.

"I assume you won't stray from the path again."

"You're the boss, Jack."

"Well put."

WE'RE HEADING FOR what looks like low hills, but as we get closer, it's really an area where the streets have buckled wildly, like black icebergs jutting up from the street. Eleusis is on the other side.

We turned off the dusty street twenty minutes earlier. Most of the signs in this neighborhood are in Spanish, but the residents are the same mix of dazed Hellions and lost souls we saw in Hollywood. They sit in cars and wander between strip malls like sleepwalkers.

Where the hell are you, Alice? What are you doing right now, Candy? I'd rather be having the worst time possible with either of you than having the best with my knife-happy tour guide. I know I told Candy to take the blood cure from Allegra, but I wouldn't mind letting her show Jack here what a Jade looks like. Try to hurt *this* woman, you little shit.

Every couple of minutes a lone man runs across the street. He's easy to spot when everyone else is going half speed. When he's settled somewhere he whistles an all clear. Soon a group of eight or ten Hellions comes up the same way. A mix of men and women, they whoop it up, running into stores, busting the places up, and coming out again with stolen wine and food. The ones with working guns take potshots at cars and store windows.

Jack says, "Raiders."

He starts running for the back of a half-burned building off to our right. I follow. When he can't get the rear door open, I push him out of the way, jam the black blade into the door frame, and push. Metal pops and wood splinters. I shove Jack inside and we head to the front of the place. The door is open a crack, giving us a good view of the street.

The Hellions stroll by like the street is bought and paid for. Some are still in their uniforms. Others only kept half of their uniforms and replaced the jackets or pants with formal wear or stolen motocross gear.

"Where are the Raiders from?"

"As the war with Heaven grows closer, there are more and more deserters from the armies. They raid the provinces and live on anything they can find. I once drove the master on a mission to arrest a group hiding in Eleusis. That's why I know where it is."

The raiders stop in front of the building we're hiding in. Suddenly I wish I'd brought a shotgun or two. But they're not looking at us. They're looking back down the street. When they get a look at what's coming, they sprint, run, and disappear over the fence behind a convenience store.

Moving lights sweep the street. The posse has grown to several vehicles. How did they get ahead of us? They must know where we're going.

There are about twenty Hellions on tricked-out ATVs and Unimogs. They have hot-rod flames on the sides and animal skulls mounted on the roofs and hoods. Their spotlights are LAPD issue. When they hit you with one from a helicopter, it's instant daylight and you better stop and look happy about it. Jack and I duck behind the door as the light moves over the front of the building.

A ticking, whirring sound follows the posse. I don't need Jack to tell me what that is. A pack of hellhounds. There wasn't much in Hell that gave me the creeps as much as the metal hounds. Maybe my subconscious really is shaping the place. The hounds are the only things I've seen that look just as hard and awful as they do in regular Hell.

The hounds move in packs. They're clockwork war dogs bigger than a dire wolf and are run by a brain suspended in a glass globe where their heads should be. A hellhound is smart and dangerous on its own. In packs, they're like a herd of velociraptors driving tanks. The best way to fight them is to run away and hope they die of old age.

The mechanical hounds lope behind the noisy trucks, their gears ticking quietly in the dark.

"Goddammit, Jack, how much longer before we get there?"

"If we cross over to the street behind this one, with luck we can beat them all to Eleusis. I know of a wall with just a little bit of a hole in it."

"Let's get moving."

"On the other hand, it might not be a bad idea to let the raiders or the men following them get there first."

"Why?"

"You know of the asylum, but do you know that as Pandemonium has fallen apart, so has the asylum. Most of the inmates have escaped and wander the streets. The old pagans to whom the place was a paradise have all been killed or driven into the wilderness. All you're going to find in Eleusis are madmen, raiders, and thieves hiding from the war."

I go to the door to look out again, and something crunches under my boot. I reach down and pick it up. It's a little wooden umbrella.

Something has been bugging me ever since we came into this place. I look at the dusty hula girls against the wall and tiki lamps and it finally sinks in that this half-collapsed shit shack is the Bamboo House of Dolls. The roof is down over the bar, but the jukebox is where it belongs. The glass dome in front is broken. Dust lies around the interior in small dunes. The player is cued up to Martin Denny's cover of "Miserlou."

"A friend of mine is still in the asylum. Do you think there's a chance if she's still in there that she's alive?"

"I couldn't say, but it's my understanding that whatever inmates remain in the asylum are of a more benign nature. The ones with strength and will escaped long ago."

Something tickles my hands and legs. Drytts. Hell's sand flies. They're not dangerous, just disgusting. If they find you and you stay still too long, others will come and you'll end up buried in them.

"We can't stay here. You have one hour to get us to Eleusis."

"One hour or what?"

He sounds defiant, like I hurt his feelings.

"Or I'm going to think you've been fucking me around this whole time. Don't forget. I'm the one with the knife. Let's start there and let our imaginations go."

He nods at the back door.

"The quickest way is that rise a hundred yards off. It's also the steepest and most dangerous."

"Lead the way."

"Is that an order?"

"A polite suggestion."

THE RISE JACK was talking about is a whole intersection that's been punched up out of the street at nearly a forty-five-degree angle. A couple of restaurants, a small shopping center, and a gas station hang in the air over our heads. The sinkhole below is so full of wrecked cars and motorcycles that it's nearly level with the street. The junk stews in the same bloody sewage that was in the sinkhole outside Hollywood Forever.

I start climbing, hanging on to gas pumps at the bottom and moving up to the empty garage. When I make it around there, I pull myself up on metal parking-lot crash posts. I turn around to check, and see Jack slowly following me up. I don't think he's happy to be around me anymore. His whole theory about fate having a reason for tossing us into the same salad has evaporated. He looks like all he wants is to get through this without ending up in Tartarus with Mammon.

As Jack climbs, cracks form under his handholds. He's followed me through the garage and is pulling himself up the crash posts. As he puts his weight on each post, the cracks under it widen. The last two posts wiggle like rotten teeth. My arm is wrapped around the solid base of the shopping-center sign. I move up to a newspaper vending machine that's anchored in the sidewalk. Jack grabs onto the solid foundation of the shopping-center sign before the posts give way.

When he's secure I crawl into the entrance of a liquor store. If you cut through the place, the back door will take us to the top of the rise.

The liquor store stinks inside. A thousand broken bottles of wine, vodka, beer, scotch, and soda have soaked through a mountain of junk food and the whole mess is piled against the front counter and front wall. The floor is sticky with dried booze and sugar, which is disgusting but helps me keep traction as I climb to the storeroom in back. Jack is right behind, baby-crawling past the empty shelves.

I'm at the back door when the shaking starts again. It's so subtle that it's almost not there. It feels like the muscle memory of a nasty dream. I thought it was an earthquake, but I think our climbing has upset the delicate balance that's kept this slab of L.A. junk wilderness upright.

The shaking turns into a steady vibration. Two heavy bodies scraping against each other. The bottles beneath us clatter together. Softly and then like a truckload of xylophones being pushed down a long flight of stairs. It's hard to hold on to the shelves as the tremors deepen. Parts of the ceiling fall down on us. There's a sick liquid moment when the whole intersection shifts. Up ahead, the rear wall cracks and the rest of the ceiling starts coming down. The whole liquor store is sliding forward.

"Move your ass, Jack."

I scramble past the shelves and kick off the top one, grabbing onto the door frame at the top. I climb to the back of the storeroom and pull on the door. The twisting building has jammed it shut. I grab the doorknob and shove the black blade into the metal lock. It pops out and clatters against the wall like a bell. The door swings open and I pull myself up onto the rear step.

Jack is stumbling over office furniture. Cracks open at my feet. The store is breaking away from this last anchor of ground.

The building growls and creaks like an iron elephant with the bends. It lurches. Slides left and down. Jack is pulling himself up on the door. I grab his wrist as a subterranean shriek of snapping concrete and sheering metal launches the liquor store down the way we came. It crashes into the garage and both structures shatter like hundred-ton dollhouses before disappearing into the sinkhole below. The slab sways like it's bobbing in a bathtub and begins to fall. I grab Jack and jump to the roof of a dry cleaner's beyond the edge of the slab.

I tuck and roll as we hit. Jack flops like a sockful of oatmeal thrown from a speeding car. When the section of road hits, one of the cleaner's walls collapses and we slide down the roof like worn-out kids at the worst amusement park in the world.

Jack and I lie on the broken pavement until the dust settles. We only slid a floor, so our asses are spanked and bruised but we're pretty much intact.

Jack was right. Eleusis is right where he said it would be. There's a twenty-foot stone wall topped with broken glass across the street. It's exactly how I pictured it. It wouldn't be Eleusis without the wall, Heaven's vision of paradise in the abyss. Hell's only gated community.

JACK IS STILL on his back when I get up and head for the wall. A couple of minutes later I hear him behind me.

"Thank you for saving me back there."

"Don't mention it. Really. Don't."

"I still think we were brought together to accomplish something bigger."

"If everything works out, maybe I'll get a chance to stop a war. That's pretty big, don't you think?"

Jack grunts.

"Anyway it's all, as the big brains say, academic, Jack. I saved you from Mammon and you got me to Eleusis. We're even-steven."

Up ahead, a gutted city bus has jumped the curb and

plowed into the stone wall. The damage is mostly blocked by the bus's body, but through the windshield I can see where part of the wall has collapsed. I glance back at Jack. He looks nervous and a little confused. Is that a good look or a bad look for a serial killer? Whichever, I want to cut this freak show loose. I climb into the driver's-side window and call back to Jack.

"Take it easy, man, and thanks for the memories."

He yells something after me, but I don't stop. I kick open the front door and head into the city.

Finally Eleusis.

Fuck me.

I wonder if Kasabian is watching me through the *Codex*? Is he eating pizza with Candy and giving her a blow-by-blow? He must be laughing his ass off by now.

Eleusis, God's city in the Inferno, halfway across Hell from Pandemonium, is part of goddamn North Hollywood. *Light Bringer,* Lucifer's biopic, was supposed to be shot in a Burbank soundstage just a couple of miles up the freeway. I'm still in L.A. This whole fucking world is L.A.

I'm almost there, Alice. I think. I hope. Who fucking knows anymore? I could walk a block and end up back in Venice or the cemetery. We seem to have come in a big circle from Hollywood back to Hollywood. But it's not the same Hollywood. And where I am can't be entirely random. Mammon was taking me somewhere and Jack has been taking me somewhere and I don't believe Mammon but I do believe Jack. He didn't have any reason to lie. He thought we were partners, Hope and Crosby on *The Road to Zanzibar.*

This is what I get for putting my life in the hands of a crazy road spirit. Mustang Sally would love wandering around like I have. More streets, more roads, more crazy-ass tracks in the dirt for her to claim. You're going to get a lot more salty peanuts than candy the next time we meet, Sally. No more sugar rushes for you.

I hear stones crunch and fall behind me. I'm not scared. I recognize Jack's footsteps. Don't get too close, Loony Tune. I really want to punch something right now.

On the other side of the rubble is a big intersection. Malls and parking on one side. A forties-style apartment house on another. The Scientology Celebrity Center nearby. There are bodies curled up under the dead trees and bushes where they've turned the celebrity center into a pagan flophouse. Most are dressed in hospital greens and bathrobes. A few are in straitjackets that look like they've been gnawed apart. There are even a few demented hellions with them. Refugees from the asylum. Finally something like good news. I'm getting closer.

There's faint noise in the distance. Yelling. Gunshots. Maybe even engines revving. Someone is having fun somewhere in Eleusis.

I should probably wait and get the lay of the land but one of these Sleeping Beauties knows where to find the asylum. I step down from the rubble and head across the street to the parking lot.

I don't get ten steps when Jack grabs me. I spin and come up with the knife under his chin.

"Do not even begin to try your Ripper act on me. I'm not one of your scared Whitechapel girlfriends. I'll teach you what every slash and cut you gave them feels like. I felt them in the arena and they don't feel good."

Jack looks past me, shaking his head. He raises his hand and points.

"Look at the street," he says.

I look over my shoulder, keeping the knife at his throat.

"I don't see anything."

"The sidewalks. The buildings. The windows. There are no proper joins. No right angles anywhere."

"Why would there be? Downtown is getting shaken to death like Lassie with a rat."

"It's not the tremors, sir. Look across the street at where the pavement is falling away."

"Don't call me 'sir.'"

I look to where he's pointing. The corner by the apartment building is shattered and sinking in the middle. The soil under the street is a mix of black mud and red muck.

"We're standing on a suicide road," he says. "The blood tide rises from beneath and eventually everything above drops down into it. This entire street could become a sinkhole at any moment."

I try to read him to see if he's bullshitting me. He looks as calm as can be expected with a knife at his throat.

"Then what are all these sleepyheads doing here?"

He looks at me like he's trying to teach a few first words to a particularly dumb parrot.

"These are the only safe parts of the city. Thieves and raiders won't come down here."

"'Safe' is a pretty loose term around here."

"Not for this sad lot. It's hide here or end up skewered."

"You'd know all about that, wouldn't you?"

"Yes, as a matter of fact. That's why I'm not anxious to go any farther."

"No one asked you to come this far."

"Have a wander on a suicide road and you could truly die down here."

"Are you still here, Jack? I didn't see you there."

I put the knife away and head to the parking lot across the street. As soon as I step into the intersection, I see that Jack was telling the truth. The pavement crunches under my boots like an eggshell suspended over quicksand. An image of Alice dead down here and stuck in the Limbo between Heaven and Hell flashes in my head. I hear Medea Bava's voice: *Alice was ours.*

No. She wasn't, you old witch. I would have known.

Are you really going to sacrifice yourself to save your great betrayer?

I push it all into the dark. Let the angel explain it to her. He's Mr. Sensitive. Medea will like him.

It's one thing for me to know that Jack was telling the truth and another for Jack to know I know it. I keep going. If I step lightly, the worst that happens is I sink an inch or so into the road at the weak spots. I don't look back or acknowledge Jack. The last thing I want is to owe him any more favors. Not that ignoring him means anything. Halfway across the street, I hear him behind me. It sounds like he's trying to crush wine out of cornflakes.

"Stay the hell away from me, Jack. This road won't hold if we bunch up."

That was the wrong thing to say. He thinks I'm leaving

him on the suicide road. I can hear him hurrying to catch up with me.

The road goes *snap, crackle, pop* and drops a few inches. Cracks shoot out from under us like black lightning. I run for the sidewalk. I sink lower into the road with each step. The lower I sink, the more the sewage muck tries to suck me backward and down into it. By the time I hit the sidewalk, it's like I'm doing some kind of hick aerobics, stumbling like a pig farmer through shit while trying to get my knees up high for a real Jane Fonda workout. Feel the burn, Jethro.

The corner of the sidewalk crumbles as I jump from the muck, but a couple of steps in, it holds. I finally turn around and there's Jack. Up to his knees in blood and mud. It's where he belongs. Still dreaming of knives and all the women no one knows about because he dumped them like fish food into the drink. Fuck him. Let him go.

But I know the look on his face. It's what I looked like when I fell from the sky into Pandemonium. It's a feeling way beyond fear because your brain can't get hold of it enough to be afraid. You want to be afraid. Afraid would be a hundred times better than this. This is total fucking incomprehension at what's happening and it's all happening to you. It's being sane one second and stark raving spiders-tunneling-their-way-out-from-under-your-skin insane the next.

I kneel by the edge of the corner far enough back so I know the ground is solid and I hold out my hand. It's the least I can do. Literally the least.

Jack scrambles for it in a panicked stumbling slog, sinking faster now that he sees a lifeline. He's almost up to his waist by the time he reaches the corner.

"Help me!" he yells. I move my hand half an inch closer.

He's practically swimming when he reaches the corner. God-dammit. He gets close enough to grab a couple of my fingers. I close my hand around his and pull. It's the very least I can do. I'm amazed and a little pissed off when he swings a leg onto the sidewalk. I let go and let him get out the rest of the way on his own. I look over at the celebrity-center bushes where the asylum refugees have been passed out. They took off. They're crazy. Not stupid. The street was sinking. I lean back against the low wall around the mall and look up at the black boiling sky. Are you explaining to Candy for the five-hundredth time what an asshole I am, Kasabian? Is she pissed at me for saving this walking, talking piece of shit? Candy wouldn't have done it. She'd have put her boot on Jack's head and helped him down under the muck. And I would have loved her for it.

Panting and stinking like sewage and rotten fish, Jack pulls himself onto the sidewalk and collapses. I light a Male-diction.

"Stay over there, Jack. You smell like what comes out of Moby-Dick after a truck-stop burrito."

He just lies there gasping and trembling like a trout tossed on land by a passing boat.

I smoke for a couple of minutes, until Jack stops shaking.

"You scared off all my crazies, you know. I was going to get them to take me to the asylum. Now they're gone. Do you know where it is? Be very careful how you answer. If you lie, I'll know it and I'm going to feed you back into the muck face-first."

He points to a dome on top of a hill that's mostly mud and dead grass. Huts and lean-tos made of scrap lumber, flattened aluminum cans, and drywall from the asylum flow from the top of the hill and down the sides like junkyard lava. Looks like a lot of the crazies had it together enough to escape, but not enough to cut the apron strings and leave home.

I shake my head. I smoke.

Maybe this jigsaw-puzzle L.A. is God's payback for burning Eden. In the old days, when I was killing for Azazel down here, I hardly ever thought about the guy. Now I can't get him out of my head. He's like the high school sweetheart you moan about whenever you've had a few too many highballs. You don't want to think about her. In fact, you never think about her until you've poisoned your brain with umbrella drinks. Then she's one big whiny question mark in your life. Where did it all go wrong, baby?

Only God and I never went steady. I barely thought of him in the world and only thought of him Downtown because in the brief time Mom sent me to Sunday school, they taught me that he was a God of love and forgiveness. Just what the doctor ordered. Forgive me for all the scams and games and shenanigans and rain down that love on me or at least call me a cab. Even Hitler got to die before climbing into the coal cart. Nothing. Nada. Turns out when I reached into the hat, I didn't pull out the shiny happy Sunday school God of Love. I got the Old Testament God of wrath. Cities turned to salt. Newborns killed in their cribs. *Twin Peaks* canceled when it was getting good again. No one came to save my charbroiled ass. Just like Mason. But ever since then I think the big man has had his eye on me, slipping me a rubber cigar every now and then. Like right now.

Where Jack is pointing is the Griffith Park Observatory.

James Dean shot part of *Rebel Without a Cause* there. Any tourist with cab fare can visit the damn place. Back home it would take me an hour to get there and back to the hotel, where Candy and I could break more furniture. But no. I have to dodge sinkholes, earthquakes, Hellions, and serial killers to get somewhere that in any sane universe I could take the bus to. I wish I could say, "No more Mr. Nice Guy," but the boat sailed on that one a long time ago.

I take a drag on the Malediction.

"Hey, Jack. What were you before you became a monster?"

He pushes himself onto his knees, stands, and tries to wipe the mud and blood off his clothes.

"An upholsterer," he says.

"Seriously?"

He looks at me.

"Yes."

"I guess 'Ripper' sounds better in the papers than 'Jack the Ottoman Repairman.' "

He ignores me, knocking mud off his feet until you can see his shoes. Maybe he's right. Who needs Heaven when Hell makes so much more sense?

"Okay, Jack. This is where we part ways. I'm heading straight up that hill. You can go anywhere you like, but I'd stay out of Pandemonium for a while. They'll have probably noticed they're down one general."

"You can't just abandon me here."

"I think I just did. You're in paradise. It's a world of shit, but it's better than being in a sardine can for the next million years, isn't it?"

"Can I at least come with you? You won't have to take care of me."

"I just saved you a second time. I don't care what you do. You want to follow? It's no skin off my ass, but get in my way once, and I'll kill you just like I'd kill any Hellion."

He says, "Understood," but I'm already moving.

I RUN AT a steady pace, but I don't sprint. The street is straight, but there's plenty that can come at me from side streets and the scorched foliage around the old buildings. I let the angel out a little to expand my senses and look for trouble. Even this far off the suicide road, the land under the buildings isn't stable. Walls sag on old apartment houses and wooden Victorians have their walls held up with tree trunks and wooden power poles cut to length.

The palms that line both sides of the road burn like the ones on Sunset, turning the dark street orange and brighter than streetlights would.

There are more pagan souls on the street as I go deeper into Eleusis, away from the wall and the suicide road. They duck under cars and cower in burned-out buildings when they see me coming and I remember that I'm wearing a Hellion face. Thanks for reminding me. It still burns a little and it's starting to itch as it heals. One more level of bullshit to deal with, but at least it's clearing the streets.

A block ahead, one of the big apartment buildings has collapsed across the road. I slow down as I get closer. Plenty of places to hide in all that rubble. A Hellion dressed in army-issue pants and a red leather jacket sprints around the corner, sees me, and hauls ass my way. I grab the na'at from my coat. Alice is right up the hill and I'm not stopping now for anyone. I twist my wrist so the blade pops out at the na'at's tip. The Hellion is female, soon to be a dead female. As she gets closer she barks at me in frantic Hellion. She's out of breath and her voice is rough. It takes me a minute to figure out what she's saying and then I get it.

"Run, asshole!"

A second later more of them come tearing ass into the street. Maybe twenty of them. Like the woman in half a uniform, they're deserters, though they don't look like they have enough gear or sense to be raiders. Just a bunch of non-coms who'd rather live on what they can steal from empty homes and liquor stores than get stomped by God's golden hordes. I can sympathize. They're running straight at me, but from the looks on their faces, they're not stopping anytime soon.

I sprint toward them, the na'at up and out. I'm not letting a few purse snatchers and shoplifters get in my way. They part like the Red Sea when they see me coming. I pick up speed. If there are more raiders on the other side, they won't be expecting me. I can see Griffith Observatory from here, so I'm not heading down any streets so God can get his rocks off by dumping me in Malibu or Disneyland.

A metallic roar fills the air and echoes off the buildings. Telltale mechanical clicking after that, like a thousand clocks ticking out of time. A few last deserters make it around the collapsed house just long enough to see freedom before being snatched back by steel claws like a fistful of butcher knives.

They're bunched together when they make it around the building. All the light shows is a mass of gracefully moving shoulders and flexible backs so they look like a clockwork flood. A Hellion dressed in priest's robes gives up and stops running. The hellhounds don't even slow down. The Hellion disappears into a wet spray of bones and thick, clear blood.

Like on a synchronized mechanical cue, half the hell-hound pack rears up and attacks the raiders from the back. Ambush predators. They get their steel teeth into the prey's throat and choke them or drive them headfirst into the ground and snap their necks. Hellhounds are strange and beautiful things. Candy would dig them. I'd love them more if I were seeing them from a little farther away. Like, say, France. The part of the pack not having thieves for lunch breaks from the larger pack and heads down my way. I look like a Hellion. To their bottled peanut brains I'm part of the gang they're turning to chum. The strategy in this situation is simple. Run the other way.

I keep the na'at open. Waving it at these clockwork poodles would be like trying to scare King Kong with a lit cigarette, but it'll clear the street of slow Hellions if they get in my way.

Jack's been following me after all. He's in the middle of the street a block down. I think he's hypnotized by the hounds. He's probably never seen them at work before. When he sees me coming, it snaps him out of it and he starts running. He's not fast enough. I pass him easily, thinking of the old joke. When you're running from a bear, you don't have to be the fastest runner. You just have to be faster than the guy behind you.

I hear Jack behind me whining and shouting something. I

don't look back. I can hear the hounds' clockwork legs and jaws closing in. They're too fast. I'm not going to make it.

I cut from the street and onto the sidewalk. We're not back to the suicide road, but maybe we can make our own killer road right here.

I slow down just a hair. Let the hounds get a bead on me and close in. I hold out the na'at. If I'm wrong, this is going to be a messy way to go, but it's better than old age or being poisoned by bad clams.

We're near a block of half-collapsed houses. As the hounds close in, I hold out the na'at and let it rip through the support poles holding the walls up. At first nothing happens, but then there's a crash behind me, followed by another and another. It sounds like the whole block is coming down, but I'm not slowing down to look.

I hear a hound right behind me. It's scraping and clatter-ing like it's taken heavy damage, but it's gaining on me. I cut to the side, hoping the huge thing's momentum will carry it past. It does and it runs right into a support post on the side of a house. I see it just before it happens and cut back into the street so I don't get crushed. I outrun the wall. Too bad I can't outrun the falling debris. Something clips me right above my left ear and that's all she wrote. Hello pavement. I love you, pavement. I think I'll stay here a while.

WHEN I OPEN my eyes a billowing black snake is crawling over me. Its belly is a furnace and its body is the whole sky and it will take the rest of eternity to pass. I can wait. If this universe burns, I have the other one that Muninn gave me in my pocket. Let the show roll on.

I WAKE UP flat on my back and moving. I'm on a flatbed with heavy wire mesh over the top. It's being towed by a Unimog. Someone shifts and grinds the truck's gears. There are maybe eighteen Hellions back here with me. Some sitting up. Some on their backs. Others are leaking clear blood where they were ripped open by big hellhound jaws. I recognize some of them. They're the Hellions that were running from the hounds.

The Unimog hits a bump and one of the leaking Hellions blips out of existence.

Someone says, "That was a good trick back there with your na'at."

I turn my head so I'm looking up. There's a smiling Hellion looking down at me.

"So good I coldcocked myself with a brick," I say.

Like a lot of Hellions, he looks like a spiky horned toad after some Hollywood plastic surgery. Slim down the cheeks and neck. A chin implant that gives him a long horse face. He's bruised and battered. It looks like the beat-down took his stubby horns, too. But his big white canines are still there. Those really hurt when they dig into you. Trying to get a Hellion off when he's got a good hold of you with his choppers is like trying to coax a moray eel into a round of minigolf with knock-knock jokes.

I rub the side of my head. There's sticky blood in my hair. I pull the hood back up, covering up the blood. I touch my face. Good. Mammon's skin is still there.

I lean on my elbows and look up front. The flame job and animal skulls wired to the front of the truck look familiar. This is the same damned posse that's been chasing Jack and me since Pandemonium. The saps caught me and they don't even know it. If I wasn't flat on my back being hauled around suicide roads in a wire-mesh chicken coop to who the fuck knows where, I'd feel like a real winner right now.

"Where's the guy I was with? A damned soul."

"Oh, him," the Hellion snickers. "He seemed like a nice guy. When you were out cold, he stole your bag and ran off."

I feel around for the leather satchel with my face in it. It's gone.

"A real nice guy," snickers the Hellion.

I reach into my coat for Mammon's flask of Aqua Regia, but it's not there. The little prick even stole my booze. Now he really has to die.

I should have cut Jack loose the moment we saw Eleusis. I should have let the sinkhole take him. The goddamn angel in my head softens me up at those moments. Every time I think we've found a balance point, it shifts its weight one sneaky gram at a time until it's standing straight and I'm flailing around like a blind man on black ice. I will not let God's little bootlicker win. I'm a nephilim, you haloed fuck. You're part of me and you better learn to take the bad, me, with the good, you, or I swear I'll put a double barrel to my head and do a Hemingway. Then we'll see which one of us is left to Mr. Clean the wall.

"I'm Berith," says the Hellion. "Who are you?"

Shit. For fifty points, name a Hellion I haven't killed.

"Ruax," I say. I wait to hear "Ruax is dead" or "He's my brother-in-law," but Berith just nods.

I sit up and lean against the wire-mesh enclosure.

"Where are we headed?"

"No idea. Jail I suppose."

A Hellion with a mangled arm pipes up.

"Then back to Pandemonium. We're so fucked."

Berith looks out at the road.

"I don't want to think about that."

The truck rolls steadily, but it's not in a rush to get any-where. The posse up front is passing bottles around. I don't suppose they'd be too keen on sharing with us prisoners. Maybe I can put my fist through the mesh and ask one nicely with my boot on his throat.

I get up and grab hold of a section of the fence. And promptly land on my back, feeling like someone just handed me a glass of whiskey with a thousand-volt chaser.

Berith laughs.

"Neat trick, eh? One of the Malebranche's hexes. You can touch the walls of your cell all you want, but the moment you come at it with attitude, well, you see what happens."

"Thanks for the warning."

"We're all going to be dead soon. We need to have a few laughs along the way."

I put my hand on the fence. Nothing happens. Holding on to it, I pull myself to my feet. We're past all the houses and apartments and into a wider main street. Somewhere around Western maybe. Lots of burned-out buildings, but with a little something extra. My face.

Wanted posters offering a hefty reward cover every building, signpost, and bus kiosk still standing.

I guess someone figured out that Mammon and his staff are missing. Mason will know who did it, but that's still goddamn fast to get posters plastered all over the place. Even with all the map games this place has been playing on me, the angel, who's better at these things than I am, is sure we haven't been here more than a day. And how does Mason even know I'm heading for Eleusis and not wandering the streets of Pandemonium like the Flying Dutchman? Jack couldn't have made it back yet and ratted me out. With my face in a bag he can claim he killed me and get the reward. The bastard will be drinking mai tais and eating prime rib before I get near the asylum.

I hear cheering voices. There must be a lot of them if they're loud enough to hear over the Unimog's rumble and grinding gears. A couple of more blocks down, there's a stadium. It's not as big as the L.A. Coliseum. It's more like the place well-off parents pay for so their sprogs can play soccer on a regulation field that's not full of beer cans and gopher holes. From the tone of the crowd, they're not playing in there.

We turn off the main road and onto a two-lane driveway behind the stadium and roll alongside what looks like a holding area for the posse's prisoners. Big wire-mesh pens and RVs with blacked-out windows hold dozens of dirty, frightened Hellions. The fact that they're being held in a stadium tells me that the posse isn't above having a little fun with their prisoners before they're shipped back to Pandemonium.

The truck stops. Six Hellions in SWAT body armor, carrying shotguns and homemade morning stars, hustle us off the flatbed and into the pens, where we have a clear view of the playing field.

Some people have dreams where they show up for final exams in their underwear or for a course they didn't know they were taking. Other people wake up in the middle of the ocean. There's land in the distance, but no matter how hard they swim, they never get any closer. Me, I dream about the arena. Shrinks call these "anxiety dreams." I call them road maps. They show you where you've been and where you're headed. A dream about being lost at sea doesn't mean you're going to end up as an extra on *Gilligan's Island,* but it probably means you've gone off track somewhere. For me it's even simpler. I don't dream in metaphors. When I dream about the arena, I'm really dreaming a dream about the arena.

In my heart of hearts I've always known I wasn't finished with the place. It's like a drunk who goes on the wagon but decides to pitch his tent in the Jack Daniel's parking lot. Yeah, he cleaned up, but he didn't run very far from what made him a lush in the first place.

Once I'd killed the other members of my old magic Circle and sent Mason Downtown, I should have walked away from the whole hoodoo world and become just another brain-dead civilian. Take a mail-order course in taxidermy or sell maps of the stars' homes to tourists. Instead I hung around with Lurkers, renegade angels, and Jades. I'm surprised it's taken me this long to get back here. If the Bamboo House of Dolls didn't have such a high-quality jukebox and Carlos didn't make such good tamales, I would have been back here months ago and this would all be over with.

All those dreams about tests and being lost and being back

in the blood and the dust are just lines on a map. The elevation marks reveal that no matter how low you get, there's always somewhere lower to fall.

Some of the Hellions from the flatbed go right up to the fence to get a good look at the current fight, trying to convince themselves they're not seeing what they're seeing. Others, the ones with a firmer grip on reality, are at the far end of the pen puking and shitting themselves. They're not in denial about what's coming.

The arena isn't much to see. Just a flat soccer field with semis parked a hundred feet apart to mark the boundaries of the killing floor. Hellions and even a few pagan collaborators fill the stands between the trucks, drinking, cheering, and throwing bottles and rocks at the Hellion prisoners forced to fight each other. I shake my head. Lucifer wouldn't have put up with the peanut gallery getting his arena floor messy. These small-time bullies have no class.

I look around the stadium, not really paying attention to the current fight. There's the unmistakable sound of metal smashing into meat and bone. The crowd cheers. The bone crunch comes again. A cheer. Then a bigger cheer. I go to the fence and look through. It looks like the Hellion who was to be chopped into McNuggets got the other fighter in the throat with a knife when he got too close. They both fall over and disappear. Cue the crowd. People drink and pay off wagers. It's a party and they take their time about it.

A few minutes later armored guards grab more prisoners from the pen. Berith is with them. He looks at me like he thinks I'm going to do something about it. All I do is stay by the fence to watch. The guards walk the group out to the middle of the killing floor and hand them weapons. Every Hellion was a soldier once. They were all part of the rebel legions in Heaven, but that was a long time ago. In the arena the prisoners look at the rusty swords and shields in their hands like they've never seen anything like them before. That's the lousy thing about shock. It makes you look stupid.

I remember my first time in the arena. It wasn't like this bumpkin retrofit. The arena in Pandemonium was built for blood sports and nothing else. It was like the Roman Colosseum, but clad in plates of bronze and ivory and hung with sculpted bone chandeliers over each entrance. It was full of false walls that could be moved to change the fighting floor. There were trapdoors and chutes where beasts and fighters could be lifted or shot into the arena in a few seconds. The crowds were connoisseurs of pain.

My first fight was against a human soul. The arena bookers thought it would be a hoot to put the one living guy in Hell up against one of his dead brethren. The thing is, the guy I was up against was from one of the lowest regions, one reserved for child killers, so I didn't exactly think of him as one of my brethren.

I'd been in Hell long enough to have built up a thick skin of fury. I was still a circus attraction back then. The living freak to be passed around and used and gawked at like a pickled punk. And I was sure as shit a long way from being Sandman Slim.

I went into the fight all teeth and claws and righteous idiot fury. It was the first time I used a na'at and I had no idea what to do with it. I can't say I was scared going up against a real killer. I was too crazy for that, and when I did think about it, more than anything I was amazed at where my life had taken me. The unreality of Hell became even more unreal. That's probably what saved me.

The Kid Killer knew how to use blades and I didn't. He gave me my first scars. Later they changed me, made me stronger, and I became a kind of living body armor. But that night in the arena, the slashes just hurt.

I tried using the na'at the way I'd seen Hellions use it, but I mostly bounced it off the ground and hit myself in the face when it sprang open into different configurations. That routine went for big laughs.

I wish I could say I finished the Kid Killer with a flashy na'at move, but the blood and pain nudged me from crazy into Norman Bates territory. And the crazier I got, the more the crowd cheered. When I managed to knock the Kid Killer down, I climbed on top of him, pinned his arms, and choked the fucker until his eyes bulged out like twin eight balls. You haven't seen surprised until you've seen a dead man realize he's about to die again. Later, one of my guards explained to me about Tartarus and the double dead.

I'd never killed anyone before and knew I was supposed to feel bad about it, but I didn't. I felt just the opposite. These geniuses were training me to kill, building up my strength and turning me into the monster I was always meant to be. Later, when Azazel made me his assassin, I thanked every Hellion I killed for their contribution to my schooling. The looks on their faces when I cut their throats never got old.

I'm glad Alice never saw me in the arena. I hope Kasabian has the brains not to show Candy.

What none of the Hellions except maybe Lucifer understood was that when I stepped onto the killing floor, I wasn't fighting an opponent. I was fighting all of Hell. When I killed a beast or a soul, I was killing every leering, putrid Hellion in existence. The nouveaux riches in the stands came for a fight. I was there for extermination, and every time I murdered them, it felt like Christmas morning. That's what I don't want Candy to see. Back in L.A. we talk about being monsters together, but it's not the same thing. I don't have any problems with my L.A. monster side, but I don't want her to see the kind of monster that comes out when I'm the real Sandman Slim.

I don't want to watch Berith and the other lead-footed fighters. I know how this is going to go. I don't want to see it again. The angel wants me to shout some strategy or encouragement to Berith. But it's already too late for him. He's down in the dust and disappears less than a minute later. The crowd cheers the winners, but cheers even harder when the guards knife each of them in the back. Hellion humor isn't what you'd call sophisticated.

I want out of here, but I don't want to get stomped by a hundred armed Hellions. I look around for a good shadow. There's one on the ground at the far end of the pen. I walk over, trying to look like I'm going over to puke. When I stick my foot into the dark, the ground is solid. The posse has thrown up an antihoodoo cloak around the place. I can't use any decent magic in here. What's Plan B? Hiding is my favorite choice, but everyone in the holding cell is trying to hide behind everyone else. It's like the saddest square dance you ever saw in here.

I still have on my coat and hoodie, so my human arms are

covered up. I feel inside the coat. The na'at is still there. So's the knife, Lucifer's stone, the plastic rabbit, and Muninn's crystal. I check my leg. The pistol is still taped to my ankle. The posse must have just tossed me into the flatbed. Good. That means they're drunk or just plain stupid. I like stupid. There are lots of possibilities in stupid.

Instead of hiding in the back, when the guards come back looking for someone else to toss to the wolves, I move up by the gates. The two closest guards look me over and whisper to each other. The talker motions me to come closer so I'm right against the gate.

The talker walks over to me. He has a sickly green complexion and a smashed cheekbone. In one hand he's holding a long truncheon. A piece of flexible metal covered in leather. When we're close together he reaches between the gates and pops me in the face with the truncheon's butt. The guards just about bust a gut at me holding my bruised nose. He takes a step forward, presses his face into the space between the gates, and spits at me. I pivot and swing, catching him under the chin with my fist. His body goes limp. I reach between the gates, get a hand behind his head and the other around his throat, and pull. The gates bow in and he starts slipping through. The other guards pounce on him, pulling him out. The gates bulge in as I get his head and the tops of his shoulders through, like he's being born out of twisted wire and steel. It's a fun tug-o'-war we've got going. I wonder if this is how giraffes were invented.

The guards get together and do a nicely coordinated group pull. I've got my death grip and dig in my heels, but they're dragging both of us toward the gate. I can't hold the guard, but I don't want to let him go. When I'm sure they're going to get him away from me, I lean down, get a good grip with my teeth, and let go. The guard shoots out of the gates like they're a solid metal slingshot and lands with his hands over his face, screaming and coughing up blood. I wait for the rest of the guards to look at me before I spit his nose on the ground in front of them. I expect them to rush me, but they go into a huddle. Their buddy is on the ground screaming, but they've already forgotten about him.

The huddle doesn't last long. One of the guards takes charge and beckons over a couple of other guards to take away the idiot who lost his nose. The head guard comes close to the gate, but out of biting range. He's wearing a faux military/law enforcement uniform, the kind you see bounty hunters wear. It gives them an air of authority, but isn't close enough to any specific uniform to get them busted for impersonating an officer. It's sad the assholes they'll sell uniforms to these days.

"Come here," he says.

I stand pat.

"Come here."

"I can't hear you clear over here, Audie Murphy. Get a little closer."

He signals to the other guards. They pull their pistols and shotguns and point them at me.

"I'm going to open the gate and you're going to come with me."

"What if you forget to say 'Simon says' and I don't?"

"My men will shoot everyone else in the pen."

So much for honor among thieves. I try to look like it's

a hard choice, but all I want is out and I'm not sticking my neck out for any more psycho killers today thanks. It's all I can do not to jump into his arms and say, "Home, Jeeves." Finally I nod.

"Yeah. Okay. I'll come."

Audie gestures a couple of other guards over to open the gates. Everyone keeps their guns on me as we walk past the pens and RVs to the killing floor.

The place reeks of dust, sweat, and blood. When I step onto the floor, the crowd shrieks like banshees at spring break. The scene is twisted and familiar and, in a terrible way, comforting.

The guards lay out weapons on the ground. I start to reach for the na'at in my coat, but decide that no one around here needs to know anything about me other than that I don't like getting spit on.

The gear on the ground looks like it was pulled out of a garbage dump. Rusting swords and battle-axes. Spears with broken shafts repaired with duct tape. I stroll around the weapons like a window shopper at Christmas, taking my time. I find a battered old na'at and pick it up. It's stiff, and the first time I try to open it, it jams. I get down on one knee and whack it against the steel toes on one of my boots. It springs out to full length and holds. I notice guards haven't hauled out any other prisoners for me to fight. That means they're going to throw guards at me to fight. I wonder how many.

Turns out it's just one.

When my opponent comes out, I'm not sure if it's a Hellion or someone is backing a moving van into the arena. The guy is big the way a sonic boom is loud. Just a big knot of muscles with a head on top, like a cherry balanced on a fist. He's holding a shield the size of a car hood in one hand and has a Vernalis over his other. A Vernalis is like a metal crab claw that extends up to the fighter's elbow and is as long as an average person is tall. When it snaps shut, it can cut a tree in half. Maybe I should have stayed in the back of the pen with the other scaredy-cats. I'm giving serious consideration to cutting and running, but the guards are still holding guns on me. And I can't do any hoodoo here, can't even click my heels three times and say there's no place like home.

No one gives a signal, blows a whistle, or drops a hanky. Crab Man just howls and charges me. I get out of his way, but not too far or too fast. I stay put and try to look confused long enough to spring the na'at's blade and slice the Crab Man's Vernalis arm. I leave a nice gash but don't do any real damage.

He howls, some in pain and some because he didn't get to draw first blood. He swings the Vernalis at me like a club, but it's a feint. When I move in to stick him, he brings the shield around like a battering ram. I throw myself on the ground just before the shield splatters me like a dump truck. I roll to my feet and Crab Man and I circle each other. I try to extend the na'at again, but the mechanism jams when it's just halfway out.

I can't fight him like this. The Vernalis gives him too much reach. I need to get in close.

I attack this time, feinting left and right. Getting the shield and claw swinging at me just a little too late. I duck forward, closing the distance between us. Crab Man is used to fighters not wanting to get near him, so he doesn't have a lot of inside defense. I spear him in the side, but he's fast for a guy his size. He catches me in the back with a big elbow and I fall against him. He snaps his knee up hard enough to toss me on my back ten feet away. The Vernalis crashes into the ground near my head. I roll out of the way just as Crab Man spits a ball of fire at me. I reflexively block it with a kind of shield hex that bounces the attack back at the opponent. Goddamn. They left a hole in the cloak for the fighters. We can throw hoodoo out here. If the Andes Mountains weren't trying to beat me to death, I could probably get right out of here.

I throw a blinding hex at Crab Man's eyes. Part of it hits his arm, so I only get one eye. He howls like I pissed on his Batman #1 and a bolt of lightning hits the ground a few feet behind me. He has some big bad hoodoo under that claw, but I have an angel in my head and it can see the flash of power when he throws the big stuff.

I move around him, trying to stay on his blind side and draw him in closer. The magic he tosses at me is like the rest of him. Big and powerful, but not all that fast or creative. Being in the arena with him is like playing tennis in a meteor shower, but one where I can see the meteors a second before they hit. I keep tossing sharp little barbs of hoodoo at him. Waves of white-hot razors at his legs. Blasts of arctic cold at his eyes and balls. Muscle disruptors that have him shaking and spasming like an epileptic. But I can't pull out the big stuff. I could air-burst this place and turn the air into a blowtorch, but Crab Man is too close and the arena's too small and burning myself up with him isn't part of what little strategy I have.

Crab Man keeps on with the blockbuster spells, raining fire and brimstone. If he keeps on tossing the big stuff this fast, all I have to do is keep out of his way and he'll wear himself out.

I toss a starburst into his face. It starts as a fist-size ball of plasma that explodes into a thousand burning pieces of shrapnel. Crab Man raises his shield to block the hex and I slide in underneath, thrusting the na'at at his gut, going for a kill shot.

The fireballs chew up his face, but he protects his one working eye and brings his shield down at me like a guillotine. I get the na'at into his gut a few inches, but not far enough to finish him. He swings the shield at my head, but I duck it. He raises it high and brings it straight down on the na'at, snapping it in half. That's not supposed to happen. When a na'at is hit like that, it goes limp and bends in the middle like rubber. Mine shatters like glass. The break is clean and bright like someone's taken a hacksaw to the thing and cut partway through it. I look at Crab Man. The na'at was rigged and he knew it. In the second it takes me to understand that, he gets my left arm in the Vernalis and closes the pincers. There's a single white convulsion of pain as he crushes my arm and snaps it off a few inches below my shoulder. It's a race between the arm and me to see who can hit the ground first. I win.

The crowd is going completely apeshit. For a second, the mad screaming and stomping sounds like I'm back in the real arena. I relax. I don't want to croak in a backwater Hooverville soccer-mom park, but being back in the real arena, I can die happy.

Crab Man is bowing all the way around the stadium. Me, I

just lie there and bleed. I'm done and he knows it. I want to go to sleep and stay that way. The angel in my head starts shouting. He reminds me that if I go out, I'll die and so will Alice.

I let my mind float away and the pain takes me over completely. The agony of crushed muscles and bones revs my engines nicely. I bark a Hellion combat spell to slow the bleeding and another to suck the blood into the dirt so no one will notice it's human.

Crab Man is soaking up the love. A few more bows and he'll come back and finish me.

John Wayne wouldn't shoot a man in the back, but that's my favorite target.

I manifest the Gladius and drag myself up. I'm not what you'd call steady on my feet, but I'm close enough that I don't have to be. I raise the Gladius as high as I can and slice off Crab Man's Vernalis arm. The crowd goes silent. Crab Man stares at his stump. I take off one of his legs next. He falls on his face, balancing on one arm and one leg. He's trying to move around to face me so he can attack. He swings his shield blindly, hoping I get too close and he can crush me. I let him close the distance before taking that arm, too. I keep waiting for the armed guards to open up with the shotguns, but they're watching, as stunned as the drunks in the stands. I stagger around in front of Crab Man. I want him to see this.

He's got one leg left and I slice that off at the knee. I want him to look in my eyes. I want the crowd to soak up every minute of this. I'm killing all of them. Every portion of pain I bring on Crab Man I'm bringing down on them. Genocide is evil and evil tastes good right now.

I slash Crab Man from right to left, through his chest. Before he comes apart, I swing the Gladius up and over, slicing him neatly from skull to ass. He falls apart in four big cauterized chunks of honey-baked ham.

That, ladies and gentlemen, is what we call showmanship, with love from Sandman Slim.

The stadium is still quiet, like all the air has been sucked out of the place. But all it takes is for someone to drop a bottle and the sound sets everyone off at once. You didn't see that coming, did you? Some ugly half-dead Hellion foot soldier that could pull out a Gladius. Sleep tight wondering what other secret things us infantry grunts can do.

My left arm has stopped bleeding, but it's still a big open wound. I bark a pain spell, hold the Gladius to my arm, and burn the wound closed. Then I fall over and drift into a comforting blackness.

I feel a couple of guards drag me back to the holding pens. I don't go back into the pen with the other prisoners. They toss me into one of the blacked-out RVs alone. Even through the half-dead haze I can see they're scared shitless. Maybe I'm a spy or an officer from Pandemonium come to check up on them and they just tossed me into a death pit with a roid-rage moron. The smell of my burned skin is making me nauseous. Damn I could go for a cigarette right now.

I feel around for the Maledictions. This really is Hell. One cigarette left and it was crushed beyond all recognition in the fight. I toss the pack into the dark. The angel is trying to remind me of something. I reach back into the pocket and find Muninn's hoodoo healing egg. I bite into it and something soothing and sweet flows down my throat. In a few seconds my head is clear. I'm still weak, but the pain is gone and the world feels firm under my ass.

I let the angel loose. I need to think through this, because unless my new stump has a 007 plan to get us out of here, I'm going to have to call leaving my arm back in the arena a major setback.

I wonder if there's a way to turn off the antihoodoo cloak around this place. I'm not too proud to crawl into a shadow and whimper in the Room for an eternity or two. Mason's already putting up wanted posters. He knows I'm here. What do I care if one of his pet magicians detects me using the key? But I'm back in the holding area and the cloak is on, so I can't throw any hoodoo. And there's no way I'm fighting my way through all those guards with a wing clipped.

I need to stop for a minute and catch my breath. I don't know how long Muninn's egg is going to last. I need to keep moving while it does. I let the angel take over my senses. It can see right through the RV's tin-can walls.

I expect to see Rommel and the Afrika Corps around the place, but there isn't a Hellion within a hundred yards of me. I'm Chernobyl in a white-trash pied-à-terre. The angel does a three hundred-and-sixty-degree scan around the place. The few Hellions brave enough to be within eyesight are all on the arena side of the RV. Behind me is an empty field. But the RV is protected by the same Malebranche hex that zapped me good back in the flatbed. I cut a person-size hole in the wall and fall through. If I keep the RV between me and the posse, I just might be able to slink away into the dark with my tail tucked between my legs.

I guess this is Plan B.

JUST A FEW blocks away the streets are packed. I'm not sure where I am. I try to look nonchalant with my missing arm and the side of my coat soaked with dried blood and scorched by the Gladius. The crowd makes it easy to disappear. So does the fact that a lot of the losers lying in the street and begging around the food stalls don't look much better than me.

I wonder if any of the big brains back at the stadium have figured out I'm not in the RV anymore. One of the brave ones is going to check out the arm I left behind, see that it's human, and eventually figure out who it belongs to. My wanted posters are all over, so knowing the arm is mine doesn't bother me, but I hate the idea that some Hellion cocksucker is going to stick it on his wall as a trophy.

This is the first crowded patch of land I've seen in Eleusis. Hard-core raider country. Instead of hitting the individual corner markets, the enterprising ones have cleared them out and set up their own stalls. It's a county-fair midway, full of ugly Hellspawn and starving pagans desperate or brave or stupid enough to pick through the gutters and garbage for leftovers. Looking at what's going on at the stadium and the ruthless bastards picking the city clean out here, I can't see much difference between the raiders and the posse that followed Jack and me except who pays their salaries. It makes me wonder how many soldiers in Lucifer's legions were true believers and how many were simple mercenaries. Another nice design job, God. You ate your roughage and shit out an angelic army that could be bought off with beer and Twinkies.

There are impressive cracks in the sides of some buildings. Like the houses, some are supported by power poles. Others by gas-station hydraulic lifts and broken-down backhoes. There are open cesspits on the side streets near piles of trash two stories high. That's where most of the crazies and the pagans hang out, picking up and pocketing anything they can eat or trade. Cracks in the sidewalk ooze sewagey blood, but I don't see any big sinkholes. That's probably why everyone is bunched up in this part of town.

Being crippled like this isn't going to make getting Alice out of the asylum any easier, but nowhere's going to be safe when Mason starts his war. There's no way around it. The trip is a package deal. I have to get Alice and I have to stop Mason. One doesn't mean a goddamn thing without the other.

I keep touching my left side, looking for my missing arm, wondering if I made a mistake. Maybe I'm still lying on the street where the brick tagged me on the side of the head. Maybe Crab Man hit me with an illusion hex and my arm is still there. I swear I can feel my fingers move. But that's just phantom limb syndrome. It'll take a while for all the nerves that went to the arm to realize there's nothing there and die. Maybe when I get home, Allegra can set me up with a big steel Iron Man mitt. That would scare the ugly off the baddest Lurkers. Sandman Slim, the cyborg nephilim.

The street is full of stalls, and raiders make the place almost look like regular Hell. But it's not and I still don't know where I am. It looks like Eleusis's wall goes all the way around Griffith Park from the 101 on one side and the Golden State Freeway on the other. I can still see the Observatory asylum dead north. If someone around here had a cannon, they could shoot me straight up the hill and I'd be there. I need to find one of the tourist roads. If I tried climbing the damned hill through the trees, I'd still be going an hour after the universe ended. I need some elevation to get my bearings.

A few Kissi wander through the crowd. They trail raiders, making them jittery and paranoid and looking for a fight. They whisper to merchants who start screaming arguments with their customers. There's one on a side street tossing lit matches into empty windows. Nothing's caught yet, but give it time. I don't dare try to scare them off. I don't want to give myself away and I'm too weak to threaten them.

Right now the hard thing is keeping my head straight and my thoughts focused. Muninn's egg isn't going to last forever. I can feel an edge of pain in my arm already. Maybe that's normal and maybe it's a sign the egg is wearing off. This is the first time I've been dismembered. I'm not an expert. I stumble against a table. Booze, cigarettes, and bottles of potions clatter against each other. A few fall. I bend down like I'm helping pick things up, but I'm really trying to pocket a pack of Maledictions. The owner comes around the stall and yells at me, punctuating his point by kicking me on the left side, where I can't do anything about it.

I come to a large intersection. Eleusis isn't burning, but L.A. glows like coal and spits fire into the sky. I duck into a four-story parking garage. The bottom floor is set up like a squatter camp. There are pagans and crazies from up the hill, cook fires and tents. The place stinks from bodies and waste. I go up the ramp to the second floor. There are fewer people and no one bothers me. I keep climbing.

The third floor is trashed, almost like a bomb went off.

Every inch is blackened and scorched. It doesn't look like a bomb. More like a fire, one big enough and hot enough so it didn't leave anything but half-melted car frames. I'm exhausted after walking from the stadium. I find a spot in the dark back by the elevators and lie down. The cool concrete feels good against my head. I'm glad Alice isn't here to see me like this. It might shake her confidence in my knight-in-shining armor act.

The air is relatively clean up here, but I still get whiffs of the body stink from down below. One smell doesn't belong—the overwhelming vinegar reek. I tilt up my head and Josef is standing on the melted frame of a MINI Cooper.

"This isn't exactly the progress I was hoping to find," he says.

"Get out of here, man. Someone's going to see you."

"So? Do you think any of the mob out there would be willing or able to do anything about it?"

"My point is, I don't want to find out. No loose ends. Remember?"

I sit up and lean my back against the wall. Josef looks at my empty sleeve and shakes his head.

"You're ridiculous. Crippled. Locked up by idiots and robbed by a dead psychopath." He kicks some loose rocks from near his feet and uncovers a pair of crushed reading glasses. "We're tired of waiting. We're coming in now."

"Be my guest."

He picks up the glasses and holds them over his eyes, squinting through the lenses. They must not be his prescription. He makes a face and tosses them out over the wall.

"Aren't you going to try and talk me out of it?"

"No. Be my guest. Pandemonium is that way and so are

about ninety percent of Hell's legions. If you and your friends think you can take on a million or so Hellion soldiers all by yourselves, be my guest."

He leans in close, bringing his stink with him.

"You don't think we can handle these Hellion idiots?"

"Maybe when there weren't enough in one place for a decent tailgate party, but these boys have just about put the original rebel angel legions back together."

"So? They lost their war in Heaven and now even Lucifer is gone. They're weak."

"Yeah, but there's the other thing."

"What?"

"Do you have a cigarette?"

He reaches into his breast pocket and pulls out a pack of regular human cigarettes. Never count on a Kissi to give you what you really want. I light the cigarette with Mason's lighter and pull the smoke deep into my lungs. It's better than nothing and it helps cover up Josef's smell.

"You said there was something else," Josef says.

"Do you ever watch the Discovery Channel? They had a show on where a colony of little tiny red ants all got together and killed a full-grown wolf. See my point?"

"No."

"Just because you're the wolf at the top of the food chain doesn't mean you're bulletproof. You and your pals might be able to wipe out the Hellions, but they won't go down easy, and by the time you're done, you're going to be blind and crippled. That doesn't sound like the big win to me."

Josef takes a deep breath and turns his head to the sounds from the street.

"How much longer are we supposed to wait?"

"Just a few more hours. I need to get up this hill and then get General Semyazah. He's the one guy who can turn this whole thing around."

"He's in Tartarus."

"I know."

"You think you can help him? How?"

"I'll tell them I'm the pizza delivery boy. They'll never suspect a thing."

"Don't be cute. No one's ever returned from Tartarus."

"Maybe they were going the wrong way."

His expression changes to genuine interest.

"You know a secret way out?"

I drag off the cigarette. After Maledictions, regular human cigarettes are like inhaling the steam off a cup of herbal tea.

"If you're so concerned about winning this thing, why don't you go and do your job and let me do mine? If I'm not back in Pandemonium in, say, twelve hours, you'll know I'm stuck in Tartarus and I'm not coming back. After that, you can do what you want, but give me the time to do this the smart way."

He gets closer, picks a bit of lint off my shoulder, and tosses it away.

"This is the last time. The tide is rising and you can't hold back the sea. Besides, you're not an easy man to trust."

"Yeah, but nobody else wants to play our reindeer games, so we're stuck with each other."

Josef fingers my empty coat sleeve.

"How are you going to pull this off with only one arm?"

"I'll manage."

"Meaning you're going to let your ego ruin everything."

"It's my plan. It's mine to blow."

"No, it's not."

It's easy to forget that Kissi are a kind of angel. A factory-second, thrown-in-the-Dumpster-and-left-in-a-landfill angel, but still an awesomely powerful creature.

When Josef grabs me there isn't a damned thing I can do to fight back. I'm one-handed, off balance, sick, and dizzy. He throws me onto my knees, pulls off my coat, and takes out the black blade. I try to back away, but he grabs my empty left sleeve and pulls me back like a fish on a reel. He slices through the cauterized stump of my arm, reopening the wound. My knees buckle. I hold on to him with my one good hand, trying to get my fingers around his throat or push him off. Something. Anything. He shrugs me off and pins me against the wall. With the black blade he cuts an X on the palm of my right hand and presses my bloody palm to the arm stump.

I'm sicker than ever. Not blacking-out sick or throwing-up sick, but lost in space. Like my body and brain have given up trying to register things like up and down or sane or insane. I keep waiting for the angel in my head to jump in and handle things, but he's as floored as I am. The stump itches and the nerves that feel like they're still connected to fingers feel even more like that. I look to see what's happening and find something white and pulsating hanging off my body like a giant maggot. Great. Now I'm going to have to change my online dating photo.

The maggot grows veins and arteries. Five twitching tentacle-things wiggle out the end. The maggot shrinks and turns almost black. The veins and arteries toughen until they're cables within thick dark muscle. Shiny skin glides over and around the growing structures. It shines like metal or a scarab's carapace. My fingers are delicate but strong, half organic insect and half machine. They flex when I tell them to. I touch each fingertip to thumb, counting one, two, three, four. They move easily. Josef is back by the MINI Cooper wiping my gore off his hands with a white handkerchief.

"That should give you a decent chance of not fucking things up entirely."

He folds the handkerchief and puts it into a back pocket.

"I could lie and tell you that I can't make the arm look any more human than that, but we both know I'd be lying. Wear that and don't forget who your friends are."

"You're a Georgia peach."

The pain and nausea are gone. I stand up. Josef comes over and helps me get my coat back on.

"Get used to your new arm quickly. You have twelve hours from now or we go without you."

He walks down the ramp and disappears before he reaches the bottom.

I flex and move the arm. Pick up a piece of concrete. Toss it from my good hand to my new one and back again. The biomechanical hand feels pressure, heat, and sharpness, but not like my regular one. It'll take some getting used to, but it's better than a burned stump.

The arm isn't the only thing I have to work out. I don't know a secret way out of Tartarus. I don't even know the way in. But I'll find it, and if hoodoo and bullshit won't get me out, I'll hold my breath until I turn blue. That always worked on Mom.

I walk up to an open level at the top of the garage and look out over the city. On top of a hill less than a mile away is the asylum. If Eleusis is as weirdly laid out and fucked up as the rest of this L.A., Alice might as well be on the moon. I don't know if I can even get to her in twelve hours, much less get her and Semyazah. I should have asked Josef for a jet pack instead of an arm.

Escaped lunatics are warming themselves around a fire of old furniture and my wanted posters.

Maybe I should steal a car and take my chances on finding a road to the Observatory somewhere.

"Still trying to get up that hill, eh?"

I look over my left shoulder and then my right. There's a small round man in a red tailored suit sitting on the edge of the wall with his feet dangling over the edge. I look at him and he glances at me.

"Is he gone?"

"Who?"

"Your pal Josef. Is he gone?"

"He's not my pal and yes, he's gone. Who are you?"

"I've had my eye out for you and then I see him fitting you out with a bug claw. I just naturally assumed that you two were buddies."

I circle around behind him, trying to get a better look.

"Who are you?"

He shrugs.

"Who is any of us really?"

"Don't get cute."

"I was born cute. You're the monster."

I get out the na'at and hold it where he can't see and walk over until I'm close enough to get a good look.

It's Mr. Muninn. Only not. It's one of his brothers. They're not just twins, they're the same in every detail including the clothes, except that where Muninn is all black, this one is all red. The angel in my head makes a sound I've never heard it make before. I put the na'at back in my coat.

"What's your name?"

The round man bounces his heels off the side of the building.

"Kid, you couldn't pronounce my name with three tongues and a million years to practice."

"Muninn told me his."

"Did he?"

"Didn't he?"

The red man holds up his hands, the fingers spread wide.

"Five brothers. Each of our names and consciousness corresponds to a color. Yellow. Blue. Green. I'm red, as you might have noticed. Muninn is black, the sum of us all." He ticks off each color with a finger. "Now, if you were the literary type or had ever read a book in your life, you might know that the mythical Nordic deity Odin traveled with two black ravens. One was called Huginn. Guess what the other was called?"

"Muninn named himself after a bird?"

"It's his idea of a joke. Don't hate him. He's the youngest."

The angel in my head stops making the funny noise and finally gets out a single word: *Elohim.*

The red man is looking at me. I get the feeling he can read me a lot better than I can read him because I can't read him at all.

"Are you . . . ?"

"Yep."

"All five of you are?"

"Yep."

"Mr. Muninn, too?"

"I think we established that when we established that he's one of us five brothers."

My head is going funny again. My stomach twists. I'm swamped by a fascination and anger that I've been carrying around a lot longer than the eleven years I spent Downtown.

"Muninn lied to me. I thought he was one of the few people I could trust."

"Calm down. He didn't lie to you. He just didn't come up and say, 'Hi, kid. I'm God. How's tricks?' Would you have believed him? I wouldn't, and I'd know he was telling the truth."

"At least I can call him Muninn. What am I supposed to call you? Santa Elvis?"

"How about Neshamah? That's one I think you can pronounce without breaking your jaw.

"What are you doing down here?"

He holds out his hands.

"Surveying my handiwork."

I lean on the wall with him and look out over the city. Something explodes a few blocks north. A fire starts in a building down the block. I guess the Kissi with the matches got his wish.

"If this was my Erector Set, I'd return it and get my money back," I say.

Neshamah shakes his head and shrugs.

"It wasn't supposed to be like this, you know. Eleusis was a beautiful place once. The whole universe was. We . . . well, it was still *I* back then . . . were building perfection, but it went wrong."

"Did you invent understatement back then or did you come up with it later?"

"At least we, I, dreamed big. What do you dream about?"

"You know exactly what I dream about. It's why I'm here."

"A dunce on a white horse tilting at windmills. Very original. You know what my brothers and I did? We invented light. And atoms. And air."

"If you get the credit for light, you deserve the credit for skin cancer, too, so another bang-up job on that one."

He puts his head in his hands in an exaggerated gesture.

"Cancer. Damn, you people are a mess."

"You made us, so what does that make you?"

He watches smoke rising from the nearby fire as it drifts up to meet the burning cloud of the sky.

"We were so sure we got you right the first time. Then there was the whole Eden debacle and it was all downhill from there. But don't worry, the new ones are a lot better."

"You're done with us and on to Humanity 2.0?"

"Oh, we're way beyond 2.0. The new ones are nearly perfect. Nearly angels. You'd hate them."

"Fingers crossed I never have to meet one."

He leans over to me and speaks in a fake conspiratorial whisper.

"You won't. I put them far, far away from you people. Why do you think space is so big?"

He sits up and laughs, pleased with his vaudeville act. I always wondered if I'd run into him sometime. I'm not sure what I was expecting. A muscle-bound Old Testament Conan

Yahweh. Maybe a pothead New Testament love guru. Something. But not Muninn. And especially not a bad Xerox asshole version of Muninn.

"Why did you leave me down here all those years?"

"You mean why do I allow human suffering?"

"No. What I mean is why did *you* leave *me* down *here*?"

"You don't belong anywhere, so what difference does it make where you are?"

"You really hate me, don't you? I'm every fucking mistake you ever made all rolled into one."

"That's about the size of it."

"Aelita murdered Uriel, my father."

"Yes."

"Did you tell her to?"

"Aelita and I aren't really on what you'd call speaking terms these days."

"Is my father stuck in Tartarus?"

"No."

"Where is he?"

"He's gone."

"Where?"

"He's just gone."

"The other dead nephilim, are they gone, too?"

He raises one hand and drops it back in his lap.

I ask, "What's in Tartarus?"

He doesn't say anything for a while.

"I'd appreciate it if you'd put that cigarette out. It bothers my allergies."

"You have allergies?"

"Only down here."

I flick the cigarette over the side into the crazies' bonfire below.

"What I don't get is the disappearing act. You hate me. That's a given. But if you were done with all us mortal slobs and moving on to 2.0, why didn't you just kill us? Or didn't you care enough to put us out of our misery? Is that who you are? One of those people who forgets their kid in the car on a hot day until it has a stroke?"

He doesn't move or speak for a while. He just looks down into the street. A couple of raiders walk by, passing a bottle back and forth. Neshamah leans over the edge and spits, hitting one of the raiders on top of his head. He laughs.

"You broke my heart. Not you in particular. All humanity. And then there was the incident in Heaven with Lucifer and his juvenile delinquent friends. I had to throw a third of my children into the void. I think the ones that stayed, the quote 'loyal ones,' were just as bad if not worse. So puffed with their importance and self-righteousness. The funny thing is, I never really believed that Lucifer wanted my throne, but I think a few of the angels who stayed did. They saw my failure and felt entitled to it after they fought and won."

He shakes his head. Looks down while he bounces his heels off the building.

"Like any decent God, I willed myself into being. I created time, space, and matter and set out to construct a universe. When I was finished, nothing quite worked the way I wanted. The angels rebelled. The Kissi wreaked havoc. And all of you on earth, well, you were just you. Then one day I realized I wasn't me anymore. I'd gone from one big me to five smaller ones. I never bothered trying to put myself back together.

What was the point? Some of me wouldn't want to do it and I didn't want to fight with myself."

"You know, I'm sure if you asked nicely, they could find a bed for you at the pretty hospital on the hill."

"Watch your tone. I could turn the rest of you into an insect to match that arm."

Just what I need. For this whole thing to turn even more Kafkaesque.

Adjust course.

"I've been wondering, who would build an asylum in Hell and who'd it be for?"

"Ah, that's the first interesting thing you've asked," says Neshamah. "Originally it was for the Fallen. Some of them went mad when they realized what they'd done and gave up. Occasionally damned human souls develop a similar condition, so when I took back this portion of Hell to create Eleusis for the heathens, I left the asylum intact. It's pointless to punish the insane—they don't understand what's happening or why. Treatment helped them come back to themselves so they could properly resume their suffering."

I rub my new arm where it meets my shoulder. The contrast between soft flesh and hard chitin is startling.

"You are one cold fucker," I say.

"Coming from someone who blissfully hacked another sentient creature to death not an hour ago, that's quite something."

"Father Traven said something interesting about you. He used a word I'd never heard before, so I looked it up online. There was this Greek bunch called the Gnostics . . ."

He rolls his eyes.

"Not the fucking Gnostics, please."

"They didn't call you God. They called you the demiurge. They didn't believe you're an omnipotent übermensch. You're more like one of those dads who tries to build a barbecue in the backyard only you can't follow the instructions, so you lay out the bricks wrong and the cement dries too fast and the thing comes out as crooked as poker in Juarez. Then, around sunset, you announce it's finished even though it looks like a brick cold sore. You throw some T-bones in the fire and pretend it's what you were going for all along. That's what you did to the universe."

He swings his legs back over the wall and hops down onto the garage roof. He smiles at me.

"You actually read something? There's evidence of a true miracle, right up there with the loaves and fishes."

"Why are you such an asshole when Muninn is such a good guy?"

He throws up his hands in disgust.

"Everyone is so in love with poor sweet Muninn. It's why he's always gotten his way. He hides down there in his cave collecting toys, holding on to the past because he doesn't want to have to deal with any of this." Neshamah gestures to the burning city. "But he's part of our collective being, and as responsible for this disaster as any of the rest of us."

"At least he's not a whiner."

"Take away his toys and see how long that lasts. Why do you think he's hiding? He never learned to share."

Neshamah takes a flask from an inside pocket. He unscrews the top and takes a long drink.

"Do you think I could have a hit off that? It's been a long weird day."

He shakes his head.

"You wouldn't like it."

"I drink Aqua Regia; how bad can this be?"

He shrugs and hands me the flask. I upend it and spit out everything that touches my tongue. Neshamah takes the flask away and bursts into belly laughs.

"What is that shit?"

"Ambrosia," he says. "Food of the gods."

He takes another sip and puts the flask back in his coat.

"So, if you're down here and Muninn is on earth, where are the others?"

"Around. We travel a lot."

"Are any of you in Heaven?"

"Always. At least one of us."

"Lucifer knows you're broken, doesn't he?"

He nods.

"Lucifer was always the smart one. That's why he and the kid never got along. One's all heart and one's all head."

"This all happened after Lucifer left. Why don't you send him down here to fix it?"

"It wouldn't help. You're right about one thing. I didn't build everything as well as I might have. This was going to happen sooner or later."

"Do the five of you know what the others hear and see?"

"Not everything. We like some privacy, too. Otherwise we'd all still be together."

"Do they know about us talking right now?"

"They can hear every word."

"Then you got the message I sent back with the angel from Eden?"

"We got it. You didn't have to cut him up like that." He nods at my new metal bug arm. "But I guess you're even."

I look away. The building the Kissi torched is really roaring. I can feel the heat all the way over here. I wonder if we should move, but Neshamah doesn't seem worried, so I decide not to be.

"Maybe I was a little harsh. I'd just gotten over being dead. And he threw the first punch."

"I guess that makes it all right, then."

Neshamah walks across the parking lot and looks out over another part of Hell. The view isn't any better from over here. I don't say it because I can see it on his face.

He says, "He's not Lucifer anymore, by the way. He's Samael."

"So I heard. Speaking of your kids, what's the story with Aelita? She makes Lilith look like Mother Teresa. Didn't she get enough face time with Daddy?"

"You're not a parent. Don't tell me how to raise my family."

"I don't know if she has Electra complex or Oedipus complex or diaper rash, but she really wants you dead. You need to get her some Prozac."

We walk all the way around the roof. The sky remains a solid mass of smoke. Earthquakes rumble on the horizon.

"I knew that Lucifer was a troublemaker, but I also knew he'd grown out of it. But I never saw this coming with Aelita. I've tried talking to her, but she might be a lost cause."

"You could always kill me. That's what she really wants."

"Don't think I haven't considered it. And that's not what she wants. You're just a symptom of what she sees as a larger condition."

"Sounds like she's gone Gnostic on you and thinks Daddy's the demiurge, too."

He turns and looks me in the eye.

"Who the hell are you to talk about misbehaving kids? Your whole life has been about breaking things. You're not a dumb kid. Why do you go looking for trouble?"

" 'Cause one of your angels ruined my mother and father's lives and made me an Abomination. When I finally found my real father, he told me that all I was and ever will be is a killer. Not exactly *Leave It to Beaver*, is it?"

"We've all got our troubles. Look at this mess."

Neshamah leans his elbows on the low wall. I do the same.

"Some of those old Greeks thought that the world couldn't be such a cruel mess without it being on purpose. They said that who or whatever made it deep down inside had to be evil."

"What do you think?" he asks.

I feel in my pocket for a cigarette my brain knows isn't there, but my body has to check for it anyway. I flex my new hand and run it over the concrete, feeling the rough surface.

I say, "I'm not a hundred percent either way. But off the top of my head, I don't really think you're evil. Just out of your depth. Or like a kid who gets a note on his report card. 'If Chet applied himself, I'm sure he could do better in class.' "

"Funny, that's how we feel about you."

"I'm a nephilim and a killer. Do you think I'm evil?"

"I'm not a hundred percent either way. Besides, there are worse things to be than a killer."

"What about 'Thou shall not kill'?"

"What about the Egyptian army Moses drowned when he closed the Red Sea on them? Do you think he could have turned them around with a few kind words? Do you think I could do that here?" He points to the city below. "Do you want to know the difference between a killer and a murderer?"

"Sure."

"It's where you aim the gun."

That sounds more like the Old Testament guy I was looking for.

"Well, chatting has been a little slice of heaven," I say, "but I have to figure out how to get up that hill so I can do a couple of miracles and save the universe. You wouldn't be in the mood to help or anything?"

He looks into the distance and smiles.

"I think you have it in hand."

"Was that a fucking joke?"

"Sorry. I couldn't resist."

I take a couple of steps to go when I hear him clear his throat.

"I think you have something of mine."

"Oh, right."

I walk over and give him the crystal.

"Muninn says that's your insurance policy. If everything ends, you can start over again."

"Is that what he told you? The truth is no one knows what it will be, but something is better than nothing."

"You and Muninn, it's like Jesus and Lucifer, isn't it? One's all heart and one's all head."

He puts the crystal in a pocket of his red waistcoat. It's a tight fit.

"He's the youngest. I'm the oldest. You do the math."

"What happens if Aelita kills one of you?"

He leans over the wall and looks down at the street.

"See that manhole down there? I have a feeling if you went down inside and walked exactly three hundred and thirty-three paces west, you'll find where you want to go."

"Seriously? Why that number?"

"Because that's how many it is. Not three hundred and thirty-two or three hundred and thirty-four. Count off three hundred and thirty-three and look around. You'll be there."

"Seriously? Thanks, man. And after all the things I've said about you over the years."

"Don't worry. I've said the same about you."

"Will you be here when I'm done up the hill?"

He shrugs.

"Hard to say. I work in mysterious ways."

I start for the ramp wondering if I'll need something to pry up the manhole cover.

"Nice meeting you, Spider-Man!"

I look back. Neshamah is waving, a shit-eating grin plastered on his face. I have no choice. I start an old tune my mother used to belt out when she had just the right number of martinis.

> At the Devil's ball
> In the Devil's hall
> I saw the funniest devil that I ever saw
> Dancing with the Devil
> Oh, you little devil
> Dancing at the Devil's ball

He turns back to the city.

"Yeah, fuck you, too, kid."

THERE'S A KID'S game that goes something like this: "Don't think of a white bear for half an hour and you win a dollar." No one ever wins because the moment anyone says "white bear," that's all you can think about. Being told your life depends on walking exactly 333 steps is a lot like that. You count on your fingers, but what if you get distracted and drop a number? What if you repeat one? How do you know each step you're taking is the same distance as all the others? I should have a calculator, a tape measure, and Rain Man as a guide. If I count wrong and don't find a way out, maybe I should keep on walking. No. I could end up in here forever, and if it's only one Apocalypse per customer I don't want to miss it.

330. 331. 332. 333.

I stop and look around. Light comes through a crack in the wall to my left. I dig a finger into the crack. It feels like a service door that's been welded shut but it was a sloppy job and the dampness in the tunnels has been working on the joins ever since. I push my new hand into the crack, gouging out layers of corroded iron and faded paint. The new hand works pretty well. It feels the shape and roughness of the metal, but it doesn't bleed or register pain. I might just have to keep it.

When there's a clean clear crack an inch wide in the door, I brace my feet and put my shoulder and body into it. The metal slides away, scattering sewer fungus and oak-leaf-size sheets of rust.

Ragged lunatics are asleep on the floor and dirty mattresses dragged down from the wards upstairs. They don't look so different from the ones I saw on the street. Maybe these are a little farther down the road to Candy Land. The others managed to run away, but these bedlam sheep never left the pasture. They drool and stare at me as I step through the old service door.

I'm in the lobby of what back home is the Griffith Park Observatory. This version doesn't look like Galileo would stop by for a piss. The floors and walls are bare cement. A large open ward and single cells in a circle are around the bottom floor. All the cell doors are unlocked or have been smashed open.

The loons over here watch a couple of old souls, maybe witches, spin a dust of tiny emerald pyramids into orbit around crystal glass cubes like imaginary constellations.

The second floor is for more impressive head cases. Jack said there were Hellions in the asylum and for once he wasn't lying. There are several, mixed in with the human souls. They're playing games that only they can possibly understand, tossing potion bottles and human or animal bones, then drawing symbols on the floor in blood and shit. When the drawing is done everyone takes a step and contorts into a strange new position. Dungeons & Dragons for actual monsters in an actual dungeon.

The third floor is the old-fashioned black-and-white Boris Karloff Bedlam I've been looking for. Dim, wet, and stinking. This is where they keep the one-percenters. All the cells on the lower two floors are open, but these have double-thick bars surrounded by bonding hexes. And they're working because most of the cells are still occupied.

The good news is that the few third-floor patients who've

escaped their cells look more dangerous to themselves than to me. Two grimy Hellions roll around on the floor, each gnawing on the other's straitjacket. I can't tell if they're trying to help or eat each other. Going by the holes in the material and their broken teeth, it looks like they've been going at it for quite a while without getting anywhere. Still, you have to give them points for hanging in there.

A Hellion as big as Crab Man emerges suddenly from the dark and lumbers past without looking in my direction. He must have been shackled to the wall of his cell. He has metal cuffs and chains attached to his wrists and is hauling two huge carved stones behind him. Going by the deep scratches on the floor, it looks like all he's done since getting out is drag his heavy chains and rocks around and around the third floor. As he passes each locked cell, damned souls and Hellions pound the doors and howl at him.

There's a short hall off the main corridor. The worst of the worst will be down there. I go through the hall quietly and peer around the corner. Just two guards at the end. That's where Alice will be. My breath catches in my throat. This is the closest I've been to her in over eleven years and there's only a couple of bored doormen in the way.

For the first time I've been down here, I'm scared. Normally I'd get out the na'at and go completely brontosaurus on two lousy guards. But if I do anything spectacularly stupid, there might be another guard in the cell who could kill Alice. The angel reminds me that I'm also wearing a brand-new arm that I've never used in a fight. For once I need to think this through.

A couple of minutes later the rock-dragging Hellion makes

the turn to this end of the corridor. The guards by Alice's cell don't even look up. They've heard him walk by a hundred times. The guards couldn't look more bored.

I flatten myself against the wall. As the backwater Sisyphus passes, I get out the black blade and slice through his heavy chains while giving him a little kick in the ass. Not enough to hurt him. Just enough to push him into the side hall so that the guards will be the first thing he sees when he realizes he's free.

At first he stands there, probably feeling off balance with the big load off his back. Then he looks at his empty hands. Sees the dark and gangrenous flesh around the shackles where they've been biting into his wrists for who knows how long. The guards aren't pleased. They want him to keep dragging the stone exactly the way he always has. They don't want him to improve himself. The boy with the wrist shackles must be picking up on the guards' negative waves because he heads right at them for a heart-to-heart. I can't be sure exactly what they're saying, but I hear a lot of "ows" and "don'ts" along with the kind of crunching I've come to associate with smashed bones. The angel reminds me to be patient and wait for the conversation to die down by itself.

In a couple of minutes a still-disoriented giant wanders out of the side hall. He's covered in blood and other colorful fluids that I don't want to think about. He stares at his stones, lost and desperate without them. I go over and pick up the end of one of the chains. He looks up when he hears the links rattle against each other. I hold the chain out to him. He eyes me for a full minute. I'm not sure what he sees. I wonder if the insane can see through glamours? I still have Hellion skin plastered on my face, so I'd be pretty confusing to look at if he can see my living body.

Slowly, he puts out a hand. I wrap the chain around his palms and close his fingers over the metal. He leans forward. The weight is different, but familiar enough that he knows what to do. The moment he puts his head down, he forgets about me. He leans into the weight and pulls. The stones scrape reassuringly along the floor behind him.

I go down the side hall, stepping over pieces of the guards, until I come to the door in the back. It's locked and the sliding viewing panel is welded shut. I can't be a hundred percent sure what's on the other side. I slash open the iron padlock with the blade. Before the lock hits the floor, I kick the door open as hard as I can. It swings back and one of the hinges pops as the door swings open and hits the wall.

As I step inside I hear a stifled scream from the farthest, darkest corner of the cell. It sounds awfully human.

"Alice?"

Nothing.

"Alice?"

And a second later there she is. Eleven years I've been waiting for this. I've lost track of how many beings I've killed, and destroyed everything in my way. I've been beaten, stabbed, burned, and maimed across two planes of existence to get to this moment. And here I am and here she is and we're together in the same room maybe a few hours before the end of everything. I want to grab her and kiss her, but I don't think the feeling is mutual.

She has her back to the far wall and her teeth are bared.

She's holding a wooden stake. It looks like she broke the leg off a chair and sharpened it on the floor. That's my girl.

"Alice . . ."

"Keep away from me!" she screams, and kicks a metal dish covered with foul-smelling slop at me. Have these pinheads been trying to feed her Hellion food? Even I wouldn't eat most of that stuff and I didn't come here on a direct flight from Heaven.

"It's okay," I tell her. "It's me. I've come to take you out of here."

She holds the stake higher.

"I'm not going anywhere with you, asshole! Leave me alone!"

There's only one small oil lamp in the cell. All she can see is my shadowed profile from the light in the hall. I get closer so I'm not a ghost anymore.

"Alice. I've come to save you."

She lunges and jams the stake deep in my chest. I fall back against the wall. A couple of months ago Candy gave me the zombie-bite antidote on the point of a knife and now this. Why do all the women I like end up stabbing me?

In this case the answer is obvious. I got so excited at the idea of finally seeing her that I forgot I'm sporting a robo-bug arm and a Hellion's face.

I pull the wood out of my chest and toss it into the hall. Even unarmed, Alice looks like she's ready to go Frazier and Ali with me. She's always been like that. She was never big on backing down from anything.

Are you really going to sacrifice yourself to save your great betrayer?

Shut up, Medea. We're having a moment. And I know you were lying now, so can it.

Getting staked isn't going to kill me, but it hurts like a rhino giving you a flu shot with its horn. I sit down on a wooden chair Alice didn't break and push the hoodie back from my head with my new bug arm. My boots are slick with the dead guards' innards. My coat is covered in blood and smells like the sewer. And then there's my face. For those few seconds when I first saw her, it felt like I wasn't Sandman Slim anymore. I was plain old boring James Stark. With the pain the truth comes back. I'm in a Hellion asylum, rank, mangled, and horrible. I'm finally the monster I always said I was.

I have to laugh. There isn't much else left to do. Go down into the deepest darkest parts of Hell, and you'll see what I mean. They laugh all the time down there.

I reach into my coat pocket and feel around. For a second I don't even know what it is I'm looking for. I pull out what Mustang Sally told me to bring through the Black Dahlia. My hands are bloody from my chest wound and I've left sticky red fingerprints all over the small plastic rabbit. I wipe it on my coat, but that just smears the blood. Fuck it.

I toss the rabbit over to where Alice is hiding in the corner.

"I was going to bring you a turkey dinner since we missed Christmas, but it wouldn't fit in my coat, so you'll have to settle for that."

I see a hand dart from the blackness and disappear back inside. My chest burns, but the wound is already closing up. My legs are cramping. I want to stand, but I don't want to spook her. I wish God hadn't made me put out my cigarette.

Soon I hear, "Jim?"

I can't see her, but the angel in my head can. He shows her to me outlined in the deep dark. The atoms that hold her together are the same as the air around her, her clothes, the walls and floor. And me. There's no difference.

"Jim?"

"Hi, Lucy. I'm home."

She comes over to me slowly, still afraid it's a trick. I know the feeling.

"Jim. Are you . . . ?"

"I'm not dead and I'm not a Hellion. I just needed to borrow a face to get here. Trust me. This isn't the weirdest thing I've done since we last saw each other."

She kneels down and looks into my eyes but keeps some distance between us.

Alice was always the smart one. She read books and thought about what she was going to say before she said it. Sometimes she said the most important things without talking. It was all little physical reactions.

She shakes her head a tiny bit, an almost subliminal movement.

"Is that really you in there?"

"You tell me."

She looks down at my human hand. I turn it over so she can see the back. It's like she's trying to read a secret in the lines. But the hand is so scarred I doubt she'll find anything familiar about it.

"Whoever you are, you really need to do something about those cuticles," she says.

"All the beauty parlors down here are closed or on fire."

She gets up and looks down at me.

"Say something only Jim would say."

"Oh shit."

"Nice start. Keep going."

I try to think, but my brain is freezer-burned.

"Vidocq has our old apartment. He uses a potion that makes it invisible and makes everyone else forget it's there so he doesn't have to pay rent. He lives there with a nice girl who's a hoodoo doctor but originally worked in my video store. Oh yeah. I own a video store. Remember Kasabian? The store used to belong to him, but I cut off his head, so now the store's mine. Kasabian's head is my roommate. He steals my cigarettes and drinks my beer. We usually live over the store, but it's being fixed up, so now we're in a hotel. I finally met my real father. He was an archangel, but now he's dead. I really missed you."

She crosses her arms. Nods at me.

"What happened to your face?"

"I had to get rid of it to get here and this one was available."

"Put it back on. I want to see the real you."

I look at the floor, smiling.

"Of course you do. But it's not here."

"Where is it?"

"Jack the Ripper stole it."

She takes a deep breath and lets it out. I'm never going to get used to seeing the dead breathe. Or mimic the memory of breathing. I don't know which it is.

"I almost believe you. Say something else."

"For almost a year I've had the strangest dreams about you. I know some were just plain old dreams, but others were different. It's like you were really talking to me."

She grunts faintly.

"I had dreams about you, too. Some were like you said. Just dreams. But I think a few were something more. Like we were talking to each other. I saw another girl in one of them. She had an accent."

"That's Brigitte. She's Czech. And a zombie hunter. You'd like her."

"Sounds fun. Is she your girlfriend?"

I shake my head.

"I almost got her turned into the undead, so it didn't really work out. But I started seeing someone recently. You'd like her, too. She's a Lurker, and when she gets mad she eats people."

Alice gives a little laugh.

"They make me sound so boring."

"That's the last thing you were."

She sits on the table and leans in close, like a scientist examining a new kind of bug.

"We need to find your real face because, seriously, human or not, no girl is going to stick her tongue in that thing." She sits up. "And for the record, I missed you, too."

She reaches out to touch my Hellion cheek but her hand goes right through me.

"Damn I was afraid of that," she says.

"What the fuck just happened?"

She stares at her hand.

"It happens with everything down here. I guess since I was in Heaven, Hell things can't touch me."

"How did you get dragged down into this cell?"

"It was that crazy angel, Aelita. She had some interesting things to say about you. She said you aren't human."

And Medea Bava said some things about you.

"I'm humanish. I'll tell you about it later."

"What happened to you all those years ago? Where were you? I know it had something to do with Mason. He's been behind every lousy thing that's happened to us."

"Like Parker." Mason's Sub Rosa attack dog who murdered her.

"Parker." She nods. "Whatever happened to him?"

"I killed him."

Alice looks at me and turns away. She's not sure if I'm kidding or not. I want to ask how Parker did it, but I can't.

I say, "I know that Mason's running what's going on down here. And to answer your question, I spent eleven years right here in Hell."

She turns halfway back.

"You seem a lot saner than I would be. I've only been here a couple of days and I'm starting to lose my mind."

"You want to know something really funny? I'm the one who sent Mason to Hell in the first place."

She shakes her head.

"This is officially the worst three-way ever." She finally looks at me again. "I'm sorry I stabbed you."

"That's okay. The nonhuman thing helps me heal fast. Also, I can park in handicapped spaces."

"So, are you going to rescue me or what? Aelita is going to drag me off to Mason soon."

"That doesn't make sense. Our deal was I had three days. And Mason is still waiting for soldiers and arguing strategy."

"Whatever he's doing, Aelita made it sound like I'm part of

it, so I'd really like to not be here." Her eyes narrow and she looks out the cell door. "How did you get by all the guards?"

"There were only two."

Her eyebrows go up a fraction of an inch.

"There are a hell of a lot more than two."

Shit.

I let the angel loose and my senses expand across the floor. The entire ward beyond the hall is filled with Hellion guards. The fuckers were hiding in the locked cells.

"Why don't they attack?"

"They're probably waiting for Aelita. She seems to be the one in charge around here."

There's no way I can get us past all the guards outside. But we're only on the third floor.

"Step back. This is going to look strange, but don't ask any questions. Just jump when I tell you."

Alice goes back to the wall. I manifest the Gladius and smash it into the floor. It cuts through the stones like a blowtorch through a marshmallow. It doesn't even make much noise. Just a low sizzle. Three hits and a section of the floor gives way.

"Jump," I say.

I don't have to say it twice. She hops into the hole and I follow her. The second-floor crazies are still playing their game. A couple glance at us when we hit the floor, but we're not nearly as interesting as the game, so they turn away. I hack another hole in the floor and we drop through to the first floor.

There are a few Hellion guards stationed downstairs, but

only a couple by the stairs. They're surprised when Alice and I come falling out of the ceiling, but shocked when they see the Gladius. One of the guards tries to shout, but I take his head off before he can make a sound. Unfortunately, the second guard shouts a Hellion alarm command. I stab him in the heart and he disappears. I try to push Alice into the tunnel, but my hand goes right through her. She's staring at me. She's never seen me kill anything before.

"Go," I shout, and she snaps out of it and jumps into the tunnel. When I get out I pull the door back into place and slash at the tunnel ceiling and walls, knocking down as much debris in front of the door as I can.

I let the Gladius go out and we head back to the manhole. She stops and looks at me a little like she did when I first walked into her cell.

She says, "What the hell was that in your hand?"

"It's called a Gladius. It's just something I found I can do." There's no goddamn way I'm explaining to her how only angels have them.

"You killed those guys and didn't even flinch," she says.

"First off, they weren't guys, and second, I've killed a hell of a lot more than them. How do you think I got here? Do you think I got these scars on the debate team? Killing is what I do down here. And it's what I still do."

"But only bad things, right?"

"We're in Hell. I don't think Mother Teresa or Johnny Cash are in much danger."

She has to think about it for a minute. It'll take her a lot longer than that to make sense of the last few minutes and we don't have time.

"We need to keep moving."

"Okay."

As we go, she tries to take my hand. It goes right through me.

"Shit," she says.

I lead her back to the manhole and we climb the ladder out.

I WALK ALICE up the garage ramp, skirting the crazies and the squatters. She can't take her eyes off them. I get the feeling Aelita dropped her straight into the cell, so she hasn't seen much of Hell. Lucky girl.

Neshamah is on the roof looking through Muninn's crystal like a jeweler checking a diamond for flaws. He shoves it back in his waistcoat when he sees us.

"The prodigal son returns. I wasn't sure you had enough fingers and toes to count to three hundred. I see you've brought back a friend and that you have a hole in your chest. Just another day at the office," says Neshamah. He turns to Alice. "Was he this clumsy on earth or is all this blood a Sandman Slim thing?"

"A who?"

"Alice, this is Neshamah. Neshamah, this is Alice. Neshamah is the one who told me how to get into the asylum."

"Thanks for helping Jim get me out of that place. I would have gone crazy if I'd been in there much longer."

Neshamah holds out his hand to Alice. She looks at it like he's holding out a dead squid. But out of a kind of doomed sense of politeness, she puts her hand out, too. She looks at their hands and then at him when they touch. She starts to say something, but Neshamah cuts her off.

"If it's any comfort, you wouldn't have been in there

much longer. Probably just a few hours. A day at the most. Wouldn't you say?"

He looks at me.

"If I don't get to Pandemonium in about seven hours, the Kissi are going to come down hard on the place. The way Josef is acting I don't know if they're going to start a war down here or join up with Mason's boys and make a play for Heaven."

He shifts his weight from one foot to the other. The angel in my head squirms like something is trying to get inside. I think he's losing.

"I noticed Kissi lurking about. What exactly are they getting out of all this?" Neshamah asks.

"They'll get what I give them. Nothing more and nothing less."

His eyes narrow.

"Do you think it was a good idea to ally yourself with such, let's say, touchy creatures?"

"I knew I was going to need help to stop Mason and I never got anything but the silent treatment from your bunch, so who was I supposed to go to? Besides, Aelita wants you out of the way, and for all I knew, she was the new CEO of Heaven Inc."

"Boys? I'm new here," says Alice. "What are Kissi? Why did Mason bring me here?"

I say, "Kissi are like angels, only worse. I'm not sure why you're here now. I thought it was just to get rid of me, but with what Aelita said to you, there might be something more." I look at Neshamah. "You want to jump in here with any insights?"

He shrugs.

"Mason wants to get into Heaven. She's from Heaven. Maybe he thinks she hid a key under a flowerpot."

"I don't even know how I got here," Alice says. She notices the sky behind Neshamah's head and it must have just registered that the darkness isn't night, but a coffin lid of smoke blotting out the sky.

Alice looks at me.

"Did you just say you're friends with Lucifer?"

"Not friends really. We're more like professional assholes who play golf occasionally and get drunk at the clubhouse before talking business."

Neshamah smiles and addresses Alice.

"Actually, there is no Lucifer at the moment. The old one is retired. Your friend James here is up to replace him. As is Mason."

Alice gives me that I-don't-know-who-you-are look again. Wraps her arms around herself.

"Is that really why you're back? You're finally going to whip them out and see whose is bigger?"

I look at Neshamah.

"The Gnostics were right about you after all, you evil motherfucker."

I turn to Alice.

"I came back here because I love you. But I'm also here to kill Mason because he needs killing. He's not going to be Lucifer or this sack of shit," I say, nodding at Neshamah.

"What does that mean?"

"I have to go. Let Rain Man here explain it to you."

Alice stares at Neshamah.

"Do I know you from somewhere?"

"You might have run into one of my brothers."

"Do you think you could possibly not be a prick long enough for me to go and finish this?" I ask.

"Are you running off to Pandemonium alone? That's magnificently stupid."

"I'm going to Houdini someone out of Tartarus, but I don't even know where it is. Do you have a map of the stars' homes or something I could borrow?"

Neshamah scratches his chin.

"I have to hand it to you, kid. You're a pain in my ass but you're not boring. Tartarus is in the Badlands."

Alice reaches for my arm but her hand goes through me.

"Wait. We finally see each other again and you're dumping me here with a stranger?"

"I know this stinks. But trust me, getting you out of the asylum wasn't rescuing you. What I'm about to do is."

She turns to Neshamah.

"Who are you? You're part of this, aren't you?"

"He can explain it to you after I go."

Neshamah pats Alice's shoulder.

"And indeed I will."

"So how do I get to the Badlands?"

"Are you sure you want to do this? Once you're in Tartarus, there's nothing I can do for you. It's not my domain. It belongs to my brother Ruach. And if you think I'm a bastard, you should meet him sometime."

"If he's around, I'll give him a peck on the cheek for you. How do I get there?"

"The same way you got to the asylum. Three hundred and thirty-three paces, but in the opposite direction."

"You really like that number."

He nods.

"Actually I like nines. Sacred numbers. You've got to love them. If you people were better at math, you'd be as smart as me."

I nod in Alice's direction.

"You can take care of her while I'm gone, right?"

"She was taken from her place in Heaven, so unlike some people, she's one of mine. No one will hurt her."

I start down the ramp. Alice follows me a few paces. I stop.

"Can you for sure stop Mason?"

"I don't know."

"Then promise me this. If you can't win and everything is going to fall apart, you come back here so we can ride it out together."

"I promise."

"Okay, then," she says.

I half turn away then pivot back.

"Did you spy on me for the Sub Rosa?" The question just charged out on its own. I can almost feel the angel trying to reach into my mouth and snatch the words back.

Alice stands still. I can read faces pretty well. If she had a heartbeat, it would be spiking right now. That's all I need to know.

There's a crack like a cannon going off as the building the Kissi set on fire collapses. I wave to her once and go.

I COME UP in the Badlands, though I don't see how this parcel of the L.A. shit-scape is supposed to be worse than any of the others I've seen. In fact, I'd find the area downright restful if it wasn't for all the blood.

I'm in a deserted industrial area surrounded by collapsed warehouses and bent and twisted railroad tracks following the L.A. River. The river's concrete banks are stained the color of old bricks from a rushing river of blood, a tributary of the Styx. I guess this is the source of the blood bubbling up out of the sinkholes.

There's nothing here that points to Tartarus. No signs, burning bushes, or sphinxes playing *Jeopardy!* for clues. The one time a sphinx tried that with me, I held it down and shaved it until it looked like one of those hairless cats you see in Beverly Hills pet stores.

I'm not far from a burned-out, crumbling version of the old Fourth Street Bridge. It's all big Roman arches with a few out-of-place Victorian streetlamps to class up the thing because you don't want your industrial wastelands to look tacky.

There's something strange under the bridge. A bright patch of green. There are palm trees on either side and they're not on fire. The green looks like fresh, healthy grass. In the middle of the little oasis is a white stucco forties bungalow. It has red slate shingles and it's styled with the vaguely hacienda look you see on the older places. I go up the pristine walkway out front and knock on the door. It opens and the woman inside smiles at me. Her face shifts and re-forms, showing the phases of the moon.

"I told you that in the end you'd come to me," says Medea Bava.

"So this is your dirty little secret. Tartarus is the Inquisition."

"No. I'm the Inquisition. Tartarus is your fate. The Dies Irae," she says, and recites, " 'Just judge of vengeance, grant me the gift of forgiveness before the Day of Judgment.' "

"I like the sound of that forgiveness part."

"And some receive it, but I'm afraid you're a bit too late for that."

I step out of Bava's way, tromping on her perfect lawn with my bloody-sewage-waste boots.

"Then why don't you scoot us on over to the Club Double Dead and let me in?"

She comes out, locking the door behind her.

"Seriously? You think someone's going to steal your stamp collection all the way out here?"

"You're not the only one in Hell with a chip on his shoulder. I don't believe in taking foolish chances."

"That sounds boring."

She leads me to a rickety-looking metal staircase leading up to the bridge through a hole chiseled in the roadbed. Medea gestures for me to go first. I take hold of the railing and shake it. The stairs wobble a little, but it looks like they'll hold. I start climbing.

"You know, I've been waiting here for you your whole life."

"I hope you've got cable, or you've missed a lot of good TV."

When we reach the top, she heads for the far side of the

bridge and I follow. She stops abruptly halfway across and looks at me.

"You know that once you get inside, you can never leave."

"That's what Angie Summers said in the back of her daddy's Cadillac on prom night. If I can get away from her, I can get away from you."

"It's refreshing to meet a man so anxious to embrace annihilation."

"Okay. You've had your supervillain moment, now can you show me to the front door?"

Medea steps back a few paces and holds out her arms.

"We're here. Behold Tartarus."

I turn around, looking for something.

"We're nowhere. Behold fuck-all."

"Look down," she says. "Then jump."

I look over the edge. We're right over the Styx.

"In your dreams, Vampirella."

"Is Sandman Slim afraid of a little blood?"

"He's afraid of how deep that is. You want me to jump and crack my head on the bottom."

She shakes her head. Shadows make her shifting features even more disturbing.

"This is the way in. You can keep a little dignity and jump, or I can push you."

"Try it."

I start for her and suddenly I'm airborne. When I land I slide about twenty feet. Medea just smacked me with a hex that felt like a tornado giving birth to a hurricane. I climb to my feet and brush the dust off my coat.

"If you put it that way, maybe I'll just go ahead and jump."

"That's the first sensible thing you've said since you've been here."

I climb onto the wide concrete railing and tightrope-walk down to where Medea is waiting.

"You've got the home-field advantage here, but I bet you can't throw hoodoo like that back on earth."

"We're not on earth, and whatever power you have in this place, I will always have more. Now jump."

"I'm going to look you up when I get back to L.A."

"You're not the first person to say something like that."

"Yeah, but I'm the first one who means it."

She gestures impatiently toward the river.

"Go."

I glance down at the bloody waves and turn back to her.

"I don't have time for one last smoke, do I?"

"Jump or I'll throw you."

I put my arms out and take a breath.

"As a great man once said, 'I should never have switched from scotch to martinis.' "

I lean back and let myself go over the edge, tumbling through the air and slamming into the red river.

I hit flat on my back. It feels just as good as falling fifty feet into blood sounds. I hold my breath and try not to breathe in anything.

I sink and keep sinking, like the gravity in the river isn't the same as the gravity outside. I'm pulled down into soft mud at the bottom. At least I hope it's mud. Another gladiator once swore to me that he'd sailed to Pandemonium on a river of shit. I hope there wasn't any backwash down here.

I'm instantly engulfed in the muck. My lungs want to

crawl up my throat and hitch a ride back to Hollywood. The angel in my head chants a serenity prayer. If I could punch my own brain, I would. The angel stops long enough to remind me that everything has a bottom, even Hell.

I'm being squeezed down through sediment that gets harder every inch I go. The sucking soon turns into pushing, like a hydraulic press is pounding me down into the riverbed. This must be what pasta feels like coming out of a spaghetti extruder.

Then I'm fucking falling again. But only a few feet this time. I slide through a tight fleshy opening in the roof and down a steep incline, like a garbage chute. Nice touch.

I slip down another level and slam into the ground. At least I'm not moving anymore. I lie on the floor and breathe. My heart is pounding. I know I'm surrounded by souls, but they're not paying any attention to me. They're used to hard-luck cases sliding down the poop shoot.

The angel is awestruck by where we are and pissed about being stuck inside me. It never really believed I'd take us this far. The absolute end of the line.

Welcome to Tartarus.

I FELL THROUGH what felt like a mile of blood, but when I get to my feet, there isn't a drop on me and my clothes are dry.

It's cold here and dim, like light that can't decide what it wants to be. Dark. Light. Or some strange wavelength that's simultaneously the opposite of each.

The walls and floors are dull gray metal. There are gleaming conveyor chains overhead. Souls hang from hooks by their ankles. They're being taken away, but I can't see where from here. If we were on earth, I'd swear that I'm in a busy industrial meat locker.

The place is packed shoulder to shoulder with double-dead Hellions, human souls, and Lurker spirits. I can even see Kissi scattered around in the mob. It's like a strange exodus, frozen just before it got started.

Aside from the overhead conveyor and the distant hiss and bang of machines, the place is almost silent, like the tens of thousands of dead around me and the thousands in the adjoining lockers have sunk so low in their misery that they can't even acknowledge each other.

I didn't think seeing Tartarus would get under my skin the way it is. I always imagined it would be Hell cranked up to eleven. Torture, chaos, and cruelty on a planetary scale. Mountains of flensed flesh. Mad bone seas. But this is worse. Tartarus is a dim, crushing despair. Heaven might not have been where you were headed, but now even Hell is a long-gone distant memory. Dante got it wrong when he put the "Abandon All Hope" sign at the entrance to Hell. This is where all hope dies, even for monsters.

I've only been here for a few minutes and the place is starting to bring me down like the permanent residents. I think about Candy, but it's already hard to remember her face. I can make out the ghost of her body, but not her voice or how she felt. When I try to remember our room at the hotel, it feels as dismal and dead as this place. What am I doing getting close to her? Even assuming I get out of here, do I want to drag her into this life? Look what happened to Alice. Look where I am now. I've been here ten minutes and I already miss Hell.

Candy is a big girl and can make her own choices, but what if she chooses wrong? Will I be doing this again in a year when someone murders her and steals her soul?

The angel in my head isn't handling any of this well. Tough shit. I didn't exactly enjoy the ride when it took over while I was sick with zombie hoodoo. I suffered through its choirboy routine so now it can limp along while I figure a way out of here.

What looks like mist in the distance shifts and parts. It's steam coming off an enormous old-fashioned open-face furnace beneath a gigantic boiler with transit pipes on top. Like a scene out of *Metropolis,* blank-faced but efficient workers take souls off the conveyor chains and toss them into the fire. The ones who aren't frying the double dead are adjusting iron valves and enormous levers. They inspect gauges and bleed off hurricanes of steam to keep the pressure steady.

I push my way through the mob. It's like walking through a wheat field. They're so insubstantial that I can barely feel the spirits around me. The meat locker goes on for miles in every direction. I could wander down here for years without ever seeing a familiar face.

I yell, "General Semyazah!"

Heads slowly turn in my direction. The motion ripples out in small waves, like I dropped a rock into a pond of the dead. No one here has paid attention to anything in a long time.

"General Semyazah!"

Nothing. I feel around in my pocket and pull out Mason's lighter. I spark it and hold it high like I'm hoping for an encore of "Free Bird." The room fills with light. Thousands of souls that haven't made a sound in years suddenly try to speak. It sounds like a wind from the far side of a hill. Some souls rush to me and fall to their knees, holding their hands up in prayer. They think I'm Jesus at the final judgment come down to save them. Sorry, but I don't think any of you are high on the Rapture list.

"Semyazah!"

Someone yells back at me. The voice is faint at first, but it gets louder as the crowd shifts, parting for someone muscling his way through. I can't tell much about him except that he's wearing the filthy remains of a Hellion officer's uniform. I head toward him with the lighter over my head.

It takes about twenty minutes for us to meet in the middle.

"General Semyazah?"

He hesitates, not sure if he should admit it.

"Yes," he says.

"I'm here to get you out of here."

"Are you? And why would the Father send an angel for me, one of his most devoted betrayers?"

"God wouldn't send you a pizza even if it was your birthday. And I'm no angel. I'm Sandman Slim."

Semyazah is thin but moves gracefully, like he was built to always be in motion. His face is almost as scarred as mine. When he smiles half of it doesn't move.

"Another one? I've met a hundred Sandman Slims down here. You're not any more impressive than any of them. Less, in fact, in those filthy rags. Besides, Sandman Slim is mortal. You're Hellion."

"No. He's not. It's him," another voice says.

I close the lighter and turn. The crowd sighs and groans when the light disappears.

It's Mammon.

"Enjoying my face, are you?"

Where his face should be is all raw red pork roast.

"Hi, General. How's the neck feeling?"

Semyazah looks at me but talks to Mammon.

"This is who butchered you?"

Mammon nods.

"I'm afraid so."

I hold out my hand to Semyazah.

"Shake my hand, General," I say.

He looks at me like it's the last thing he wants to do.

"I'm not asking you to be roommates, but I've come a long way to see you. It's the least you could do."

He lifts his hand slowly and puts it in mine. It has weight and mass. I can feel it.

"Mammon was telling the truth. They stuck you in here alive."

"And they took great delight in watching me go."

"I know the feeling."

We're both looking at Mammon, who looks right back at us.

"Rumor is you're not a fan of Mason Faim. How would you like your legions back and a chance to stop Mason's war from destroying your world?"

He straightens and squares his shoulders.

"Our war with Heaven was just. It was for the worthy cause of releasing angels from our existence as slaves. Mason Faim's war is pure vanity. He's used that and fear to gather the generals who've fallen in with him. I want no part of it and I believe that other generals agree with me but are too frightened to say so. As you see from my circumstances, public disagreement has a high price."

"So you'd like to stop him."

"Very much."

"Good. Then let's get you out of here."

I didn't realize how hard I'd been concentrating on Semy-azah until the conversation stopped. Talking to another living being was like being sucked into a different whirlpool of light down here. When I look around we're surrounded by souls. I recognize a lot of them. Most at the front are military men and women I killed. Azazel, my old slave master, the Hellion who made me into a killer, is there. Beelzebub. Amon. Marchosias. Valefor. Maybe a dozen others. There are members of Hell's nouveau riche in ghost furs and jewels. Beyond them are rows and rows of other Hellions and human souls. More than a hundred. I've never seen them in one place before. I had no idea I'd killed so many down here. They press in from all sides, trying to crush me. But Tartarus has reduced them to empty spirits with no substance. Shadows on panes of glass. I manifest the Gladius for a second and they stumble back, leaving a no-man's-land around me.

"What a lovely trick. If I'd known you could do that, I wouldn't have bothered giving you the key," says Azazel.

"How's retirement treating you, boss?"

Azazel is the Hellion general who put the key to the Room of Thirteen Doors in my chest. I used it to move around Hell and kill for him. I slit his throat before he had a chance to ask for it back.

"I wondered if I'd ever see you down here someday, and here we are. Reunited at last."

"Don't get too choked up. I walked in on my own."

"I showed you your power. I made you what you are," he says. "You could show a little gratitude."

"I could have tortured you to death, but I killed you quick."

Semyazah's eyes narrow.

"You came into Tartarus voluntarily. Why?"

"To get you." I glance at the crowd. It's still packed with dead generals. I speak louder so they can all hear. "I've got good news and bad news for you. The good news is that you won't have to suffer down here much longer. The bad news is that Mason Faim is going to burn the universe to the ground. He doesn't care about Heaven. He just wants the high ground for his attack. And he's probably going to do it in the next few hours."

That gets their attention. I hear whispers and then actual voices from the crowd.

Semyazah says, "You intend to take me out of here?"

"Yes."

"That's absurd. Tartarus has been here for hundreds of thousands of years. If it was possible to escape, someone would have done it by now."

"That's the great part. Who do you think Hell's armies would rather follow, a mortal who made a lot of promises but hasn't delivered on anything or the biggest baddest general ever? The only Hellion who ever walked out of Tartarus."

That starts the chatter again. Generals lean together like they're forming battle plans.

"So how can we do it?" I ask.

"You can't," says Azazel. He looks at Semyazah. "You can't trust this creature."

"Why should they trust you?" I ask. "They all know you sent me to kill them. Now you want to keep them in Tartarus just because you can't get out?"

There's a slow murmur as faces turn in his direction. In Tartarus's gloom and despair, a lot of the dead forgot that it was Azazel who's responsible for sending them here. Some old wounds are fresh again. Azazel looks around and fades back into the crowd.

"How does this place work? Is this meat locker Tartarus or is the machine?"

Semyazah says, "The place and the furnace are parts of a single punishment device. Tartarus is the machine that runs the universe. It provides heat and energy to light the stars, Heaven and Hell, and every place where mortal and celestial life dwell. And we're the fuel."

Mammon gives a mad, gleeful little nod. He says, "We're the souls judged so worthless or relentlessly vile that the universe has no more use for us. All we're good for is fuel for the fire."

Did Muninn, Neshamah, and his brothers think up Tartarus on a particularly good day or a bad one? Did they mean to create this place or is it another one of their mistakes? I'm going to have to reconsider whether the demiurge is evil or not because this place is on a whole new scale of evil.

I watch the *Metropolis* proles working away at the furnace and boiler. Gears and pipes and valves stretch from the floor, spread to the three enormous pipes that disappear into the ceiling.

This is it. God's ultimate revenge for his kids letting him down. Eventually we'll all end up down here. Right now it's only the most monstrous souls, but Muninn and his brothers will get tired of watching humanity fuck up and we'll end up cordwood, too. So will the rest of the angels. Even Humanity 2.0, 3.0, and 100.0 will eventually disappoint them. When there's no one left to punish, why would they keep Hellions around? We'll all end up in the furnace, warming the brothers' palace, a tiny dot in an empty universe, while they sit around arguing like old biddies for the next trillion years. Or until one of them gets fed up enough to crack open the Big Bang crystal and put them out of their misery, too.

The furnace workers cut down more souls from the conveyor and toss them in the fire.

"We can't get out the way we came in, but what about up there?" I point to the machine. "Are there any maintenance areas or access tunnels? Someone built this place. Someone has to maintain it."

"No. God in his infinite wisdom built the furnace well," says Semyazah. "It might be his greatest achievement. His perfect creation."

Even Mammon doesn't argue with him.

When I think about leaving Alice with Neshamah, I get a bad feeling in the pit of my stomach. He knew what I'd find down here. Wouldn't it be the biggest joke in history to have survived Hell, Lucifer's games, and Mason's bullshit just to have God murder Alice while my back is turned? I can't even go back and check on her. All I know is that they're in a parking lot in Eleusis. In L.A., gosh, there can't be more than fifty of those in the area.

"Has anyone tried attacking the workers?"

Some of the generals nod.

"The furnace has divine protections against that. We have some of the most powerful witches, warlocks, necromancers, and djinn in existence here. They've tried every imaginable type of magic to destroy the furnace or break down the walls. They've even combined their powers. Nothing has worked."

"Where exactly does the furnace go?"

A female Hellion general with a hole in her chest says, "One conduit goes up to Heaven. One to Hell, and one to the rest of the universe."

"Then that's the way out. How do we attack?"

The souls nearby whisper to each other like they're going to be held after school if they get caught talking. Azazel smiles smugly. With his meat-loaf face, it's hard to tell if Mammon is smiling, too. Even Semyazah has turned away.

"Hey, assholes, I only chanced coming down here because there were supposed to be a lot of sharp G.I. Joe types. You've been standing around with your thumbs up your double-dead asses for years, so you've had time to suss out the weak spots in the machine's defenses. What are they?"

Semyazah points to the furnace.

"An attack is simple in theory. We're deemed powerless, so there are virtually no defenses around the furnace."

"Who are the salarymen bleeding the steam? Are they fighters? Can I take them?"

"You don't have to. They're the Gobah. Angels who rebelled after we were thrown from Heaven. Their punishment was that Father took their minds and sent them here."

"If they're not in charge, who do I go after?"

"Chernovog," says Mammon.

"He was the leader of the second rebellion."

"Where is he? I can't see him."

"No. You can't. The Father took away his visible form, leaving him nothing but an empty space in the air."

"How do you know he's there?"

"Beelzebub. Come over here," yells Semyazah. I remember Beelzebub. He put up a pretty good fight when I crept into his palace. I had to cut him up pretty bad to kill him. He seems to remember, too, because he's not in any rush to get near me.

"Stand at an angle," Semyazah tells him. "Come here," he says to me. When I get there: "Look."

It takes a minute to see it. Beelzebub was always a flash boy and his armor is like a gold mirror. As I stare at the reflection of the furnace, a seventh worker slowly comes into view on a platform high above the others. He's bigger than the other Gobah. He moves well and seems to still have a mind. He climbs all over the furnace on his arms and legs like a spider monkey, making tiny adjustments. He leaves the heavy work to the drones down below.

After a minute, Beelzebub lurches away and sinks back into the crowd.

"You see? No soul, angel, or Hellion can attack Chernovog," says Semyazah.

I think I just found out why Heaven calls me an Abomination.

"Then it's lucky for you that I'm none of those things. I'm a nephilim."

A few of the Hellions laugh. Mostly the military types. The rich ones roll their eyes. Most just stare.

"The nephilim are dead," says the female general. I think I might have put the hole in her chest with the na'at. "Before we fell, I commanded one of the companies dispatched to hunt them down. The few we didn't kill killed themselves. Temperamental children, all of them."

"I'm the last one because I was born after you pricks played Kristallnacht with the others."

It's the same as before. Laughs. Eye rolls. Stares.

"I'm Uriel's son."

That shuts them up.

"I notice he's not here with us. Someone is going to have to talk about that. But right now I have to kill another angel. See if it brings back any fond memories."

I look around for Beelzebub, but he's long gone. Just as well. His armor is as ghostly as he is, so I can't steal it off him and use it to see Chernovog.

"General Semyazah, come with me but don't get too close. The rest of you can follow or you can stand here and generally fuck off. I don't care. But if you get in my way, I'll put you in the oven myself, feetfirst."

It's a long way to the front of the chamber. Tartarus would be a lot more fun with Segways.

Christ. Look at the shit I do. How can I drag anyone into a life like this?

I've never tried to kill a God before, but if Neshamah has put a scratch on Alice, I'm going to try.

The front of the crowd is exactly what I thought it would be. Hellion garbage collectors, street sweepers, and small-time merchants. The officers and Hellion elites are all bunched at the far end of the place, leaving mortal souls, Lurkers, and working-class Hellion slobs to be fed into the furnace first. I bet some of those Hellion heavyweights have been hiding at the ass end of Tartarus for centuries. You'd think one of the drones would break up the tedium and take souls from the back of the room once in a while. I'd volunteer to sharpen the hooks for them.

The crowd gives me a wide berth when I make it to the furnace. I walk up to the machine slowly, waiting for the Gobah to react. I don't think they even see me. They're drones that service the dead. I bet they can't even see the living. They don't even twitch when I stroll past them. I jump up, grab a valve, and pull myself onto the machine, heading to where I saw Chernovog working. I whisper some simple hoodoo as I go.

Steam bleeding from pipes rolls down and wraps the upper boiler in a hurricane of opaque heat. I reach Chernovog's platform and hoist myself over. A few feet over my head I see him. Chernovog is a negative space in the steam. An angel-shaped ghost enveloped in burning mist. It's goddamn hot up here. If I'd thought about it, I'd have gone for him Greco-Roman style. Oil up and take him down naked instead of wrapped in a wool coat and heavy boots. I'll put that in my memory book for the next time I destroy one of God's perfect creations.

Chernovog is banging on the furnace controls with a monkey wrench, trying to stop whatever is causing the boiler to bleed so much steam. I manifest the Gladius and take a swing at his leg. He screams as I burn off part of his left foot, then does his spider-monkey thing up into the mist. I go to the middle of the platform, looking for any odd movement in the steam. Listening for movement overhead and feeling for weight shifting on the platform. Chernovog drops down behind me. I pretend I don't notice. When he's close I drop to one knee, spin, and swing at his legs. I catch the edge of one. He screams again. But even with a leg wound, he jumps straight over my head and onto the boiler before disappearing.

Chernovog is somewhere overhead. I catch glimpses of empty spots in the steam. Sweat is rolling into my eyes. I have to keep rubbing it away with my coat sleeve just to see. The hissing of the steam makes it hard to hear his movements.

Something smashes into my left arm. Chernovog swings his heavy wrench. I dodge it and he disappears. I look at my robo arm. Not a scratch on it. I admire it just a little too long. Chernovog slips up from behind and gets a better shot at my right shoulder. The pain blinds me for a second. I fall forward and almost burn a hole in my own leg with the Gladius.

I look up in time to see Chernovog scrambling up and away on all fours. I get to my feet, trying to see where he went, when he jumps onto my back from behind. I spin and push back, driving him into the hot metal on the front of the boiler. Chernovog squirms a little, bites down, and tries to take a piece of my ear. When I shake him off, he disappears.

I don't even get a chance to look for him this time. He rolls past me and hits my leg with the wrench. I slash down with the Gladius but miss him by an inch. Then he's on my back again. Then gone. He hits my arm with the wrench. Slams into my chest and drives me down on my back. Gone again. The prick's actually getting faster. I get to my knees and use the railing to pull myself to my feet. Between the steam and the sweat in my eyes, I can't see a thing. I turn in circles, swinging the Gladius randomly at the steam just trying to keep him off. The angel in my head says something terrible and I want to shove him back into the dark, but I'm afraid he might be right.

I'm playing Chernovog's game. And I can't beat him.

I slash the bars off the side of the platform with the Gladius. I'm exhausted. The steam makes it almost impossible to breathe. I catch glimpses of Chernovog shooting back and forth on the face of the boiler. I let the Gladius go out. Is it technically playing possum when you're about to do something that might amount to suicide?

I know what he's going to do and I wait until I see him do it. An empty spot in the steam streaks toward me as Chernovog leaps from high up, hoping to land on me and crush my chest. I bark some arena fighting hoodoo, holding off on the last syllable until Chernovog is a foot above me. Then I say it and roll off the platform as the air turns to fire.

Who needs Mason? It feels like I just blew up the universe myself. I've never done the air-burst hex inside before. I figured it might work since the only things not ghosts already are Chernovog, Semyazah, and me. After you set off a hex like that, the trick is to stay out of its way. Falling from the furnace, I stay just ahead of the blast. I chant one more arena hex and make an air pocket to cushion my fall. It isn't exactly like landing on a feather bed, but it keeps my bones from turning to butterscotch pudding.

I still can't see a thing. Steam is everywhere and the heat from the furnace feels as hot as ever. Souls howl and scramble away from the explosion. In a few minutes, the steam drifts away and the temperature cools. Like a magic trick, the boiler emerges from the mist. It's caved in on itself, the bottom twisting as the face and overhead pipes came down. The bottom is twisted slag and the transit pipes droop from the ceiling like metal stalactites. Chernovog and his drones are gone daddy gone.

Cold air and a white celestial light streams down one of the pipes and lights up Tartarus for miles. I don't even bother checking what's on the other end of that one. I hope they have electric blankets in Heaven because it's going to get cold tonight.

The light from the second pipe is bright, but flickers and is colder than Heaven's glow. That's the way to the stars and earth. I hope Neshamah, Muninn, and Ruach up in Heaven and the other two brothers heard what just happened here. Cleanup on aisle two, boys.

Nothing comes out of the third pipe. No light. No air. No nothing. I crawl up into the bottom. There's a breeze, but it flows almost imperceptibly upward. The angel feels it long before I do. But I know what's important. Overhead, the ground is blown open. Beyond it are rolling black clouds lit underneath by fires in the hills. Hell's half acre never looked so good.

I yell, "Semyazah!"

He stands under the pipe and peers into the sky.

"I never thought I'd see the sky again."

"You can write a sonnet about it later. Get up here and get climbing."

I manifest the Gladius, shove it into the pipe, and pull it out quickly. I do it again at an angle to the other hole and again a few feet higher. I put my foot into the first hole and my hand in the second, pulling myself up. I punch climbing holes all the way to the top.

When I get out I can see the Fourth Street Bridge. Sweet. It's close enough that Medea Bava had to feel the explosion. I hope the falling sparks kill her pretty lawn.

Semyazah yells down the pipe for the others to start up. Lurkers are scrambling up the sides of the pipe, holding on like geckos. They reach the top and run into the gloom, whooping as they go.

Scrub trees and dry weeds growing along the sides of the railroad tracks are burning. A pile of abandoned railroad ties makes a pretty bonfire. Too bad there aren't any marshmallows in Hell.

"Come on, General. Let's get you to Pandemonium."

He looks around at the industrial waste.

"How? We're halfway across Hell."

"See those nice fat shadows by the railroad ties? I'll show you a shortcut."

We go to the fire, but before taking him into the Room of Thirteen Doors, I stop.

"What happened to Uriel? I know Aelita killed him, so he must have ended up in Tartarus. If he's still down there, he would have found me."

Semyazah nods but doesn't look right at me.

"I wasn't there when Uriel came to Tartarus. I heard that the Gobah were waiting for him. He was taken to the furnace immediately."

That's pretty much what I imagined. Aelita's a planner. She'd have everything set up in advance. Smart woman. Dead woman.

I shake my head, trying not to show anything other than information received.

"Okay. Let's go."

We step into a shadow.

TWO POTENT LEY lines meet where Beverly Drive and Wilshire Boulevard cross. Beverly Hills is a major power spot in a city that's a major power spot. The layout of Convergence L.A. might be twisted all out of shape, but power is power and Lucifer's palace is right where the two lines meet. But his palace is different here. And it's not his palace anymore. It's Mason's. Other than that, I'm right about everything.

Back on earth, the Beverly Wilshire Hotel has some of the most expensive rooms in the world. The nicer ones average around 10K a night, but that's okay because the mints on your pillow are extra big. The hotel was built in the twenties, when movie stars were still movie stars, rich people skin-popped monkey glands to stay young, and black people had to come in through the kitchen. Except for the big screen TVs, Louis XIV wouldn't feel out of place there. In case you're slow and haven't figured it out yet, the Beverly Wilshire is Lucifer/Mason's palace in Convergence town.

Semyazah and I are on the roof of a Bank of America building a few blocks down Wilshire. An earthquake has smashed most of the first three floors and fires gutted the rest. The roof seems stable enough, though I wouldn't want to be us if a big quake hits right now. From here, Semyazah and I can see most of Beverly Hills. It's filled with Hell's legions, attack vehicles, and weapons. Many, many troops and weapons. They stretch for over a mile in every direction. On another day, seeing all this Infernal firepower would make me consider wetting my pants, but today it's just one more thing to cross off my bucket list.

"We need to talk over some things before you go to your troops."

Semyazah only half turns. Most of his attention is focused on the soldiers in the street.

I say, "I'm going to tell you a few things and you're going to have to go along with them or all of this is going to fall apart."

Now he looks at me.

"I've been a general in the Infernal legions since we fought in Heaven. I'm not used to taking orders from a mortal. Especially one who's killed my people, good soldiers, for eleven years."

"At least you chose to be down in Heaven's toilet. I was shanghaied."

Semyazah touches a finger to his lips.

"We seem to have reached an impasse."

I shrug.

"Stay up here in the cheap seats if you want, but I'm going to try and stop this thing, and if that means killing every one of your pals in uniform, oh well. And after I save your shitty little world, we can call the movers for your stuff. I hear there's plenty of room in Tartarus these days."

I start for one of the fat shadows cast by the hill fires.

"Try to understand my position," says Semyazah. "I can't very well rally troops to my side by telling them that I allowed myself to be rescued by our worst enemy."

I look back at him.

"That's the best part. You're not going to mention me at all. You broke out of Tartarus on your own. You got all the *brujas* and wizards and table tappers together, organized them, and you led the final assault on the Gobah yourself."

"I don't know. It's easier for them to believe that I've been cowering in a hole somewhere."

"Mammon knew where you were in Tartarus, so the rest of them will know, too. And I guarantee they all heard the explosion when the boiler blew. Between that fucked-up uniform and the blisters on your face, they'll believe you."

"Possibly."

"Tell them you broke out to save your men from Mason's war."

Semyazah grunts.

"It's a good line because it's true," I say. "Mason is as suicidal as he is homicidal. He wants to burn down everything you ever cared about."

Semyazah looks at the palace and absentmindedly touches the blisters on the side of his face that was toward the blast. They probably hurt like hell, but they'll help convince the other officers he was in a serious fight.

"There's one other thing," I say. "It's going to piss you off, but you can use it to persuade any of the holdouts."

"What is it?"

"The Kissi are coming. I cut them into the game. It wouldn't be a party without them."

He's back over to me in three quick steps.

"Are you mad?"

"Relax. Just because they're crazy doesn't mean they aren't useful. But when it comes to dealing with them, you need to listen to me."

His eyes narrow. He's wondering if Azazel was right and I'm the liar who's going to get them all killed.

"I'll need to hear your plan before I agree to anything."

"Fair enough. You're going to need whatever generals you still trust and some goddamn fast runners."

IT ISN'T HARD to guess where Lucifer's office is. The penthouse is huge. It's basically an old-school Hollywood mansion bolted to the top of a classy hotel, with multiple bedrooms, a kitchen, I don't know how many goddamn showers, plus expensive furniture and enough art to start a tacky museum. San Simeon meets the Playboy Mansion.

In the middle of a large meeting room is a table with the same floating 3-D map I saw at Mammon's palace. A gaggle of Hellion generals and staff officers are gathered on the balcony talking, arguing, and waving their hands describing details of battle maneuvers.

I stay half a step behind Semyazah, playing the humble underling. No one turns our way until I clear my throat extra loud. The officers turn. Then do nothing for a few seconds. A couple head over to Semyazah.

"General?"

"You look surprised to see me. When Hell is at war, then I'm at war and nothing could keep me away from my legions. Not even Tartarus."

More officers come over.

"Did Mason free you?" asks a general who, if I remember right, might be Belial.

I say, "No one lets anyone out of Tartarus. The general led the escape himself."

They seem to notice me for the first time.

"Who is this?" Belial asks.

"Just a guide," I say. "The general freed us from Tartarus, so in gratitude I showed him the quickest route back here."

The oldest and most battle-worn of the officers steps out in front of the others. It's Baphomet, one of Lucifer's first converts.

"That's quite a story, General," he says. "It might answer a troubling question. When we heard the rumbles to the south, Mason Faim ordered us to use artillery to lay waste to that entire region of Pandemonium. I refused an order. Firing on my people was never part of our plans. I persuaded much of the officer corps to join me. Now it seems that Mason Faim has disappeared, allegedly preparing his own alternate war plan."

"What plan?" asks Semyazah.

"I have no idea."

A pale officer comes to stand beside Baphomet. I think it's General Shax.

"The truth is that many of us have been having increasing doubts about this mortals' war. What will it profit either of us if both Heaven and Hell are laid to waste?"

Semyazah steps forward and gestures for the other officers to come closer.

"The destruction of both worlds has always been Mason Faim's plan. Let me tell you what I know and you'll understand why he banished me."

While they talk, I slip back out the same shadow we used to come in.

I COME OUT in Lucifer's old office. Mason has taken it over completely. All the Hellion art and tapestries showing the fall from grace are gone. Maybe they weren't ever here. This version of Lucifer's office looks like a top-floor office at the New York Stock Exchange. Nice paneling. Cushy chairs. A lot of expensive-looking paintings on the walls. I prefer Lucifer's slaughter art. At least that didn't look rented.

Mason's office is part office and part lab. A lot of the equipment is the same kind of alchemical gear that Vidocq uses. There's an area with machining tools and a home-brew blast furnace that's scorched one wall black. It's surrounded by stacks of raw iron slugs. The floor and tables are covered with dozens of failed copies of the key to the Room of Thirteen Doors. I wonder how many of those keys I can shove up Mason's ass before they come out his eyes.

Papers, blueprints, scrolls, and spell books are scattered all over Mason's desk and the floor. Someone has dumped the contents of the drawers on the floor. I sit in Mason's desk chair, close my eyes, and step aside so the angel can take over for a while and read the room. It feels around for any signs of him, not just in the room, but also in the aether, where hoodoo leaves trails and powerful magic leaves the magician's fingerprints. There's nothing there. Not an easy trick. He really wants to keep his backup plan to himself.

There's something familiar in a wooden box doubling as a trash can. I upend it and the leather satchel Jack stole from me falls out. I open it and take out the carefully folded cloth. My face is still there. At this point I'm so far past numb that I'm not even happy to find it. More like relieved that there's one less thing to run around after.

I push everything off Mason's desk with my robo-bug arm and lay out my skin. I chant, letting the rhythm and the hougans' words drift back into my head. I rub my temples until the flesh goes soft. When it feels loose I pinch the edges and pull. Mammon's face peels away like the bandage off a wound. I concentrate, keeping the rhythm going while I press my face into place. The skin burns slightly as it settles and re-attaches itself. I stop the chant and take my hand away, go to Mason's worktable, and paw through the junk for anything reflective. I find a polished metal toolbox and hold it up.

I recognize this guy. He smokes all my cigarettes and gets me in trouble. And when I find Alice this face won't scare her as much as the other. Of course, she hasn't seen all my scars. She might not think this is an improvement.

If the bag is here, it means Jack must have made it back. But if Mason tossed it, that means he wasn't much interested in Jack's swag. I'm a little hurt. I thought he'd at least have my face stuffed and mounted like those mariachi frogs you get in Tijuana.

"Is that you, Stark? Or are you another bad dream?"

The gurgling voice drifts in from an open window. Something is moving out there, casting a wavering shadow on the floor. I get out the na'at and push aside the curtains.

There's a heavy chain and something wet and red dangles from it, swaying gently with the breeze. It's too small to be a side of beef and too big for pork.

The meat smiles at me.

"Are you real?" it asks.

"Hello, Jack. You're not looking so good."

"I'm not, am I?"

He gurgles the words. There's a lot of blood in his throat, just one of the many downsides to being skinned alive (or as alive as Jack can be). He giggles high and crazy as the breeze moves him in gentle circles. Suddenly being tossed into the Tartarus furnace doesn't seem so bad. At least it's quick.

"As you can see, I received somewhat less of a reward than I'd hoped for," Jack says. He grimaces, grinding his teeth as the pain cuts through whatever mad place his mind has gone to.

"What happened?"

Jack kicks his fleshless legs in frustration.

"He didn't even want it. He was disgusted by it and by me for bringing it. He said he already knew where you were."

"Did he say how?"

Jack giggles again.

"It wasn't much of a conversation. My contribution consisted mainly of screams."

This time the laughing doesn't stop. It goes on until it's kind of a mantra. It stops when he coughs up a bucket of blood.

Why do I feel sorry for this murdering thieving psychopath? He's getting exactly what he did to all those women.

"I've got to go, Jack."

"Toodle-oo," he says. "Toodle-oo. Toodle-oo. Toodle-oo . . ." He sings it like a kid's song.

The angel in my head prods me.

When the wind blows Jack around so his back is facing me, I jam the black blade between his ribs and into his heart. He stops singing. Twitches for a few seconds. Then slows. Then stops. Then vanishes.

Even a bastard like him doesn't deserve what Mason did. Soon he'll wake up in the ruins of Tartarus and climb out like the rest of the double dead. He'll wander there forever, a ghost among the ordinary souls. I don't know if that's justice, but sometimes you take what you can get.

I say, "Olly olly oxen free, Josef. It's showtime."

A second later the Kissi's standing by the desk.

"I hope this isn't another excuse or delay," he says.

"Delay? You're already late for the ball. Get the kids in their Sunday best and bring them out front. It's time to go."

He struggles not to let his smile get too broad and loses.

"It's about time. When we destroy Heaven's armies and the Hellion legions are gone, I think I'll take this palace for myself. I like the desk and have always admired that little furnace. What happened to the hanging man outside? I was thinking of getting several of them and using them as wind chimes."

"Bring your troops out front with the legions. Feel free to make a gaudy entrance."

Josef disappears. I pronounce a few words and the glamour that's hidden my being alive fades away. There's no point to that anymore. I go to the nearest shadow and disappear, too.

I COME BACK out on the reviewing balcony. The officers are in a ring around the floating map as Semyazah explains the plan. I shoulder my way into the ring before anyone can react.

Knives come out, but no one throws any angel hoodoo. I'm next to Semyazah and they don't want me quite enough to risk making him collateral damage. Baphomet, the oldest, isn't intimidated. He heads straight for me, a long curved blade in each hand.

"I've waited a long time for this."

Rule one in wolf-pack territory is stand your ground. I

manifest the Gladius and hold it up to his face. Curses and gasps erupt around the room.

Semyazah pushes me back and gets in front.

"Enough!" he barks at Baphomet. The old general stops, confused. I guess even he can't do the sword trick. If any of the others can, Semyazah has intimidated them enough to back down.

"Sandman Slim fights with us against Mason Faim."

Baphomet says, "Why should we trust this monster now?"

I say, "I'm not here for your piano recital. I'm here because the enemy of my enemy isn't exactly my friend. But he isn't my enemy until this shit is over."

"You haven't been here for months. How could you know what's happening in Hell?" asks Baphomet.

"Didn't Lucifer mention it to you? He gave me his password to *The Daimonion Codex*. If you squint hard enough, you can see past the words and into every nook and cranny in Hell. I watched every one of you assholes betray each other, trying to get just an inch closer to Mason." I look at Baphomet. His eyes are red with fury. "Mammon, who poisoned your troops before the attack exercise in Dis. He's dead now, by the way. You're welcome." I look around at the circle. "Do you want a laundry list of which one of you shafted the other and how? How about it, Shax? Belial?"

Semyazah says, "Lower your weapons, both of you. Sandman Slim fights with us, and whatever happened in the past can be dealt with after the battle."

Baphomet sheathes his knives like a kid who has to put back the cookies he stole before dinner.

Shax says, "I still don't trust him. You said he's involved with the Kissi. They don't have a stake in this fight. Why would they come?"

I look up at the sky.

"Why don't you ask them yourself?"

Shax and the others follow my gaze.

Something bursts through the burning clouds. It comes in a long solid line that snakes from the clouds. It spreads out, staining the air black. Then the dark breaks apart into a thousand pieces and settles to the ground like a plague of giant locusts. One bug heads straight for us and lands on the edge of the balcony. Josef steps down and bows. Not Aryan supermodel Josef. Kissi Josef.

He looks like an unfinished insect angel. His features are half melted, like sculpted wax. Josef glows faintly with a blue-white light that makes him look like a bottom-of-the-ocean predator. He's so awful he's almost beautiful.

He walks to the circle of officers. Stops and waits when he reaches the line. A hole opens up and Josef steps through. When he reaches Semyazah he gives a bow small enough to be a head bob.

"I'm honored to meet Tartarus's destroyer, General Semyazah."

Josef offers his hand to shake. Semyazah reaches for it. It's a pure act of will. It will be inexcusably rude if he doesn't and Josef will read it as fear, not disgust. The general barely gets through it.

"Did you get the battle plans to the right people?" I ask Semyazah.

He nods, trying to make the comment look casual.

"As best as we can spread the new strategy to so many in so little time. We'll know soon enough if it's worked."

"A new plan?" asks Josef. "Why have you changed your attack so close to battle?"

He's suspicious. I don't have to be able to touch his mind to see that.

Semyazah says, "Because Mason Faim is no longer a part of this battle. You are. That changes how we deploy our troops."

"And how is that, General?"

"Heaven knows we're coming, but they don't know about you. As the Kissi's leader, you will ride point with Sandman Slim and myself. Your troops will travel in tight formation behind a legion of our infantry. This will hide the Kissi until the last minute. Before we reach Heaven's gates, our legions will part to reveal you. The shock will allow us to flank Heaven's battlements and crush its armies between us. Is that clear?"

"As the pristine vacuum of space."

Semyazah turns to his men.

"And to the rest of you?"

Heads nod. There are noises of agreement.

Semyazah goes to the edge of the balcony. The legions are spread out below him in every direction.

He shouts, "Release the hellhounds!"

There's a whir like prop planes and clanking like all the garbage cans in L.A. are being pounded on the ground at once. A mechanical hound the size of an elephant walks across the hotel lawn. Soldiers move back and leave a lane for the hounds to pass. Behind the elephant hound, the regular hellhounds come pouring from their pens in the underground garage. They paw the ground and snarl. Brains slosh in spinal fluid within the glass globes that are their heads. That's how you motivate your troops. Get them anxious to start the war just so they can get away from the dogs.

Out in the street, Unimogs and flatbeds arrive. In regular Hell it would be the big hounds pulling carts loaded with trebuchets, siege towers, and Hellion versions of Roman ballistae. Here it's trucks pulling cannons, rocket launchers, and mortars. The vehicles have huge animal horns on the front and metal barbs around the body and over the top. I wouldn't want to have to attack one.

"It's time to go, gentlemen," Semyazah says. "Our fall from Heaven took nine days, but our rise will take mere hours."

He looks at Josef.

"I'll meet you downstairs with your army."

Josef nods, spreads his wings, and launches himself from the balcony.

Semyazah pulls me aside.

"Are you sure your people are going to go along with this?" I ask.

Semyazah watches Josef go.

"We'll know soon. If not, we'll both be dead. Even if we win, we could be killed, so what does it matter?"

"You didn't get the pep-talk badge in Hellion Boy Scouts, did you?"

IN FRONT OF the hotel trainers gather the smaller hellhounds into packs by the giant hounds. Weapons specialists with faces like children's nightmares do last-minute adjustments on their equipment. A lot of them recognize me. Their eyes go a little wide when they see my new arm and all the dried blood on my coat. I was expecting more hostility, but they know I'm here with Semyazah, so maybe having Sandman Slim on his side gets him extra brownie points. I'll be his beard if it gets the job done.

Semyazah says, "My men are bringing up your transport. Which would you prefer, a male or female hellhound? The males are stronger, but the females are faster."

"Fuck you. I didn't sign up to be Tarzan. Get me a truck or a Harley or anything else, but I'm not riding one of those things."

One of his officers drives up in a red Ferrari Testarossa. He gets out and hands the keys to the general.

"This is Mason Faim's vehicle. I thought you might be more comfortable in it," says Semyazah.

I walk around the car, running my hand over the nearly frictionless surface.

"Damn, General. I think you almost made a joke a second ago."

Semyazah tosses me the keys.

"If both you and the car survive the battle, I suggest you use it to get away from Pandemonium. When the fighting is over, Sandman Slim will be the next target for a lot of my men."

I rub my shoulder where the new arm is attached.

"Let's hope there's enough of us left to worry about that."

Semyazah walks around the car. His lips are drawn and thin. He hates the mortal stink on it.

"You'll be able to keep up in that. You, Josef, and I will be in separate trucks at the front. Can you handle a vehicle like this?"

"Just keep the trucks and hellhounds off my back. I'm not looking to pull a Jayne Mansfield down here," I say. "One question. This isn't a convertible. If I'm tucked up in here, how is anyone going to know it's me?"

"Mason Faim might have driven this, but he wouldn't have taken it into battle. You're the only one stupid enough to do that."

"Cool. That's even better than vanity plates."

As Semyazah goes he calls over his shoulder.

"Meet me where the Kissi are massing on the other side of the palace."

It feels a little weird using keys to start a car. I turn them in the ignition and the engine roars like a stealth fighter. I give it some gas and pop the clutch. Hellions scatter as I blast across the lawn straight at Josef and his big boys.

The Kissi formation wavers and falls apart as I drive right at them. Josef doesn't move.

At the last minute I downshift, crank the wheel, and grab the hand brake, spinning the car in a one-eighty and stopping in front of him.

"Very funny," says Josef. "You always were the king of comedy."

"And I don't work blue. You'll play the big rooms if you work blue."

Semyazah, in full battle armor, rides shotgun in a Unimog. The armor is dented where it was hit with bullets and crossbow bolts and slashed with heavenly swords. Another truck pulls up next to it for Josef. He doesn't try to hide his disgust when he sees it. Kissi fly into battle. He must feel like an invalid having to ride. I just hope he doesn't do anything clever and fuck things up. I gun the Ferrari and wait for the order to move.

Climbing on top of the Unimog, Semyazah gives the signal to fire up the vehicles. The growl of a thousand engines and gears shifting is something you feel as much as you hear. Your rib cage shakes and your heart bounces around in your chest. I could do this every night.

Fireworks burst overhead. Skyrockets burst in spiderwebs of green, gold, and red across the sky, lighting the bottom of the roiling clouds. That's our cue. I pop the clutch and we roll forward.

Good night, moon. Good night, world. Whichever way this turns out, nothing is ever the same again.

You'll never know how stupid I feel, Candy, fucking off to war in this four-hundred-horsepower road rocket when I should have stolen one back home and taken you to Mexico or Vegas or even the real Venice Beach. I wish we'd had more time and gotten a chance to bust up more hotel rooms. Vidocq once told me that you can't judge your life by the moments you missed, but only by the ones you got. We didn't get many measured against eternity, but it's better than nothing.

I hope Lucifer is Upstairs and knows what's coming. He's known how my head works for a long time. Fingers crossed I know something about how his works, too.

I hope Neshamah is taking care of you, Alice. This is going to work or it's not. It's that simple. I've never strung together so many strands of bullshit before. If God won't save us, maybe tall tales and lies will. Maybe all the crap I've pulled my whole life will turn out to be useful for something besides cadging drinks and pulling girls, and my still being alive will mean something. I let the world kill you once and I'm trying like hell not to let it happen again.

I wonder if Neshamah has the crystal out, ready to break it if Heaven burns and Hell cracks open and swallows itself? Be cool, old man. Wait till the credits roll. No twitchy trigger fingers tonight.

We're heading south toward the port and the refineries. The trucks, APCs, and tanks spread out across the empty freeway, ripping the roadbed to pieces. It trembles and cracks, kicking up a hailstorm of concrete and rebar and tossing it back at the trucks in the rear. I keep up the Testarossa's speed. I don't want to end up in that rolling shit storm. The hill fires have rolled down through the city and flames rise up around us on both sides of the road.

A couple of miles ahead, the top deck of the freeway has collapsed and one end is lying on the street below. Semyazah and Josef either don't care or don't notice. I do. I'm goddamn concerned that my kidneys don't end up as hood ornaments. If I stop, the trucks riding my bumper will crush me. There's no shoulder to pull off on and no detours. Fuck it. I jam the accelerator to the floor. Let's see how far this little red wagon can fly.

The collapsed slab shudders and pieces of roadbed follow the Testarossa over the edge. It's not a fall. It's more like shooting down from the top of a roller coaster. The car plummets and gradually levels out on a pristine lower freeway level a hundred lanes wide. The road is stained with thick patches of solvents and petrochemicals, but in this twisted light they shine like jewels and fallen stars. The Glory Road to Heaven.

It's not long before we see a glow ahead, like the sun has set the other side of the world on fire. But there's no sun here, just smoke and the glow, and I know the moment I see it that the light ahead is Heaven. I look around for Semyazah and Josef. We have to stay together for this.

Finally I can see Heaven itself.

It spreads out straight across the whole horizon, a monster parody of L.A.'s southern refineries. God's little acre in the gleaming industrial skeleton of a prehistoric beast. Mountainous burn-off towers, catalytic crackers, and soaring distillation units are steel spines along the beast's back. Heaven's steel-pipe bones glow gold, illuminated by a thousand sodium-vapor lights. And on every catwalk, crow's nest, and gantry, armed angels are waiting for war.

I hold my breath and wait for something to go wrong. Slowly let the air out of my lungs. Don't think too much. Don't jinx it. Just drive. I tick off the seconds, imagining Heaven's golden pipes exploding and the place burning. It turns to rivers of molten metal that flow down the Glory Road to flood Hell and then the rest of Creation.

We're right at the refinery's gates. I can't believe how high they are and how close we are to them.

War whoops blare from loudspeakers mounted on the trucks. Fireworks explode overhead. The signal.

Semyazah and I peel off from the point of the attack. It's like when I spooked the Kissi at the hotel. I crank the Testarossa's wheel hard, hit the brakes, and use the hand brake to send the car into a hundred-and-eighty-degree spin. Then I floor it, following Semyazah back the way we came, staying close to the edge, inches from the guardrail. The Kissi army blasts straight at Heaven's gates as the Infernal legions close in behind them.

There's a noise like a nuke going off. Heaven has opened fire. With the halo polishers in front and the Infernal legions at their backs, the Kissi are the bologna in a death-row sandwich. Adios, Josef. Send me a postcard from the Big Nowhere.

Something slams into my rear bumper, knocking me into the guardrail. I scrape along it for half a mile, peeling metal off half the side of the Testarossa. I'm swallowed in blackness as something huge jumps over the car, heads down the freeway, and turns to face me. It's one of the giant hellhounds. It bellows and lowers its head until I can see Mason on its back wearing Lucifer's golden armor. Momentum carries me toward him, and the hellhound raises one of its front feet to stomping position. I hit the accelerator. The hound is strong but it's not as fast as a Ferrari.

When I'm about to go under the stomping foot, I spin the wheel right, slamming into the other leg. The hound wobbles. When I pull away, the car is making nasty sounds and shudders every time I pick up speed. I think I just broke the frame. I should have bought the rental insurance.

I'm almost clear of the hound when one of its legs kicks the rear end. The car almost stands on its nose and flips. Now it's making a brand-new bad sound. The rear axle might be cracked. Nothing to do now but see how long this heap holds together.

Every time I try to get up speed, the car shudders like it's going to fall apart. I can't get it over sixty. A grinding and thumping comes up through my feet. The rear axle is definitely cracked. No way I can outrun the hound.

It charges me again. When it gets close enough to flatten me, I hit the brake and slide underneath it.

The hound gets one of its paws under the hood and rips the top off. I stick my Kissi arm out the window and slash at the hound's leg as I go by. Something splashes over the windshield. Hydraulic fluid.

I keep running. Mason's hound is still in my rearview mirror, but it's slowing down. The hydraulic line to one of the hound's front legs spews fluid all over the freeway. It can't get enough pressure to bend the leg. The hound sways from side to side, looking like it's about to fall.

As a group of Semyazah's Heaven-bound hellhounds passes us, Mason throws a hoodoo power bolt, knocking the rider off a medium-size hound. He jumps onto it as his dog stumbles off the edge of the freeway and crashes in a burning ditch. Mason turns the hound around and heads down the freeway back toward L.A.

He pushes the dog hard. I try to catch up, but he's way ahead of me and soon disappears. I keep the Testarossa pegged at sixty. Metal grinds against metal. *Please hold together just a little bit longer, just until we get off this road and I can find somewhere with deep fat shadows.*

As the Testarossa closes on the collapsed freeway section, I get a bad feeling. It won't make it up to the top. The rear end screams and drops. The car is still moving, but suddenly I'm dragging an Italian precision-engineered plow, kicking up sparks and digging a deep furrow as I go. Up ahead is a minefield of broken pavement the trucks kicked up. I can't steer clear in time. The car's cracked frame bottoms out and the shudder nearly shatters my teeth. I hit the brake and let the car roll to a stop.

I have to kick the door open to get out. Fires burn along the freeway. I'm back by the furnace in Tartarus again, except this time there's enough light to make deep fat shadows. I dive in.

At least one thing has gone right today. The Kissi are being taken out of the picture. They did their job. They made me look strong enough and crazy enough to be part of the war. Now I have to move on to the hard part, but all I want is a cigarette, a drink, and a nap. I probably should have just blown the universe up with the Mithras when I first got back to earth. This caring about stuff is too much goddamn work.

I GO THROUGH the Door of Fire and come out in Mason's office. It's the last place he should come, but I know he'll be here. People are funny. When they're dangling at the end of a rope, they head back to where they feel most secure, even if it's the dumbest thing they can do. But Mason is a bit smarter than your average thug. He has one thing none of those others have. He has Alice.

Mason is perched on the edge of his desk trying to affect exactly the kind of cool he doesn't have or he wouldn't be here. Alice is sitting in his desk chair. Her eyes are red like she's been crying. There's a black bone knife sticking point first into the top of the desk. It's hard not to charge him. I can probably get him before he throws a hex. Who am I kidding? The angel in my head points out that I'm not exactly in prime shape and that attacking Mason is what he wants. I go for him. Mason grabs the knife. Alice dies again and I get to watch.

I'm not even sure I want to kill Mason anymore. I want to force-feed him Vidocq's immortality potion. Then I'll do to him what he did to Jack. He can hang from the chain on the balcony, a chunk of raw red meat turning in the wind for a million years.

"Are you okay?" I ask Alice.

She nods.

"Where's Neshamah?"

She shakes her head.

"He's dead. Aelita came with raiders. She killed him and took the crystal. Then she brought me here."

Mason tosses the Singularity back and forth between his hands.

He says, "Do you know what this is?"

"No," I lie. "But I have a feeling you don't want to break it."

He smiles.

"So you do know what it is."

"I just try not to break anything angels steal from deities. Call it a fetish."

"He says it's a weapon," says Alice.

Mason catches it with a flourish, like a juggler.

"When I couldn't get the key to work, Aelita told me about the Singularity. It's been my private project ever since."

"If you want to blow up everything, you have what you need right there. Go ahead and do it."

He holds up the crystal.

"With this? It will just start another universe and all the whole humans-versus-God-and-monsters game will start all over again. No. When this place goes I don't want anything coming back."

"Neshamah never said it could do that."

"It can't. I can. That's why it was easy to duck out when Baphomet turned the generals against me."

Mason puts the Singularity in his pocket.

"The trick is to contain the explosion. Allowing the blast to happen, but preventing it from coalescing back into a new universe."

"How can you do that?"

He walks behind Alice.

"By setting the Singularity off within a divine object. Say a soul fresh from Heaven."

He puts his hands on Alice's shoulders.

"Her divine spark will increase the strength of the new Big Bang so that the new universe will blow itself apart before any of it can come together."

"I bet I can yank out your spine before you do anything with Alice and that goose egg."

"I don't need long. I was hoping for just a few more minutes before you got here."

"Where's Aelita? Did she desert you in your hour of need?"

He rolls his eyes.

"The silly bitch went back to Heaven. You know her obsession with killing God? She got Neshamah but she wants the brother still in Heaven. Ruach."

"She knew all about the Singularity," says Alice. "She said Ruach told her."

"Why would he give her something that could wipe out everything, including him?"

Mason wipes a few spots of hydraulic fluid from his cheek.

"Apparently, he thinks he's figured out a way to survive the blast. It's not possible, but he believes it and it got me what I wanted."

"So, you've got Alice, the Singularity, and the big knife. But you haven't done anything with any of it yet. What do you think happens now?"

"I'm going to set off my bomb and you're going to try and stop me, which means that one of us is going to kill the other one. Or we kill each other."

"I vote for the first one."

"Me, too."

Mason puts his hands together like he's praying. Something in the ceiling explodes, covering me with white powder. Does he want us to make biscuits together or fill me full of anthrax? The room turns to water and I fall through.

I wake up in our bed in the old apartment. I hear Alice showering in the bathroom. My head is a little fuzzy. I drank too much again last night. I'll cool it tonight. We'll stay in and watch the Argento marathon and order pizza.

Alice comes out of the bathroom toweling herself off. She's naked. She comes over to the bed and hands me the towel.

"Do my back, will you? And my hair?"

She asks like it's a burden to run the towel and my hands over her. I bend her forward and pull her against me, carefully toweling her from the small of her back to the nape of her neck. I start rubbing the towel through her hair and she leans back into it like a puppy being scratched.

"Kasabian called," she says. "Your little magic Circle is supposed to meet at Mason's place at ten."

I say, "They're going to have a long wait. I'm not going back. I'm quitting."

She turns around and hugs me to her naked skin.

"Really?" she asks. "I was hoping you'd say that. I don't like those people. Mason gives me the creeps."

"Me, too. I'm going to call some Sub Rosas I know and see if they can help me find a legit job. Nothing behind a desk, but not like the apocalyptic power stuff we've been playing with in the Circle. It's giving me bad dreams."

"That and the beer."

"You're right. We should buy better beer."

"You always know how to fix everything."

Alice pushes me down and climbs on top. She leans down to kiss me and her wet hair brushes my face. When she sits up again, her face isn't right. She morphs into a small brunette and we're not in the apartment, we're at the Beat Hotel in a room filled with broken furniture. Her face changes into a distorted combination of Candy and Alice. There's pressure in my head, like hands are pulling me apart from inside. I try to make sense of the woman's contorting face but I can't.

My vision explodes into different spectrums of light. I fall a long way, no longer seeing light, but separate photons working their way through the air.

My eyes snap open. I'm lying flat on my ass. The angel took control and pulled me out of Mason's hallucination. For the first time in a long time, I'm glad the angel is there.

I say, "Damn. Can I get a six-pack of that stuff before I go? That was more fun than trucker speed."

The prayer hands caught me off guard the first time, so when Mason curves his fingers into a new configuration, I throw up a defensive shield.

His hex flies past me and hits the office's big double doors. They turn bone white and fall apart, the dry wood turning to dust before it hits the floor.

That prick almost hit me with a ball of time. I've never tried that. I'm going to have to steal the idea.

I hit Mason with a quick series of hexes, alternating ice and fire, freezing and heating his skin so it splits open like the fault lines in the street. Follow it up with shots of pure pain to make his nerve endings sing. I finish by tossing a dozen pit vipers Mason's way. Their venom dissolves skin, turning blisters into what look like third-degree burns. They swarm Mason. I hear Alice gasp.

Mason isn't moving. The vipers haven't hit him that many times, but he seems out of it. I can't hear a heartbeat or his breathing. It could be anaphylactic shock.

Standing over him, I should at least be able to read that he'd had life in him once. When I touch his body, it falls to the floor like candy glass. Touching the phantasm broke the illusion. I spin around, looking for the real Mason.

Something crunches through my left shoulder. The pain turns off my brain. When I'm thinking again, I realize I've been stabbed three more times. I mumble a healing spell, but Mason is ahead of me, delivering a counterspell before I've finished mine. I'm suddenly exhausted. The angel reaches down and reads my body. There's something funny in my blood all of a sudden, but it's a Hellion brew he doesn't recognize. I fall to my knees and Mason pushes me down onto my back.

"I always admired your black knife. So, when I couldn't make a key to the Room, I made myself a knife. I think I even made some improvements. Let me show you."

He jabs the blade into me just under the collarbone and makes a downward cut to my sternum. He does this again on the other side so there's a big V sliced into my chest. He carefully puts the tips of the blade into the bottom of the V and pulls down my body, heading south of the border. Even through the pain I can tell he's not trying to kill me. He's looking for something. He drags the knife down my chest and something clinks. He's found the key. If he's going for my heart, I'll return the favor. I shoot my hand out and through his skin and bones, feeling around inside his chest cavity.

But whatever is in my blood is making it hard to keep my eyes open. Mason is playing operation, cutting me up like a weekend surgeon, but it doesn't even hurt anymore. I have my hand in his chest, but when I find his heart, I don't have the strength to grab it. My hand falls out of him as my muscles decide it's break time. I can't even keep my eyes open. It finally occurs to me that this isn't sleep. I'm dying.

The last thing I see before I'm gone is Mason pulling a piece of glowing metal from my chest. Then the lights go out.

AND I'M REALLY no-shit, no-fake-outs-or-take-backs, no-paralyzing-spells-or-glamours dead. I don't know how I know I'm dead, but I do and all I have are questions. Like, where's all the light coming from? I thought death would be a lot blacker than this. Also, it feels like I'm stuck in someone else's death because this one is two sizes too small. Death doesn't feel much like dying. More like being on a crowded bus. And what's with all the jagged edges that keep poking me? Maybe I'm still stuck in my dead body while it's on ice. Fucking great. My body's gone because one asshole stabbed me and now my soul is going to get the flu because another asshole stuck me in a morgue deep freeze. I fucking hate Mason. He can even make death a pain in the ass.

Somewhere far, far away, Alice is screaming. Then Mason screams. A pattern is developing. I don't know what's going on, but someone's moved my body. It's dark again, but I'm not on ice anymore. There's more screaming. It hurts my ears and I would really appreciate it if whoever's doing it would shut the fuck up and let me be dead. I sit up to tell them that, but it feels like I gained a thousand pounds since I died. My head and arm weigh a hundred pounds each. I open my eyes to see what's wrong with them, but they're fine.

Why are my eyes open if I'm dead? And why is there a second me standing there with Mason in one hand and a Gladius in the other? Alice kneels down in front of me.

"Are you all right?"

I try to tell her yes but all that comes out is, "Being dead is stupid."

Did I say that? I'm not sure, but it's true. I'm pretty sure I'm alive again because there's a big hole in my chest and it hurts like I got shot with rock salt and porcupine quills.

The other me drops Mason, kneels down, and puts his hand against my chest. I feel the hole closing, the bone, muscle, and skin knitting back together. I stare at the other me and my face stares back at me.

"Goddammit, did someone cut my face off again?"

The other me helps me to my feet. This close I see that

he's exactly me. He's me without the scars and eleven years younger.

"How do you feel?" asks the other me.

"Like Lazarus if Jesus brought him back to life by having Mike Tyson use him as a speed bag."

"He's all right," says the other me.

Mason is on his back where the other me dropped him. I go for him, but I'm still a little limp, so I don't so much attack him as fall on him like a cow thrown from a blimp. The other me pulls me to my feet.

"I know who you are," I say to the other me. "It's quiet all of a sudden. You're the Boy Scout who's been squatting in my brain. You owe me back rent, fucker."

"Why don't you take it out of Kasabian's beer money? Or yours."

I look at Alice.

"Is this real? Or am I back in Mason's hallucination?"

She shakes her head and comes over like she wants to put her arm around me but remembers she can't and ends up standing a few feet away looking awkward.

"It's real. He appeared the moment you died and took the key back from Mason."

"Is Mason still alive?"

"Unfortunately. He's playing possum now," says the angel. "First he was afraid of me and now there are two of us."

"What just happened?"

"You died. The mortal part. But I'm not mortal. Cutting us like that wasn't going to kill me, so I brought you back."

"How?"

The angel smiles and picks up something small and black

from the floor. It's about the size of a robin's egg and smells like cordite.

"It was Lucifer's stone. That stupid white rock we've been carrying around for months. It's a soul trap. When Mason killed you, it released me and sent your soul into the stone."

"He put it in your chest and touched your heart with his Gladius," says Alice. "It released your soul back into your body."

"And then you spackled me shut. You're a lot better roommate than Kasabian."

I go over to Mason and kick him a couple of times.

"Where's his knife?"

"Over here," says Alice.

I go over and pick it up.

"Good. I think it's time to wrap things up. Don't you?"

"The faster the better."

Angel me gestures at Mason.

"He's wearing Lucifer's armor. He can't die as long as he has that on."

"Get him out of it, will you?"

"My pleasure."

While angel me strips Mason, I get Mason's desk chair and roll it to the middle of the room. I get a chair from his worktable and set it facing the other.

"When you're done, bring him over here."

The angel drops Mason into his chair and I spin his knife in my hand.

"It's been a hell of a day," I say.

Mason nods.

"A little busier than most."

He keeps an eye on the knife. I'm tempted to tease him

with it, but this whole thing has been about us playing kid games with each other, so I let it go.

I shrug off my coat and the hoodie, giving Mason and Alice their first really good look at my Kissi arm.

I look at Alice and what she said to me in that last dream comes back to me. "I love you, but I'm over your moony guilt trip. Dream about that girl you're lying next to for a change." She was right. I love her but that part of our lives is over with. Besides, Alice can't stand looking at the Kissi arm. Candy would love it.

I pull up my pant leg and cut the duct tape that's holding the .357 snub-nose in place. I toss the knife and it sticks into the floor between us.

I say, "I finally know why you left the lighter for me to find in your basement. It was so no matter how lost I got, I could always find my way through the dark and get right here, right now. It's taken a few twists and turns, but here we are. A couple of little lost lambs who finally found their way home."

Mason nods at the pistol.

"That was real poetry. If you shoot me with that thing, you're going to spoil the moment."

"I used to think we were connected because we're badass hoodoo men. But it's because we're losers. We can't kill the universe, and after all the shit we've pulled, we can't kill each other. And we can't keep doing this forever. So let's just do what we've both been wanting to do since we met."

"What did you have in mind? One of those retreats where men sit around in drum circles and talk about their fathers? Or take your gun and male-bond while knocking over some liquor stores?"

I open the chamber and tilt the pistol so the shells fall out. I put one back in, spin the chamber, and slap it closed.

"Let's keep it simple," I say. I pull back the hammer. "Since we can't seem to kill each other, we're going to let the universe decide which one of us dies. I'll go first."

Alice turns away. The angel has his arm around her.

I put the pistol to the side of my head. Pull the trigger.

Click.

I'm still alive.

I hand Mason the pistol, butt end first. The angel comes up behind him and grabs his shoulder. I toss the angel the knife. He holds it to Mason's throat.

I say, "Here's the thing. I didn't use magic just then, so neither are you. That angel on your shoulder can look inside you all the way down to your atoms, so he'll see if you try to throw any hexes. If you cheat or even think about cheating, Johnny Angel there is going to cut you a new blowhole."

Mason sits for a minute, both hands on the gun, letting it dangle between his knees, barrel to the floor.

"Before Christmas, please," says the angel.

Mason sits up. He doesn't like being told off by a halo polisher. But he still doesn't move the gun.

I hold out my hand.

"If you're that chicken, I'll take another turn."

That hits him where it hurts. He puts the gun to his head and cocks it. He looks straight at me. And blows his brains out.

Of course he blows his brains out. I'm not stupid. I said he couldn't use magic. I didn't say I couldn't.

The palace sways under me like it's a cruise ship. This isn't hoodoo or regular tired. I slide from my chair to the floor. The carpet is soft and comfy.

"What's wrong with him?" yells Alice.

"He's mortal now that I've left him. Get him into Lucifer's armor."

Someone straps big slabs of metal over my chest and back. When did we get to the Ren Faire?

Alice is in Mason's chair.

"Jim, can you hear me?"

"Yeah."

She waves her hand in front of me.

"How many fingers am I holding up?"

I squint.

"When did you get thirteen fingers?"

"He's all right."

I stand on my own. The dizziness is gone. I feel better than I do 90 percent of the time. Sharper, stronger, and better focused. Lucifer wore this armor in Heaven. He fought in it. Killed in it. Bled in it and almost died in it. He's left a part of himself in it. I feel as strong and clear as I felt when the angel was running things.

"It feels good. Like someone put a V-8 in a MINI Cooper."

Alice says, "I don't think you should take the armor off while you're down here."

"Hell, I may never take it off."

The angel clears his throat.

"We're not done here."

"I suppose you're right."

"Mason is dead. Isn't it over?" asks Alice.

"You might want to stay here and skip this next part," I

tell her. "One of us has to put on a show for the wolf pack outside."

"I'll do it if you aren't up to it," says the angel.

"No. I'm the killer, not you. And I have the armor. It should be me."

I look at Alice.

"Stay with her. Don't let her get grabbed by any angels or gods or elves."

The angel nods.

"What are you going to do?" asks Alice.

I pick up Mason's body and toss it over my shoulder. It hardly weighs anything. This armor is definitely coming home with me.

"Got to go out and become a god, baby."

Alice looks at me. I shift Mason so his blood runs down my armor.

"There are so many at this point, what's one more?"

I start to go out through a shadow, but bump into a solid wall. Ow. I forgot I don't have the key right now. Allegra can put it back when she splices us back together. It feels funny not having someone inside me looking over my shoulder.

In the elevator I take the Singularity from Mason's pocket and put it in mine. At the lobby, I go out onto the hotel's wide lawn.

The Infernal legions, fresh from slaughtering the Kissi, are spread out in every direction. Soldiers show each other fresh Kissi pelts and wings. For all the fallen angels have built down here, at heart they're still a bunch of morons pulling the wings off flies. Someone needs to work on that. Maybe I can set up a time-share for the angel. He can come down and teach them table manners and I can take care of business upstairs. Right now, though, I'm in wolf-pack country and this million or so killers are wondering who's the alpha dog.

I climb on top of Semyazah's Unimog and hold up Mason's body so everyone can see him. A cheer goes up. It's decent as cheers go, but it's not a Steppenwolf playing "Born to Be Wild" to a sold-out crowd cheer.

I manifest the Gladius and hold it up high. And swing it down. Mason's body drops and I kick it off the truck. When I hold up Mason's head, that's when the Thank-God-Bruce-is-finally-playing "Born to Run" roar hits. When I stick the head onto a set of longhorn antlers mounted on the truck, the screams get even louder. I stand there in Lucifer's armor with the Gladius burning, shining like a blood-soaked star.

A group of generals comes across the parking lot. I keep the Gladius burning but lower it to my side. If they're looking to pull an Ides of March thing, I have no problem whatsoever with running away.

General Semyazah is up front with Baphomet and Shax behind. Other officers spread out around them. Halfway to the truck they stop. Time for the bum rush. I should have kept Mason's head. I could beat a couple of them stupid with it before it fell apart.

The officers don't attack, but I still have a significant urge to run away. Semyazah kneels and one by one the other officers get down on one knee.

He shouts, "Hail horrors! Hail Infernal world! Hail Lucifer!"

The air is full of the thundering of the "Hail Lucifer!" Shit. No wonder rock stars go crazy. A mob like this can love you or rip you to pieces in a hot minute. And I don't have a tour manager to tell me what to do next. Time for one more slice of bullshit.

I hold up my hands and the crowd goes quiet.

"Tonight was a great victory against a great enemy. In the coming weeks and months you'll see some changes around here. Tonight, though, forget about war and blood and be happy that we're still where we should be and Heaven is still where it should be. Both could be gone now, but they aren't and it's because of your fearlessness. So tonight Lucifer bows to you."

I do it. I get down on one knee like Semyazah. The crowd goes apeshit. I get up while they're still screaming. Always leave your audience wanting more. I get my ass back into the elevator and up to the penthouse. My guts are in knots, but no one's taken a shot at me yet.

When I get upstairs Lucifer is there, chatting casually with Alice and the angel like they're deciding whether to rent *Bambi* or *Beaches*. Lucifer looks my way and claps his hands.

"Wonderful speech. I couldn't have done better myself. Well, actually I could have done much better, but that was a good first effort. What sort of changes are you planning?"

"I don't know. It was just something to say. First thing I'm going to do is haul that broken-down Bamboo House of Dolls in from the desert and rebuild it here. Maybe I'll drop back down here every now and then and bartend. I'm making sure someone puts the roof back on Tartarus and let Semyazah toss Mason's soul down there. He can have the whole place to himself."

Lucifer narrows his eyes.

"You ruined the furnace."

"Tell Ruach if he wants to send down a plumber, we'll welcome him or her or whatever else you have up there with open arms."

"You might not make a terrible Lucifer after all," says Lucifer.

"How's the bleeding?"

God bodyslammed Lucifer out of Heaven with a thunderbolt during their war and his wounds have never healed. He's been hiding the open, bleeding wound from other Hellions for how long? Thousands of years? A million? The linen bandages are still there when Lucifer opens his shirt, but just a few drops of blood have soaked through.

He says, "Healing nicely. The climate up north is excellent for the health. You should come visit sometime."

"Don't get too cozy up there. I was more than happy to put Mason in the ground, but I told you before that I'm just a temp. The gig is done. Hell is yours."

Lucifer loops his arm through my Kissi arm and walks me to a window.

"You still don't grasp the situation. I'm not Lucifer anymore. I'm Samael, and Samael is a creature of Heaven just like Lucifer is the lord of Hell. As of tonight, you are the new Lucifer."

"Fuck that," I say, backing off. "I quit. I abdicate. I'm impeaching myself. No way am I staying down here a second longer than I have to."

"Actually, I think you are and it's not my doing," says Samael.

He looks at Alice.

"Are you ready to go home, my dear?"

"No," she says. "If Jim is staying, then I'm staying, too."

"Yeah, except I'm not staying. Get it?"

"I'm afraid you are," says the angel. "I'm holding on to the key for safekeeping. With all due respect, you aren't to be trusted with it."

"We both have to go back so Allegra can put us back together."

"I'm going back alone. You go ahead and make changes here. I'm going to make some changes up above."

"You're fucking ditching me?"

The angel walks to a shadow on the wall.

"I could give you a million reasons, but the simple truth is that I'm sick of you, your moods, your anger, and your hangovers. And the way you kept me chained in the backyard like a bad dog. I'll go back to earth and pick up where you left off."

"You don't have any scars. And you're too young. Everyone will know you're not me."

He smiles and points a finger.

"But will anyone care? I might not be as colorful as you, but I'm much less likely to get everyone around me killed. That goes a long way toward making friends."

He steps into the shadow.

"Wait! Come back. I promise I won't try to stop you."

The angel steps back in but doesn't move from the shadow.

"You need to take some things with you. Take Kasabian a crate of Maledictions. And have one of the soldiers bring you a hellhound. I figure there has to be a Sub Rosa engineer or charm maker who can modify the mechanics so it can move upright, more like a person. Kasabian can go where the brain went. Voilà. He has a body."

The angel sighs and squints at me.

"Is there anything else? Maybe I can get Bob Geldof to do a benefit to help you rebuild the place."

"That would be awesome, but in the meantime . . ." I take out my black blade. The angel flinches, but takes it when I hand it to him butt first. "Give this to Candy and tell her to keep it safe for me. Tell her I'm coming back for it soon."

The angel slips the knife into his waistband.

"I'll get your cigarettes and your dog, but I'm not coming back here."

"You're really going to hate L.A., Clarence."

As he goes I yell, "And tell Muninn to send care packages! He owes me that."

Lucifer looks around and says, "I think that's my cue to go. I'll stop by from time to time to see how you're faring. And, Alice, if you ever change your mind and want to come home, just whistle. I'll be here in a flash."

"Thank you," she says.

"No," I say. "I'm changing your mind for you. Go home. I know this place and I'm the boss now. I'll be fine."

"I can't leave you here alone."

"You know what's worse than me being alone? It's you hanging around out of guilt or obligation or something. I came down here to free you so you can go back where you're supposed to be. So please do it."

She looks between Lucifer and me. Samael, I mean. I'm Lucifer. That's going to take some getting used to.

"I don't know."

"You made it Upstairs and that's where you belong. I'm where I belong."

She crosses her arms.

"How do I know this isn't you conning me? Trying to be all noble. I don't need you noble."

She takes a step toward me. I take one back.

I say, "You don't need me at all. Remember that last dream? All those times we talked. They were more than dreams, weren't they?"

"Yes. I didn't plan them. They seemed to happen when I slept too. Upstairs they told me it wasn't all that uncommon for people who died in a violent and unsettled state. You're still tied to a person or place like a ghost. Those dreams were me kind of haunting you."

"That's funny. It always felt like I was calling you."

"Maybe it was fifty-fifty."

"I'm just glad it wasn't all me. I felt pretty pathetic when I thought it was."

I pick up a rag from the workbench and wipe Mason's blood off the armor. She doesn't need that to be her last image of me.

I say, "But that last dream was different, wasn't it?"

"Yeah."

"We both knew it, but you were the one with balls enough to say it. It's time to let go."

"We can't go on haunting each other forever. Actually we could, but what kind of life is that?"

I toss the rag on the bench and walk over to her.

"You really like your friend, Candy?" she asks.

"I really do."

"Is she going to wait for you?"

I shrug.

"Who knows? I'll wait for her and the rest will go however it goes."

"What happens now? We just say so long and never see each other again?"

"No."

I want to talk but my jaw doesn't want to move. I have to concentrate to get the words out.

"I've been ducking something ever since I first got out of here. I didn't think I could stand to hear it but things will never be right between us unless I say it."

My Kissi arm throbs. I rub it but the pain doesn't let up.

"How did you die? How did Parker kill you?"

She starts to say something, shakes her head and starts again.

"All this time I thought you knew."

She looks at me.

"Parker didn't kill me. I did. Parker broke into the apartment, cuffed me, and dragged me to a crack head motel on Sunset."

"The Orange Grove Bungalows? The magic Circle used to rent the rooms for rituals sometimes." The Grove is also where I killed Parker back on New Year's Eve. There's a kind of funny symmetry in that that was probably lost on him.

"That's the place. Parker called Mason when we got to the room so I knew this wasn't his idea. I asked Parker what was going on and he laughed and said Mason had plans. He was going to do to me what he did to you but he didn't say what that was. Before then, he said, we were going to have some fun together. All there was in that shitty little bungalow was a bed and a filthy bathroom so I had a pretty good idea of what he had in mind."

My throat is closing up. I can't stand this. I need to make her stop but I don't. I let her keep talking.

"He took off his jacket, pushed me down on the bed, and climbed on top. I didn't even fight him. He was twice my size. He had a gun. And he was Sub Rosa so he could use magic."

She smiles to herself.

"Parker was never the brightest penny, remember? When he climbed on I held on to his shoulders like I was getting off on the scene. The horny asshole must have thought Mason was going to take a bus or something. He was shocked as hell when Mason magicked himself into the room. Parker didn't get more than two minutes of fun. When Mason got there, let me tell you, he wasn't laughing when he saw what was happening. He got hold of Parker with a ghost hand spell, lifted him off the bed without touching him and bounced him off the walls like he was playing air hockey, yelling the whole time about damaged goods. Neither of them noticed that I'd gotten the gun out of Parker's shoulder holster while he was on top of me.

"When he was done with Parker, Mason did another spell and a hole opened in the floor of the room. I couldn't see where it went but I knew damn well I didn't want to go down there. So I shot him."

She cocks her head for a second.

"I shot at him. But I missed. He looked at the hole and he looked at me and I knew what was coming next. Before he could grab me with the ghost hand I put the gun under my chin and pulled the trigger."

The pain in the new arm won't stop and my vision is getting tunneled. It could be a stroke but I know it's just my brain trying to crawl out of my body and away from the sound of Alice's voice.

"You can stop there," I say. "I get the picture."

"For the record, shooting myself wasn't my first choice. I thought of you when I did it. I thought, 'What would Jim do if he was here and he knew he couldn't beat the other guy and something horrible was going to happen when he lost?' And it came to me. Mason might have won the fight, but that didn't mean he got to keep the prize. I took it away from him and all he could do was stand there and watch me pull the trigger. Mason didn't win. I did. And it was because of you."

Because of me. It's because of me she was in that room at all. There's nothing I could have done about it then and there's nothing I can do about it now and that's what I have to live with. Maybe that right there is the definition of life. Being alive is learning how to live with the intolerable. I'll be explaining that to Parker soon enough. I'll send a search party for his soul and teach him all about the intolerable.

I look at Samael.

"How is it she went Upstairs instead of down here? I thought suicide was a sure ticket on the coal cart."

"Usually, but under extreme circumstances the rules can become flexible. Especially for me."

Thanks, you pointy-tailed lunatic. Thanks a lot.

"Now it's my turn to say something I've been avoiding,"

says Alice. "You asked me before if we got together because the Inquisition wanted me to spy on you. The answer is yes. And that's why I came to you."

"That's what I thought. But it's old news. I don't care anymore."

She puts her hands over her mouth. There's a moment of silence.

"Medea Bava told me about how dangerous you were and how you were going to expose the Sub Rosa to the whole civilian world and get us killed. I was afraid for my family."

"Makes sense."

She blinks. Half smiles.

"When I got to know you I knew Medea was half right. You were dangerous and I liked it. By then I didn't care about the rest."

"It's okay. I believe you."

"Really?"

I nod.

"That's why it's okay. Whatever Bava says we were to each other we know different and that's all that matters."

"Thank you."

"Hell. Thank Medea for getting us together. I owe the old witch a candygram."

She looks at Samael.

"You'll look after him, right?"

"For you, dear, of course."

"That's sweet, Sam," I say. "You're getting as sentimental as the angel."

He gives me a look that's a lot more like the Infernal prince than I'll ever be.

"Because I am an angel. And you're the Scarecrow. A charming fellow. Now, if you only had a brain."

"I wonder if they still get cable down here? I'm going to have to check that."

Samael looks at Alice.

"See? He's already tackling the big issues. I think we should leave him to it."

I sit in Mason's desk chair.

"I really have no fucking idea what I'm supposed to do. The angel was the smart one."

"Try reading a book. There's a library one floor down. Try reading up on how some of the smarter Greek kings did it."

"None of them are audiobooks, are they?"

"I'm afraid not."

"Damn."

"Good-bye, Jim," says Alice.

"That's 'Lucifer' to you, girlie."

She smiles a crooked smile.

"See you around, you devil."

I blow her a kiss.

They're gone. And I'm alone in Hell again.

That's not a bad title for a song. Maybe I'll look up Hank Williams tomorrow.

They're gone maybe thirty seconds when someone calls my name from the balcony. I pick up Mason's black blade and go outside.

It's Josef. He looks like he went in through a meat grinder and got hit by a truck on the way out.

He whispers in a broken, damaged voice, "You betrayed us."

"All I did was betray a betrayer, so if you're here for an apology, you can kiss my ass on the way out."

"I never betrayed you."

"Really? The thing with the wanted posters kept bugging me. Jack couldn't have made it back in time. Mason was still into his war plans, so he wouldn't have made the posters unless he knew I was going to Eleusis. That's where you come in. You knew that's where I was going."

"What about your so-called friends? The chattering head. Or the disgraced priest. He's consorted with darker souls than yours."

"Maybe. What turned it for me was when I called you to Mason's office. You already knew the layout. You knew Mason had strung up Jack. You'd been in Mason's office before. It's where you told him everything I was going to do."

Josef shuffles away, leaving bloody footprints behind.

I say, "If it makes you feel any better, you didn't disappoint me. I never trusted you."

"Then why call us back from the void?"

"Hey, I was improvising most of the time. But you were my ace in the hole. I knew you couldn't beat Hell or Heaven on your own. But if I couldn't stop the war, I figured I could put you together with whatever side I decided should win."

"But instead you murdered us."

"The only reason you haven't killed off humanity is that we're your food, and then where would you be?"

His swollen eyes widen. Kissi are so ugly that it's usually hard to tell if one's been hurt or not. But not tonight.

"So genocide is the first order of business for the new Lucifer. What a fine start to your reign."

"It's not genocide. You're left."

Josef climbs onto the balcony railing.

"This isn't over. If I have to come for you alone, I will."

"No you won't."

I throw my knife. It goes into Josef's throat and out through his spine. He falls backward off the balcony.

And I was this close to letting him go because I did kind of fuck him over and he was so beat up and pathetic I felt sorry for him. But I let my guard down with Jack and he stole my face. I trusted Mason and he dragged me to Hell. Even Lucifer used me so he could go home. As of today, this is an official zero slack zone for the true monsters.

I wander back to a window and look out over my weird Convergence kingdom. It isn't Hell and it isn't L.A., but I've been to Fresno, so I've seen worse. I take the Singularity from my pocket and watch the black and white pinheads spin around each other.

I survived the arena and Mason down here, and I survived Wells, Aelita, and the Golden Vigil up there. I still have two legs, two eyes, an arm, and something pretty close to an arm. I'm back in Pandemonium, so I bet Kasabian can see me. Maybe I'll learn semaphore Morse code so I can send messages to Candy. And I wouldn't mind killing Aelita. She goes right at the top of my Infernal to-do list. Yeah. This might not be so bad.

You think I can't cut it down here anymore? I grew up

in L.A. and lived to tell the tale. Hell is just L.A. with lousy head shots. We're balls-deep in the shit Downtown, but we know it and admit it. Someday I'll get back home, and when I do I'm going to find an angel with my face and kick his bony ass from Roscoe's Chicken and Waffles to the Pearly Gates and back. They might call me Lucifer these days, but I'm just a part-time devil, so don't count me out. And don't use up all the whiskey and cigarettes. I'll be back.

RESURRECTION SUCKS.
SAVING THE WORLD IS WORSE.

'The best B movie I've read in at least twenty
years. An addictively satisfying, deeply amusing,
dirty-ass masterpiece.'

WILLIAM GIBSON

OUT NOW AT ALL GOOD BOOKSHOPS